ACCL ... AN

Need You Now

"Wiseman gets to the heart of marriage and family issues in a way that will resonate with readers . . ."

—ROMANTIC TIMES

"With issues ranging from special education and teen cutting to what makes a marriage strong, this is a compelling and worthy read."

—BOOKLIST

"You may think you are familiar with Beth's wonderful story-telling gift b[ut] ... [th]at will stay with you for ... [a] life seems hopeless. It's ... [seemi]ngly unre-deemable. It' ... [t]o hear."

... [A]UTHOR OF
GOD LOVES BROKEN PEOPLE

"Beth Wiseman tackles these difficult subjects with courage and grace. She reminds us that true healing can only come by being vulnerable and honest before our God who loves us more than anything."

—DEBORAH BEDFORD, BEST-SELLING AUTHOR
OF HIS OTHER WIFE, A ROSE BY THE DOOR, AND
THE PENNY (COAUTHORED WITH JOYCE MEYER)

The Land of Canaan Novels

"Wiseman's voice is consistently compassionate and her words flow smoothly."

—PUBLISHERS WEEKLY REVIEW OF
SEEK ME WITH ALL YOUR HEART

"Wiseman's third Land of Canaan novel overflows with romance, broken promises, a modern knight in shining armor and hope at the end of the rainbow."

—ROMANTIC TIMES

"In *Seek Me with All Your Heart*, Beth Wiseman offers readers a heart-warming story filled with complex characters and deep emotion. I instantly loved Emily, and eagerly turned each page, anxious to learn more about her past—and what future the Lord had in store for her."

—SHELLEY SHEPARD GRAY,
BEST-SELLING AUTHOR OF THE
SEASONS OF SUGARCREEK SERIES

"Wiseman has done it again! Beautifully compelling, *Seek Me with All Your Heart* is a heart-warming story of faith, family, and renewal. Her characters and descriptions are captivating, bringing the story to life with the turn of every page."

—AMY CLIPSTON, BEST-SELLING
AUTHOR OF *A GIFT OF GRACE*

The Daughters of the Promise Novels

"Well-defined characters and story make for an enjoyable read."

—ROMANTIC TIMES
REVIEW OF *PLAIN PURSUIT*

"A touching, heartwarming story. Wiseman does a particularly great job of dealing with shunning, a controversial Amish practice that seems cruel and unnecessary to outsiders . . . If you're a fan of Amish fiction, don't miss *Plain Pursuit*!"

—KATHLEEN FULLER, AUTHOR OF
THE MIDDLEFIELD FAMILY NOVELS

The House That Love Built

Also by Beth Wiseman

Need You Now

The Land of Canaan Series
Seek Me with All Your Heart
The Wonder of Your Love
His Love Endures Forever

The Daughters of the Promise Series
Plain Perfect
Plain Pursuit
Plain Promise
Plain Paradise
Plain Proposal

Novellas included in
An Amish Christmas
An Amish Gathering
An Amish Love
An Amish Wedding
An Amish Kitchen

The House That Love Built

BETH WISEMAN

THOMAS NELSON
Since 1798

NASHVILLE   DALLAS   MEXICO CITY   RIO DE JANEIRO

Published in Nashville, Tennessee, by Thomas Nelson. Thomas Nelson is a registered trademark of Thomas Nelson, Inc.

Thomas Nelson, Inc., titles may be purchased in bulk for educational, business, fund-raising, or sales promotional use. For information, please e-mail SpecialMarkets@ThomasNelson.com.

Publisher's Note: This novel is a work of fiction. Names, characters, places, and incidents are either products of the author's imagination or used fictitiously. All characters are fictional, and any similarity to people living or dead is purely coincidental.

Library of Congress Cataloging-in-Publication Data
Wiseman, Beth.
  The house that love built / Beth Wiseman.
     pages cm
  Summary: "Brooke has only loved one man. Owen's heart is filled with bitterness. Can a mysterious house bring them together for a second chance at love?"-- Provided by publisher.
  ISBN 978-1-59554-889-4 (pbk.)
  1. Single mothers--Fiction. 2. Dwellings--Conservation and restoration--Fiction. 3. Texas--Fiction. I. Title.
  PS3623.I83H68 2013
  813'.6--dc23
                                          2012047037

Printed in the United States of America
13 14 15 16 17 18 RRD 6 5 4 3 2 1

To Diana Newcomer

One

rooke Holloway woke with a start, then felt her stomach lurch when she recalled her dream. She rolled over and threw her arm across Travis's side of the bed, wishing she could will him to be there. She lay there a few more minutes before forcing herself to get up and dressed before she went downstairs.

She pressed the button on the coffeemaker before facing off with the calendar that hung on the wall to the left of the refrigerator. She reached for the black marker dangling on a string nearby and drew a big *X* across today's date, as she did every morning, then scribbled "45" in the upper-right-hand corner of the square. The kids liked to keep up with the countdown to July 10.

Two cups of coffee later she still yawned as she headed back upstairs and down the hall to Meghan's room.

"Up, sleepyhead." Brooke flipped on the light and walked toward her precious six-year-old, whose blond hair crumpled in a mass on the pillow. "Time to get up." Brooke sat on the bed and kissed Meghan on the forehead, Travis still fresh on her mind. He used to wake up the kids each morning, said that seeing their faces first thing always made for a better day.

"Two more days of school after today." Meghan sat up and pulled down the pajama pants that had inched up her calves during the night.

"I know." Brooke stood and clapped her hands together. "So let's don't be late."

She headed down the hall to Spencer's room. Brooke had learned, after being reprimanded more than once, to always knock first.

"Come in."

Spencer was already sitting on the side of the bed when Brooke took two steps into his room. He no longer wanted her hugging and kissing him in the morning. Or any other time, for that matter. He'd grown up too much these past couple of years. Brooke wondered how much of that was her fault, if she'd handled Travis's death correctly with the kids, particularly Spencer. Either way, her ten-year-old son had made it clear she couldn't be "huggy and kissy" with him anymore.

"Glad to see you're up. I'm going to make some eggs and bacon, so I'll see you downstairs. Okay?"

Spencer nodded as he rubbed his eyes and yawned.

Thirty minutes later they were eating, and running late as usual. Brooke glanced at her watch, hoping the kids wouldn't miss the bus. Again.

"I miss Grandma," Meghan said through a mouthful.

"I know. Me too." Brooke stuffed the last bite of bacon in her mouth, chewing as she got up and tossed her paper plate in the trash can. "We'll go see her tomorrow after school. She's playing bingo this afternoon."

"She'd rather play bingo than see her grandkids?" Spencer stood up and also tossed his plate in the garbage.

Brooke looked at her watch again and grinned. "Yes. I believe she would." She snapped her fingers. "Now, chop-chop. We need to go."

Brooke had tried repeatedly to talk her mother out of moving to the assisted living complex here in Smithville, but once Patsy Miller had a notion in her head, there was no changing her mind. "They have bingo, card games, pottery, and painting classes," Mom had told her. "And Gladys told me they have dances too. You never have to cook, they give you rides to the doctor, and they have a maid service. Sounds like heaven to me, and I'm going to live there!" she'd said. That had been two months ago.

"We're going to miss the bus again." Meghan grabbed her backpack by the front door and slipped it over her shoulders.

"Not if you hurry!" Brooke kissed her on the cheek. "Love you."

Then she grabbed Spencer and planted a kiss on his forehead. "I know, I know," she said when he squirmed away. "But humor me every once in a while."

Brooke watched from the porch until the kids were safely on the bus, then started her ten-minute walk to Miller's Hardware Store.

Francis Tippens, affectionately called Big Daddy, was unlocking the door when Brooke walked up. At almost seven feet tall, the man commanded respect, and no one dared to call him by his given name. Even though he had a permanent scowl on his face, Brooke was pretty sure he would go to his grave to protect her and her children.

"Mornin', Ms. Brooke." Big Daddy held the door open for her. As she reached for the light switch, she tripped over the entryway rug. *Gonna get rid of that thing one day.*

Brooke stopped at the counter while Big Daddy walked

toward the back of the store to begin unloading a recent order. "Have a good day, Big Daddy."

He didn't turn around, just waved. Brooke walked behind the front counter, sat on the wooden stool, and unlocked the register. She pulled yesterday's cash from her purse and was loading it in the machine when the door flew open again.

"Good morning, sunshine." Brooke put her hands on her hips when Juliet came scurrying in, shaking her head. Brooke braced herself for whatever excuse Juliet might have for being late.

"I am so sorry." Juliet brushed a strand of long blond hair away from her face, hair that didn't look like it had seen a comb this morning. She readjusted her silver purse on her shoulder and tucked her pink blouse into the short blue-jean skirt. "I couldn't find my keys this morning." She let out an exaggerated sigh. "Then I remembered it was Wednesday and I had to put the trash out."

"It's okay."

Juliet had grown up in Smithville and had worked part-time at the store during her high school years. Now she attended Texas State in San Marcos, but Brooke hired her to help do inventory and catch up the filing in the summers.

"I'll go start the coffee." Juliet headed toward the back office. "Want some?"

Brooke nodded. "Yes, please. Thanks."

She closed the cash register and stared out the plate-glass windows that ran the length of the store. Across Main Street she could see Travis's old business, the windows boarded up. Right out of high school, he'd used inheritance money from his grandparents to open the Treasure Chest, a store he'd filled with old books, photographs, antique toys, and other vintage items. Brooke would joke that most of the inventory consisted

4

of stuff Travis had collected since he was a kid. She was pretty sure he'd overpriced everything in the store because he really didn't want to sell any of it. Luckily, they hadn't depended solely on Travis's income.

Brooke wished someone would lease the space and open something new. Maybe a candy store. Then she'd just eat herself happy.

⚜

Owen Saunders walked across the concrete floor and up to the counter of Miller's Hardware Store. He was surprised to see how far back the full shelves ran in the shop. He'd been traveling to Austin for supplies, assuming Miller's wouldn't stock what he needed. Maybe he'd been wrong. But this excursion wasn't so much about buying something as it was about looking for advice.

A woman wearing a navy baseball cap looked up as he walked in. His gaze drifted, and he wondered if she knew she had a big black smudge on her white T-shirt.

"Oops," she said as she pulled the shirt away from herself and examined the dark spot. "And I haven't even been here fifteen minutes." She paused, smiling. "Can I help you?"

"I hope so." Owen rubbed his chin, knowing he was three days without a shave and not looking his best. His blue jeans and brown T-shirt were splattered with white paint, and he probably didn't smell too good. "I'm restoring a house I just bought here, and—"

"Oh. Which one?" She thumbed through a pile of papers on the counter, not looking at him.

"Uh, the old white one on Olive Street, about three houses from the corner."

She stopped what she was doing and lifted her head. "You bought the Hadley mansion?"

"Well, I wouldn't exactly call it a *mansion*."

"Around here, that's a mansion." The woman cocked her head to one side. "You must have a big family. That place is huge. Six bedrooms and, if I remember right, two and a half baths—quite unusual for the time." She tapped a finger to her lips. "Plus a big parlor entry, nice-sized kitchen. I think there's even a basement—also uncommon around here." Pushing back the rim of her cap, she looked at him. "No one has lived there for at least ten years."

"No family. Just me."

That was the thing about small towns—everyone knew everyone's business. He'd told Virginia that, but she hadn't cared. His former wife had always wanted a big house in Smithville, the small town where the movie *Hope Floats* was filmed. After their divorce, he'd bought the place to spite her.

"I'm Brooke." She extended her hand. "Welcome to Smithville. I haven't been in the Hadley place since I was a kid, but I imagine you'll become a pretty good customer." Grinning, she lifted one eyebrow.

She was attractive, in a tomboyish sort of way. Full lips covered straight white teeth, and she had gorgeous big brown eyes. Her long, sandy-blond ponytail protruded through the opening at the back of her cap. He thought about Virginia. His ex-wife wouldn't be caught dead in a baseball cap.

"I'm Owen Saunders," he finally said, noticing her hands weren't smooth like Virginia's, nor was she wearing a ridiculously large rock on her left hand like his former wife. No ring at all. *Stop comparing everyone to Virginia.*

"So what brings you here today?" She placed her palms flat on the counter and sat a little taller.

"I painted the entryway yesterday, and the paint is already flaking off." Owen shifted his weight and sighed. "I'm not sure what to do next, whether to paint another coat, maybe thicker this time."

"Did you sand it really good before you started? Those old houses usually have oil-based paint, and you've got to get most of it off before you apply the primer."

Owen swallowed. He didn't know one single thing about renovating an old house. Virginia had hired out even the simplest repairs at their house in Austin. Always the perfectionist, she'd never wanted Owen to attempt home improvements. Thinking about her brittle ways made him wonder why he'd ever married her.

"I must not have sanded it well enough." Owen wasn't about to tell her he hadn't used primer. "What should I do now? Maybe you can ask your boss or something?"

The corner of her mouth curled up on one side. "I *am* the boss, and all you can do now is sand it off and start over."

"You're kidding." Owen sighed again, shaking his head. He'd wanted this project to keep him busy, and apparently it was going to. "Then I guess I need some sandpaper."

She got up and walked around the counter, motioning for him to follow her. She was about average height for a woman, but there was something not so average about the way she walked, and after a few moments admiring how well her jeans fit her, Owen reminded himself that it didn't matter if she was attractive, married, single, or from Mars.

Not going down that road again.

"Here's what you need." She pointed to a box on her right, tapping it a few times with her finger. "This is the biggest, baddest sander we have for the price. It will still take you a long time, but I guarantee this will get the job done."

Owen looked at the price. Three hundred dollars. He decided not to think of this as an expensive mistake. He needed an electric sander for the rest of the house anyway. It didn't really matter if it took him years to finish. He didn't have anything else to do. He pulled the box from the shelf. "Then I guess I better get this one."

She smiled, and he assumed she was happy she'd just made a three-hundred-dollar sale. Owen couldn't help but smile along with her. They were walking back to the counter when he heard footsteps behind them. He turned around to see a young woman with long blond hair and a short blue-jean skirt gaining on them, heels clicking. A skinny little thing.

"Brooke! Brooke!"

Owen stopped when Brooke did. "What is it?"

The young woman was breathless. "I have to talk to you right away." She turned to Owen. "Please excuse us for one moment." She held up a finger as she pulled Brooke around the corner. Owen waited, eyeing some of the larger sanders, wondering if he should step it up. But the women's voices caught his attention.

"I saw that man out the window of my office when he passed by on the sidewalk, and that has to be the new guy people are talking about. He is *hot*, and he looks about your age."

"Lower your voice. And . . ."

Owen couldn't make out anything else they said. He grinned, appreciating the compliment. But what neither of these gals knew was that he was done with women. Forever. He was still in love with a woman he couldn't stand.

And for that . . . he didn't like himself very much either.

Brooke finally got Juliet to hush before she made her way back to the new guy, a bounce in her step. Finally, something to get mildly excited about, and it wasn't Owen Saunders or the prospect of a new love interest.

"Sorry about that," she said as she met up with him again. "So . . . are you doing mostly cosmetic work on the house? Or are you restructuring, like knocking out walls?" She punched keys to ring up the sander. "Cash or credit?"

"Just trying to get it livable." He handed her a card. "I guess you could say it's mostly cosmetic. But there's a lot to do."

"I imagine." Brooke bit her bottom lip as she swiped the card. "Have you found anything . . . unusual?" She held her breath as she recalled all the stories she'd heard about the Hadley place.

"Does a raccoon in the attic count?" He smiled as he put his hands in his pockets.

In another life, she might have found him attractive, even with his scraggly chin and paint-splattered clothes. But Travis had been her one true love, and she was sure no one could replace him.

Owen Saunders did have something she was interested in, though, and she got giddy just thinking about it. If she played her cards right, this might be a chance to finally get in and look around his house.

To see if what she'd heard was true.

Two

Every time Brooke walked into her mother's small apartment at the Oaks Retirement Villa she questioned Mom's decision to move here. Mom had sold her house and moved in with Brooke and the kids after Travis died, and Brooke had thought the arrangement worked well. Her four-bedroom home had plenty of room, and she and the kids had enjoyed having her mother around. Mom had liked being with them too. Or so Brooke had thought.

The simply furnished apartment featured a compact living room, plus a tiny bedroom, a bathroom, and a half kitchen with a microwave, a small sink, and a few cabinets. Lunch and supper were provided in the main dining room, and Brooke kept her mother stocked with fruit and cereals for breakfast.

"Grandma, you look pretty," Meghan said when they walked in. Brooke froze in the doorway, momentarily caught off guard. She couldn't remember the last time she'd seen her mother so done up. Mom's graying brown hair looked freshly cut and set and . . . was that blue eye shadow? She wore a navy pantsuit Brooke didn't remember ever seeing.

"Where are you off to?" Brooke set her purse on the couch

as Spencer gave his grandmother a hug that warmed Brooke's heart. Mom hadn't driven for the past three years, since her glaucoma had gotten so bad that she could no longer pass the eye exam.

"Just to supper," Mom answered with a shrug, then she held up a finger, smiling. "But they have a band tonight." She walked over to the couch and sat down. "Gladys, Audra, and I thought it would be fun to get a little dressed up. We don't do that very often."

"Well, Meghan's right. You do look very pretty." Brooke sat down beside her mother. Meghan snuggled up close on the other side, and Spencer planted himself in the nearby rocking chair. "Do you need anything? More cereal? Anything else?"

"Hmm." Mom adjusted her thick gold-rimmed glasses and then drummed her fingers against her blue slacks. "Can you pick me up some perfume? Do you remember the kind I like?"

"Chantilly, right?" How could Brooke forget? Her mother had always favored the same flowery scent, never opting to try something new. "But you haven't worn any perfume in a long time."

"I know, dear. But the girls always smell so good, and I smell like Ivory soap." Mom frowned as she cupped the back of her hair and gave it a little lift. It was the same haircut she'd always had—short, with a little poof on top.

"I'll pick you up some perfume." Brooke touched her mom on the leg. "Anything else?"

Mom shook her head. "No, I don't think so."

For the next fifteen minutes, her mother quizzed the children about school and their plans for the summer, but Brooke noticed that she repeatedly looked at her watch. Then, as if she'd dutifully fulfilled her grandmother role, Mom stood up and hugged each of them.

"Thank you for coming by. I don't want to be late for supper tonight." She walked to the door, obviously expecting them to follow.

Brooke glanced at the clock on the wall as she stood. "Supper's not for another thirty minutes, Mom."

"Yes, but I want to get us a good seat." Her mom kissed the children on the cheek, leaving lipstick on each of them. "You know, because of the band. It will be extra crowded in the main dining room."

Spencer ran the back of his hand across his cheek, scowling, as he walked out the door, followed by Meghan. Brooke hugged her mom. "Okay. I'll come by tomorrow."

Mom's eyebrows puckered. "Brooke, I love you. But you don't need to check on me every day."

"I don't come *every* day. I come every other day, or sometimes every three days." Brooke folded her arms across her chest. "Getting sick of us?"

Mom grunted. "Oh, of course not." She patted Brooke on the arm. "But you need your own life, honey. Have some fun."

Fun? "I do have fun." Brooke felt like a little girl, and her voice rose defensively.

"Like what?"

Brooke looked toward her children, who were climbing into the minivan. "Me and the kids do fun things all the time. We go to the park, movies, make cookies—"

"No." Mom shook her head. "You need some grown-up fun. When's the last time you went to dinner with friends or spent the day shopping with the girls?"

Brooke honestly couldn't remember. Most of her and Travis's friends had been couples, and Brooke had edged away from those relationships. Navigating the memories was just too hard. "Not that long ago," she finally said.

Mom frowned. "You're lying." She moved closer to Brooke, almost pushing her out the door. "And it's been almost two years. I think it's time you considered dating again." She put up a finger when Brooke opened her mouth to argue. "And I know what you're going to say. But those children need a father figure in their life. And you're too young to give up on finding love again." Her expression softened, and she laid a hand on Brooke's arm. "I know it hurts, honey. Travis was a wonderful man. But you need to move on."

Brooke blinked. Of all the people she knew, her mother had always seemed to understand and sympathize with her the most. Even though Brooke's father hadn't died, her mom had suffered from a broken heart for years. Why was she being so pushy now?

"I'm not ready." Brooke forced a smile before she turned and headed for the parking lot.

⚜

Patsy closed the door behind her daughter, breathing a sigh of relief that they were gone. She loved her family dearly, but she needed time to touch up her makeup, apply some scented hand cream so she didn't smell like an old woman, and put on some earrings. And she wasn't ready for them to know about Harold.

She'd barely done all that when she heard the knock. She flung the door open, and there he stood, looking dashing in his tan khakis, white pullover, and white tennis shoes. His bald head shone like a polished stone, and his bushy gray eyebrows arched above the most beautiful pair of pale blue eyes. Patsy's heart rate doubled at the sight of him.

"Hello, handsome." She smiled, hoping she didn't have lipstick on her teeth.

"Hello, beautiful."

They'd been greeting each other that way for two weeks, and Patsy felt like a teenage girl, a wave of excitement rushing through her at the sound of his voice.

Harold offered her his elbow. "Shall we?"

Patsy looped her arm in his, still smiling, and together they walked to the dining hall around the corner. Harold was three years older than Patsy—seventy-two—and even though his recent health issues had aged him considerably, Patsy still thought he was the most handsome man alive.

Gladys and Audra were already seated when Patsy and Harold walked into the dining room. The band was still setting up, and Patsy felt like a prom queen as she approached her friends, Harold on her arm.

She'd moved into the Oaks so she could participate in all the activities she'd heard Gladys and Audra talking about. Dating Harold was a bonus she hadn't foreseen. She hadn't felt so alive in years. And as a breast cancer survivor and the mother of a young widow, she knew how precious time was. Briefly, she thought about Brooke and hoped her daughter would realize that as well.

"You look very pretty, Patsy," Gladys said when they arrived at the table. It was the third time she'd heard that this evening. Patsy beamed. She *felt* pretty.

"Doesn't she, though?" Harold pulled out her chair, smiling, and Patsy felt her cheeks warming. "And you ladies look lovely as well."

"Oh, go on." Gladys was clearly pleased, despite her protest. Harold wasn't a resident at the villas, but he had come to dinner with Patsy three times and quickly won over her friends.

"I'm sure they are going to destroy the lobster bisque today." Audra shook her head. "People who don't know how to cook French food shouldn't do it." She took a deep breath.

"And I'll bet you all the ants in a hill that they won't get the crème brûlée right either. They'll probably slap some boxed pudding together, throw some sugar on top, and then light it with a cigarette lighter."

The others paid no attention to her rant. They were used to Audra's role as resident food critic. She'd been a chef most of her life, even preparing food for the rich and famous in New York City. But Patsy thought the food here was just fine, especially since she didn't have to cook it. "Maybe it will be all right, Audra." Patsy smiled. She was so happy, not even Audra's negativity could bring her down.

She glanced at Harold. He met her eyes, and she felt a tingling in the pit of her stomach—a sensation she loved and feared at the same time.

❧

Owen sat down on his front steps and gulped from the glass of iced tea he'd brought outside with him. He'd managed to sand off the new paint he'd applied and the coat underneath that, then he'd taken it down to the original wood. Six thousand square feet of house, and he'd managed to tackle about three hundred of it so far. And those three hundred feet had just about done him in.

He swooshed ice around the empty glass, wiped his sweaty face with the tail of his T-shirt, and decided he needed to rethink his plan. The May heat was a challenge, but July and August would be impossible. He remembered it getting up to 112 degrees in Austin last year. He'd known when he bought the place that the central air-conditioning didn't work, but he'd thought he could put off the repairs until later. *What was I thinking?*

15

He reached into his back pocket and pulled out a card someone had given him a few weeks ago: Smithville Heat and Air. That was his new first goal, to get the central air repaired. He'd already installed a small window unit in the master bedroom so he could sleep. But to work on the rest of the house, he needed it not to feel like the African Sahara.

Pressing the cold glass against his cheek, he looked across the street, then down to the left and right. He couldn't have picked Virginia's dream location any better than he had. All around him were beautifully restored turn-of-the-century houses with front porches and great landscaping. Some even had white picket fences. It was everything his wife—ex-wife—had ever wanted. And though Owen had put off leaving the city, eventually he would have gotten it all for her. For *them*.

Sirens in the distance jerked him out of his thoughts, and he sat taller as the cop car drew closer. It wasn't a sound you heard very often here. Maybe the occasional ambulance, but not police sirens. Owen had done a short stint as an EMS worker right after he graduated from college, so he could tell the difference.

He stood up as the sirens blared even louder. But long before the police car turned onto his street, a lanky red-headed boy rounded the corner, huffing and puffing as he tore past Owen. The kid wore ragged jeans and a yellow T-shirt. Tattoos ran the length of one arm. That was all Owen saw. The kid was around the next corner before the police car turned onto Owen's street.

Hmm.

Wonder what he did?

⚜

Hunter Lewis squatted in the Parsonses' flower bed, wishing he hadn't worn a yellow shirt today. The plants came almost to his waist, so he bent down and crawled beneath the leaves, tucking his head and holding his breath. One more trip to jail and he was gonna do some real time, not just an overnight thing. At least that's what the judge had told him a couple of months ago.

Another thirty minutes or so, and it would be dark. A gnat buzzed near his ear, and he slapped at his cheek without thinking, then peered out between the long stalks to see if he'd drawn any attention to himself. So far so good. The sirens moved farther away, and Hunter was pretty sure they were giving up for now. But they'd be looking for him again at daybreak, so that meant no going home tonight.

Another gnat tickled his nose. Hunter pinched his nostrils and shook his head, swatting at the space around him. If he could just get away this time, he'd leave town. That's what everyone wanted anyway, even his grandma. He'd need some money, though, and he couldn't take any from her. She needed every penny for all those pills she took.

Hunter's heart began to race so fast he couldn't breathe, and if he hadn't known better, he would swear someone had their hands around his throat. He hated this feeling. Grandma said it was panic attacks, but to Hunter it always felt like he was going to die.

He took a few deep breaths, hoping to slow his heartbeat and make the dizziness go away. He tried to focus on something else, on where he would go. He didn't have any other family besides Grandma. Well, none to speak of.

The invisible hands closed in tighter, and his vision narrowed. This always made him wonder where he'd go when he croaked. He was only seventeen.

Covering his hands with his face, he wanted to cry. Such a sissy thing to do. But so much had gone wrong in his life, and he didn't have a clue how they could ever be right. Not that he could blame it on everyone else. That would be a cop-out. No one had forced him to rob a store a couple of years ago or to steal Ms. Skaggs's computer so he could pawn it a few months back. But Mom and Dad without drugs was like living with two wild bobcats that hadn't eaten in a month of Sundays. Seemed easier to get them the money.

At times like this, he figured he'd be better off to just cut his wrists open and bleed to death. It would be better than this awful feeling that swept over him. What did he really have to live for anyway?

Right then he felt a sharp pain against the back of his neck. A hand. And a strong force yanked him to his feet. Like the little sissy baby that he was, he barely kept from crying as he tried to struggle free.

He was caught. And the guy was strong. He quickly had Hunter's arms behind his back with nothing but the firm grip of one hand. With the other hand, he held Hunter's arm.

"I think the cops are looking for you."

Hunter didn't say anything or struggle. The Parsonses' porch light came on. Crazy Mr. Parsons came out with a shotgun, and Hunter thought he was lucky this strong guy had found him first. Otherwise, Mr. Parsons most likely would have just started shooting. As many times as Hunter had thought about dying, a gunshot wasn't the way he wanted to go.

"Don't shoot!" Strong Guy said as Mr. Parsons held the shotgun toward them. "I found this kid hiding in your flower bed. Call the police. I think they were looking for him earlier."

Mr. Parsons inched closer, all bent over, probably a hundred years old. *And they let people like him have guns?*

"It's that Lewis kid! Hunter Lewis. I'll go call the police. No telling what that piece of trash has done now."

Trash. That's what Hunter was. And everyone knew it.

⚜

Owen had to give his statement at the police station, an inconvenience he hadn't foreseen. He'd tried to tell the cop on the scene how he'd walked around the corner and spotted the kid, but they insisted he go down to the station.

Hunter Lewis was being charged with robbery and evading arrest. They weren't his first offenses. Hunter had a long record, and from what Owen gathered from the police, he was the town troublemaker. His parents were druggies in court-ordered rehab. Hunter lived with his grandmother, who clearly couldn't control him.

Apparently Hunter was seventeen, but with his red hair, freckles, and lanky build, he didn't look that old. Owen would have pegged him around fourteen or fifteen. Owen could see him from here, leaning against the brick wall in the cell with arms folded across his chest and the kind of scowl that only a teenager can hold for long. He was the only one in the small jail tonight.

Owen looked at his watch, surprised that it was nearly midnight. *Nothing moves fast in a small town.*

"You guys done with me?" Owen stifled a yawn.

The arresting officer, a stocky, middle-aged man, didn't look up as he glanced back and forth between his computer and a file on his desk. "Uh, yeah. You can go."

Owen turned around to leave, but a memory from his past kept slamming into the forefront of his mind. *Push it away. Just go home.* After taking a few more steps toward the exit, he turned and walked back to where the officer sat.

He glanced at the name plate on his desk. "Uh, Officer Ward?" Owen waited until the man looked up. "What happens now?"

Officer Ward raised one bushy brow and grunted. "Oh, he'll be in here for a while. This ain't his first rodeo."

Owen nodded again, scratching his chin.

"Is there something else, Mr. Saunders?" Officer Ward didn't try to hide the irritation in his voice.

Owen took a deep breath, stifling a yawn. "No. I guess not."

He left the police station with a strong urge to pray for Hunter Lewis, even though he hadn't talked to God since the day he and Virginia called it quits.

Three

Brooke woke up on Saturday to sun rays streaming through her white lace curtains, and she felt movement on Travis's side of the bed. She eased one eye barely open and found herself gazing into the most beautiful pair of brown eyes.

She quickly lowered her eyelids, scrunched her face into a contorted expression, and deepened her voice. "Who is this in my bed?" Keeping her eyes closed, she reached a hand toward the small bundle next to her.

"*Me*, Mommy." Meghan laughed. Brooke knew she would never tire of hearing that sound.

"Me *who*?!" Brooke growled as she continued to poke her hand toward Meghan, keeping her eyes closed.

Meghan squealed, giggling as she tried to squirm away. "You know who! It's me!"

"I don't know anyone named *Me*." Brooke pulled the covers over her head, knowing what was next. She braced herself.

Meghan pounced on top of her. "It's Saturday, Mommy. Get up! It's pancake day."

Brooke threw back the covers and came face-to-face with

her little angel. "And who gets pancakes?" Brooke pointed a finger to her cheek and waited as Meghan planted a kiss there.

"Me and Spencer."

Brooke had been making pancakes on Saturday mornings since way before Travis died. Spencer and Meghan used to love going to the Treasure Chest with him after those breakfasts while she worked at the hardware store. Later, after her mother moved in, the children had stayed with Mom after school and on Saturdays. Nowadays, both kids were *forced*—Spence's word—to go to work with Brooke. Their lives were definitely not the same, but pancake Saturday had kept its spot on their schedule. Brooke sat up, stretched her arms, and swung her legs over the side of the bed. "I'll meet you downstairs shortly."

Meghan scurried out the door, and Brooke shuffled to the closet to pull out a pair of jeans and a T-shirt. Ten minutes later she was in the kitchen, keeping their pancake tradition alive. She served Meghan the first two cakes, then walked to the calendar and marked an X in the appropriate square.

"How many days left?"

Brooke wrote in the number, then turned to her daughter just in time to see her upending the syrup bottle over her flooded plate. "Forty-two," she said as she rushed to Meghan, frowning down at her plate as she took the bottle from her. "That is way too much. Your pancakes are swimming in it."

"She does that every time." Spencer rolled his eyes. "And now she won't want them 'cause they're soggy."

Brooke knew he was right. "Do you want new ones?" she asked her daughter.

Meghan was nodding when someone knocked on the door. Brooke glanced at the digital clock on the stove, wondering who would be visiting at eight o'clock on a Saturday morning. She turned the burner off, pulled the pancake from the griddle, and put it on a new plate for Meghan.

"Here. Now go easy on the syrup." Brooke hurried out of the kitchen, through the living room, and toward the front door, almost tripping over Kiki, their big orange-and-white cat. She pulled the door wide, then blinked, stunned by the dazzling floral arrangement the man on the porch was holding.

"Brooke Holloway?"

"Yes."

"For you." He held out the colorful mixture of tulips, orchids, and daisies toward her. As soon as Brooke latched onto the white vase, he turned and left.

She noted the small white envelope stuck in the middle of the arrangement. Austin address. *Who in the world ordered me flowers from an Austin florist?* "Or any florist, for that matter," she mumbled as she made her way back over the cat and into the kitchen.

"Mommy!" Meghan bolted out of her chair and ran to see the flowers. "They're so pretty!" She bounced on her toes as Brooke lowered the arrangement so Meghan could see it and get a whiff of the sweet aroma. "Where'd they come from?"

"I have no idea." Brooke couldn't imagine who would send her flowers. *Duh. Open the envelope.* She gently eased a card out with no idea what to expect. But as she read the message, inscribed in blue ink, she felt her legs go weak beneath her. Stuffing the card into the back pocket of her jeans, she set the flowers on the counter.

"Well? Who are they from?" Spencer's chair scuffed against the wooden floor as he pushed away from the table and stood up. He slammed his hands to his hips. "Who are they from?"

Her son had made no secret about his thoughts concerning

another man in their lives. "You better not ever try to replace Dad," he'd said almost venomously on many occasions. She'd assured him that Travis could never be replaced.

Now she was faced with lying to her kids about the sender or facing off with them about a subject that they didn't have time to get into this morning. "No one you know." It was a truthful answer, but Brooke could feel Spencer's eyes boring a hole through her.

"They're from a guy, aren't they?" He ground the words out between his teeth.

"Spencer, they aren't from anyone you know, and it's not what you're thinking." Brooke shook her head as she began clearing the table. She took a quick look at two pancakes on a plate next to the stove, but she'd lost her appetite.

"I think they're from a man." Meghan leaned toward the flowers, lifted up on her tiptoes, and her big eyes rounded as she smiled and took another whiff. "Juliet said yesterday that there is a new man in town, and he's about your age, and his name is Owen. And Juliet said—"

"Stop, Meghan." Brooke blew out a breath of frustration. She looked back at Meghan, who was grinning. Unlike her son, Meghan had often asked if they'd have a new daddy someday. Brooke couldn't imagine it, but she'd always just said, "You never know."

"Don't listen to everything Juliet says," Brooke told her. She would have to speak to Juliet about this later. For now, she was concerned about her son, who stood with his fists clenched at his sides. He wouldn't meet her eyes. "Spencer . . . ," she began, but he stormed out of the room. Brooke followed him to the front door, but Spencer was already running down the street. She yelled after him, hoping he could hear her. "Spencer, we have to go to work! Get back here! The flowers aren't from Owen!"

Sighing, she closed the door, knowing he wouldn't go far and would probably show up at the hardware store shortly. There were advantages to small-town living. When one of your kids got mad, there wasn't far for them to go. And an ice cream at Miss Vickie's Emporium would cure just about anything that ailed a person.

Just the same, Brooke would go look for Spencer after she got dressed.

⚜

Owen tightened the last screw into the porch ceiling, sweat dripping down his face, then stood back and admired his new swing. He was tired of sitting on the steps, and the small grocery store in town had been selling porch swings out front yesterday—locally made, already painted, and with room for two. *Gonna just be me.*

He eased himself down, letting the swing get used to his weight, and hoped he'd hit a stud overhead. Once he felt the screws weren't going to pull loose over his head, he pushed with his boot until the swing fell into a rhythm, then he closed his eyes and smiled. *You always wanted one of these, Virginia.*

His bitterness should have suffocated him, but some days it was all that gave him comfort. He opened his eyes, still smiling, and noticed a kid walking up the sidewalk.

"Hey, there." Owen slowed the swing to a stop, noticing the frown on the boy's face. "Everything okay?" The kid walked right up to Owen, stuffed his hands in the pockets of his blue-jean shorts, and wagged his head back and forth. His brown hair looked freshly cut into a burr, and he didn't look older than nine or ten.

"Are . . . are you named Owen?" The boy squinted from the sun's glare.

"Yeah, I'm Owen. Just moved in not too long ago." Owen draped one arm over the back of the swing, tapping his fingers against the wood. "And you are?"

"Spencer."

Owen dropped his hand to his knee and waited, wondering if the boy's sole purpose was just to introduce himself. "Well, nice to meet you, Spencer."

The kid clenched his mouth tight and looked to his left, then right. His eyes landed back on Owen, and the boy raised his chin. "I'm looking for my mom."

Owen slid to the edge of the swing. "Are you lost? Do you need me to call someone?"

Spencer shook his head as he glowered. "No. *I'm* not lost. My mom is." He paused, looking around again. "Her name is Brooke Holloway."

Owen recalled the woman who'd helped him with his sanding issues. "Yeah, I know your mom." He scratched his forehead. "What do you mean she's lost?"

Spencer took a step closer, then spoke almost in a whisper. "My mom, she has . . . problems."

"Problems?"

"She's not right in the mind." He pressed his lips together. "And sometimes she gets lost." He shook his head mournfully. "She just walks right out the door and doesn't know where she's going. It's real sad."

Owen stood up from the swing and came down on one knee in front of the boy as he wondered if Brooke was okay. She'd sure seemed all right at the hardware store. "Do you want me to call someone?"

Spencer sighed, a hint of annoyance hovering in his eyes.

"No. I always find her, then I take her back home. I take care of her."

"All by yourself?" That sounded unlikely. Owen kept his eyes on Spencer's, watching for any clue that the kid might be making this up. Owen didn't know much about children this age. Did they usually make up tall tales for total strangers?

"My grandma helps take care of Mom too."

This sounded more plausible. Sad, though. He hated to think of a young boy having to shoulder that much responsibility.

"Anyway, I was checking around. I'm sure she'll show up soon. She runs the hardware store in town." Spencer squinted one eye. "Guess you might already know that."

Owen nodded, then held a hand to his forehead, blocking the sun, as he looked down the street. He still wasn't sure whether to call someone in case it was Spencer who was in some kind of trouble.

"I'm pretty sure that's where she got that bad rash all over her back, being 'lergic to something at the store." Spencer scrunched his face, closing his eyes. "It never goes away. Just big red bumps all over her back, oozing stuff all the time."

Owen tried not to cringe. He well remembered the backside of Brooke moving down the aisle in front of him. Now he could add oozing red bumps to that mental image. "That's, uh . . . that's a shame," he finally said, wanting more than ever to doubt this kid's credibility. But Spencer's face was utterly sincere. And what reason would he have to lie about something like that?

"Anyway, I better keep looking for her." Spencer smiled and took a deep breath. "Gotta get her to work on time." He turned to leave, then spun around with a quick wave.

"Nice to meet you, Spencer." Owen watched him walk

away, and the kid was almost to the street when he turned around again.

"And she's real 'lergic to flowers too!" Spencer gave another wave and ran down the street.

Owen watched him until he turned the corner, then he sat back down in his new swing and kicked it into motion. He shook his head sadly.

You just can't tell about people.

⚜

Brooke dropped Meghan off at the store to stay with Juliet so she could go look for Spencer.

"And I'll chat with *you* later." She pointed a finger at Juliet.

Juliet gave her an innocent shrug but began nervously twisting a strand of long blond hair.

Brooke wound her way to the front of the store, where Big Daddy sat at the cash register. "I shouldn't be long. I'm sure Spencer didn't go too far."

"No problem. I was just sorting through some deliveries in the back. Nothing that can't wait." Big Daddy opened up the newspaper on the counter and picked up a cup of coffee. "What's he mad about anyway?"

Brooke didn't want to explain about the flowers, so she just waved a hand in the air. "Who knows."

She had searched up and down Main and was halfway down Olive Street when Juliet called to say that Spencer was there at the store.

"Thank goodness." She stuffed her phone in her pocket and made an about-face in the middle of the street, swiping at the sweat trickling into her eyes. Her pink T-shirt was damp with perspiration. Twisting her hair into a ponytail, she secured it with the hair band she kept on her wrist during the hot summer months. She picked up the pace to get back to the store, but slowed down when she heard someone call her name. She turned to see Owen Saunders running toward her.

"Hey, Brooke." He reached out like he was going to touch her arm, but then didn't. "Can I help you?"

Brooke dabbed at her forehead with the palm of her hand. "Uh, no. But thanks." She turned and started walking again, but Owen caught her by the arm.

"Really. I don't mind. Where are you trying to go?"

Brooke pulled her arm away and let out a small grunt. "I'm going to work." She forced a smile, then kept walking. *Weird.*

Owen got in step with her. He looked about the same as the last time she saw him, but even with his paint-splattered clothes, scuffed work boots, and sweaty white T-shirt, he still managed to look good. The broad outline of his shoulders strained against the T-shirt. He was taller than Brooke by several inches, and his dark hair looked like it had been parted on one side earlier today. At the moment, it was wind tossed and a bit wild.

"How's the house coming?" she finally asked, wondering why he was walking with her.

"Slow." He smiled, but then stopped suddenly. "Crud!"

Brooke stopped too. "What? What's wrong?"

He put a palm to his forehead and squeezed his eyes closed for a few moments. "I think I left water boiling on the stove to make some iced tea." He paused, frowning. "I'm going to need to go back to the house."

"Uh, okay." Brooke shrugged. "Bye." She took off walking again, only to have him catch up with her.

"Are you going to get there okay?"

Brooke turned to face him but kept walking. "Get where?" *What is wrong with this guy?*

"Can you find your way to work okay? I can call someone . . . or go get the car."

Brooke stopped and stared into his blue eyes. She spoke slowly. "Yes. I can find my way to work just fine. Thank you." She put her hands on her hips and nodded toward his house. "Can *you* find your way back home?"

He chuckled. "Well, of course."

"Excellent!" She slapped her hands together, then took off in another brisk walk, not looking back, hoping he didn't follow. His looks were clearly deceiving. He looked like a normal guy. Had even acted like one the other day at the hardware store. *But there is something seriously wrong with him.*

She shook her head, then thought about the flowers she'd received. A recollection that caused her stomach to twist into knots.

Something odd about this whole day.

Four

rooke tried to pay attention to the pastor's message on Sunday, but she'd had another dream about Travis last night, and thoughts of him distracted her. She couldn't remember much of the dream except that she, Travis, and the children had been all together. They'd been happy.

She glanced to her right at her mother. Mom hadn't looked this good in years, and Brooke was pretty sure that peach dress with the ruffled ivory collar was new. Once a week a van from the Oaks took the residents to the mall, and apparently Mom was taking advantage of the field trips. Brooke noticed a hint of blue eye shadow again, and Mom's cheeks were a bit rosier than usual. Brooke had given her mother the bottle of perfume she'd asked for, and as always, her mother had insisted on reimbursing her. Mom must have been in between field trips when she asked Brooke to get the perfume for her.

Clearly, the retirement villa was agreeing with Mom, and Brooke hated to mess up her mother's day. But she'd decided she had to tell her about the flowers . . . and why she'd tossed the lovely floral arrangement in the trash can.

She waited until after lunch at the house before she broached what she knew would be a painful subject for both of them. Spencer was upstairs in his room, playing video games, most likely, and Meghan was in the fenced backyard swinging. She spent every free moment doing that. Brooke watched her through the kitchen window. She could almost see Travis standing behind her, laughing and pushing her higher and higher.

"I need to tell you something, Mom." Brooke pulled her gaze from the swing set and turned to face her mother. Mom sat at the kitchen table sipping on a glass of iced tea. Brooke closed her eyes for a moment, wanting to bypass this conversation. But she'd never really kept much from her mother.

"What?" Her mother set the glass down, pushed her glasses up on her nose, then slowly laid her palms on the table as she sat taller. "Is everything okay? With you? The kids?"

"Yes, yes." Brooke pulled out a chair across from her mother and slowly eased into it. "Everything is fine with all of us. I—I just . . ."

"Spit it out, dear." Mom reached over and laid a hand on top of Brooke's. "What is it?"

Brooke leaned her head back, blew out a long breath, then looked back at her mother. "Daddy sent me some flowers." She watched her mother's face, waiting for sadness or anger to creep across her expression, but Mom wasn't giving anything away.

"Oh," she finally said before she took another sip of tea.

Brooke watched her and waited. *That's it? Oh?*

Her mother rubbed her forehead for a few moments before she looked up at Brooke. "I'm guessing you aren't happy that your father did that."

"Uh . . . no. I'm not." Brooke leaned back in the chair. "I

don't care if I ever see him, and I threw his stupid flowers in the garbage." She could hear how juvenile she sounded, but she didn't care.

Her mother tapped freshly painted pink nails on the table. "Was there a card?"

"Yes." Brooked rubbed her arms as she spoke. "It was all a bunch of . . ." She took a deep breath and blew it out slowly.

"What did it say?"

Brooke tried to recall the exact wording on the card. "It said . . . um, 'I miss you, Brooke, and I have always loved you. Hope to see you soon. Love, Daddy.' She blinked back tears as she shook her head. "Something like that."

"You need to forgive him, Brooke." Her mother's matter-of-fact tone was not the reaction she'd expected.

"No. I don't." She thought briefly about all the times Travis had given her the same advice, saying she needed to forgive for her own sake.

"And saying he loves me? I mean, really, Mom. You don't walk out on the people you love. I don't care if I never see him again." She swiped at her eyes.

"Hmm." Mom laid her hands flat on the table again and stared into space.

"That's all you have to say?"

A smile tipped at the corner of her mother's mouth. "No, Brooke, that's not all I have to say, but I can see that you aren't ready to *hear* what I have to say."

"If you're going to tell me to reach out to Daddy, save your breath, Mom. I quit caring about him a long time ago."

"Yes. I can see that by the way you're crying." Her mother propped her elbows on the table and cupped her chin in her hands. "Why don't you tell me how you really feel?"

Brooke lifted her hands in the air. "Mom! I watched you cry

about him for years. He left us both. And maybe you still care about him, but I don't. I don't want him near me or my children!" She let her hands fall. "A few birthday cards or phone calls here and there does not a father make."

"Hmm."

"Quit doing that. I know you have more to say about this." Brooke raised her eyebrows. "Has he sent you flowers too?"

Mom smiled. "No, dear. He hasn't."

"Well, I'm just not going to acknowledge the flowers or the note." Brooke snorted. "Not that I could anyway. I have no idea where he is." She leaned forward. "Mom, are you over him? Or are you hurting so much inside that you're going to cry your eyes out when you leave here? Talk to me. Why do you think Daddy is contacting me after all this time?"

"I don't know." Her mother stared long and hard at her. "Sounds to me like he is seeking forgiveness."

"Well, he can seek all he wants. Seek 'til the cows come home. I really don't care."

"This attitude is hurting you more than anyone else."

Brooke thought about Travis again but just shook her head. "I get it, Mom. But I still don't want anything to do with him."

"Well, that's your choice, I guess."

They were quiet for a while. Brooke knew that her mother still talked and corresponded with her father occasionally. "Have you forgiven him?"

Her mother's gaze drifted to the far side of the kitchen. "I forgave your father a long time ago."

"How? How could you do that after . . . after everything that happened? I remember how it was, especially in the beginning."

"It was hard." Her mother sat there silently for a few moments, then reached over and put her hand on Brooke's again. "But it was the only way to heal my heart. And you need that healing too."

"Well, I'll have to find it some other way, because I'm not talking to him. That other person whose genes I share lost the right to be my father a long time ago, and a bunch of stupid flowers and a card isn't going to change that." She pulled her hand out from under her mother's. "Mom, I'm glad you've found some sort of peace about all this, but I can't. I'm sorry."

"You'll have to come to terms with all this on your own." Her mother stood up, shaking her head. "I'm at a new place in my life, and I choose to let go of that heartache." She walked toward Brooke and touched her arm. "As you well know, life is short. You were dealt a terrible blow with Travis, but I was so proud of you. Somehow you got through it, and you clung to God, even though I know it was impossible to understand how this could be His plan for your life." She stared into Brooke's eyes.

Brooke lowered her head, knowing that wasn't entirely true. Yes, she'd clung to God, but she'd also questioned Him for a long time. Still did sometimes. She let out a heavy sigh. "I love you, Mom, and I'm glad you're in a happy place and you've forgiven Daddy." She paused. "But I just can't do it right now, and I still have a hard time understanding how you can. Mom, he cheated on you and left us for another woman."

Mom pulled Brooke into a hug, ignoring the mention of the infidelity as she always did. "Okay, dear, I think you'd better call in the children and then get me home. I feel a nap coming on."

"*This* should be your home, Mom." Brooke headed toward the door to call Meghan.

"We've been over all this." Her mother shook her head.

Brooke yelled for Meghan to come in, then smiled at her mom. "I know. And I really am happy if you're happy."

Her mother smiled. "I am *very* happy."

And for that, Brooke was thankful.

❦

Patsy called Harold as soon as she got home, and he promised to come right over. Fifteen minutes later he was knocking at the door. Patsy rushed into his arms as soon as she saw him. She'd managed to hide her tears from her daughter, but now she just wanted to cry in Harold's arms.

"Oh, my sweet Patsy," he said as he held her.

Patsy basked in the comfort of his arms for a few moments before she backed away, pulled him inside, then closed the door behind him. She motioned him to the couch, then sat down beside him. Harold grabbed both her hands, brought them to his mouth, and kissed each finger tenderly. "Everything is going to be all right, my love."

Patsy felt the weight of the world struggling to lift from her shoulders at the sound of his voice. That was the way it had always been. Harold had the ability to calm her soul.

"I'm sorry this is causing friction between you and Brooke." Harold pulled her close and kissed her on the forehead.

Patsy snuggled into his chest, listening to his heart and wondering if he could hear hers. She lifted her head. "Do you know how much I love you?"

Harold blinked his eyes several times. "Yes. Almost as much as I love you."

Patsy stared into his eyes as she reached up and touched his cheek. She forced a smile. "But I don't think our daughter is ready to accept you back into her life."

❧

Hunter covered his face with his hands as his grandma swung her arms in his direction, catching the side of his face twice. When she finally ran out of energy and plopped down on the couch, Hunter eased his hands away. "I didn't do nothin', Grandma! I swear it. Not this time!"

"Shut your mouth, Hunter." Grandma grabbed her chest as she leaned against the back of the worn blue-and-white-checked sofa. "I'm tired of your lies. Just plumb tired of 'em, ya hear me?"

Hunter shifted his weight from one foot to the other and waited for her to go on. There was no talking to her when she was like this. She'd never really hurt him during her rants, and it seemed to make her feel better, so Hunter always just let her swing at him a few times.

"So who paid your bail, or did ya pay it yourself with what you done stole?" Grandma reached for her pack of smokes on the TV tray by the couch. She lit one and blew a puff of smoke in Hunter's direction as she crossed her legs.

"I told you. I didn't steal nothing." Hunter waved the smoke from his face as he stared at her. "You ain't supposed to smoke. Doctor said so." She looked real old, older than sixty-two. She'd already had two surgeries for some sort of cancer. It wasn't a cancer most people got. He could never remember the name of it, but Hunter knew she wasn't supposed to smoke.

"I'll worry about me, Hunter." She drew in a long drag, held it, then turned her head this time when she blew the smoke out. Reaching for a pill bottle on the tray, she struggled to open it, so Hunter walked toward her, opened it, and handed it back. Grandma popped two pills and added, "But I sure don't need to be worrying about you too. Why you got to go pulling a stupid stunt like that?"

Hunter hung his head. He'd been plenty guilty of lots of bad stuff in the past, so it was no wonder Grandma didn't believe him now. Truth was, he didn't steal anything this time. But he shouldn't have run when he heard the sirens. Habit, he supposed.

"So how'd ya get out of jail?" Grandma coughed, and Hunter cringed. It was a deep, raspy cough. Reminded Hunter of when she first got sick.

He sat down in the recliner on the other side of the den, edging around the exposed spring on the left side. "Somebody posted my bail."

Grandma coughed some more, the smoke lingering in the air all around them. "On a Sunday? Who?"

Hunter shrugged. "I dunno."

His grandma took another drag and scowled.

"Really, Grandma. I ain't got no idea."

She took a deep breath, shook her head, then stubbed out her cigarette. "They feed you in there?"

He'd been eating bologna sandwiches for days. "Yeah."

Grandma nodded toward the kitchen. "Get on in there and getcha something decent to eat, then. I got a pot of spaghetti and meatballs on the stove." She slid her legs up onto the couch and lay back, pointing toward the kitchen. "And get you some bread. You're too skinny, boy."

Hunter hurried to the kitchen, hungry as a hostage, and loaded himself a plate of Grandma's spaghetti and meatballs. He was pretty sure there wasn't a better meal on the planet. Grandma always made sure he had a hot meal and clean clothes, and she never allowed him to curse around her.

As he stuffed a meatball in his mouth, he thought about all the beatings he'd gotten from both his parents. 'Course, he deserved them. He was a bad kid. They'd told him so since he was barely old enough to go to school. He'd quit school when he was sixteen, as soon as it was legal to. Momma had told him he needed a job, so he'd gotten one. Then another. Then another. Things always started off real good at his workplaces, but sooner or later Momma would show up there, all high on crack and making a scene. Next thing Hunter knew, he was being let go for something stupid.

Dad had a job. He was probably the best drug dealer in the tri-county area, and he barely spent any time in jail. Until this last go-round with the judge, when both Momma and Dad got sent away to rehab. Hunter knew he was a bad person for thinking it, but he was glad they were gone. Glad it was just him and Grandma.

"You getting enough to eat in there?" Grandma yelled from the living room.

"Yes, ma'am." Hunter swallowed as he watched a big black cockroach walk across the table in front of him. Not much point killing the poor fellow. A thousand more were probably hiding all around. He glanced at the sink full of dishes from the past week and thought about cleaning them, but he suspected he better go out and look for a job. Grandma's money from the government didn't pay for all her medicines. Or if it did, it didn't leave money for things like electricity and food. He'd been told that at least a thousand times.

He'd have to leave this area to find work, though. Nobody would hire Hunter Lewis around here. He thought about what Old Man Parsons had said. *"It's that Lewis kid! . . . No telling what that piece of trash has done now."*

Hunter stuffed another meatball in his mouth as he watched the roach trailing across the table toward an opened loaf of bread.

Five

Owen thought about Hunter Lewis as he finished a late breakfast at the Comfort Café. Getting the kid out of jail on a Sunday had been a challenge, but Owen had woken up this morning with the boy on his mind. He couldn't help remembering his friend Bruce from high school. Something about Hunter reminded Owen of Bruce—always in trouble, but deep down a good person. No one had ever given Bruce a chance, though. He'd gotten into the system and never managed to break free. Two years after Owen graduated, he'd learned that Bruce had been killed in a parking lot scuffle.

He glanced around him at all the dresses and suits. He figured he was probably the only one in the place who hadn't come straight from church. Worship services weren't on his agenda these days, and he doubted they ever would be again. Posting bail for a kid he didn't know anything about, based on a hunch and a memory, would have to be his good deed for the day. His reward? Poached eggs from the Comfort Café, which made some of the best he'd ever tasted. After scooping up the last of the eggs, he paid his bill.

He was crossing Main Street to get to his car when he noticed the enormous painted gingerbread man standing to the left of the Chamber of Commerce office. One of these days he was going to remember to ask one of the locals why it was there. He shook his head, wondering if he should make a closer inspection. Maybe there was some other explanation aside from his speculation that the folks here just forgot to take down all their Christmas decorations. But he was in a hurry to get home. He'd gotten up early and finished painting his entire bedroom this morning before he left—after sanding down the woodwork with his handy sander—and he was hoping the paint was dry enough now to peel the tape away. He'd painted the room Virginia's favorite color, a dusty purplish color. Maybe he'd snap a picture of it on his cell phone and send it to her. Surely by now she'd heard from mutual acquaintances that he was living in Smithville. *Eat your heart out, baby.*

A few minutes later Owen was ripping the tape from the trim in the spacious room. At least twice the size of his and Virginia's old bedroom, it would easily hold a couple of armoires—the closet was minuscule—and a sitting area.

He stood there for a few moments, mounds of used trim tape all over the floor, and just stared at his purple room. It made him want to vomit. Or cry. He wasn't sure. The entire room just screamed Virginia. And he hated armoires. He kicked the tape around the floor, then couldn't seem to shed a large mass stuck to the tip of his boot. Ripping it from his shoe, he threw it across the room and slammed the bedroom door behind him. For the first time since he'd moved to Smithville, he wondered if this entire spiteful venture had been a huge mistake. Was he going to think of Virginia constantly while he meandered around this big old house every day?

His stomach had soured with regard to business too. He

had Gary to thank for that. Together, they'd built a successful public relations firm. But for the past two years, apparently, Gary's preferred relations had been with Owen's wife. Owen had sold out to his former friend and had no plans to go back into that line of work.

A loud thump turned his attention to the porch, and he was pretty sure he knew what it was. He walked outside and, sure enough, one end of his new swing was on the porch. He'd missed that stud after all.

Fearful he was about to blow, he slowly walked into the house, grabbed his keys, and headed to his car. Four clicks of the key later, it was clear that the black BMW wasn't going to turn over. The car was only a year old, and he'd never had a problem with it. *Why today?*

He climbed out of the car, slammed the door, and kicked his foot back. *This is what I have insurance for.* He was just about to ram his foot into the side of his car when Brooke Holloway walked up. Just what he needed right now—the crazy mom.

"Hi, Brooke." He forced a smile.

She folded her arms across a white T-shirt. Same ponytail as before, minus the baseball cap, and her jeans had holes in the knees. Her pink flip-flops matched her toenails. No one could make that look work the way she did. But even though she briefly took his breath away, Owen quickly reminded himself about the conversation with her son. Was she really, um, mentally disturbed?

Brooke raised her chin, grinning. "I'm not for sure, but I think I stopped you from kicking your car."

Owen swallowed hard. "Uh, yeah. I was considering it." He felt his face turning red. *Who's the crazy one now?* Regrouping, he edged closer to her. "Are you lost again?"

Her smile faded. "What?" She put a hand on one hip. "Why do you always think I'm lost?"

He pictured large, oozing red bumps all over her back and cringed for a moment, then forced a smile. "I just . . ." He shrugged, not wanting to get her kid in trouble for either telling on her or spinning such a tale. "I don't know."

"Did you check the battery cables?" Brooke shifted her weight, her other hand landing on the opposite hip.

Owen didn't know a thing about cars. He was missing the male mechanic gene. "No, but I will."

She raised an eyebrow as one side of her mouth curled into a smile. "You do know how, don't you?"

"Well, yeah." He rolled his eyes, wishing she would leave. "What are you doing here, anyway?"

"I just walked my daughter to a friend's house, and I'm on my way home. I heard you trying to start your car, then looked up just in time to save Mr. BMW from a good kick in the door." She laughed—more like a cute little giggle—and Owen couldn't help but smile.

"Well, thanks. You probably just saved me a five-hundred-dollar deductible and a lot of grief."

She tapped a finger to her chin. "Listen, I have to ask you something . . ."

Oh no. "What's that?"

"Have you found the bunker?" She bit her bottom lip and bounced on her toes, and for a moment, she looked about twelve years old.

"What bunker?"

Brooke moved a little closer. "I bet you didn't know that there is a story behind your house."

"Uh, no. What's the story?" Owen was intrigued, if a bit skeptical—unsure what to believe from anyone in her family.

43

"Well . . ." She took a long breath. "According to some of the older locals, John Hadley built the house for his bride in 1939. He was still a young man but impressive—had built the lumber business he inherited into quite an operation. He met Adeline Doyer on a trip to San Antonio, and apparently theirs was quite the love story. They were both more or less alone in the world, and they dreamed of having a large family." She waved an arm toward the house. "Thus, the size."

Taking a deep breath, she went on. "Anyway, John and Adeline still didn't have any children two years later when the Japanese bombed Pearl Harbor, and Mr. Hadley enlisted to fight." She paused, holding up a finger. "But then, just a few months after he was sent to the Pacific, Adeline received word that he'd been killed in action."

Owen scratched his forehead. "I thought this story was about a bunker."

"I'm getting there." She reached both hands to her head and pulled her ponytail tight before she took another deep breath. "Apparently, when John Hadley went to war, Adeline had her hired man build a small bunker somewhere in or under the house."

"Why would she do something like that?"

"It actually wasn't uncommon back then. We can get pretty big storms around here—hurricanes and such."

"This far inland?"

"You'd be surprised. We can still get lots of wind and rain and sometimes tornadoes. But I suspect Adeline was just feeling really insecure, being there alone without her husband. And remember, Pearl Harbor had just happened, and no one knew if there would be other attacks. She wanted to feel safe, and the bunker seemed a way to do that. Anyway, when Adeline got word of Mr. Hadley's death, she bolted out of town and disappeared, leaving nothing but a note for her attorney on the kitchen table." She grinned broadly. "Guess who has that note?"

"I'm guessing you?" Owen smiled at her enthusiasm.

Brooke nodded. "Yep. Before the attorney died, he gave it to my husband, knowing that he was a preserver of old letters, photographs, things like that. He owned a store here in town called the Treasure Chest. He loved anything old—books, antique toys, and all kinds of other vintage items."

Owen's curiosity was growing. "What did the note say?"

"I'll find it and show it to you, but it basically left an Arkansas forwarding address and instructions for him to sell the house and all the furnishings. And it said . . ." She closed her eyes for a moment. "Trying to remember the exact words." Her eyes flew open as she snapped her fingers. "Oh, I know. It said, 'All of my worldly treasures are those of the heart, buried safely beneath this house that love built.'" She shrugged. "Everyone around here thinks that Adeline Hadley stashed something of importance in the bunker before she fled town."

"Like what?" Owen shifted his weight as he folded his arms across his chest. "I haven't found any bunker."

Brooke frowned. "Neither did the two women who bought the house from Adeline. They were sisters whose husbands had both been killed, and they took in boarders to make a living."

"Hmm." Owen wasn't sure he bought the story. "How do you know the bunker isn't outside somewhere on the grounds?"

"I don't for sure." She shrugged. "And maybe there is no bunker at all. But like I said, folks around here think that the bunker is somewhere in the house and that Adeline left something important there."

"Hmm," Owen said again as he waited for her to go on.

Brooke pushed back a strand of blond hair, her features

animated. "The two sisters didn't do much to the house, except to have central air installed back in the seventies."

"Which isn't working," Owen grumbled.

Brooke frowned. "Well, it's disappointing that you haven't found the bunker either."

Owen chuckled, still unsure if she was making all this up. "Maybe the two women found the *treasure* and just never told anyone."

She shook her head. "I don't think so. They lived there until they died, and once they'd stopped taking in boarders, they were pretty reclusive and kept to themselves. The handyman who built it left town about the same time Adeline did—just kind of disappeared without telling anyone where it was. And the house has been vacant since the last sister died—well, until you bought it."

"So no one's found Adeline's bunker."

"Not that I know of. Even Mr. Hadley doesn't know where it is."

"Wait a minute. I thought you said he was killed."

"Apparently that was a mistake. In fact, Mr. Hadley is still alive today, in his nineties. He's in the same retirement villa where my mother lives."

"So did he and his wife get back together?"

"That's the really sad part. She left town before the mistake was discovered. He'd been badly wounded, then captured by the Japanese. He spent the duration of the war as a prisoner on some Pacific island, with everyone here thinking he was dead. They didn't find out he was alive until the end of the war."

She smiled. "I'm told the entire town gave him a big party when he returned. But by that time his house was sold and his wife was gone, and he wasn't able to track her down for a long time. He finally learned she'd remarried and left Arkansas, moved around a bit, and then died in childbirth out in Wichita Falls. Not sure when that was, but I do know Mr. Hadley never saw her again. And he never remarried."

Owen shook his head. "That's a sad story." *And you seem so normal right now.*

He waited to see if there was more. Apparently there wasn't. They stood there awkwardly for just a minute as he remembered Brooke's mention of her husband.

"So . . . are you divorced?" It was totally off topic, but maybe the woman despised her ex-husband, and they could find common ground and entertainment by bashing their exes. Or maybe her husband had left because of her illness.

Brooke's face instantly went somber. "Travis died two years ago in a car accident."

"I'm sorry." Owen had wished on more than one occasion that Virginia was dead, although he knew he didn't mean it. As painful as divorce was, he couldn't imagine what he would do if she'd died.

"We would have been married twelve years next week." She stuffed her hands in the back pockets of her jeans. "What about you?"

"Divorced." That's all he had to offer at the moment.

Brooke nodded. "Do you have children?"

Owen felt himself tense. "Uh, no. No kids."

"I have two. Meghan is six, and Spencer is ten."

"I met your son. He stopped by yesterday morning." Owen avoided her eyes, scratched his forehead. "He was, uh, looking for you."

She chuckled. "I doubt it. He was probably hiding from me. He got upset with me about something and ran out the door. Yesterday, when I saw you, I'd just gotten a phone call that

47

he was at the hardware store." She paused. "I hope he didn't bother you too much."

Oh, he was a regular cornucopia of information about you, lady. "Absolutely no bother."

"So how are the renovations coming?" She peered around Owen toward the front door.

"Well, my paint is sticking this time." His dark eyebrows slanted in a frown. "Although I wish it wasn't sticking in my bedroom. I hate the color I just painted it. I'm hoping I can just paint over it."

"What color is it?"

"The name on the can is 'Dusky Mauve.'"

She grinned but quickly covered her mouth.

"I know." Owen had to laugh. "It's a little bit girly."

"Well, now, I didn't say that." She reached up and tightened her ponytail. "What color do you want it to be?"

"Black." That just came out, but Owen didn't even try to withdraw it.

"Really?"

"No. Guess that's just my mood today. I hate the purple bedroom." He pointed over his shoulder. "Also, apparently I missed a stud hanging the porch swing, and it fell." Nodding toward the driveway, he added, "And my car won't start."

"Hmm. That all stinks." Her voice was firm, but Owen could see the hint of a smile playing on her lips. "Could always be worse."

He grunted. "I guess."

"Where were you headed?" She nodded to the car. "Do you need a ride somewhere?"

"No, but thanks. I wasn't really headed anywhere. Just too mad to stay and look at my girly bedroom and my broken swing. Guess I'll add broken car to the list."

"Jack's Auto will be open at seven thirty tomorrow morning. They are your best bet. Good guys, and fairly cheap." She peered around him toward the house. "You know, my husband was always fascinated by this house—and the letter the attorney gave him. I hope you find the bunker."

Owen grinned. "You're really intrigued about that, aren't you?"

She was quiet, still staring at the house, then she looked back at him. "I can show you the letter, although there wasn't much else in it except what I already told you. And I think there might be some photos at my husband's store that could help you restore the house to its original state—if that's what you're trying to do."

"Sure. I'd like to see the pictures." Owen wasn't sure if he'd be able to restore the house to its former glory, but it would still be fun to see what it looked like in its prime. "And the letter, I guess. I can stop by the store to get it anytime that's convenient for you."

"Anytime?" Brooke tipped her head to one side. "Don't you have a job or something?"

"I used to. I was in public relations but recently sold out to my partner to move here." He was hoping she wouldn't ask any more questions.

"I haven't been in the Treasure Chest, my husband's store, since . . ." She paused, took a deep breath, and stared to her left. "Since before he died. The landlord let me leave the inventory there until he found a new tenant, and no one has ever wanted it." Her voice trembled just slightly. "So all Travis's stuff is still there."

"Hey, don't get the pictures if it's going to upset you." Owen didn't want her to do anything that might cause her some sort of emotional setback.

Brooke stood a bit taller and gave her head a decisive nod. "No, I probably need to take that next step. It's been almost two years." She blinked several times and then gazed off down the street as if lost in thought.

Owen forced himself to think of that alleged rash on her back. Otherwise he'd have to admit how attracted he was to her. That surprised him. Brooke didn't look anything like Virginia, who spent countless amounts of money on her hair, makeup, and who knows what else. Brooke was more of a natural beauty. Without a speck of makeup, she was gorgeous.

Think about those terrible bumps. But even that thought was doing little to deter Owen's eyes from running the length of her body. Luckily, she didn't seem to notice. She was staring around him at the house again.

"I'll tell you what," she finally said. "I'll get the letter and the pictures for you sometime this week. But"—holding up one finger, she locked eyes with him—"I get to have one really good look around your new house."

Owen laughed. "You want to look for the supposed bunker."

"Yeah, I guess I do. And I want to see the house too. It's been locked up so tight for the past ten years."

"Sounds like a deal. Any day is fine with me."

Brooke ran her hands along the sides of her jeans and nodded. "Great." She turned to leave, but spun around. "Do you want me to bring a pizza or something?"

Owen's entire body went stiff as the warning bells sounded loud and clear in his head. This was starting to resemble more than a quick tour through the house—and that was not good.

Normal or nuts, Brooke was probably looking for a husband and father for her children, and Owen was not what she was looking for. He certainly didn't want to do anything to lead her on, especially if she was a bit off in the head.

But as she stood there smiling at him, Owen's mouth seemed to have a mind of its own.

"Sure. Pizza sounds great."

⊰❧⊱

Brooke reprimanded herself all the way back home. She'd been right that it was time to open up Travis's store. Maybe getting the pictures and letter for Owen could be the first step. But what in the world had made her offer up pizza, almost like it was a date or something—a date she'd set up.

If she was honest with herself, she'd have to admit that Owen Saunders was the first man she'd been attracted to since Travis, but it wouldn't be fair to lead him on. Brooke knew in her heart that she would never love another man the way she loved Travis. Everyone else would come in a distant second, and that made having any kind of relationship seem selfish. She would only be using a man for companionship—maybe someone to say she looked pretty from time to time or a strong guy to help with chores around the house. And that person would have to love her children. But Travis had been her first. Her only. She couldn't imagine kissing someone else, much less . . .

She shook her head to clear the thoughts. She'd wanted to investigate that house for years, but the two sisters who owned it after Mrs. Hadley had been very private back when Brooke was growing up. She had gone over there once when she was about ten to sell Girl Scout cookies. The older of the two women had left her standing on the front porch while she went to get her checkbook, dashing her hopes of seeing inside. The most she'd done over the years was look in the windows.

51

If nothing else, she now had a chance to poke around the old place. She was doubtful that the bunker even existed, but having a look around would be a nice distraction from, well, other things in her life—like the flowers from her father. What nerve he had, thinking she'd want anything to do with him. Not only had he cheated on her mother, but he had abandoned both of them. Mom had been young enough to find someone else back then, but she'd always said she could never love another man the way she loved Harold Miller. *How could she say that about a cheater?*

Brooke felt the same way about Travis, but her husband hadn't been anything like her father, thank God. She wished her mother could have found someone to share her life with over the years.

She rounded the corner toward home, feeling a bit agitated. Upset about the flowers from her dad. Nervous to face the Treasure Chest. Excited to look around the Hadley mansion. And strangely unsettled by the tingling that ran up her spine at the thought of seeing Owen Saunders again.

Six

By the time Friday evening came around, Owen had decided that Brooke must have changed her mind about bringing the letter and photos . . . and the pizza. And that was okay. Over the past five days, he'd traveled to Austin, bought khaki-colored paint, and managed to paint over the purple color in his bedroom with ease. He'd also figured out that there was a way to expand the room's tiny closet without any major remodeling. He'd had to buy one of those how-to books to get going, but he'd made great progress. So if Brooke Holloway didn't show up, so be it. He'd avoided going to her hardware store for reasons he couldn't quite explain.

He was sitting on his newly hung porch swing about eight o'clock when he saw her walking down the street toting a pizza box, the sun barely starting to set behind her, the oak trees forming an arch over the street. It was a picture-perfect street with an awesome view. Virginia would have loved it. Owen stood up when Brooke got closer.

"I was starting to think you'd changed your mind." Owen immediately took note of the white capri pants she was wearing and the fitted pink blouse. Pink was a good color for her.

His eyes drifted to her white flip-flops and pink toenails. Even her feet were cute. Her hair was down, no baseball cap. He'd had trouble keeping his eyes off her before, but this new look was intoxicating.

She walked up the porch steps and held up the pizza box. "I'm afraid I didn't keep up my end of the bargain." She pushed the box toward him. "I don't have the pictures or the letter yet, but I did promise pizza." Smiling, she nudged the box toward him until he took it.

Owen wasn't sure what to say. Maybe going back into her husband's store had been too much for her. "It's okay."

"Oh, I'll get the pictures and the letter for you tomorrow." She shook her head, grinning. "I got myself all prepared to go in last night, and I couldn't find the key anywhere. It's an antique lock, so I hated to jimmy it open. Lennie Potter is the locksmith we use, and he's out of town until tomorrow. So I'll get him to cut me a key then."

"Oh." Owen couldn't take his eyes from her.

"Anyway"—she tucked her hair behind her ears—"if you're busy, you can keep the pizza, and I'll go. I just didn't want you to think I forgot, and I found myself without my children tonight, so . . ." She blushed, shrugging.

"No way," he said loudly. "I'm not eating this all by myself. I eat alone every night, so I was looking forward to some company." It was true, but he made a mental note not to do anything to lead her on. Then for reasons he would later analyze, he faked a sneeze.

"Bless you."

"Thank you." He opened the front door to let her walk in front of him. "Lots of allergies here in this part of Texas."

She looked over her shoulder at him and smiled. "I guess I'm lucky. I'm not allergic to anything."

Hmm. He followed her in.

"I love the smell of fresh paint," she said as she stopped in the entryway. Owen waited for her to finish her inspection. "This is a great color."

Owen walked to her side and gazed upon his first project. It had certainly been a pain—the painting, scraping, primer, then repainting. And the wall color didn't look anything like the sample strip. It was supposed to be a very pale grassy green but had turned out much darker. But it contrasted nicely with the cream-colored woodwork.

"You think this color is okay?" Owen balanced the pizza box in one hand and touched the wall in front of them with the other.

Brooke smiled. "I love bold colors." She turned to him. "What accent pieces do you have for this room?"

Owen laughed. "Accent pieces? Uh . . . none. Yet."

"There's a great store farther down Main Street that sells décor from this time period."

Owen was in new territory, for sure. He'd never picked out a piece of furniture or art in his life. "I'll have to check it out." He motioned her down the hallway and to the kitchen, where he had set up a small table and two chairs near a large window. He put the pizza down on the table, then scurried around the outdated kitchen to find a stack of paper plates and a roll of paper towels. "I'm afraid I can't offer you fine dining on good china."

Brooke laughed. "Well, that's a disappointment." She accepted the paper plate and lifted the lid on the pizza box. "I just got plain ol' pepperoni. Not sure what you liked."

"Plain ol' pepperoni sounds great." Owen piled his plate with three slices as a bead of sweat slipped down the side of his face. Even with the kitchen windows open and a box fan on the counter turned up high, they were both dripping. "I hope you won't think this is out of line, but we're both going to melt in here. The only room I have air-conditioning in is my bedroom."

Brooke pressed her lips together and raised an eyebrow.

Owen scratched his chin. "Best pick-up line you've ever heard, huh?" *What is wrong with me? Stop flirting.*

"Yes, I do believe it is." She dabbed at her forehead with her paper towel. "But I think I'm going to have to accept your offer."

Owen walked to the small refrigerator-freezer he'd bought to store a few things and make ice until he could figure out exactly what he was going to do with the kitchen. He pulled out two bottled waters. "This okay?"

Brooke nodded as she picked up their plates. Then she followed Owen down the long hallway to his bedroom.

Opening the door, he mentally kicked himself. Why hadn't he thought about this scenario earlier? He kicked a pair of underwear under the bed, hoping she didn't see, but there was no hiding the two piles of clothes in the corner. On the left was dirty. Clean ones were to the right. "Sorry. I bought a bed, and that's about as far as I got."

Brooke walked to the frame of the new closet as she bit into a slice of pizza. "This will be a great closet." She turned to him, grinning. "I bet you hate armoires. Most men do. My husband couldn't stand ours. We had two in our bedroom." Gazing around the room, she continued to smile. "This is a huge room, and I love the color in here too."

Owen pulled up the brown comforter on his bed, then sat down. Brooke walked over and sat down beside him. Frowning, she said, "You're not going to keep this comforter, are you?"

Owen loved that comforter, but he knew it was worn out. Probably the only reason Virginia had let him have it. It also made for a lot of brown in the room. "I guess not."

"So many times I wanted to change out the comforter in our bedroom, but Travis insisted we keep the one we had." She shrugged. "It was really old, but he said it was broken in."

She'd mentioned her husband twice in the last few minutes. Owen wondered if that was the norm. Not that it mattered. "Where are your children tonight?"

"My friend Judy invited them over. Her kids are the same ages as mine. So I have a much-needed night to myself." She took another bite of pizza.

For the next thirty minutes or so they covered the basics—where they'd grown up and where they'd gone to school—or hadn't. Neither Brooke nor her husband had gone to college. They'd done well in high school but chose to stay in Smithville afterward and run their businesses. Owen told Brooke a little about his days at Texas Tech, but didn't bother to mention that's where he'd met Virginia. Though Brooke liked to talk about her husband, Owen preferred to avoid mentioning his ex-wife.

"Didn't you ever want to leave here?" Owen took a gulp of water. "I mean, I thought people who grew up in a small town always looked forward to the day they could leave."

"Well, us country bumpkins actually do go to the big city from time to time. Travis and I were huge fans of the theater. There's a small theater here in Smithville. Maybe that's how we first got hooked, but we branched out to Houston and Austin. We even went to New York for our anniversary one year."

Owen felt himself blushing. "I didn't mean to insinuate that you're a country bumpkin."

She laughed. "Sure you did. But that's okay." Brooke sat

taller. "I reckon us country folks don't get 'round as much as you city folks."

Owen laughed out loud at her put-on accent. "I stand corrected."

"Seriously, though, we thought about leaving. But this was a great place to grow up, and it's still a wonderful place to raise kids." She paused to take a swig from her water bottle. "It's slower here. And truthfully, I don't think I'd be happy in a big city."

The jury was still out on that for Owen. He'd grown up in Austin. City life was all he'd ever known—until now.

Brooke set her empty pizza plate on the bed and picked up a paper towel to wipe her hands.

"More?" Owen started to stand up.

"No. You go ahead. I'm full."

Owen ate two more pieces of pizza and still wasn't ready for her to leave. When she pulled a band from her wrist and twisted her hair into a ponytail, Owen was drawn to the way her blouse cut to a low V down her back. There were no oozing red bumps that he could see. She seemed perfectly normal. Better than normal. And no allergies? *Hmm.* All of a sudden his blood seemed to be pumping harder, and he thought it might be best to get her out of his bedroom.

"I bet you're ready to look at the rest of the house." He paused. "It's really hot, though."

She stood up, grinning. "That's okay. I'd love the grand tour."

"Are you going to be pushing on walls to find the bunker?" He chuckled. "There's one built-in bookcase upstairs, but I've never leaned against it or anything—you know, to see if it rotates into a secret room."

"Well, I just might." She slapped her hands against her

white pants. "Although, the bunker would be *below* the house."

Owen motioned for her to step in front of him, a little intrigued himself. "Downstairs we have the entryway, powder room, living room, formal dining room, and kitchen—plus this bedroom, of course, and the full bath right next door. Where do you want to start?"

She shrugged. "Let's just start here and work our way around."

Owen followed Brooke around the downstairs for the next five or ten minutes. They were checking out the last room, the kitchen, when she turned to him and laughed. "This is dumb, isn't it?" She was glistening with sweat—they both were—but she was a feast for the eyes nonetheless. And absolutely nothing about her hinted she was anything other than sane.

"Listen, I have to ask you something." Owen finally led her back into the kitchen. *Don't do it. You don't care. You don't need to know.*

"What's that?" She positioned herself in front of the fan and lifted her ponytail behind her.

Owen leaned against the counter and crossed his ankles. "You said earlier that you weren't allergic to anything. Is that true? Nothing?"

"Uh, not that I know of." She scrunched her face up. "Why?"

Owen was already out there, so why stop now? "Just wondering." He held up a finger. "And one more thing. Do you get lost easily?"

Brooke's hands slammed to her hips. "Okay, what's going on? You keep asking me if I'm lost. Do I look lost?" She glanced down at herself with an exasperated grin.

"Remember when I told you I met your son? Spencer, right?"

59

"Yeah. I remember."

Owen closed one eye tight, took a deep breath, and hoped for the best. He opened his eye and looked down at her. "Spencer told me that you aren't right in the mind and that you get lost a lot."

The color drained from her face. "He did *what*?"

Owen shrugged. "That's what he told me."

Brooke shook her head, frowning. "Why would Spence say such a thing?"

"That's not all."

"Uh-oh. What else?" She sat down on one of the kitchen chairs.

"He, uh . . . well . . ."

She threw a hand up. "Just spit it out."

Owen cocked his head to one side, sighed, and said, "Well, he told me you have an allergy and that you have big red bumps all over your back." Owen squeezed his eyes closed when she jumped from the chair.

"Are you making this up?"

"No, I promise." Owen held his palms up and toward her. "He said they were big red bumps oozing with—"

"Oh good grief! Stop. Please." She bent at the waist and propped her hands against her knees for a few moments.

"I'm only telling you this because your son went out of his way to make sure that I found you totally repulsive. He even told me that you were allergic to flowers, however that is relevant."

When Brooke straightened, her face was bright red. "I am so embarrassed." Then she burst out laughing, and Owen couldn't help but laugh along with her. "I think I know what this is about." She shook her head. "I got some flowers at home last week, and somehow I think Spencer must have thought they were from you. I just can't believe he'd lie like that."

Owen's heart sped up. He shouldn't be surprised that someone was sending her flowers. She was attractive and single.

But for some reason he had to work to keep the smile on his face.

        ❧

Brooke followed Owen up the stairs, but all she really wanted to do was go home. She wasn't sure she'd ever stop blushing. How could Spencer say all that? Brooke understood that Spencer didn't want her dating anyone, but she was surprised that he would lie like that just to make sure Owen thought she was crazy and hideous.

They went room to room, and Brooke tried to pretend she was still intrigued about the possibility of a secret room or bunker. But she'd lost her excitement in light of Owen's news—until they walked into the fifth bedroom upstairs. It was much larger than the others and dirtier, almost as if no one had ever lived in there. A large water stain in the corner of the ceiling and down one wall hinted that the roof was in need of attention.

The room was also home to the built-in bookcase, which did pique Brooke's sense of adventure. She checked all around the floor before she focused on the bookcase.

"Go ahead." Owen nodded to the shelves, which were about four feet wide. "I know you're dying to put your weight into it and see if it swings into another room."

Brooke forced a smile. *Wait 'til I get my hands on you, Spencer.* The few times her children had needed spankings,

Travis had handled it while Brooke put her hands over her ears. She hadn't needed to spank them since Travis died. Now Spencer might be too old for a spanking, but she couldn't have him lying. Although she had to question what she was most upset about—the lies or the content of his stories.

"That's a very cool bookcase." She ran a hand along the dusty surface, then leaned one shoulder against it and pushed.

"If you fall through onto the other side, I'll be along shortly." Owen laughed but then tapped her on the arm. "Step aside, my dear."

Dear? It was playful, but still . . .

Owen threw his weight against the structure until he grunted, but the bookcase didn't budge. Had she really thought it would? The whole idea seemed silly now. "I don't think it's going to budge," he said as he wiped his forehead.

"Well, we tried." Brooke turned to leave the room. "I don't think the bunker would be aboveground anyway. If it exists."

"Wow. You give up easily."

I'm embarrassed and want to go home. She turned around. "Tomorrow, when I get into the store, I'll look for the pictures and the letter. Maybe that will give you some clues."

She left the room and started down the stairs. She could hear Owen following.

"Don't be too hard on Spencer," Owen said as if reading her mind.

They had reached the landing, but Brooke kept going down to the entryway before she turned around. "I'll try not to."

Owen grinned. "I'm just superglad to hear you're not crazy and you don't have those, uh, things on your . . ." He flinched as Brooke held up her palms again.

"Please. I don't want to hear." She couldn't help but grin.

"Thanks for the pizza and not making me endure another meal alone."

If that was a hint for her to invite him to dinner, she wasn't biting. Spencer would probably kick him in the shins or something. "Thanks for showing me around."

She was almost out the door when Owen said, "So . . ."

Eyebrows raised, she stopped and turned around.

"I was going to ask you when you thought you might be over with the pictures and letter, but why don't I just give you my cell number." He reached into his pocket, pulled out a card, and handed it to her. "Don't have the company anymore, but the cell number's still the same." He pointed toward the BMW in the driveway. "Can I offer you a lift or walk you home?"

"No, no. I've been walking these streets at night since I was a kid. It's no big deal."

"Do you let your children walk these streets at night?"

"Well, no. They're too young."

Owen closed the door behind him. "You don't need to be walking home alone either."

"Not really necessary, but okay."

The short walk home turned out rather pleasant. Brooke listened to Owen detail his move to Smithville—how he'd sold just about everything he owned in an effort to start fresh, and how he really didn't know the first thing about restoring an old house. This did not come as a surprise.

"So why did you do it?" Brooke slowed down as they approached her house.

Owen stopped when she did and shrugged. "I needed a change. I needed to get away from my ex, Virginia."

Clearly he was still bitter—or not over—his divorce. "I guess change can be good. For some people." She shifted her purse on her shoulder. "Thanks for walking me home."

"Thanks again for the pizza. I guess just call me when you feel like coming back over with the letter and pictures, and we can have another look around. Wouldn't it be something if we did find a hidden room or bunker somewhere in that house?"

"I'll get Lennie to cut me a key tomorrow, then I'll call you soon." Brooke's stomach churned at the thought of going into the Treasure Chest, but it was time. "Good night."

❧

Owen walked back home, feeling better than he'd felt in a long time. It felt good to have someone to talk to.

Brooke was clearly still hung up on her husband. She'd talked about him a lot. And Owen was still hung up on Virginia, despite the circumstances. But maybe he and Brooke could be friends. It would be nice to have a female friend. Maybe eventually he would feel comfortable enough to talk to her about Virginia. Perhaps a woman's perspective would shed some light on exactly what had gone wrong. Maybe he'd done something wrong he wasn't aware of. Or maybe Virginia was just a terrible person and no amount of analyzing would make any difference. Either way, he'd enjoyed the company and the pizza.

As he climbed his front porch steps, he slowed down. "Where'd you come from?"

Lounging in front of the door was a large black cat sprawled out like he—or she—owned the place. Owen wasn't superstitious by nature, but he'd had enough bad luck to last him a lifetime. He was relieved to see a small white patch on the cat's tail, but he still wished the animal would go away.

He wasn't much of a cat person. Most felines he'd met were finicky and uppity, and once as a boy he'd been attacked by a cat his mother brought home. He glanced down at his forearm. Even though the scar was gone, the memory was clear.

He stepped forward, assuming the animal would run away. It just looked up at him and blinked. He stepped around it and opened the front door. The feline jumped up suddenly and darted across the threshold.

"Oh no you don't." Owen dove for the cat, but the animal was quick, running past him and straight up the stairs. "Whatever." He walked to his bedroom and closed the door to his nice cool room, too tired to deal with the animal tonight. Maybe there was a way for it to get out. If not, he'd chase it out in the morning and take care of any accidents upstairs. That part of the house was still in rough enough shape that he wasn't really worried.

His room was silent apart from the hum of the AC. Tomorrow he was going to buy a television. He was surprised he'd lasted this long without one. Dozing off with his iPhone running Pandora was getting old.

After a quick shower, he crawled into bed and was just setting the music to play when he heard a loud crash upstairs, then footsteps that sounded like a herd of animals.

The cat.

He briefly considered going upstairs to nab the animal and put it outside where it belonged, but once he lay back on the bed, that idea got as weary as he was. Despite his body's need for sleep, his mind wouldn't shut down. Virginia's face was all over the place, occupying parts of his mind that he wished he could close off forever. Sometimes the pain and bitterness comingled with such longing for the past that it was hard to breathe. It was easiest when he was angry and could convince himself that he hated Virginia. But the anger was a loose Band-Aid that always fell off—usually late at night when he was alone.

Squeezing his eyes closed, he fought the images of that night almost a year ago—the night he walked in on Virginia and Gary. His friend and business partner had tried to tell him it wasn't how it looked, but Virginia had made no excuses. She'd filed for divorce the following week, confessing that the affair had been going on for a year.

He fluffed his pillow, stared out the window into the darkness, and wondered if he would ever stop loving her.

Seven

Saturday morning Brooke made her trek to the calendar in the kitchen and drew another big *X*. Thirty-five days left. Then, after their pancake ritual, she dropped the kids off at the store for Juliet to watch them while she went to see Lennie at his locksmith shop. An hour later, key in hand, she was crossing Main Street toward the Treasure Chest.

So far she'd opted not to say anything to Spencer about the wild tale he'd told Owen. She needed to. She couldn't have him lying. But talking to him would mean a long conversation about why her father had sent the flowers, and Brooke had no answer for that anyway. *I hope to see you soon,* he'd written on the card. What was her father thinking?

Maybe she would talk to Spence tomorrow. For today, going into the store would be enough of a feat.

She took a deep breath and turned the key in the lock, halfway hoping it wouldn't work. But it did. The door stuck a little at first, but when she pushed harder it swung wide. The familiar aroma of old books filled her nostrils and she breathed it in, closing her eyes for a moment, picturing Travis sitting at the desk in the corner. The room was dark and cool because she'd kept the electricity on to protect the merchandise. She reached for the light switch without looking, keeping her eyes on the desk, picturing Travis smiling at her.

Once the lights were on, despair filled Brooke's heart. Not only did she miss Travis more than ever in this place, but she'd allowed his most prized possessions to become covered in dust. As she moved between two tables covered with some of his favorite collections, she ran a hand along several of the dust jackets, pulling back thick powder. Now that she was here, she realized she was going to have to do more than just find the pictures of the Hadley mansion and the letter. Mr. Knopick had been incredibly patient with her, but Travis's things couldn't stay here forever.

Brooke sat down at Travis's desk and ran her hand over the dusty surface as she eyed the picture of the two of them together at the beach in Galveston a few years ago. "I miss you so much," she whispered.

She looked around the small store filled with everything Travis loved. Some of it he'd collected since he was a kid, but most of it he'd picked up at estate sales—books, paintings, vinyl records, old photo albums, and an assortment of other trinkets and antiques. On a small table in the corner was a collection of vintage toys. Brooke picked up a model airplane that she recalled Travis being really excited about. She didn't think it had ever flown and probably wasn't worth much, but he had loved it.

A whiff of dust blew up her nose when she picked up the plane, causing her to sneeze. She thought about what Spencer had told Owen, and she couldn't help but smile. *Owen must have thought I'm so gross.* It wasn't really funny, but as she looked around the store, she didn't have to try hard to keep things in perspective. Without a doubt, she was going to have to make time to clean this place up and either sell the inventory or store it, a task she hadn't felt up to doing. She still didn't, but it needed to be done. Just not today.

Pictures and the letter. Where would they be?

Brooke could see every inch of the store. There were no tall bookshelves. All the inventory was arranged on desks and tables, much of the furniture also antiques. She glanced at the boarded-up windows. Big Daddy put up the boards last year when they'd had a hurricane threat and she had left them up to protect the merchandise. But if she was going to clean things up, she needed to take those boards down and let in some sunshine. *Maybe my heart will open up and see some light someday too.*

On a narrow table that ran almost the length of one wall, books were lined vertically against the wall, and in front of them were old magazines Travis had collected over the years, even some old comic books. He had always been a kid at heart. And even though the store had never made much money, it represented everything good about Travis. Brooke picked up a comic book dated June 1965. She was flipping through the worn pages when she heard the bell on the door ding.

"Hey, buddy," she said to Spencer as he shuffled into the store. She put the comic back down. "Dusty in here, huh?"

Spencer nodded as his eyes roamed the room. Brooke watched him carefully, hoping he was ready to be here. Spence slowly walked to the model airplane.

"Do you want to keep that? I'm sure Dad would want you to have it." Brooke put a hand on his shoulder, but he eased away as he shook his head.

"It doesn't fly."

"I know. I just thought you might want it." Brooke took a deep breath and swallowed hard. "Do you see anything special you'd like to take home?"

Spencer's expression was unreadable, but he shook his head. *Lord, when are we all going to heal?* Brooke would do anything to take Spencer's hurt away. Some days she wasn't sure she could miss Travis any more than she already did, but she'd take on every bit of Spencer's heartache if she could. Meghan missed her dad too, but she'd adjusted quicker because she'd been only four when Travis died. Spencer still struggled, every day.

"I'm looking for some pictures of the Hadley mansion. I think your dad had some somewhere." She paused. "Wanna help me look?"

Spencer's eyes glazed over as his face turned red. "For that *guy*? You're giving Dad's stuff away to that guy?" He clenched his fists at his sides.

"Spencer, that guy is named Owen." Brooke pointed a finger at him before he could say anything. "And he did not give me flowers." She paused. "I know about all the things you told him."

Her son had the good grace to turn red, but he didn't say anything.

"Spencer, I don't want you lying." She walked to him and lifted his chin until his eyes were locked with hers. "Seriously, Spence." Brooke grinned. "Big, red oozing bumps on my back?"

Spencer leaned away from her grip, but Brooke saw the hint of a smile.

"Pretty creative." Brooke playfully tapped him on the arm. "And gross." She waited a couple of beats before adding, "Honey, no one is ever going to replace your dad. You know that, right?"

Spencer's eyes filled as he looked up at her. "I'm not stupid, Mom. I know that you'll probably date someone and even marry him." He pressed his mouth firmly together, his face turning red again. "But I will never like whoever it is. Not ever!"

"Okay." Brooke spoke softly, thinking the issue was probably moot anyway. She couldn't see herself with anyone else either. "But I am going to look for the pictures for Owen to help him try to find the hidden bunker in his house."

"What?" Spencer swiped at his eyes. "What hidden bunker?"

"Oh, you didn't know about that?" Brooke walked to Travis's desk, trying to be cool and casual.

"What hidden bunker?" Spencer asked again, following her.

Brooke sat down. "Supposedly there is a hidden bunker somewhere in that house, but no one knows where it is. I'm hoping the pictures might help Owen find it. If it's really there, of course."

"You mean a secret hideout, like in the movies?" Spencer leaned his hands on the desk.

"Yes. Just like that." Brooke pulled out the desk drawer, knowing the pictures weren't in there, but hoping to give Spence time to get onboard. *And where is that letter?*

"I know where the pictures are." Spencer's face brightened before he turned and walked to a small hutch against the wall opposite from the long table. He pulled the door open and peeked inside, then turned to Brooke. "They're in here."

"Really? Great." Brooke knew pictures were stored in there, and that's where she would have looked first, but she wanted to credit her son. She walked to the hutch and looked in. "There's a lot to go through." She shook her head.

"I'll help." Spencer grabbed four photo albums and a brown bag that was behind them, then Brooke pulled out a couple of albums. They both sat right down on the dirty floor where they'd been standing. Brooke's heart didn't feel quite as heavy at the moment, and for that she silently thanked God.

Fifteen minutes later Spencer had made a discovery far greater than pictures of the Hadley mansion or any secret bunker.

"Mom," Spencer said softly, as if in awe. "Look at this."

Brooke leaned over to have a look. She slowly grasped the black-and-white photo as her hand began to tremble.

Spencer edged closer to Brooke. "Who is that?"

Brooke eyed the photo of a young boy sitting on the porch steps of an old farmhouse. "It's my father—your grandfather—when he was about your age." She took a deep breath. She knew what Spencer was thinking.

"I look exactly like him!" Spencer brought the photo closer to his face.

Brooke forced a smile, knowing that Spencer had inherited his grandfather's pale blue eyes and defined features. In this photo, her father even sported the same tightly clipped burr haircut that Spencer wore now. "Yes, you do."

She recalled the day she'd been spring cleaning and found a bag of old pictures in the closet. She'd pulled out all the ones of her father, stuffed them in a separate bag, and told Travis to destroy them. She'd known her mother had her own stash of pictures, and that was her mother's business, but she hadn't wanted any pictures of her father in her possession.

Obviously Travis hadn't followed instructions.

Spencer began pulling out more pictures, and with each one Brooke felt like a wound was being ripped open.

"Put them back, Spence." Brooke hastily took the pictures and shoved them back into the bag. "We'll look at them another day."

Spencer grunted, and after a few moments he asked, "Why'd he leave Grandma?"

Because Harold Miller is a selfish, cheating man who doesn't care anything about his family.

"Sometimes things just happen between people and it causes them to split up." Brooke stood up, shoved the bag back into the hutch, then sat down again. "Let's start looking for the pictures of the Hadley place. And we're looking for a handwritten letter too."

Spencer was perfectly still for a few moments, staring up at the bag in the hutch. "Can I have that bag?"

"No."

"Why not?"

"Because I said so." Brooke opened a photo album and began flipping through pictures she didn't recognize—some old portraits and a few landscape shots.

"Grandma said you don't really hate Grandpa. You just don't know how to process your feelings." Spencer folded his hands in his lap.

Brooke bit her tongue. "Really? Is that what Grandma said? Well, I don't feel like processing my feelings today either." Being back in the Treasure Chest was bringing up all sorts of feelings to process, and she didn't plan to add her father into the mix. "Now, help me look."

"What are we looking for?" Spencer finally opened up one of the albums.

"Any pictures of the house that Mr. Saunders lives in. Also a short letter signed by a woman named Adeline."

"Like this one?" Spencer held up a yellowed piece of paper. "It was loose in this album."

"Yeah." Brooke took the letter and tipped it toward the light. "Exactly like this one." She hadn't seen the letter in at least a decade, but she recalled the shaky penmanship and the black ink. "Do you want me to read it out loud?"

Spencer nodded, and Brooke took a deep breath.

"'To Mr. Jack Cunningham, attorney-at-law, As you know, I recently received word that my beloved John has been killed in action. It is too painful for me to carry on here without him, to wander within these walls, praying for a miracle that isn't meant to be. Therefore, with haste, I have chosen to relocate. All of my worldly treasures are those of the heart, buried safely beneath this house that love built. Everything else no longer holds meaning for me. Please sell my homestead and furnishings, keeping a percentage for your efforts. My forwarding address in Little Rock, Arkansas, is below. I will be leaving on the train and will contact you soon. Best always, Adeline Hadley.'"

Spencer fidgeted with the hem on his shorts. "That's a sad letter."

"Yeah. I know." Brooke could relate to Adeline. If it hadn't been for her children and mother, she might have felt the need to flee after Travis died. She reached for the photo album in Spencer's lap. "Here, let me see if this is the one with the pictures I remember seeing." She quickly fingered through the pages. "Yep, this is it. I'm going to lend it to Mr. Saunders."

She stood up and started putting the other albums back in the hutch. "And I'm going to take it to him this week, Spencer. So I'd appreciate you not telling him any more stories about me, now that you know the flowers aren't from him."

Spencer stood up too and handed her another album. "Then who did give you the flowers?"

Brooke knew she wasn't going to get out of this. "My father. Your grandfather."

"What? Really?"

"Yes, really. I have no idea why, and it really doesn't matter." She walked back to Travis's desk and sat down.

"Does Grandma know?"

"Yes. And I don't want to talk about it." She spoke firmly, hoping to end the conversation. "Now, what should we do with all this stuff of your dad's?"

Spencer looked around. "Nothing. Leave it all here."

Brooke gazed at Spencer, whose eyes were scanning all of Travis's treasures.

"We can't leave it here forever. It's been two years, Spence. That's why I asked if you wanted anything to take home." She paused, but kept going when her son didn't respond. "I guess we need to sell it."

"No!"

"Well, Spencer, we don't have room for all of this at the house. Mr. Knopick has been very nice to let us keep storing everything in here, but that's also probably part of the reason he hasn't had anyone interested in leasing the space."

"Not yet, Mom." Spencer blinked his eyes a few times, and Brooke swallowed back a lump in her throat.

"Okay. Not yet." She picked up her purse and the photo album with the loose letter tucked inside. "Come on. Let's get to the hardware store. Juliet is probably giving your sister free rein with the candy jar." She rubbed his head, and he jerked away as expected.

Brooke stared through the glass door as she locked it, unsure when she'd go back in. It needed to be soon, before she let another year or two slip by.

As she and Spencer crossed the street, she thought about the bag of pictures. She'd been so venomous about her father, so determined to write him out of her life. Not that she still wasn't, but there must have been a reason Travis held on to those pictures. Maybe as a legacy to their children—or maybe he suspected Brooke would want to go through them someday.

Today was not that day, but she kept turning over in her mind the fact that her father was suddenly wanting to make amends after all these years.

Why?

Eight

Patsy placed a bowl of cereal in front of Harold on Tuesday morning. They'd spent a glorious three days together shopping, dining out, and lots of other things that Patsy hadn't done in twenty years. She felt like a new bride, and although she felt wrapped in a cocoon of euphoria, she knew that one thing stood in the way of her happiness with Harold.

She sat down at the other end of her small kitchen table, wearing a blue satin robe she'd picked up while shopping, and circled her spoon in her bowl of cereal.

"Patsy . . ."

She looked across the table into Harold's blue eyes and smiled. "Yes, dear."

Harold reached across the table and latched onto her hand. "I can see the pain on your face. Tell me what to do and I'll do it."

Patsy squeezed his hand and forced another smile. "Brooke is very bitter." She paused, closing her eyes for a moment. "If she knew about us, she might disown me right along with you."

76

"You don't really think that, do you?" The love of her life released her hand, then leaned back against the chair and rubbed his chin. "Because I can't live with that."

Patsy shrugged. "I don't know." She cringed just thinking about Brooke's reaction to the renewed relationship between her parents.

"I'm going to talk to her." Harold sat taller and gave his chin a taut nod.

Patsy swallowed hard. "I don't think that's a good idea. Not yet anyway. I probably need to ease Brooke into a conversation about you."

Harold blinked a few times. "Can you ever completely forgive me, Patsy?"

She smiled. "You know I forgive you, Harold—you don't have to keep asking. But when Brooke knows everything, she's going to need to find it in her heart to forgive *me* too."

"You did what you felt was best." Harold hung his head. "I deserved it. And I want Brooke to know that."

Patsy took a bite of her cereal and swallowed. "We both made mistakes. But let's not say anything to Brooke yet. We're just getting to know each other again, and I want to relish these moments before we invite the rest of the world to share with us."

The truth was that fear twisted around Patsy's heart every time she thought about Brooke's reaction to the news. Would she pressure Patsy to give up Harold—or to choose between them? Would she understand the choices Patsy had made? She was praying almost constantly these days that the good Lord would open Brooke's heart. Brooke had been through so much. Patsy didn't want to cause her daughter more pain. But she wasn't sure she could survive losing Harold again.

"I will let you set the time frame." Harold scooped the last of his cereal into his spoon. "I'll talk to her when you think the time is right."

Patsy was pretty sure that there wasn't going to be a right time. But maybe, little by little, she could casually mention Harold to Brooke, reminding her daughter of the good times the three of them had shared, what a wonderful life they'd led before Harold left. Patsy refused to focus on all they'd missed in the past twenty years. Instead she set her dreams on what they could all have in the future, for however long God's grace provided for them.

Patsy stood up, cleared the bowls from the table, and was running water in them when Harold's arms circled her waist from behind, fueling the already heady sensation she got in his presence.

"What would you like to do today?" His lips brushed the back of her neck, soft as a whisper. She turned to face him, cupping his cheek in her hand.

"I don't care what we do, as long as we're together." Standing on her tiptoes, Patsy touched her lips to his. It felt so familiar, as if no time had passed. She tried to force all her fears aside and just bask in his embrace, let the joy consume her. But she knew this wasn't forever.

One day, maybe soon, he will leave me again.

⚘

Brooke turned another page in the photo album she'd brought home to lend to Owen. Then she reached for his business card on the end table by the couch, picked up her cell phone, and dialed the first two numbers before hanging up. She'd been doing that for three days—mostly because of the two e-mails that had popped up on her phone from Travis's mother. Just knowing they were there created a rush of guilt that stopped her every time.

She loved Travis's parents. She really did. But conversations with them sometimes felt like alcohol poured on an open wound. They tried to keep in touch, and she was good about sending pictures of the kids and news about what was going on with them. But she preferred e-mails over phone calls and personal visits, and she had to admit to relief that they lived so far away. She'd taken the kids to spend one Christmas with them in Colorado, and that was all she could endure. Having them close, seeing them often, would just be too painful.

"I thought that photo album was for that Mr. Saunders guy." Spencer sat down on the couch beside her, munching on a cookie.

"It is."

"Then why haven't you given it to him yet?"

Because I'm attracted to him, and I find that a bit unnerving. "I just haven't had time."

Meghan came into the room and plopped down on her pink beanbag chair. "I thought we were going to go see Grandma tonight."

Brooke stretched her legs out on the coffee table in front of her. "We were, but Grandma said she had some other plans." She scratched her chin. Something was up with her mother. It had been over a week since Brooke and the kids had seen her, and that seemed a bit ridiculous since Mom only lived three miles away. But she'd had some sort of excuse every time Brooke called and asked to stop by. One night she was tired. Then it was Bingo night. The last time Brooke called she was going shopping with a friend. Oh, and twice she was going to visit one of the other residents. Brooke knew her mother. Mom was probably sick and didn't want Brooke to know.

Tomorrow she was going to just show up, whether Mom liked it or not.

She jumped when her cell phone rang, glanced at the caller ID, and realized she'd looked at Owen's card enough over the past three days to recognize his number.

"Well, I've covered this place over and over," Owen said when she answered. "And I'm convinced there isn't a hidden bunker." He chuckled. "But I couldn't help but wonder if you'd found the pictures you were talking about, something that might give a hint."

Brooke cut her eyes quickly in Spencer's direction, then stood and hurried out of the room. "I did," she said, talking softly until she was in the privacy of her bedroom. "And I found the letter Adeline Hadley left behind." She paused. "I was going to bring everything over, just hadn't got around to— Spencer, what do you need?" She covered the phone with her hand as her son entered the room. "Spence, I'll be out in a minute."

"Let's go tonight," Spencer said. "I want to help look for the bunker."

"No. Leave. I'll be out in a minute."

Spencer grunted but left the room. Brooke uncovered the phone when she heard Owen asking if she was still there. "Sorry. Spencer helped me find the photo albums, so now he's all interested in the bunker."

"Is he, now?" Owen paused. "Well, why don't you all come over and help me look?"

Brooke glanced at her watch. "Um, well, I still need to feed the kids some dinner, then we could—"

"Listen, I really appreciate you finding those things. I know that couldn't have been easy—I mean, going into the store and everything. So let me order some pizzas, you bring the kids over, and we'll all see if we have any luck finding this bunker I am beginning to believe doesn't exist."

"Well, I know my son would be happy about that. And both Meghan and Spence love pizza. But why don't I just pick up some on the way?"

"No. This is on me. Just head over whenever you're ready."

Brooke sat down on her bed. "How did you get my cell phone number?"

"Juliet at the store. She said you were out running errands earlier today, but I didn't want to call you while you were busy." He paused. "Is that okay—I mean, that she gave me your number?"

"Uh, yeah, it's okay. Then I guess we'll see you soon."

After they'd said good-bye, she walked into the living room. "Let's take a ride," she said to the kids. Pointing a finger at Spencer, she added, "Are you going to behave yourself around Mr. Saunders?"

"Yeah, Mom. His house sounds cool if it's got a secret hiding place no one knows about."

Brooke grabbed her keys and slipped on her flip-flops. "Remember, it might not really exist."

Either way, they were all going to eat pizza at Owen's house, and something about that gave her a warm feeling all over. She glanced down at her worn-out blue T-shirt. "I'm going to change." A quick inspection of both her children, and she realized that Spencer needed to do the same thing. She waved a hand toward the stairs. "Clean shirt, please."

Spencer rolled his eyes but complied. Brooke fed Kiki, then wiped Meghan's chocolate ring from her mouth. Ten minutes later they were on their way.

Owen wasn't exactly sure why he had invited Brooke and the kids over. Loneliness, probably, and curiosity about those pictures. It surely couldn't have anything to do with the fact that she'd been on his mind since Friday. He shook his head, reminding himself not to do anything to lead her on. Lost in thought, he didn't check his caller ID when his cell phone rang.

"Hi, Owen."

His chest tightened at the sound of Virginia's voice. He forced himself calm, if not a bit formal. "Hello, Virginia."

"How's the house coming?"

Good. She knows. "Great. You were right. Smithville is a wonderful place to live. Picture perfect." He gritted his teeth as he smiled.

"Good. I'm so glad you're happy."

Happy? You evil— He took a deep breath and was trying to dream up just the right retort when she spoke up again.

"You got a letter from your uncle. Do you want me to forward it to you?"

"Yes. Thank you." Owen paused as he thought about Denny, his eccentric uncle who was traveling the world and checking items off his bucket list. Owen rattled off the address to Virginia, half hoping she'd drive by sometime and see the picture-perfect house that she was never going to live in.

"Okay, I'll put it in the mail." She was quiet for a few moments. "I'm glad you're doing okay, Owen. I really am."

Virginia, are you serious? He opened his mouth to unload on her, but then he saw Brooke pulling into his driveway, and he decided to take another approach. "I have to go. My date is pulling in." He squeezed his eyes closed and cringed, knowing that wasn't exactly what was happening.

"Date?"

"I have to go, Virginia. Thank you for forwarding the

letter." He pushed End on his phone, pleased with the role reversal that left him feeling in control. Usually Owen ended up screaming and yelling at her, then she would hang up on him. This would give her something to think about. Maybe she'd even be a little jealous. He smiled as he walked out to the car.

"You beat the pizza delivery guy here," he said as the driver-side door opened and Brooke stepped out. *Wow.* How could anyone continue to make jeans, T-shirts, and a ponytail look so good? The kids climbed out too, and Owen decided to address the little girl first, unsure what kind of response he might be in for from Spencer. "You must be Meghan."

Her blond ponytail bounced behind her as she nodded. Big brown eyes met Owen's. She was a mini Brooke right down to her white flip-flops and painted toes.

Brooke rounded the vehicle, toting a photo album and her purse. She nodded toward her son. "I believe you already know Spencer?"

The poor kid wouldn't meet his eyes, and his face turned three shades of red. Owen decided to cut him some slack.

"Nice to see you again, Spencer." He winked, then motioned for them all to come in. When they reached the living room, Owen pointed to the wall. "I got the living room painted over the past couple of days. What do you think of the color?"

Owen homed in on Brooke's face. His work in public relations had lent him some special skills, or so he thought, and he wanted to see her initial reaction to his unusual color selection.

"It's very nice," she said in a monotone voice as she avoided his eyes.

"You hate it." Owen drew in his eyebrows and took a deep breath.

She turned to face him, expressionless. "I wouldn't say that."

"I feel like I'm inside an orange!" Meghan piped up.

"Meghan, be nice." Brooke playfully put a hand over her daughter's mouth as both grinned.

"I knew it. It's supposed to be way darker than this, sort of a dark rust color." Owen shook his head. "But I figured I'd see what you thought before I painted over it, on the very off chance you liked it."

"Lots of repainting going on in this house. I said from the beginning that you would be good for business."

Owen felt bad for not buying his latest supplies from her store, and he was considering an excuse to give her when her cell phone rang in her purse. She excused herself and walked back into the entryway, but Owen heard her.

"Oh no. What's wrong?" A long pause. "I'll be right there."

"Everything okay?" Owen asked when she walked back into the room.

"I think so, but that was my mom's retirement villas. I need to go visit with the administrator."

"Now?" Owen looked at his watch. "The pizzas should be here any minute. Do you have time to eat first?" He could tell she was getting ready to bail, and he didn't feel like eating alone.

Spencer came to the rescue. "Mom, you said we were having pizza and could look for the hidden bunker." He crossed his arms across his chest.

"Spencer, don't act like that." Brooke turned to Owen. "I'm sorry about this. Sorry you ordered pizza for us and that we have to leave."

"Just leave Meghan and Spencer here." Owen smiled as he nodded at Spencer. "We can look for the bunker while you're gone."

Brooke bit her lip. "I don't know, Owen. I'm not sure—"

"Please, Mom." Spencer batted puppy-dog eyes at her.

Owen knew she was considering whether she knew him well enough to leave her children with him. He'd do the same in her place. "I understand if you're not comfortable with—"

"No, it's okay. They can stay."

Owen saw a flicker of apprehension as her jaw tensed, but he suspected the more pressing matter at the retirement place might not be something she wanted her children to hear.

"I hope everything is okay. We'll be eating pizza when you get back. Just take your time."

She was quickly out the door, and when Owen turned around, Spencer and Meghan were both staring at him. He realized he hadn't babysat anyone's kids before. Neither he nor Virginia had nieces or nephews, and by Virginia's preference most of the couples they ran around with didn't have children either. Owen fought the bitter bile in his throat, struggling to focus on the situation at hand.

He looked at both children and took a deep breath.

How hard can babysitting be?

Nine

rooke hurried into the administration office at the Oaks. She would have never left the kids with Owen if she hadn't recalled that Juliet had run a background check on him. Once Juliet figured out how to check out a person for less than five dollars, it had become almost like a hobby for her. You were fair game if you were new to town, and Juliet paid an extra ten dollars for a more extensive search if someone was asking her out. She'd deemed Owen worth the ten bucks as well, and he'd come out clean as a whistle.

Still, Brooke didn't know Owen all that well, and her stomach was churning. She hoped to make this as quick as possible.

Mrs. Doyle's office light was the only one on as Brooke walked through the main lobby, and all kinds of crazy thoughts ran through her head as she recalled her mother's avoidance over the past couple of weeks. All Mrs. Doyle had said on the phone was that they had concerns about her mother and could she please come to the office to discuss it.

"Brooke, honey, this could have waited until tomorrow, but I could hear the worry in your voice, so I was happy to stay late this evening." Mrs. Doyle looked at her watch, and Brooke doubted that Mrs. Doyle wanted to stay much later. It was already six thirty.

"Is Mom okay?"

"As I said on the phone, she's fine. We are just . . . well . . . concerned about her, her . . ."

Brooke shifted in her seat across from the director and tapped her foot nervously. "What is it? Concerned about what?"

Mrs. Doyle was not much younger than Brooke's mother, a small woman with short gray hair, cropped bangs, and—at the moment—a face that was turning red. She placed her palms firmly on her desk and sat taller.

"We are concerned about your mother's lifestyle." Mrs. Doyle raised her chin a little.

Brooke cocked her head to one side, confused. "Her *lifestyle*?"

"Yes." Mrs. Doyle lifted her chin even higher, casting her eyes down at Brooke. "Your mother is entertaining men in her apartment—or at least one man." She leaned forward. "His car is here some mornings, and two of the residents have told me that they've seen them making out like teenagers, right outside in the parking lot or on her front step."

"What?" Brooke had a mixed reaction as she tried to process this information. She was very happy that her mother must have found someone so late in life. But Mom wasn't the type of woman who would sleep around without being married. That part was disturbing. "Maybe it isn't the way it looks."

Mrs. Doyle frowned. "I think it is. And this is a small, close-knit community." She raised her eyebrows. "People talk, don'tcha know?"

Brooke nodded, realizing that this explained her mother's desire to be left alone. *She has a man in her life.* "I will talk to my mother, Mrs. Doyle. Thank you for bringing this to my attention." She stood to leave, and Mrs. Doyle walked around to the other side of the desk to stand next to her.

"I thought you'd want to know. We try to give our residents as much privacy as they need, but if we suspect that something dangerous or inappropriate might be going on, well, we tend to reach out to a loved one."

"I understand."

Brooke couldn't walk fast enough to get to her mother's apartment.

⚜

Patsy hurried to her door and looked through the peephole, then gasped.

"It's Brooke." She ran to the couch where Harold was sitting. "Hurry. Get up and go hide in the bedroom."

He stood up slowly, floundering in place. "Are you sure, Patsy? Are you sure you don't want to just get this over with?"

Patsy shook her head as she coaxed him into her room. "No, no. Not tonight." She closed the door behind him, ran a hand through her tousled hair, then pulled her blue robe snug around her. She opened the door a few inches and poked her head out. "Brooke, honey, what are you doing here?"

"Mom, are you going to let me in?" Her daughter's tone was insistent, so Patsy opened the door wide and let her in.

"I wasn't expecting you." Patsy forced a smile, hoping Harold stayed quiet.

Brooke walked around the small living room and kitchen, eyeing every nook and cranny. Patsy was thankful she'd cleaned the dishes in the small sink and put them away.

"I'll bet you weren't expecting me." Brooke pulled her

purse up on her shoulder, scratched her forehead, then stared at Patsy.

"Where are my grandchildren?" Patsy's stomach clenched tight, and she tried to avoid looking at her closed bedroom door.

"Uh, with a friend." Brooke sat down on the couch and crossed her legs, her purse still on her shoulder.

Patsy didn't sit down. She didn't want to do anything that would encourage Brooke to stay. She cut her eyes toward the closed bedroom door, then caught herself and quickly looked back to Brooke.

"Hiding someone in there?" Brooke raised an eyebrow as she nodded toward the bedroom.

Patsy swallowed hard. "What are you talking about?"

"The jig is up, Mom." Brooke uncrossed her legs, stood up, and walked to Patsy. "I know you're seeing someone." She touched Patsy on the arm. "And that's okay, but can you be a little more discreet? I mean, really, Mom. People are talking. I got a call from Mrs. Doyle, and she said people have seen you kissing a man in the parking lot."

Patsy's knees went weak, and she could feel her bottom lip quivering.

"Momma . . ." Brooke's tone was soft and soothing. Patsy loved it when Brooke called her Momma rather than Mom. The name reminded Patsy of happy times, back when Harold had been in their lives. She waited for Brooke to go on. "I love you, Momma, and I want you to be happy, and I'm sure I'll love whoever you're seeing. But I've got to be honest with you." Brooke shook her head. "This isn't how you raised me, and I'm a bit shocked that you are . . ." She pulled her eyes away. "You know."

"It's not what you think, dear." Patsy latched onto both

of Brooke's arms. "I'm not doing anything *bad*, if that's what you're thinking."

"Mom, is there a man staying here overnight?" Brooke brought a hand to her chest. "And please tell me we are only talking about one man."

"Brooke! Of course it's only *one* man."

"Are you having sleepovers?" Brooke closed her eyes, waiting.

"Sometimes. But it's still not what you think."

Brooke's eyes flew open and she stomped her foot. "Mom, this is the first time in my life that I think I've ever been ashamed of you. This is not how you raised me, and how would you feel if I was avoiding you, having casual sex with men, then hiding it from you? Tell me, Mother. How would you feel?" Her eyes began to tear up, and Patsy's along with her. "I love you, Mom. So much. And I want you to be happy, but you're being . . . irresponsible." Brooke lifted her chin, swiping at her eyes. "And you know this isn't right."

Patsy's heart was beating fast, her palms were sweating, and her knees were weak. She opened her mouth to say something, but her lip trembled so much that only a small sound came out before tears started to pour. Hearing Brooke say she was ashamed of her was almost more than she could bear.

"I'm sorry, Mom. I'm sorry you're upset. But this just isn't right."

Patsy hung her head but managed to say again, "It's not what you think."

"At your age, I'd think you would be mindful about—"

As the bedroom door flew upon, Patsy was fairly certain she might have a heart attack.

Brooke couldn't move. She couldn't breathe. He was older, thinner, and bald now, but the man standing ten feet from her was unmistakably her father. Brooke felt like she was in some sort of time warp, because this couldn't possibly be happening.

"I'm sorry, Patsy, but I can't stay in there and listen to her talk to you like this." Her father walked to Mom's side and put an arm around her. Thankfully, he wore slacks and a shirt, not a robe like her mother. He stared long and hard at Brooke. "We wanted to tell you when we thought you were ready."

Brooke took a step backward, toward the door, one hand over her mouth.

"Brooke, please." Her mother moved toward her.

"Get away from me." Brooke held up a hand toward her mother as tears streamed down both their faces. "You just stay here with *him* and play house." *Oh, God, please don't let this be happening.*

"We're married, Brooke." Her mother cried as she spoke. "We remarried yesterday. We've always loved each other. Please be happy and—"

"Be happy?" Brooke glanced at her father, crocodile tears swimming in his eyes, then she pointed a finger at her mother. "I watched you struggle all those years after he betrayed you! And what about me? He just took off without—"

"Let me just talk to you." Her father stepped forward, but Brooke took another step back.

"Mother, I am not talking to *him*. And I can't believe you did this!" She avoided her father's gaze on her and glared at her mother. Brooke had never been this angry at her. "I can't believe this." She reached for the doorknob and pulled the door open.

"Brooke, honey, please, just listen. You know your father is the only man I've ever loved. You know that."

"Then go to him, Mom." Brooke turned around and forced a fake smile. "Because I'm done . . . with both of you."

Seconds later she was out the door. She heard her mother lean against it, sobbing, and it took everything Brooke had to keep walking to her minivan. She hated to see her mother hurting. But she hated even more to be in the same room with her father.

❧

Owen was pleased with how well his new window air conditioner was cooling the rest of the downstairs. It was going to be three weeks before the AC people could get out to repair the central air, so he'd picked up another window unit yesterday. They were inexpensive enough, and there was no way he was going to keep working in this heat without air-conditioning.

He'd also arranged for Internet service and picked up a forty-two-inch television, which he'd moved from the bedroom into the empty living room when Brooke agreed to come over. He'd brought in the small kitchen table and the two chairs, rounded up an old barstool that had been in the house when he moved in, and unfolded a lawn chair. It was the most ridiculous dinner setup he'd ever seen, but it was working fine. Brooke's kids were happily munching on pizza and entertained by the television. Spencer kept staring at Owen, though, and when Owen carried the empty paper plates to the kitchen, Spencer followed him.

"Do you want to date my mom?"

Owen stuffed the plates in the trash. "Nope." He turned and faced the kid. "Don't get me wrong. I think your mother is great, I've just got my reasons."

They stood facing off for a few moments.

"I'm sorry about what I told you—you know, about Mom." The kid avoided Owen's eyes and stuffed his hands into the pockets of his shorts.

Owen turned on the faucet and washed his hands. "It's cool. I can understand you wanting to look out for your mom." He turned to face Spencer as he reached for a kitchen towel. "So, uh, did you ever find out who sent her the flowers?" It was none of Owen's business, but he'd been curious ever since Brooke mentioned it.

"Yeah. My grandpa." Spencer leaned against the kitchen counter, frowning. "Me and Meghan have never met him before."

Owen wasn't sure what to say, or how much Brooke would want her kids sharing.

"He wants to see us and my mom, I think. That's why he sent her the flowers." Spencer walked out of the room, leaving Owen wondering about the situation, but he followed Spencer back into the living room.

"Why don't you have any furniture?" Meghan asked when they walked in.

The little girl had been asking questions all night, but she was the cutest thing—very animated when she talked, lifting her hands, twisting them together. Much like her mother in personality and looks. She had Brooke's big brown eyes and sandy-blond hair.

"Well, I have to get all the painting finished, and these floors need refinishing." Owen kicked at the worn wooden slats. "I guess I'll get some furniture after some of this is done." Although, at this rate, he'd be without for a while.

He looked at his watch. Almost eight o'clock. Now Meghan was the one staring at him, her elbows resting on the table, her cheeks in her hands.

"Do you have kids?" She smiled, as if hopeful.

"No. I don't." Owen sat down in the green lawn chair across from where Meghan was sitting. He'd found some 1980s phone books in a kitchen cabinet for her to sit on.

"Don'tcha want kids?" Meghan frowned.

Owen crossed an ankle over his leg. "I always thought I did."

Meghan threw her hands up in the air. "Then have some!" She laughed.

Spencer leaned over and whispered to Owen, "Just ignore her. She thinks babies come from a stork who leaves them on the front porch." Spencer rolled his eyes. "Because that's what Grandma told her."

"Quit talking about me, Spencer!" Meghan told him. Loudly.

"Shut up and quit yelling, Meghan!" Spencer replied even more loudly.

Brooke, where are you?

Both kids seemed to have lost interest in whatever they'd been watching, and Owen didn't have any other way to entertain them. Not even any ice cream or cookies. They went back and forth again, yelling at each other to shut up, and Owen knew he was out of his league.

He checked his watch again. "Well, your mom is taking longer than we thought, so should we look through the pictures while we wait for her?"

Spencer and Meghan both got quiet and nodded, and Spencer reached for the photo album. He opened it, pulled out a piece of paper, and handed it to Owen. "This is a real sad letter."

Owen unfolded the piece of paper and read it, a melancholy settling over him. How awful for Adeline, wandering around this big house. Alone.

He scratched his chin. *Not so different from me.*

Ten

Brooke hurried back to Owen's house with crazy images in her head of her children tied up in the basement or something worse. But as she ran up the sidewalk and onto the front porch, the sound of laughter calmed her nerves. About her children anyway.

She pulled a tissue from her purse and dabbed at her eyes before she knocked on the door. Spencer opened it, his face lit up with a smile Brooke hadn't seen in a long time. He reached for her hand and pulled her into the entryway.

"Mom, we've been looking all over the house for the hidden bunker!"

"Really?" Brooke sniffled as she let Spencer drag her into the living room. Meghan ran to her, hugging her legs.

"Mommy, we've had so much fun. This house is *so* big, and there's a big black cat that runs in and out of it and up and down the stairs, but he doesn't really live here."

Brooke glanced at Owen, who grinned and shrugged. "I guess he kind of lives here. But not by my choice. I had to put a litter box upstairs since he tends to dart up there without permission and I can't always get him down."

Spencer still had hold of Brooke's hand, which felt nice. He didn't let go until he had pulled her to a small table in the middle of the living room. He pointed to the open photo album.

"Look how the house used to look." Spencer glanced at Owen and grinned. "It didn't have much furniture back then either."

Brooke leaned down. "I see that." She looked at Owen. "Sounds like you guys had a great time." She sniffled again but smiled, glad to see everyone enjoying themselves. "So no hidden bunker?"

Spencer frowned. "No. We even looked in the basement."

"I didn't go." Meghan made a face. "It's dark and scary down there."

"I wasn't scared!" Spencer shot back. "It's like a cave, and there's all these pipes and little rooms and things to hold up the house. It was cool. But we didn't see a bunker."

"Not really much of a basement," Owen explained. "Just kind of a glorified crawl space—not finished or anything. No bunker there that I could see—or anywhere else in the house."

Spencer's face lit up. "But Mr. Saunders said we can come back and look again."

Did he now?

Owen motioned for Brooke to follow him toward the kitchen. "I want to show your mom something. We'll be right back."

As soon as Brooke was out of the children's earshot, the tears came. She put her hand over her mouth.

Owen placed a gentle hand on her arm. "I could see that something was wrong, and it looked like you were about to lose it. Is there anything I can do?"

Brooke fought to control the sob in her throat as she

shook her head, and she didn't resist when Owen wrapped his arms around her. She buried her head in his chest and cried. She knew she'd behaved like a child in front of her mother, but the sting of seeing her parents together had fanned a long-burning flame. She finally eased away from Owen and apologized repeatedly.

Owen still had his hands on her arms. "Is your mom sick?"

"In the head," Brooke blasted before she thought about what she was saying. She took a step back, and Owen's hands fell to his sides. "Thank you for watching my children, and I am so sorry that you are seeing me like this. Everything will be fine. I just need to get the kids home and figure out—" She stopped. Owen was still a relative stranger, and she wasn't about to start spilling the details of her past.

A few awkward moments went by. Then Owen said, "I'm sorry you're hurting."

He sounded so sincere. Brooke looked into his eyes. "Thank you."

She wanted to run back into his arms and cry some more, but she had to put her adult face on. She dabbed at her eyes and allowed herself one last sniffle. "We need to go."

"Okay."

Owen followed her back into the living room and stood behind her while she talked to the children. Spencer tried to throw a fit about leaving so soon. *That's surprising.* Owen promised Spencer that they'd look around again soon.

"Come on, you guys. Thank Mr. Saunders for a nice time." Brooke grabbed Meghan's hand, and Spencer and Owen followed them to the door.

"Look at Mr. Saunders's cat." Meghan pointed to the far end of the porch.

Owen raised a palm toward them. "He's really not mine. I don't even like cats. But he kept hanging around, so I gave him a can of tuna."

Brooke smirked. "Well, he's yours forever now."

"I don't know about that, but he's hard to catch. He usually stays away from people, but sometimes he does dart past me and into the house." He chuckled. "Probably to get out of the heat. But he darts out again pretty quickly."

The cat jumped off the porch as they all came outside.

"He's pretty skittish." Brooke eyed the bowl of food and water. "I see you're still feeding him."

Owen snickered. "Yeah. But if you want him, he's all yours. If you can catch him."

"Uh, no thanks. I don't think our Kiki would do well with another cat." She paused. "I really appreciate your help tonight."

Owen nodded. "Happy to do it. We had fun."

"Well, thank you again." Brooke waved as she, Meghan, and Spencer made their way to the minivan.

Once at home, she went straight to her bedroom, threw herself on her bed, and allowed herself another good cry. She'd never felt so alone in her life. Mom was her best friend, and they'd grown even closer after Travis died. Now she felt like she had no one.

Why is this happening?

❧

Owen went back into the house, which seemed quieter than usual now. For the past couple of hours it had been filled with laughter, silliness, and adventure. He smiled at how excited the kids had been about the prospect of finding a hidden bunker in his house. After an exhaustive search, Owen was pretty sure there was no such thing, but it had been fun pretending he was ten years old again.

He couldn't help but wonder what had Brooke so upset, and as he got into bed, he reached for his cell phone. He put it down and then picked it up a few times, then finally let the call go through.

"Hi. It's Owen. I just wanted to make sure you got home okay." He paused. "And that *you* are okay."

"Thank you. We're all home, and I will be all right. I'm sorry for breaking down on you like that."

Owen recalled the feel of her in his arms. "No, don't apologize."

"The kids had a great time at your house. Thank you so much for keeping them entertained."

"They're great kids." Owen propped his pillow up behind him. "Your son really wants to make sure you don't have any male suitors, though."

"Oh no! What did Spence say now?"

Owen chuckled. "Don't worry. He didn't come up with anything new. He just wanted to know if I wanted to date you. I explained to him that I didn't, for reasons of my own. I mean, not that I don't think you're—" Owen cringed, wanting to be honest without being insulting. "I think you're great. I'm just kinda messed up." He paused. "I didn't tell your son that. I just said that I had my reasons. He seemed satisfied, so I think he might *allow* us to be friends."

"Aren't we all a little messed up?" she said softly. "And that's good to know—I mean, about the dating and all. I'm just not ready for anything like that."

There was an awkward silence. Owen knew he should feel relieved that she wasn't looking for a relationship, but his thoughts felt convoluted. He glanced at the time on his phone. Nine thirty. *Don't do it.* But as he listened to the nothingness all around him, he said, "Are you going to sleep now?"

"Too early for me. I haven't slept well since Travis died, so I usually stay up until about midnight rewatching old movies. Sounds pitiful, huh?"

Nothing sounded better at the moment. "Want some company?"

Another awkward silence. "I, uh . . ."

"Just two friends watching a movie." Owen sat up and folded his legs underneath him. "It's just so quiet in here, and I guess I didn't realize it until after your kids left." He paused. "Wow. I'm being pretty insensitive, though. I know you're upset. It's okay. Maybe another—"

"It's fine," she cut in abruptly. "I wouldn't mind some company either."

Owen got up and scurried around his room, looking for his shoes. "Great. I'll see you shortly. Pick a movie."

"You know it will be a chick flick." She snickered, and it was nice to hear her sounding a little happier.

"I love chick flicks." He closed his front door behind him.

"Okey-dokey. Don't say I didn't warn you."

He climbed in his car, started it, and pulled out of his driveway. He wasn't about to tell her that he'd cried during *The Notebook*. Twice. "I'll be ready for anything."

"I see you pulling into my driveway, so I guess I'll let you go." She paused. "How'd you know where we live?"

Owen stepped out of his car and walked up to Brooke's door. "I walked you home, remember?"

"Oh, right."

The door swung wide, both of them with phones still to their ears. Then Meghan and Spencer peeked their heads around Brooke, and she grinned. "You said you'd be ready for anything."

They both pressed End, but before Owen could even stuff his in his pocket, Meghan reached for his hand and pulled him over the threshold. "We're watching *VeggieTales*!"

Spencer spoke up. Loudly. "Mom, do we have to watch that dumb DVD again?"

"It's past both your bedtimes, so I don't think anyone should get too excited. We can watch one episode of *VeggieTales*, but you're both going to bed at ten, and Mr. Saunders and I are going to watch a grown-up movie."

Owen followed Brooke into a nice-sized living room. Her house was older too, but beautifully restored. He noticed the vintage hardware on the doors, the crisp white bead-board halfway up the walls and floral wallpaper above that, and what appeared to be the original wooden floors that had been sanded and redone. He noticed things like that these days.

Brooke motioned for Owen to sit down on the couch, and within seconds Meghan was on one side, Spencer on the other.

"This is a dumb show." Spencer leaned back against the couch as the opening credits of the cartoon began to run.

Owen had assumed it would be him and Brooke relaxing, watching a movie, and maybe even talking—getting to know each other better, as friends do. But when Meghan reached over and took his hand, Owen found himself in strange new territory. And when she leaned her head against his shoulder, he stopped breathing. He glanced up at Brooke, who was smiling.

Alarms were going off all over the place, but something about being here seemed to dull the warnings. Maybe it was because he and Brooke had both already admitted that they just wanted to be friends. Or maybe it was the way the place smelled—like honeysuckle or jasmine. It was inviting and warm and incredibly different from the way he and Virginia had lived.

He briefly tried to picture how Virginia might have restored an old house like this. He imagined it would have been cold, the way she was, not warm and inviting like this house. He couldn't even imagine why Virginia had ever wanted to move to this quaint small town away from malls, salons, and all her social activities. He'd never pondered it before, but it seemed she would have been a fish out of water. Or did Owen just see her differently now? Either way, Owen made a mental note to make his home warm and inviting. And it was going to smell good.

Brooke sat down in a navy-blue recliner next to the tan couch, pushed the button to raise her legs, and stared at the television, but Owen suspected her mind was elsewhere.

It wasn't long before the episode ended. Brooke sent her children up to bed, promising to be right up to tuck them in.

"It's already ten thirty, but I'm still up for a movie if you are." Brooke's eyes were puffy, and he wanted to ask her if she just wanted to talk, but he knew from experience that sometimes a bit of distraction can be the best thing.

"Sure."

"Okay. Let me go tuck them in. There's the movie I picked if you want to get it ready in the DVD player." She pointed to a hutch on the wall near the television, then left the room to go upstairs.

Owen got up and moved toward the hutch. He saw several books stacked up on a shelf, some sort of toy . . . and a thin DVD case. He picked it up and sighed.

The Notebook.

Brooke got Spencer and Meghan all settled, even though Spencer argued with her about why he should be able to stay up and watch the movie with them. Brooke sagged with relief when she finally closed his door and started down the stairs. All she wanted to do at this point was put in another DVD and lose herself in someone else's drama. She was glad they'd be watching a movie and not having to dive into small talk—or worse, talk about why she was upset. She walked down the stairs in her flip-flops and the same jeans and white T-shirt she'd had on earlier. No wonder he had no interest in asking her out. Only once had he seen her in anything besides jeans and T-shirts— that time she wore her white capris and nice pink shirt, a slight step up. She couldn't remember the last time she'd worn a dress. Even for church, she usually wore her nicest jeans and a blouse.

Whatever. She had enough problems without worrying what Owen Saunders thought of her. Dating wasn't on her agenda either. *Unlike Mom and . . . Harold.*

"So, do you like popcorn with your late-night movies?" Brooke stopped in front of where he sat on the couch.

"I'm fine with anything. Whatever you want. I put the movie in."

"Feel free to kick off your shoes and put your feet on the coffee table." She grinned. "Because I will." She turned to leave, talking over her shoulder. "Be back shortly with some popcorn."

When she returned with a bowl of popcorn and two Diet Cokes, Owen did indeed have his socked feet up on her coffee table, and for a moment she could almost see Travis sitting there. They'd loved to stay up late and watch movies. It was their time to just sit and cuddle, enjoy some downtime. No cuddling tonight, but she hoped she could put her thoughts about her parents on pause for just a little while.

She handed Owen the bowl and one of the sodas. Then she sat down beside him, but not too close. All of a sudden this whole thing felt weird, and she wondered why he'd wanted to come over in the first place. Maybe he didn't sleep well either. Or maybe he just hated being alone. That was probably it. Brooke didn't think she'd want to be alone in a place as big and empty as the Hadley mansion. She wanted to ask him why he'd bought the place after his divorce, since it was just him, but he was already hitting Play on the remote, so she settled back and took a sip of her drink.

"Have you seen this one?" Brooke kicked her feet up on the coffee table and reached into the bowl on Owen's lap, pulling back a handful of popcorn.

"Yeah. It's a good movie."

Brooke nodded.

They made it about halfway through the movie before Brooke started to question why she'd chosen this particular film to watch—about a couple that was together, then separated for several years, then back together again. Brooke's parents had been separated for twenty years, not just seven years like the couple in the movie. And they had been married when her father left them—also unlike the movie. Just the same, Brooke began to recognize the similarities, and she wished she could turn it off, but Owen seemed entranced. She'd expected him to talk during the movie, the way guys tend to do during a chick flick, but Owen was quiet.

Travis loved this movie too.

As she watched the older version of the couple in the movie, she pictured her own parents on the screen, and her mind drifted. She wondered how her mother was doing and when she'd talk to her again. Brooke missed her already.

Lost in her thoughts, she missed the ending. But she'd seen

it a dozen times, so it didn't really matter. She turned to look at Owen and blurted, "Are you crying?"

"No." Owen blinked a few times.

Travis had cried when he watched this movie with her the first time, and every time thereafter. Another reason she couldn't believe she'd picked this movie. She and Travis hadn't enjoyed the happy ending she'd always dreamed of, and they hadn't died together in their sleep. Instead, a drunk driver had ripped him from their lives when Travis was on his way back from an antique sale in Austin.

"It's okay if you are. Travis cried every time he watched it." Brooke felt like she was betraying Travis the minute she said it. Travis had always been embarrassed when he cried, and he hadn't done it often.

She kept her eyes on Owen. He was a tall, athletic kind of guy. Actually, it was cute to see him in this tender moment. She plucked a tissue from the box to her right and pushed it his way.

"I'm not crying." He took the tissue but just held on to it. Then he turned to her and smiled. "Okay, maybe just a little." He scowled. "I thought women always boohooed during movies like this. My wife even shed a few tears, and that was a lot for her."

Something about the way he said it led Brooke to believe that he was still bitter, so she just stepped on out there. Why not? This day had been horrible, and maybe there was a story there, something to further distract her from all that was wrong with her own life. "So, can I ask you . . . why does a newly divorced man leave the big city and buy the biggest house he can find—one that needs a tremendous amount of work—in a dinky little town like Smithville? Are you planning to fix it up and sell it?" She twisted to face him, knowing she was being nosy, but too curious not to ask.

Owen rubbed his chin for a few moments and didn't look

at her at first, then turned to face her. "I guess I could give you some hopped-up version of the truth, but I really bought it just to spite my ex. She'd always wanted to live in Smithville, ever since she saw *Hope Floats*. So when we got divorced, I found her dream house and bought it." His mouth crooked into a mirthless smile. "With Virginia, bigger was always better. She'd sometimes made noises about opening a bed-and-breakfast or something, but I really think she wanted a place for her friends to come and visit—a big house to show off. I can't picture Virginia running a B&B and tending to the needs of others."

Maybe bitterness was an understatement if this guy changed cities and bought a huge house, all out of spite. "Then will you sell it?"

"I don't know. I haven't thought that far ahead." He shook his head. "You know, I always knew what I wanted. Success in my business. Virginia. Then a house full of kids. So now that it's all fallen apart, I have no idea what I want. I'm a shell of a man wandering around with no idea what to do with myself. No goals. No plans."

"That's sad." And then she couldn't help it. She grinned. "I'm sorry. I know it's not funny, and I don't mean to laugh. Really. But *shell of a man*?" She covered her mouth with her hand.

Owen lifted one bushy eyebrow. "Not very sensitive, are you? As a matter of fact, I didn't see you crying during the movie."

You didn't look close enough. Brooke recalled the way Travis used to tell her that he could see her crying even when she didn't shed any tears by the way her throat moved. She'd always been good at hiding her emotions—until earlier today. She shrugged. "I've seen the movie a million times."

"So it sounds like life threw you a curveball as well. I'm sorry about your husband."

His voice was so sincere, Brooke regretted teasing him. "I'm really sorry about you and your wife too." She paused, thinking about Travis. "Do you still talk to her? What's her name? Virginia?"

Owen shifted his weight on the couch, and his voice took on an almost-unpleasant tone, deep and raspy. "Only if I have to."

"Hmm. I'm sorry."

"Don't be. That woman is . . . toxic." Owen gritted his teeth, and Brooke wondered what Virginia had done to make Owen so bitter.

"*Toxic*. Strong word." Brooke yawned.

"Sorry. I should probably go soon." Owen edged to the front of the couch.

"So what happened? Why did y'all divorce?" Brooke scrunched her face up. "Sorry. Small-town living. You'll have to get used to it. We like to know everyone else's business."

He smiled briefly. "Well then, I guess everyone will love my story." He paused, and Brooke sat taller, eager to hear. "Virginia had an affair with my business partner. I caught them in his office one night."

Brooke wondered if that kind of betrayal could be as painful as death. Surely not. He could still pick up the phone and call Virginia if he really wanted to. "That must have been awful."

He shook his head as he stared at the floor. "Funny thing is, I always wanted children. Virginia was adamant that she didn't want any." He smiled as he turned to Brooke. "Guess the joke's on her. Virginia and Gary's baby is due sometime next month."

Eleven

Hunter leaned over the couch to make sure his grandma was still breathing. He'd been out looking for jobs all morning, and Grandma didn't look like she'd moved from the couch since he'd left.

"I'm alive, boy. Quit hovering over me."

Hunter jumped back when she opened her eyes and spoke. "You need anything?" He grabbed his belt loops and pulled his jeans up, knowing Grandma didn't like them "hanging off his butt," as she called it.

"I *need* you to have a job. You find one yet?" She grunted as she pushed herself to a seated position. She lit a cigarette, then glared at him long and hard.

"I'll find one." He slid into the recliner and leaned his head back.

"You been lookin' all week. Ain't nobody got nothing you can do? Groceries don't pay for themselves 'round here." She blew a puff of smoke in his direction.

"I'll find something. What I really need is a car to get around, to go somewhere else besides Smithville. No one likes me around here."

Grandma took a long drag, blew two smoke rings, and crinkled her face all up. "And whose fault is that?" She crossed her legs and pulled her pink robe around her. "Cars take money anyways. Gas ain't free neither."

Hunter stood up and walked to the kitchen, hoping there was some leftover meatloaf from last night.

"Meatloaf's on the bottom shelf of the fridge," his grandma said as he passed by her.

By the time he'd finished his lunch and walked back into the living room, she'd already passed out again. His eyes drifted to the half-empty bottle on the floor beside the couch. "Vodka ain't free neither," he muttered to himself as he walked out the front door. He didn't see any point in looking for jobs around here, but he hit the streets just the same, his mind wandering all over the place.

As he kicked a loose rock at his feet, he pictured himself with a real job and a normal family. A mom who welcomed him home with a kiss and a snack after school, then wanted to know all about his day. A father who wanted to play catch and take him to ball games, who would teach him how to be a man. In Hunter's mind, they'd all eat supper together at a big long table in a pretty house. No roaches, no one hitting each other, always plenty to eat . . . and no one drinking or smoking or shooting up.

"Hey!"

Hunter turned to his right and slowed down.

Great. It was Strong Guy. He lowered his head and kept walking. His gut told him to run, but that didn't get him very far the last time, only in trouble for something he didn't do.

Strong Guy yelled at him again, so he stopped. "You talkin' to me?"

Strong Guy walked across his yard in a pair of stupid-looking blue-jean overalls with paint splattered all over him. He was old. Probably thirty or forty.

"Hunter, right?"

Hunter stood taller. "Yeah. I didn't do nothin', if that's what you're thinking. Just looking for a job."

Strong Guy ran an arm across his forehead. He was sweating like a pig. "What kind of work are you looking for?"

"Anything that'll make a buck." He folded his arms across his chest. Seemed like a long shot, but . . . "Why? You got something I can do for money?"

"Plenty. You handy with a paintbrush or a hammer and nails?" Strong Guy raised an eyebrow.

Hunter tipped his head to one side, squinting from the sun's glare coming over the top of Strong Guy's house. "I reckon I can do both."

Strong Guy held out his hand. "I'm Owen Saunders."

Hunter slowly extended his own. "Hunter Lewis."

"Well, Hunter, I got a real mess here. I'm building a closet in my bedroom, trying to overhaul a kitchen, and all the floors in this house need to be redone. I've got AC people coming in another week or so, but for now I have a couple of window units cooling the downstairs, so the working conditions aren't too bad."

Hunter wasn't sure he'd ever had a job working inside, much less in air-conditioning. His last job had been working at the Oldhams' farm. He'd liked taking care of the horses, and they'd seemed to like him too. He hadn't even minded the heat or the smelly stables. To this day he didn't know why Mr. Oldham let him go. He'd said it was for money reasons, but Hunter figured someone probably got to him, told him what a bad kid Hunter was.

"You really offering me a job?" Didn't seem to make

sense. This guy already knew about Hunter. He's the one who ratted him out to the cops.

Mr. Saunders nodded. "If you're interested."

It seemed too good to be true. The guy was probably planning to pay him pennies, then work him like an old hound dog. "How much you payin'?" He knew he wasn't in a position to be choosy, but . . .

"I can start you out at ten dollars an hour. Then if you do good work, I'll bump it to fifteen dollars an hour after one month."

Hunter had never made more than seven dollars an hour, so he quickly picked his jaw up off the ground, swallowed hard, and focused on playing it cool. "I guess that'd be all right."

"When can you start?"

Hunter thought about how proud his grandma would be. "As soon as you want me to." He paused. "Mister, why are you doing this?"

Mr. Saunders scratched his chin, then let out a heavy sigh. "Because I'm tired of busting my rear all by myself. I need the help, and some company would be nice."

Even if it just lasted a couple of days, that would buy plenty of groceries. He knew he should keep his mouth shut, but this still seemed too good to be true. "But you know about, uh, about—"

"I don't know anything. I'm new here." Mr. Saunders shrugged. "So, you want the job? I'd expect you here at eight in the morning, with an hour for lunch, then stay until five."

Hunter swallowed hard again as he calculated that to be eighty dollars per day. Four hundred dollars for the week if Mr. Saunders kept him on that long. Grandma would probably cook all his favorites, and maybe she'd look at him like a good provider for the only family he had left. "I reckon I can do that."

Mr. Saunders reached into his pocket and pulled out two

twenties. "Here. You don't want to ruin your clothes. I picked these up at that resale shop, the one close to the post office." He pointed to those overalls he had on, and Hunter tried not to cringe. He reminded himself how much money he'd be making and accepted the twenties.

"Just plan on being here Monday morning. Tomorrow is Saturday, and I might do some work, but I don't expect you to work on the weekends."

Hunter figured this must be some kind of trick. Had to be. Strong Guy had hauled him off to the police, and now he was offering him a ton of money to do a real eight-to-five job. He looked down at his cheap, worn tennis shoes and shook his head for a moment, then looked back up. "Mr. Saunders, you only gonna work me for a day or two, then say I stole something? Then the cops would take me back to jail? Is that what you're wanting?"

Mr. Saunders laughed. "First of all, call me Owen. Mr. Saunders makes me feel like an old guy."

You are an old guy. Hunter waited for him to go on.

"Second, there isn't anything to steal in my house even if you were so inclined." He paused, smiling a little. "And I don't think you're so inclined anyway." He held out his hand again. "So, see you Monday morning?"

Hunter shook his hand, nodded, and went on down the street toward the resale shop. He did his best to keep a straight face, but he felt like laughing and yelling.

I got a real job. Working in the AC. And for a lot of money.

❦

Brooke's kids had been driving her bonkers since Tuesday, wanting to know when they could go back to Mr. Saunders's house. *So odd.* Spencer seemed to really like the guy, now that Owen had assured him he had no plans to date her. Maybe her children were starved for male attention. Briefly she thought about her father, but quickly disregarded that idea. Spencer was probably just intrigued about the prospect of a hidden bunker somewhere in Owen's house.

"Why can't we go over there?" Spencer leaned against the store counter in front of Brooke while she totaled store receipts for the day.

"We aren't going to invite ourselves to Mr. Saunders's house just because you want to look for a secret bunker." Brooke stapled the receipts and put them on the counter. She raised an eyebrow. "Because I know that's why you want to go over there."

Spencer shrugged. "It's just a cool house."

"And he's nice." Meghan shifted her weight on the stool where she was sitting beside Brooke but didn't look up from her coloring book as she pressed down with a blue crayon.

Brooke had more on her mind than Owen Saunders and his house. She hadn't spoken to her mother since Tuesday, and she missed her. She felt guilty too; they'd never had such harsh words. But try as she might, Brooke couldn't wrap her mind around the situation with her father. She cringed. *What is Mom thinking?* Her mother had tried to call several times, but Brooke hadn't answered, and her mom hadn't left a message.

Her cell phone chirped to indicate a text message. She glanced down at the display. It was from Judy Delgado. Apparently last week's sleepover had gone so well that Judy wanted the kids to sleep over again tonight.

Brooke had mixed feelings. As nice as it was to have some time alone, that's exactly what it was—time alone. Too much time with her thoughts, especially when it was two weekends in a row. But she conceded, knowing the kids liked being at Judy and Rick's. She did too, actually. She and Travis used to hang out with them all the time. But all their couple friends had continued their lives while Brooke had holed herself away just trying to survive her grief, and Brooke felt the distance.

An hour and a half later she had dropped off the kids, made it home, and was standing in the kitchen with the refrigerator open when her cell phone rang again. This time she was busy studying possibilities for dinner and didn't check the caller ID.

"I've been trying to reach you, and I was going to leave a message this time if you didn't answer."

Brooke closed the refrigerator, then leaned against it and sighed. "How could you do this, Mom?"

"I want to tell you how it happened. I'd heard your father had moved back to town, but that's all I knew. Then on one of the ladies' shopping trips, I ran into him at the mall. We started talking, Brooke, and it was as if no time had gone by."

Brooke grunted. "Mother, twenty years has gone by." She shook her head and pinched her eyes closed as she recalled her father walking out the door with nothing but a backpack swung over his shoulder. "And exactly where has he been all this time? Does he have another family? Has he been in jail? What? I'd like to know."

"You know he's been in Seattle working. I told you that when I received his last letter."

Brooke had quit opening her father's letters a long time ago. "Whatever."

They were quiet for a few moments before her mother said, "Due to health issues, he wanted to come home."

"Home? Is that what he calls Smithville?" Brooke laughed as she turned around and yanked the refrigerator door open again. Spying half of a chocolate bar, she grabbed it and peeled back the wrapper. She took a huge bite, then talked with her mouth full. "Mom, he had an affair and walked out on us."

"But he left us everything. The business and plenty of money."

"He broke our hearts. How can you defend him, much less . . ." She choked down the rest of the candy bar.

"Brooke, he's really very sorry. And I hate it that you're hurting, but I want us to be a family again. I want him to get to know you and to meet his grandchildren. Can't you open your heart? Even just a little?"

Brooke was quiet, wishing she had more chocolate.

"Don't you think God would want—"

"Don't throw God into this. I've relied on God for everything my entire life—when Daddy left, when Travis died, everything. But God would not expect me to just invite that man back into my life again after all this time."

"Of course He would."

Brooke ground her teeth and chose to redirect the conversation. "Mom, how did he coerce you into this? I know it's not his looks because he's skinny and bald. So is it . . ." Brooke gasped. "He wants money, doesn't he? That's why he's back."

"He doesn't want money, and he has a nice apartment outside of town."

"Then why didn't you stay at his place instead of making a spectacle of yourselves by playing smoochy-smoochy outside of your apartment?"

"Because your father knows I don't sleep well when I'm not in my own bed, and before we remarried, he was sleeping on the couch anyway."

Brooke stiffened. "Stop calling him my father. He lost that right. And you've lost your mind for remarrying him."

"Can he at least meet Spencer and Meghan?"

Brooke could hear the quiver in her mother's voice, but it didn't matter. "No, Mom. I don't want him around my children. And if you can't understand that, then search your memory and think about how it was for us after he left. He didn't care anything about his family, so why should I trust him with mine?"

They were silent for a few moments before her mother spoke up. "We all make mistakes."

"Yeah, well, his was a big one." Brooke paced the kitchen, shaking her head.

"I'm going to let you go now, dear. Give you some time. But just know that I love you very much."

Brooke blinked back tears. "I love you too, Mom. I really do. But time isn't going to change the way I feel."

She hung up feeling all the sadness and bitterness of the past two years. She wanted to kick something, hit someone, yell, or scream. She resisted the temptation to yell at God, to ask Him why all this was happening. The Lord had been her rock for her entire life, the One to see her through the tough times. She wasn't going to turn on Him now. But she felt reckless, in need of a distraction. Picking up her cell phone, she dialed Owen's number. He answered on the second ring. After a few pleasantries, she got to the point.

"I was just wondering if you wanted another movie night. My kids are at a sleepover again." She paused, taking a deep breath. "The offer comes with dinner. Nothing fancy. Just a beef and noodle casserole that I'd planned to make."

"Hmm."

Why did I do this? She shook her head. He was going to turn her down, and she was going to feel like an idiot.

"Does it mean that I'll have to watch another chick flick?"

Brooke smiled. "Maybe."

"Hmm."

"But you'll get a home-cooked meal out of it."

"I'll grab my tissues and be on my way." He chuckled.

Brooke laughed, then glanced around the house. Meghan's dolls were piled in the middle of the floor, and there was a trail of playing cards leading from the kitchen into the living room. That was just what she could see from where she was standing. "Give me an hour. Actually, an hour and a half, if that's okay."

"Sounds good. Thanks."

She hung up the phone, still feeling a bit reckless and longing for something, even though she wasn't sure what it was. She might not be able to change her mind where her father was concerned, but other areas in her mind were working overtime.

❧

After a shower and shave, Owen pulled on a clean pair of blue jeans, a light-green polo shirt, and his brown flip-flops. As he looked in the mirror, he recalled Virginia saying this shirt was his best color. *Why does every single thought have to be attached to her?*

He combed his hair, put on aftershave, and pondered why Brooke was inviting him over for dinner while her children were away. Was he reading too much into it? Maybe he hadn't been clear about his intentions. He'd thought she was pretty up front about hers.

Deciding this was just two lonely souls watching movies and having dinner, he left for her house.

But when Brooke opened the door, she didn't look like any lonely soul he'd ever seen. She didn't even look like the same person he'd been hanging out with lately.

Twelve

Owen swallowed hard and tried not to react to Brooke's new look. Her super-high heels put her almost at eye level with him. She wore a short denim skirt and a tight-fitting yellow shirt. Her hair was long and flowing past her shoulders, and she had on more makeup than he'd ever seen her wear.

"You look great," he said as she stood in the doorway, although he much preferred her baseball cap, ragged jeans, and flip-flops. He glanced down at his own flip-flops. "I, uh, feel underdressed."

"Don't be silly. Come on in." She pulled the door wide and stepped aside.

"It smells great in here." Owen didn't feel nearly as comfortable as he did the other night, and it wasn't just because her children weren't home. Something was different.

"Thanks. The table's all set." She motioned for him to follow her into the dining room. Alarms were blaring in his head so loudly that he could hardly think. Candles were lit, and it looked like the good dishes were in place. Then he noticed real napkins. Virginia used to use the cloth napkins when she was trying to impress someone.

"Looks great." Owen had pictured them in front of her television, feet propped up on the coffee table, eating off paper plates. He sat down across from her, and when she folded her hands and bowed her head, he did the same. As she blessed the food, Owen opened one eye and studied her transformation. This could only mean one thing. She was interested in him way more than as just a friend.

By the time they'd finished eating, Owen was already trying to think of a way to leave.

"I decided to let you pick out the movie," she said as she gathered up their empty plates. He had to admit she was a great cook, and the homemade meal had been welcome. The conversation had stayed light, although Brooke had fidgeted a lot. Most of the time her dry sense of humor was casually confident, but this evening she was polite and soft-spoken. Yes, this was an entirely different Brooke.

Owen helped her clear the table. Once the dishwasher was loaded, they went into the living room. *Are the lights dimmer in here?* He glanced around the room. During his last visit, there had been toys everywhere. Things were much tidier now.

"What do you feel like watching?" Brooke pointed to the hutch where she'd laid out their last DVD. "If you open that door, it's filled with movies."

Owen picked out a comedy that he knew wasn't romantic in any way. "How about this?"

"That's fine." Brooke walked to his side and waited while he loaded the DVD, then they both walked to the couch. She waited for him to sit down, and then she sat down beside him, much closer than last time. As she hit Play on the remote, he tried not to think about her outfit and how close she was sitting. For some men, this might have seemed like an opportunity, but Owen thought himself a good enough guy not to lead on a widow with two children. No matter how good she looked. Or smelled.

Ten minutes into the movie Owen barely knew what was going on. His only thoughts were of her leg slightly rubbing against his, especially when she laughed. Once, her hand landed briefly on his knee. He'd been married to Virginia for eight years, so he'd been out of the dating pool for a long time, but he still remembered what flirting was.

Somehow he made it through the movie, but there was no denying that by the end she'd edged even closer. And despite his feelings for Virginia and his desire not to hurt Brooke, he felt the overwhelming urge to take her in his arms and kiss her. It had been so long.

She flipped the television off and twisted to face him. Owen held his breath.

"Well, what did you think? Did you like it?" She smiled, and for a moment, the old Brooke was back.

"Yeah. It was pretty good." He tried not to look at her, but when he finally did, she grabbed his face in her hands and planted her lips right on his. He couldn't move, nor did he really want to, but his conscience overruled and he backed away. "Uh, Brooke, I thought we agreed that neither of us were ready for this."

Her face turned red, then her eyes began to water, and Owen felt like a jerk. Maybe he should have just gone with it, then made it a point to never see her again. "Please don't cry."

She jumped up from the couch, yanked her shoes off, and even tossed one across the room. Owen shielded his face with his hands, unsure if the other shoe would be coming his way. As he cowered on the couch, she stomped her foot and started to cry.

"I am so stupid!" She pulled at her skirt. "These clothes are Juliet's. She insisted I borrow them a long time ago, and I've never even worn them until tonight." She covered her eyes with her hands. "I guess I'm just so mad about everything in my life! Mad that Travis is dead. Mad that my parents have reconciled after twenty years apart. And now I'm mad that I threw myself at a man I barely know!"

Owen opened his mouth to try to say something, even though he wasn't sure what to say, but she started in again, standing over him, pointing a finger at him.

"You know what? I've never even kissed anyone else besides my husband. We were together since the beginning of high school." She leaned down. "Why did I do this?" She threw her hands in the air and began to pace the room, almost as if Owen weren't even there. "Maybe I just needed to act out." She stopped and turned to face him. "Maybe I just wanted to do something a little reckless." She shook her head. "This is so not me." Then she threw herself on the couch next to Owen.

Owen twisted to face her. "Look at me."

She turned to face him, her eyes red. "You can go now. I'm sure you'll never want to be my movie and dinner buddy after this. I'm really sorry. I'm just—"

"I know." He gazed into her eyes for a moment. "You're just unhappy. I can relate."

"Owen, I've never acted that way before. You must think I'm . . ." She pulled her eyes from his and shrugged.

"Brooke, you're absolutely gorgeous. Any man would be crazy not to want to get involved with you." He paused. "But I'm trying to be a good guy here. I'm damaged goods. You don't want to be involved with me."

"I don't want to be involved with anyone. Really. I guess

I just needed something. I'm so mad at my mother right now, and I guess I wanted to try to get her back somehow. And I haven't been held in so long. It was all just like the perfect storm, and I . . ."

Owen shook his head, clicking his tongue and grinning. "Yep. You pretty much threw yourself at me."

"Do you have to rub it in?"

Owen took a deep breath, unable to stifle his smile. "Yes, I think I do."

She playfully slapped him on the arm. "Look, go ahead and leave if you want, but I'm going to go put on my jeans and a T-shirt. I'm miserable in these clothes. I've been worried about tripping in those shoes all night." She stood up. "So if you're not here when I get back, no explanations necessary, and I'll see you around."

Owen didn't move. He was unsure what proper protocol would be in a situation like this, but he was pretty sure that just bailing without a good-bye wasn't the way to go. Brooke returned a couple of minutes later wearing jeans, a red T-shirt, and no shoes at all. She'd pulled her hair into a ponytail and apparently wiped off some of her makeup. She looked like the old Brooke again.

"I like this Brooke better," Owen said as she sat down on the couch.

"Wow, you're still here. Why didn't you run when you had the chance?" She leaned her head back against the couch and closed her eyes.

"Okay, here's the deal." Owen propped his feet up on the coffee table for the first time that evening. "I was married for eight years. I was madly in love with my wife and would have stayed with her forever, even though she was really hard to live with. Our only big issue was that I wanted children and she didn't. Then she slept with my best friend and business partner, and now they are going to get married and they're having a baby, as I already told you."

He blew out a puff of air. "So. I basically think all women are evil, and I'll never trust or love another one. In addition to that, I have zero goals for the future and will probably be working on my house for the rest of my life."

He turned to face her and smiled. "Your turn."

⚜

Brooke glanced at her watch and wished Owen would just go home. She'd never behaved like this in her life. "I don't think you have enough time for my saga. I don't think I can sum it up that easily."

"I have all the time it takes."

"Okay, let's see." She fought the urge to laugh. Or cry. "I married Travis right out of high school. He was the love of my life. After he died, I didn't think I'd ever be able to function again—simple things, like getting up and getting dressed in the morning. But I didn't have a choice. I had two children to take care of. My mom moved in and lived with us until a couple of months ago. Now I do get up, get dressed in the mornings, and find certain pleasure in some things— like a tub of ice cream every now and then." She smiled. "And watching my children grow into wonderful little people. That makes me happy.

"But I don't feel complete anymore. It's like my heart is just closed—forever." She glanced his way to see him nodding. "And I don't hang out with the women that I used to because they all have husbands. They've reached out to me plenty of times, but I always find an excuse not to do things with them.

I'm the third wheel, and being with them just reminds me of Travis. That he's not here."

She turned to face him. "So, despite my actions this evening, I have no desire to be in another relationship. Sounds nuts, I'm sure."

Owen shook his head. "Nope. Not at all. So what's the deal with your parents?"

Brooke told him about her father's infidelity and his leaving them when she was twelve. About growing up without him . . . and then finding him at her mother's apartment the other night.

"Wow. That had to be a shock."

Brooke put a hand to her forehead, then rubbed tired eyes. "I want my mother to be happy. I really do. But this is some kind of false happiness—I'm sure of it. She hasn't been around my dad in twenty years. I just don't believe that they had the kind of love she says they had. If they did, he would have never cheated on her, then stayed gone for that long."

They were quiet for a while, then Owen said, "Maybe you need to talk to him."

Brooke tensed. "I can't. I've spent part of my childhood and my entire adult life hating him. I can't just turn off those feelings."

"I didn't say to turn them off. I thrive on hating Virginia." He gave a humorless laugh. "But in your case, it sounds like he's going to be a part of your mother's life whether you like it or not. Maybe there's a way to work through it. Or maybe not. But it seems like a chapter waiting to be written."

Brooke forced a smile. "The book ended a long time ago for me."

"Can I tell you something?" Owen put his elbow on the

back of her couch and propped his head up, facing her. "I'm glad you threw yourself at me and we had a chance to talk like this."

Brooke slapped him on the arm. "If you ever bring this up again, we are not going to be friends."

Owen smiled, then stood up. "Brooke, I'm going to be your friend for as long as you'll have me. But eventually someone is going to come along and have more to offer you than just friendship, and that's as it should be. You'll open your heart one day. Your situation is different from mine. Travis left, yes, but he never betrayed you. And betrayal is a tough thing to get past."

She playfully held out her hand. "Friends, then."

Owen grabbed her hand, but pulled her to him and held her tight. She wrapped her arms around his waist and buried her face in his chest. "I think this is all I really wanted from the very beginning. A hug."

He kissed her on the top of the head. "From now on, when one of us needs a hug, we're going to just ask for it."

"Deal."

As she walked him to the door, she felt different. Partly about Owen, but also just in general. Calmer. Maybe her fit had been building up for a while.

She walked into the kitchen for a glass of water, glanced to her left, and made sure she'd marked through the day.

Only twenty-nine days to go.

❧

Brooke was glad when Spencer and Meghan came running into the house early on Saturday morning. She already had the pancake mix ready and the bacon cooked.

"There are my munchkins." She gave Meghan a big hug and winked at Spencer as they came into the kitchen.

"Mrs. Judy is here too." Meghan reached for a piece of bacon on the table.

"Oh." Brooke turned around to see Judy walking into the kitchen.

"Hope it's okay. I just followed the kids in. I think they all had a great time." Judy had gotten a haircut since Brooke had seen her last. Her shoulder-length dark hair had been cropped into a stylish short style that barely covered her ears.

"Your hair looks great." Brooke twisted her ponytail for a moment, wondering if she could be so brave.

"Thanks. I just needed a change." Judy bit her bottom lip. "Anyway, I just wanted to come in and say hi."

Brooke recalled all the times she and Judy had spent together, with their husbands and without. Brooke knew she was the one at fault for shying away from the relationship. "I'm glad you did. Do you want to stay for pancakes?"

Judy put a hand on her stomach. "No, I better not. I'm on this new diet, and I'm afraid pancakes aren't on it." She grinned. "But I'm glad to see you guys are still doing pancake Saturday."

Brooke poured batter onto the hot griddle. "Yeah. We try not to miss it."

Judy walked closer. "After you get done with the pancakes, can I talk to you? By ourselves."

"Sure. It'll just be a few minutes. Is everything okay? Did something happen with the kids?"

Judy waved a hand in the air. "No, no, everything is fine." She pointed to the coffeepot. "If you don't mind, I'll just have some coffee and wait."

Brooke got each of the kids started on pancakes, then set

the griddle aside and motioned for Judy to follow her into the living room. "What is it?"

Judy barely got out of earshot from the kids when she said, "Spencer was telling us all about your new friend, Mr. Saunders."

Brooke pushed back a strand of hair that had fallen from her ponytail. "Yeah, the kids seem to like him. He bought the Hadley place."

"So I heard." Judy grinned. "I also heard he's gorgeous."

Brooke briefly recalled her ridiculous behavior the night before. "He's nice looking."

"So do you think—you know—anything more than friends, maybe?" Judy raised one shoulder and lowered it.

"No. I'm not ready, Judy. Friends only."

Judy frowned. "Are you sure? Positive?"

"I'm sure." *Clearly I'm as messed up as he is.*

"I didn't think you were. But I wanted to double check, especially since Spencer told us you've all been hanging out together." Judy bit her bottom lip for a second. "The thing is, Tallie met him the other day at the dry cleaners, and I think— well, I think she gave him her phone number. I just wanted to make sure there wasn't something already going on between you two."

Brooke swallowed hard. Tallie Goodry had been divorced for about six months, but Brooke knew she still ran around with Judy, Rick, and the rest of the group. Tallie's ex-husband, Brian, had moved to Houston. Rumor was that Tallie had wanted the divorce, but Brooke didn't know for sure.

"He's fair game. There's nothing going on between us." The minute she said it, though, her stomach flipped.

"Although . . ." Brooke didn't want to spread gossip, but something about Tallie and Owen together disturbed her. "He *is* coming out of a bad marriage, and he made it pretty clear that he isn't looking to date anyone."

Judy rubbed one of Brooke's arms. "Aw, honey. You'll find someone."

It took Brooke a few moments to catch what Judy was insinuating—that Owen just wasn't interested in Brooke.

But maybe that was exactly the case.

Thirteen

Owen was on the porch Monday morning when Hunter Lewis walked up wearing blue-jean overalls and carrying a black lunch box.

"Right on time." Owen took a sip of his coffee. "I always have coffee made in the mornings. You a coffee drinker?"

Hunter shook his head, his stringy red hair blowing in the wind.

"You ever been inside this house?"

The kid shook his head again. "No, sir."

Owen swiped at coffee he'd dribbled on his overalls. "I think you can just call me Owen. No need for the 'sir.' Makes me feel old, just like calling me Mr. Saunders." He moved toward the door and opened it, then pointed past the entryway. "Right through there to the kitchen. You can put your lunch in the fridge."

Hunter shuffled in, and Owen followed him to the kitchen. "I want to finish the closet in my bedroom and the trim work in the other rooms, then we'll start in here. It's going to be a big overhaul." He looked around the spacious kitchen. Three cabinet doors were missing, and the rest had been painted a peach color at one time, but now just chips of color remained on the bare wood. The gas range worked, so Owen figured he could wait to upgrade it until after the other work was done. He didn't really cook much anyway. An old white sink was stained a dreary red-brown, despite all the scrubbing he'd done when he first moved in, and the faucet leaked.

"You can tell that someone redid this kitchen at one time." Owen pulled on a strip of peach-and-white-striped wallpaper that peeled loose from one of the walls. "I'm guessing it must have been in the sixties or seventies." He pointed up. "And it must have leaked in here at some point because you can tell where someone patched the ceiling. The leaks upstairs are a much bigger problem, though. Pretty sure I need a new roof, but I'm hoping to wait a little longer on that."

Hunter looked up but didn't say anything. Owen hoped he was going to talk at least a little.

"You ready to get started?" Owen set his coffee cup in the sink. "I thought you could paint the trim in the living room and then in the dining room. I'm going to work on the closet." He paused, thinking about all the work he'd put into the painting he'd already done, realizing that Hunter might not be as meticulous about it as he was. "Or I can start you hammering the sides on the closet?"

"Painting will be okay." Hunter stuck his hands into his overall pockets and tossed his red hair out of his eyes. The kid needed a haircut badly.

Owen took a deep breath, and Hunter followed him to the living room, where the paint supplies were laid out on a tarp. "Okay. Let's get going then."

Hunter opened a can of creamy enamel, stirred it carefully, and dipped the paintbrush. Owen lingered and watched him for a minute. The boy leaned close and made slow, straight strokes along the baseboards, some of which Owen had replaced. "Those new ones will probably need an extra coat."

Hunter nodded but kept his eyes on the paintbrush and his hand steady. After another minute or so, Owen headed to the bedroom to work on the closet.

Hunter painted for three hours before he put the paintbrush down. He walked into the bedroom where Owen was hammering and waited until Owen finished pounding a nail in. "Where's the bathroom?"

Owen pulled two nails from his mouth. "There's one right outside this room, plus a little half bath right next to the entryway. Also one upstairs, but it's kind of a work in progress." He laid the hammer on the bed. "Let's take a break. I'll get us some iced tea. Meet me on the front porch."

Hunter nodded, then proceeded down the hall. He couldn't imagine living in a big, fancy house like this. Even though it needed lots of work—and some furniture—Hunter could tell it was gonna be real pretty someday, the kind of place you'd have a bunch of kids. He thought about Jenny, the girl he'd been talking to online for the past few weeks. She lived in a real small town called Flatonia that wasn't too far away, and she had a car. They'd been talking about meeting in person soon.

He walked onto the porch, and Owen handed him a glass of tea. "I checked out your work in there. You're doing a great job."

"Thanks." Hunter sat down on the porch step and took several gulps of the cold, sweet tea. "You the only one who lives here?"

Owen sat on the porch swing. He kicked his foot until it started to move. "Yep. Just me."

Hunter rolled up the pants of his overalls. They were dragging the ground. "Why'd ya buy such a big house just for you?"

Owen shrugged. "Long story."

Everybody's got a story.

Hunter finished his tea, stood up, and was going to go put the glass in the kitchen. He could remember his momma knocking him silly for not putting dirty dishes in the sink. He'd never really understood that, since those same dishes usually stayed in the sink for a long time.

Owen reached his hand out. "Here, I'll take it."

Hunter handed him the glass, then went back into the cool living room. He could get used to working in air-conditioning.

"We'll break for lunch at noon." Owen waved his hand, then disappeared down the hallway.

Hunter's hands were occupied, and his mind was filled with thoughts of Jenny. She didn't know everything about him the way folks around here did. And last night he'd been proud to tell her online that he'd gotten himself a real good job. Jenny worked at a clothes store for ladies in Houston. The picture of her online was beautiful—long blond hair and big blue eyes. He'd talk to her more, but he had to get Internet from the Johnsons next door, and their signal wasn't always too good. Hunter was using an old laptop he'd found in his parents' room. It hadn't worked when he first found it, but once he'd got it running, he'd realized he could pick up the Johnsons' signal sometimes.

It was almost noon when Hunter felt something press up against him. He jumped. Luckily, he didn't have his brush on the wall when it happened. He looked around to see a big old black cat pressing its head against him. "Where'd you come from?" Hunter reached his hand out, and the cat tipped his head and rubbed against Hunter's hand. He scratched his ears for a few minutes.

"Well, I can't believe it." Owen walked into the living room and crossed his arms across his chest. Hunter figured he was about to get fired.

"Sorry." He pulled his hand away from the cat and hurried to dip his brush in the paint.

Owen took two steps into the room, and that cat ran past him, nails clawing at the wood floor like he was trying to get out of a burning building, his tail puffed and hair standing on end. Owen jumped out of the way, and Hunter hid a smile.

"I can't believe that cat came up to you like that." Owen sat down at one of the assorted chairs grouped around a little table in the living room. "He runs from me, hides upstairs, and won't even come near me."

"Cats know if a person likes 'em." Hunter eased the brush along the very bottom of the baseboard, extra careful since Owen was watching.

"Maybe. I don't really like cats, but that fellow has been hanging around for a while."

"What's his name?" Hunter dipped his brush and kept his eyes on his work.

"Cat, I guess." Owen chuckled.

Hunter wasn't sure how to act around this guy. He was treating him like a regular person. "You could call him Scooter." He paused, pulled the paintbrush from the trim, and shrugged. "I had a cat named Scooter once. I named him that 'cause he was fast, scootin' all over the place." Hunter squeezed his eyes closed for a few seconds as he recalled the black-and-brown tabby he'd befriended when he was ten. Dad had shot

Scooter in the head one night for getting into the trash can outside and spreading garbage on the sidewalk.

"Scooter it is, then," Owen said. "And feel free to take him home if you want. He doesn't seem to like me too much."

"Wish I could." Hunter didn't think Grandma would like that. *Another mouth to feed.* He thought about all the money he'd be making if Owen kept him on for a while. Maybe he would take Scooter home then—or even be able to save enough for a cheap car.

"Well, I say we break for lunch now. I think I can have the closet done by the end of the day, then tomorrow I can paint it while you keep going on the trim in here." Owen walked out of the room, motioning for Hunter to follow him to the kitchen.

Tomorrow. So far, so good.

⚜

Tuesday morning Brooke watched as Meghan lifted the black marker and put a big X on the calendar, then scrawled in "25." Brooke flipped the switch on the coffeepot to Off and gathered up her purse and keys.

Once she and the kids got to the store, Meghan went to the back office with Juliet, but Spencer stayed with Brooke at the register, fidgeting. He rubbed his fingers together and paced.

"What's up, Spence?" Brooke loaded the register with cash.

"I was just thinking about Dad's stuff at the Treasure Chest."

Brooke finished counting the bills, then looked up at her son, who was staring across the street. "And what do you think? Did you think of something you want to keep?"

"Yeah. The plane."

Brooke swallowed hard as she wondered what she was going to do with everything else. "Of course you can have the plane. We'll go over there again and see what else we want to keep, but eventually we're going to have to sell at least some of it. Dad would want someone to enjoy those things."

"I guess." Spencer sat down on the extra stool beside Brooke. She'd been teaching him to run the cash register. They both looked toward the door when someone knocked on the glass. They didn't open until nine, but when Spencer saw that it was Owen, he ran to the door and turned the key that was in the lock.

Brooke hadn't seen or talked to Owen since the previous Friday, and she was okay with that. She'd analyzed her conduct since then and decided she'd been due for some bizarre behavior, but she still felt a little embarrassed. Her mother had called again, and Brooke was starting to feel guilty for squashing Mom's happiness, but she didn't think she'd ever be able to look at her father. She'd never understand how her mother could remarry him after all these years. *Patsy Miller must be the most desperate woman on earth.*

Owen walked toward her, Spencer at his side. He looked rather goofy in overalls and a white T-shirt, but the outfit did nothing to take away from his good looks. She wondered if Tallie Goodry had seen the overalls yet.

"Hello, Mr. Saunders." She tipped the rim of her baseball cap. "What can we do for you today?"

Spencer spoke up before he could answer. "Did you find the hidden bunker yet?"

"Not yet. You're not there to help me look." Owen grinned and rubbed the top of Spencer's head. Her son didn't pull away the way he did when Brooke got near him.

"How about Friday night? We could come over Friday night and look some more?"

"Spencer!" Brooke stood up from her stool. "You don't just invite yourself to someone's house like that."

Owen scratched his head and avoided Brooke's eyes. He turned to Spencer. "Actually, buddy, I have some plans Friday night. But I promise that you and I will do some looking around again soon—and eat more pizza."

Brooke instantly wondered who those Friday-night plans were with. Tallie Goodry was as pushy a woman as she'd ever known. And she could picture Judy giving Tallie the go-ahead to pursue Owen "because he's not interested in Brooke."

"Can I help you find something?" Brooke sat back down and lifted her eyes to his. Before he answered, they both heard footsteps coming from the back and turned to see who it was. Big Daddy came into view and raised an eyebrow in Brooke's direction. She nodded, letting him know that everything was fine.

"Uh, I just need some more finishing nails. I know where they are." Owen glanced at Big Daddy, then hurried away down the second aisle. Spencer followed him, and Brooke could hear them talking, but she couldn't understand what they were saying.

Owen found the nails quickly, paid with cash, and made a dash for the door. *Wow, did Big Daddy spook him? Or maybe it was me the other night.* She still cringed a little remembering her clumsy attempt to be a little reckless. But hadn't everything ended on a good note? They'd talked. A lot.

"So . . ." Brooke kept her head in a tool catalog, flipping the pages and trying to sound casual as she addressed Spencer. "I heard you and Mr. Saunders talking. Did he mention what his plans were for Friday night?"

"You like him." Spencer narrowed his eyes.

Brooke looked up. *Tread carefully.* "Of course I *like* him. I thought you did too."

"No. I mean you like him, like him." Spencer lifted himself onto the stool beside Brooke and hung his head. "I like him too."

Brooke closed the catalog and twisted on her stool to face him. "Spence." She lifted his chin until he was looking at her, glad he didn't pull away. "It's okay to like Mr. Saunders. You don't have to feel bad about that. He's a nice man." She paused. "But I don't like him the way you're thinking. Mr. Saunders and I are friends, that's all."

"Yeah, I know." Spencer dragged the words out. Brooke could tell that he was disappointed, which was both good and bad. She waited to see if he would say what Owen's plans were for Friday night. When he didn't, she decided to push a little.

"I'm sure you'll get another chance to scope out Mr. Saunders's house." She waited, but Spencer said nothing. "Maybe . . . maybe another Friday."

"Maybe." Spencer picked up a pencil and started doodling on a scrap piece of paper. "This Friday he said he's taking someone to a baseball game in Houston."

Brooke took a deep breath.

"He's taking some other kid to the baseball game." Spencer stood up, crammed his hands in his pockets, and mumbled, "I've never been to a baseball game in Houston." Then he walked toward the back of the store.

Hmm. Both Brooke and her son were jealous over a man that neither one of them wanted.

Brooke felt bad for Spencer, but she was incredibly relieved that Owen didn't have a date with Tallie Goodry on Friday night.

Whatever that meant.

Patsy refilled Harold's coffee cup, then sat down at the kitchen table across from him. He hadn't said a word in almost an hour, but he'd been writing steadily. They'd both agreed that a letter might be the best way for him to approach Brooke. Maybe if their daughter knew the truth, she could find it in her to give Harold another chance. Patsy was praying about that constantly these days. It was the only way she could bear her separation from Brooke and the kids.

"How's it coming?" She held her breath and bit her bottom lip.

Harold took off his reading glasses, rubbed his eyes, and put the pen down. He tore one page from the yellow pad and pushed it toward her but didn't look up.

Patsy pushed her glasses up on her nose.

Dear Brooke,

I can still see the look on your precious face when I walked out the door all those years ago, and it's an image that has haunted me. I wish I could have seen you grow into the beautiful young woman that you are today, and I deeply regret the choices I made back then. Your mother has shown me pictures of you from the time I left until you were married. You were a beautiful bride, and I will always regret that I never got to know Travis. Your mother says he was a wonderful husband and father. And now you are a mother yourself. How I long to be a part of your life and Spencer's and Meghan's.

As I write this, I can feel your anger and hurt, and I know that no words will give you comfort. But if you'll let me, I'll spend the rest of my life trying to make it all up to you. My heart is filled with love for you and your mother. It always has been, despite the mistakes I have made.

I suppose I could tell you that I've punished myself enough, but I doubt you'd understand or believe that. And you're probably right. What is ample punishment for a man who has done what I've done? But the Lord is giving me a second chance, and I will continue to pray that you will too.

Brooke, I love you very much. I always have and I always will.

With my love always,
Daddy

Patsy pulled her glasses off and rubbed her eyes, then put the glasses back on and shook her head. She reached across the table and put her hand on Harold's.

"That's only a partial version of the truth. You omitted two important things." She swallowed back a lump in her throat, knowing that one of those things involved her own actions. "Why didn't you tell her everything?"

Her beloved husband swiped at a tear that rolled down his cheek. "Because I just can't."

Then he reached for the letter and tore it into pieces.

Fourteen

Hunter handed his grandma half of what he'd made this week so she could get her medicines and some food. She'd been up and about more the past couple of days, and she seemed to not be coughing so much.

"Why's your boss man taking you to a baseball game? Them tickets cost an arm an' a leg. Ain't like you been working for him very long." Grandma groaned as she got off the couch and started toward the kitchen. Hunter followed.

"I dunno. He asked me if I'd ever been to a game in Houston, and I told him no. Then he asked me if I wanted to go." Hunter glanced down at his green T-shirt, blue jeans with a hole in the knee, and tennis shoes and hoped Owen wouldn't be embarrassed. Getting some new clothes was first on his list this weekend. He was hoping Jenny could drive to Smithville tomorrow night like they'd talked about. But so far, any plans they'd tried to make hadn't worked out. Jenny's car was on the blink a lot, and her parents didn't want her going by herself to meet a guy she'd only talked to on the Internet.

"Well, I reckon he's done you right so far, giving you a job and all for fair wages." Grandma pulled a soda from the refrigerator, and Hunter swallowed hard. He'd only told her that he was making seven dollars an hour. Three empty vodka bottles on the counter was one of the reasons.

"I'm going now. I told him I'd walk over there." Hunter waited for her to take a swig of Coke and wondered what it would be like if she hugged him good-bye. His family didn't do that, but sometimes he thought it would be nice.

"You embarrassed about our home?" Grandma leaned against the counter in her robe and crossed her ankles.

"No." It was another lie. No way he wanted Owen Saunders to see this place. "I gotta go."

"Be quiet when you come in this evening," she yelled from the kitchen as Hunter made his way through the living room, sidestepping a stack of dirty towels on the floor and several pairs of his grandma's shoes.

By the time he got to Owen's house, he was dripping in sweat. He was sure there wasn't a place in the world as hot as Texas. He ran his short sleeve against his face, then pushed his hair back. Now that he had some money, he was planning to get a haircut too.

"You should have let me pick you up." Owen met him at the car. It was a black BMW with 552 horsepower, super-high performance. *I bet this baby flies.* He'd never been in anything like it.

"It's no big deal." Owen opened the passenger door, and it was as nice inside as it was outside. Black leather, digital dashboard, and it didn't smell anything like the old Chevy his grandma used to drive before she got sick and sold it. He was buckling his seat belt when Owen turned the key. Nothing but a clicking noise. He tried to start the car about six more times before he slammed his hand against the steering wheel.

"I just had this car fixed!" He leaned his head back

against the headrest, and Hunter waited for him to start cursing or something, but he just took a deep breath and got out of the car. "I'm going to assume there aren't any taxi services near Smithville."

Hunter had never been in a cab, but he doubted it. "Aren't you gonna look under the hood? Maybe it's something we can fix real easy."

Owen made this weird sound. Not really like a laugh, more of a snort. "I'm afraid I don't know much about cars." He paused, shook his head. "Actually, I don't know anything about cars."

Hunter had been tinkering and fixing things for as long as he could remember. They never had money to take things to repair shops. He was doing brakes on his grandma's car by the time he was eleven, and he'd overhauled the motor a couple of years ago.

"I can look if you want. Might just be a loose battery cable or something like that." Hunter walked to the front of the car and started looking for a hood release.

"Hood release is in the car." Owen opened the door and reached in, and the hood popped up. Hunter couldn't believe how cool this engine was. He hoped he could find everything.

It took him a minute to figure out that the battery was actually in the trunk. That freaked him out at first—when he didn't see it under the hood. Then he remembered he'd seen something on TV about that. He had Owen pop the trunk and even checked the little diagrams in the manual. After that it was pretty easy to locate the battery cables and the generator belt. Sweat was running down his face, but he sure did want to go to that baseball game. He smiled when he saw the cable to the back of the generator hanging loose. He knew then that the generator wasn't charging the battery. He snapped it into place.

"Go give it a try now," he said to Owen, his head still under the hood. Owen got in the car, but the motor wouldn't turn over, just kept clicking. "We need jumper cables to help boost the battery."

Owen climbed out of the car and slammed the door. "I've got jumper cables, but who is going to jump—" He stopped and pointed a few houses down. "Do you know that man in the front yard?"

Hunter squinted to see. "Yeah. That's Bart Murphy."

"I'll go see if he'll give us a jump." Owen took off jogging in that direction and returned a couple of minutes later riding alongside Mr. Murphy in his Ford Explorer.

Once Hunter had the cables connected, Owen hurried into the driver's seat, and the car started on the first crank. Hunter avoided Mr. Murphy's stare as he handed the jumper cables back to him. Hunter was sure Mr. Murphy was wondering what Owen was doing with someone like Hunter. He slammed the hood and got in on the passenger side. Owen thanked Mr. Murphy, got in the car, then turned to Hunter and smiled as they both buckled up.

"Wow. You know your cars. Thank goodness you got it fixed. I just had it in the shop."

"They just didn't tighten a cable, that's all. No big deal." Hunter shrugged, glad to be on the road and away from Mr. Murphy's peering eyes.

"It's a big deal if you don't know anything about cars." Owen shifted the gears, and once they were on the freeway, he really opened it up.

"How fast does this car go?" Hunter watched Owen passing the cars around them.

"Fast enough," Owen answered as he switched lanes. "You can drive it home if you want."

Hunter jerked his head toward Owen and blinked a couple of times. "Are you kidding me?"

"Nope." He turned to face Hunter. "You do have a driver's license, don't you?"

"Yeah." He'd taken driver's ed in school before he dropped out. It was the only class he'd ever really wanted to pass. But he'd only had his license a week before Grandma sold her car so she'd have money for doctors and medicines.

"You know how to drive a standard?" Owen flipped through stations on the radio.

"Yeah. My grandma's car was a standard."

"What does she drive?"

Hunter looked out the window. "Nothing now. She had to sell it when she got sick. We don't have a car now."

"So it's just you and your grandma?" Owen whipped around another car, and Hunter wasn't sure what he was more excited about—the baseball game or getting to drive this car back home.

"Yeah. Just the two of us." Hunter didn't really want to talk about his messed-up life.

"What's wrong with your grandma?"

He shifted in his seat. He didn't like to talk about Grandma being sick either. "She's got some kind of cancer, some rare kind, but I can't ever remember the name of it." He paused as he recalled something his grandmother had said once. "She said God struck her down with the cancer because she'd lived such a bad life."

"I don't think that's how God works. Lots of people who have lived very good lives get cancer."

Hunter shrugged. "I don't know. I don't know if I believe in God."

Owen came close to saying, "Neither do I," but he knew that wasn't true. He believed in God. He just didn't have anything to say to Him. And he found it disturbing to hear a kid Hunter's age say that he didn't believe at all.

"Oh, there is a God." Owen glanced at Hunter.

Hunter was quiet for a while before he spoke up. "You a churchgoer?"

Owen pushed the knob to turn up the air conditioner. "I used to be."

"I ain't never been to church."

Owen pressed hard on the brakes as he edged too close to a car in front of him. He turned to Hunter. "Never? Really?"

Hunter shook his head. "My folks aren't much for it." He paused, shifting his weight beneath the seat belt. "And Grandma don't go either."

Owen had grown up in the church. He'd even had a pretty strong faith—until recently. But shouldn't everyone have an opportunity to know about God before they decide whether or not to dismiss Him?

There was probably more to be said about a relationship with the Lord, but Owen wasn't sure he was the one to say it. So he changed the subject to cars. And Hunter talked more on that subject than he had since Owen met him, rattling on about engines, horsepower, and things Owen didn't know about, but it was nice to see the kid excited about something.

"Is that Minute Maid Park?" Hunter pointed to his left.

Owen nodded as he took the next exit and smiled at the excitement etched across Hunter's face, as if Hunter were a young boy untarnished by life—not a teenage hoodlum with crackhead parents.

If Hunter could have handpicked a father, it would have been someone just like Owen. He didn't seem like the kind of guy who would hit you or make you feel worthless. He drove a fancy car, had a big house, and must have tons of money. Owen Saunders was the luckiest man on earth, and Hunter felt lucky just knowing him—and being able to work for him. When Owen asked him if he wanted to get a bite to eat after the game, Hunter was glad the day wasn't over yet. He wanted to tell Owen that this had been the best day of his life, but he knew that would sound real dumb, so he didn't.

"I'm glad the Astros won," Owen said as they got in the car. "Although I thought they were going to blow it in that last inning."

Hunter closed the door. "Yeah, that was a great catch." He paused, looked out the window, and could feel his face reddening. "Uh, thanks for taking me."

"Sure. You're welcome. Where do you want to eat?"

Hunter thought about the best meal he'd ever had. When he was thirteen, Brooke and Travis Holloway had taken him out to eat with them and their kids. They'd gone to a real fancy seafood restaurant called Pappadeaux. That was back when he was mowing yards for money, and he'd just finished mowing their yard when Mrs. Holloway came out and asked him if he wanted to go to Houston with them. He'd showered, had a great meal, and gone shopping with them. They'd bought him a shirt. Hunter cringed and tried not to think about the Holloways—and what he'd done to Mrs. Holloway a few years later. He didn't want to ever go back to that restaurant. Or think about the Holloways. He even avoided walking by their hardware store.

"It don't matter. Whatever you want to eat is okay with me."

Owen pulled into a Mexican restaurant, and Hunter had

the best enchiladas ever. They talked about all sorts of stuff. Owen was an only child, like Hunter, but other than that they didn't have much in common. Owen had gone to a big fancy college, owned his own business, and already been married and divorced. He didn't want to talk about that part too much, but Hunter figured that Owen wasn't over it yet.

The best part of the day for Hunter was when they left the restaurant and Owen handed him the keys. Hunter felt like an upscale type of person behind the wheel of the BMW. Owen made some phone calls and didn't even seem worried about Hunter wrecking his car.

When they stopped to get gas, they were already in Smithville, so Hunter gave Owen the keys back. "Thanks, man. Great car."

"You're welcome." Owen finished pumping the gas, then got in the driver's seat. "Where's your house? I'll just drop you off."

Crud. "Just go on to your house. I can walk from there."

Owen frowned. "Don't be silly. It can't be too far from mine. Where do I turn?" He slowed down on Main Street.

"Two streets up, turn left. Then you go down for about six blocks, over the railroad tracks."

Hunter stared out the passenger window and wondered what Owen was going to think when he pulled up to their run-down house with an old oven on the front porch, a busted rocker, and several days' worth of piled-up black bags full of trash. The trash people had stopped coming since they hadn't paid the bills. Then the neighbor's dog had gotten into the bags. It was a real mess, and Hunter was going to have to clean it up. *Should have cleaned it up before now.*

"Hope you had a good time," Owen said as he pulled up to Hunter's house.

But Hunter didn't face Owen, didn't see his reaction to Hunter's house or hear anything else the man said. All Hunter saw was the beat-up red Chevy pickup in the driveway. His heart sank, and he suddenly felt like he might vomit.

❧

Hunter walked in the front door and into a cloud of smoke. It wasn't even close to dark, but he had to blink his eyes a few times to adjust to the dim lighting and see his parents sitting there.

"Hey, Hunter. I hear you been out partying with the rich folk. Good for you." Hunter's mother was dressed in the last outfit he'd seen her in when they left for the rehab facility—jeans, a white T-shirt, and a pair of red spike heels. She'd put on some weight, though. He didn't remember her stomach hanging over her jeans like that. Her blond hair had really dark roots for several inches down the sides of her head.

"Hey, Mom." *Is that pot I smell?* He waved his hand in front of his face, then focused on his father. "Hey, Dad."

"Hey, boy. Good to see you." His father stood up and walked toward Hunter with his hand outstretched. Hunter shook his father's hand and wondered if his parents were home for good.

Mom crossed her legs and grinned. "So, Momma tells us that you got yourself a real good job."

Hunter nodded. Grandma was propped up on pillows on the couch, still in her pink robe. His parents were in the recliners. No other place to sit. "Yeah, painting and stuff."

"I hope you're taking care of things around here, like keeping the electricity on and food on the table." Mom lit a cigarette, although Hunter was now sure that wasn't all they'd been smoking. The sweet smell still lingered in the air. His chest tightened up, and it felt like someone had their hands around his throat.

His father chimed in, "After we leave, I don't want to hear you ain't been using that money to take care of your grandma."

Music to his ears. They were leaving. *When?*

"We got us a weekend pass," Mom said before chuckling. "For good behavior."

Hunter struggled to breathe—from the smoke and what he now knew to be an anxiety attack.

"You having another one of them attacks?" Grandma edged herself up on the couch until she was almost sitting. She looked at his mother. "I told him to take some of my Xanax, but he just chooses to be miserable instead. Hope you're not having those on the job, Hunter."

He shook his head, which made him feel like the room was spinning.

"Good grief. What in the world do you have to feel anxious about?" His mother actually laughed, and Hunter wished she'd have this feeling—just once—to know what it feels like to think you're going to die. Then maybe she wouldn't be laughing.

"Go on in your room, Hunter." Grandma walked toward him and put an arm around him, which almost made the anxiety attack worth it. "Lay down and take some deep breaths. You know it will go away." They were almost in his room when she whispered, "Remember, you're not going to die. Everything is all right."

Hunter nodded, thankful for his grandmother. In spite of everything, she really did love him.

After she closed his bedroom door, he lay down on the bed

and tried to think about the day. About Owen, the baseball game, the great meal. But the sound of his parents laughing in the next room was making that nearly impossible. At least he only had to make it through the weekend.

He turned his face away from the sounds in the living room but then sat up quickly, knocked himself in the forehead with his palm, and held his breath. His dresser drawer was open a little. He hurried across the small room and pulled the drawer all the way open. He reached to the back and felt around for the envelope with one hand while he clicked his lamp on with the other.

Tears built up in his eyes.

Gone. All the money he'd made this past week, less what he'd given his grandma. Twenty dollars in his pocket was all that was left.

He burst out of his bedroom door, head throbbing, heart racing, palms sweating. His father stood up before Hunter could even say anything. Dad puffed out his chest as Hunter walked toward him. "You got a problem, Hunter?"

Something about the way Dad said his name made Hunter real sure that he'd take him out back and beat the snot out of him if he accused anyone in the room of stealing his money. Grandma didn't allow no beatings in the house, and a few times she'd even cried and begged Hunter's father to stop hitting him.

He walked out the front door and slammed it behind him.

rooke was sitting at the counter early Saturday afternoon when Owen walked in. Juliet was in the back entertaining Meghan and Spencer, and Big Daddy was stocking shelves nearby.

"I see you're busy painting today." Brooke eyed the dark-colored splotches on Owen's hands. "Interesting color."

Owen looked down at his hands. "Actually, it's stain. I'm staining the inside of my closet. And myself, I guess." He smiled. "Do you want to have dinner with me tonight?"

Brooke's eyes widened. "Uh . . ."

"Not like pizza at my house or hanging out on your couch. A real dinner."

Brooke frowned. "I thought my cooking was a *real* dinner."

Owen laughed. "I know, I know. I just meant like at a restaurant. Somewhere here in Smithville."

Wow. Sounded almost like a date. "Okay. I guess so." She paused, wondering about Meghan and Spencer.

"Can the girl who works in the back keep your kids? Or maybe your mom could watch them?" He held up a hand.

"Not that I don't like your children. Meghan and Spencer are great. But . . . you know."

Yikes. This is *a date.* A bubble of excitement rose in her stomach, along with a little guilt and some surprise.

"Juliet can probably keep them." She pressed her lips together, struggling not to smile.

"Can you go ask her?"

"Uh, now?" She raised her eyebrows, still stifling a smile. He was almost being pushy, and that was strangely flattering. It felt good to know he wanted to be alone with her.

"Yeah." Owen nodded. "Then we can set a time."

Brooke shrugged. "Okay." As she turned and walked toward the back, the smile did indeed fill her face. She wasn't sure she was ready for this, but the prospect of going on a real first date with Owen felt better than she'd expected.

They were friends. Was he wanting it to be more? She recalled the time they'd spent together, how good he was with her children. *Hmm.*

Juliet could barely contain her excitement when Brooke pulled her out into the hallway and asked her to babysit. "Are you going to wear that outfit I loaned you awhile back?"

Brooke tried not to cringe. No way she was wearing that. "I don't know. I'll figure something out." She pointed back to the office. "And don't mention this to Spencer or Meghan yet. I'll talk to them tonight. I'm not sure how Spence will feel."

"Just go!" Juliet was practically dancing. She pointed to the front of the store where Owen still waited. "Tell him yes!"

Brooke returned to the counter, hiding the smile she felt trying to resurface. She'd been asked out plenty of times since Travis died. This was the first time she'd accepted.

"Juliet can babysit."

Owen clapped his hands together. "Great. Where should

we go? It needs to be somewhere really popular around here. Where do all the locals go? I want everyone to see us together."

Brooke pulled her eyes from his, blushing. "I guess either Pocket's Grill or the Back Door Café. Why . . ." She paused, unsure how to ask what she was thinking.

"I've been to both. Which one do you think more people will frequent on a Saturday night?"

She finally asked, "Why does it matter?"

Owen put his palms on the counter and leaned a little closer to her on the other side. "Do you know someone named Tallie Goodry?"

"Yes." Brooke folded her arms across her chest. "Why?"

"She came to my house this morning unannounced." He squinted one eye, frowning. "She practically asked me out. I had to do some major sidestepping, but she bullied my phone number out of me." He paused. "Anyway, I've told you how I feel. I've got some major issues to work through, and I'm not ready to date anyone. If everyone thinks you and I are a couple, it will keep people like her at bay." He shook his head. "She called me around lunchtime . . . after she'd already been by this morning."

Brooke felt her face flame and her heart raced. "So you want me to give up any opportunities that anyone might ask me out by pretending to be your girlfriend. Is that correct?"

"I thought you didn't want to date anyone. I thought you weren't ready." Owen stuck his paint-covered hands into the pockets of his silly overalls.

"Maybe I just haven't met the right person to even consider it."

Owen grinned. "I think you were considering it the other night when you came on to me."

Brooke tipped back the edge of her baseball cap and

stared into his eyes. "Go find yourself someone else to keep away all the hundreds of women who will surely be banging down your door to date you!" She turned and walked toward the back.

"Brooke. Wait!" He followed her, and when she didn't slow down, he grabbed her arm. "Stop."

"You're mighty arrogant, Mr. Saunders." Brooke glared up at him, feeling ridiculous, angry, and embarrassed.

He let go of her and looked away, then met her eyes again. "See why I'm undateable? I'm a jerk." He held up one finger. "But in my defense . . . I just assumed that every guy around here has already made a play for you. I didn't think I'd be messing up your social life. I thought you made it pretty clear you weren't ready to move on."

Brooke shifted her weight and tapped one foot. "I guess that's a decent apology."

"I tell you what. Forget all that about being seen together. Tallie Goodry will most likely figure out what a jerk I am anyway on her own. Why don't we just go out tonight? You have a babysitter. We can just sit and talk and have a good meal. I don't care where."

As much as a night out sounded good, Brooke hesitated. For a few moments, she'd actually looked forward to a real date with Owen, and that was concerning. Did she really want to put her heart out there like that?

"Please." He leaned down and tried to woo her with his blue eyes and charming smile. When he started batting his eyes, she smiled.

"A grown-up dinner out would be nice."

"I'll pick you up at seven." He winked, then turned to leave.

Brooke stood there for a few moments, trying to figure out what had just happened.

❧

It was six o'clock when Owen wrapped up his work for the day, pleased with how his closet had turned out. He eyed the clothes on the floor and decided that was a tomorrow project. He needed to shower so he could pick up Brooke at seven.

What a mess that whole scene in the hardware store had been. *Women.* He was never going to figure them out.

Based on her previous actions, Owen decided that Brooke was teetering on the edge, unsure if she wanted to start dating or not. So he made a mental note not to do anything to lead her on. His heart wasn't up for grabs, but he certainly didn't want to do anything to hurt her.

He showed up at seven, and when she opened the door, Owen had to question the pep talk he'd given himself. She wore a green-and-white sleeveless dress, flat sandals, very little makeup, and her hair was long and flowing loose past her shoulders. She was stunning, and for a few moments, he was speechless.

"I already took Meghan and Spencer to Juliet's, so I'll just grab my purse." She left the door open and walked to her couch to pick up the bag. As she turned the key in the front door, then turned and smiled at him, Owen felt like he'd just moved into dangerous territory. Nothing could be more irresponsible than to lead her on, but Owen was going to have a hard time keeping himself in check. What had he been thinking?

"You look great," he said as he opened the car door. She blushed right away.

"Thanks." Grinning, she added, "You clean up pretty well yourself."

Owen went around the front of the BMW, glancing down at his yellow short-sleeved shirt, then climbed into the driver's seat. They were at Pocket's Grill in less than two minutes. It was a casual place, but roomy. Smithville had been the locale for quite a few movies, and film memorabilia lined the walls of the restaurant. He and Brooke were led through a crowd of patrons to a seat at the back.

"Well, the place is packed. Lucky you," Brooke said as she opened a menu the waitress had just handed them. Her words held an edge, but she was smiling.

"I told you to forget about that plan. We're just two friends enjoying a night out."

"Your plan wouldn't have worked anyway. My friend Judy already asked if there was something going on between you and me, and I told her no." Brooke peered at him above her menu. "And she mentioned Tallie, so I'm not surprised you heard from her."

Owen closed his menu and rubbed his forehead. "Not my type. At all."

Brooke slowly put her menu on the table. "Do you really think we all have a type, or do we just see things in people that we find attractive in a lot of different ways?"

Owen thought about how completely opposite Virginia and Brooke were, yet he couldn't deny he was attracted to Brooke on several levels. And the things he found appealing were qualities Virginia lacked. Brooke was a good mother, and Owen found that very attractive. She also didn't go out of her way to make herself something she wasn't. He thought about all the appointments Virginia kept every week—nails, hair, facials, massages, and most recently a plastic surgeon for what she'd called some "minor work."

"I don't know. I guess maybe you're right. We can find attractive qualities about people who are nothing alike." Owen smiled. "But Tallie is still not my type."

"Because you are damaged goods." Brooke didn't smile, and her gaze was sympathetic. "Why do you say that anyway?"

This was starting to get heavier than Owen was up for, but he didn't want to do anything to hurt her feelings again. "My ex-wife ruined me."

Brooke waited. Owen should have known that answer wouldn't satisfy her.

"After what she did, I just don't think I can trust anyone again. We'd been married for seven years when she started sleeping with Gary." Owen paused, thinking. "And I didn't suspect a thing until I walked in on them. Virginia made a full confession and said it had been going on for a year. A year!" He shrugged. "And the sad thing is . . . I still love her. But I hate her too, so that makes me a pretty messed-up guy."

After the waitress returned, they both ordered, then Brooke leaned back in her chair and stared at him.

"What? Why are you looking at me like that?" Owen laid his napkin in his lap as he locked eyes with her.

"I'm just thinking."

Now Owen waited.

Brooke sat a little taller and folded her hands on the table. "We can't stop loving someone overnight, no matter what they've done. And I can see where you'd have trust issues." She paused. "But I think maybe presenting yourself as damaged goods might not be accurate. I'm thinking it would just take a long time to get over something like that."

"It's so ironic." Owen took a sip of iced tea. "I wanted a child so badly, and Virginia was dead set against it." He shook his head. "And now she is having a baby. I can't help but wonder if she just didn't want to have a child with *me*." He tried to picture Virginia pregnant. He couldn't help but feel a little smug knowing how much she'd hate being fat. How she would have to forfeit all the big plans she'd had for her life, plans that didn't include having a baby. "I guess I'm just bitter about all of it. I mean, what kind of guy buys a house just to bother his ex-wife? What does that say about me?"

The waitresses brought them their burgers and fries, and Brooke cut hers in half. "When Travis died, I don't think I was bitter, but I was just incredibly sad. It wasn't like anything I'd ever gone through—just total devastation. If it hadn't been for Meghan and Spencer, I think I would have stayed in bed the rest of my life." She took a bite, and when she was done, added, "But they needed me, and they were having a hard time, so I didn't have a choice but to pick myself up and keep going."

"I can't imagine losing a spouse. As much as I despise Virginia, it would be awful if she died."

"You just don't think it will happen to you, you know?" Brooke pushed her fries around with her fork. "You get up and kiss your spouse good-bye, then go to work—with no way of knowing that you'll . . . never see him again." She picked up a fry and poked it absently in her mouth, her face bleak.

It's not fair that You took her husband like that! Owen startled himself with his first spontaneous prayer in a long time. Brooke didn't deserve that. Nor did her children.

He kept his eyes on Brooke. "Is it hard for you to talk about this?"

"Sometimes. But it gets easier." She paused, another fry in hand. "That's not to say that some days I don't want to just lie in bed and cry. That still happens. Maybe it always will."

Owen took a bite of his burger, thinking about his own situation. "I probably cut off my nose to spite my face by buying this house. Virginia has gone on with her life, and I'm all by myself, redoing a house that's big enough for an army of people. Sometimes, especially at night, I wonder if maybe a smaller place would have been better. Maybe the loneliness wouldn't settle all over me so much."

Brooke nodded. "Nighttime is when it all hits me, after the kids are asleep."

"I bet they give you a lot of comfort though." Owen smiled. "By the way, does Spencer know we're having dinner?"

Brooke smiled. "Yes. And he was very okay about it." She pointed her fork at him. "But I'm pretty sure he just wants another shot at looking for that bunker."

"You have great kids." Owen thought about sweet little Meghan and the way she'd taken his hand and snuggled up against him. He figured by the time he got over Virginia—if that ever happened—and found someone else to love, he'd probably be too old to have children. He hated her for that too.

"Thank you." Brooke's face lit up. "They really are great."

They both passed on dessert, but Owen wasn't in any hurry to go back to his lonely old house. Brooke was great company, easy to talk to, and he felt they were crossing over into more of a real friendship. It was nice. For the next hour, they sipped coffee and talked. Brooke shared her frustration about the situation with her mother and father. Several times she'd blinked back tears.

"I hope you can forgive your father," Owen finally said. "For your sake. Life is short."

Brooke looked at him long and hard. "The pot calling the kettle black, wouldn't you say?"

Owen nodded. "I guess so. I don't see myself forgiving Virginia anytime soon." He paused. "But I'm fortunate to have a good relationship with my parents—even if they deserted me and moved to Florida." He grinned but quickly grew serious. "He's the only dad you've got, Brooke."

"I know it's wrong for me not to forgive him. I really do. And I've talked to God about this. But I just can't do it."

It was the first mention of God between them, and Owen wanted to know if she was as angry at God as he was. "Did you, uh, have a strong faith before Travis died?"

She smiled. "I still do. Without God, I don't think I would have survived everything. Have you joined a church since you've moved here?"

Owen just stared at her for a few moments. "No."

"Our church is great. It's small, but we have a really good pastor and a wonderful group of people."

Owen avoided her eyes. "I don't think church is for me. Or God." When he looked up at Brooke, her expression was more solemn than he'd ever seen.

"You don't believe in God?"

Owen thought she looked like she was holding her breath. "I guess I believe in Him. I just don't have anything to say to Him."

Brooke nodded. "I guess it could have gone that way for me when Travis died. I was so angry. But not at God."

"How could you not be angry at God? He ripped your husband out of your life and left you to raise your children alone."

"Yes." She leaned back as if she'd just been splashed in the face with water. "And I'll probably never understand why."

Owen shook his head. "Sorry. But I lost my faith the day I walked in on Virginia and Gary."

"Maybe you just need time." She pulled her napkin from her lap and put it on her plate—a clear signal that she was through with this meal.

"Nope. I don't think so." Something had drastically changed between them in the past minute. "You ready to go?"

"Yeah, it's getting late." She looked at her watch. "Wow. We've been here for almost three hours. Thank you for dinner and the conversation."

She was being overly polite, and Owen had the strangest feeling she wouldn't want to spend any more time with him. That should have been okay, but it wasn't.

He prayed silently for the second time this evening. *Go ahead, punish me some more. Take away the only friend I've got in this town.*

When they pulled into her driveway, he wasn't sure what to do. He knew that a gentleman would walk his date to the door. But this wasn't really a date. And what was he supposed to do when he got there? Hug her good-bye?

The problem was solved when she took off her seat belt, then leaned over and kissed him on the cheek. "Thank you again for dinner."

"You're welcome."

She was just about to close the car door when she pulled it wide again.

"Owen?"

"Yeah?"

She bit her lip for a moment. "Would you like to come with me and the kids to church tomorrow?"

Owen swallowed hard. "Brooke . . ."

She waited, her eyes pleading with him. It wasn't her job to save him, but it was sweet of her to try. Selfishly, he didn't factor God into the request, but instead wondered if maybe his presence at church would ensure that they would stay friends. But he just couldn't bring himself to say yes.

"I can't, Brooke. Sorry."

Sixteen

When Hunter didn't show up for work Monday, Owen was angry. But about an hour into assessing everything he needed to do, his gut told him to take a drive.

When he pulled up to the curb at Hunter's house, he almost felt guilty about the way he and Virginia had lived when there were people like Hunter and his grandma living like this. He'd enjoyed the baseball game with Hunter, and he'd thought Hunter liked his job. So where was he?

He knocked on the door, and when no one answered, he pounded on it.

"Hang on. Just a minute!"

It was a woman's voice—Hunter's grandma, he presumed. Hunter had said she was sick, and Owen hoped he hadn't awakened her. She opened the door a few inches, scowling, her gray hair tousled as if she'd just gotten up.

"I'm looking for Hunter Lewis."

The woman pulled the door wide as she tied a band around a bedraggled pink robe. "What's he done now?"

"Nothing. I'm Owen Saunders. He works for me." Owen tried to see past her and into the house, but she blocked his view.

"I told that boy he was going to blow this job." She huffed, shook her head. "Wait here."

Owen could hear her muffled yelling. A few minutes later Hunter was at the door, head hanging.

Owen folded his arms across his chest. "You quitting on me already?"

Hunter didn't look up or say anything.

"Look, if you need a day off or something, you just have to ask me. But don't just not show up."

Grandma was no longer in sight. Hunter stepped out onto the porch and closed the door behind him. "Sorry."

Owen was thinking he should have known better than to hire this kid. "That's it? Sorry? So are you done? You quit?"

Hunter looked up, and Owen wasn't sure he'd ever seen a shiner like the one on Hunter's left eye. Owen swallowed hard. "Who did that?"

Hunter didn't say anything, but his bottom lip was starting to quiver.

Owen was trying to picture how that small, frail woman could do this to Owen, and he quickly ruled that out. Had Hunter done something to get himself into more trouble with the police?

"I hope the other kid looks half as bad as you do." Owen leaned closer to get a better look, and Hunter started to shake.

"It weren't with no other kid, okay?" He shook his head. "Just go. You would've fired me pretty soon anyways." He turned to go back in the house, but Owen grabbed his arm.

"Hey." He kept a firm grip. "I thought you were doing great work at my house. I didn't have any plans to fire you. If someone did this to you—and it was unprovoked—then you should press charges."

Hunter shook loose, turned, and half-smiled. "You're

kiddin' me, right? Guess I'm supposed to go to that judge who hates me already and tell him my dad knocked the you-know-what out of me. I bet they'd send someone right over to pick him up."

Owen didn't say anything for a few moments until his blood cooled. "Is your father here now?"

"No. They was only here for the weekend." Hunter chuckled, but then grimaced as he reached for his eye. "Just long enough to come home and—"

"Get your shoes on. We're going to go file charges." Fury was about to choke him, but Owen kept his voice level and calm.

Hunter shook his head. "They're gone, and I imagine when they get back to that rehab place and have to take a drug test, they ain't gonna get back out for a while." He paused. "But they're gonna get out someday, and I don't wanna have to deal with my dad about this." He pointed to his eye. "I doubt next time it would be just a black eye."

Owen let out a heavy sigh. "I think you ought to report him." When Hunter didn't say anything, Owen said, "If it hurts too much to work, you could have just called and told me."

"We don't got a phone."

Owen scratched his head. "Or maybe you could have walked the few blocks to my house? Or something?"

Hunter shrugged and looked away.

"Did you think I'd fire you when I saw your eye?"

Hunter shrugged, and Owen figured he was just embarrassed enough to lose his job over this.

"Look, we're supposed to have some bad weather coming later in the week. I've got a roof that leaks, several trees that need to be cut down before they fall down, cracked windows upstairs . . . the list goes on. I really need some help getting my house at least a little weatherproofed. A lot of the bad roof damage was done in a hailstorm a few months before I moved in, and I haven't had time to get to that." It was all true. "So if you choose to keep working with me, we're going to have to spend a little time in this heat for a couple of days."

Hunter furrowed his brow, but then flinched again from the pain. "You still want me to work for you even though I didn't show up or call or nothin'?"

Owen shrugged. "Everyone deserves a second chance, don't they?" He patted Hunter on the arm. "Go get your work clothes on. Lunch is on me today."

Hunter stood and stared at him for a few seconds, then finally turned to get his shoes. Owen heard him telling his grandma he was leaving. "Good thing you got that job back, boy. I was wondering what we was gonna do. Don't be so stupid from now on."

Was this job all that Hunter and his grandma depended on, outside of government assistance? What had they done before Owen hired Hunter? Owen rubbed his chin and thought about all the trouble Hunter had been in, the life the kid had lived so far.

Maybe I need to be grateful for what I do have, not what I've lost.

⚜

Brooke was sweeping around the counter at the store Monday morning, her mind filled with thoughts of Owen. They'd had such a great time . . . until the end of the evening. It saddened her to think that Owen had given up a relationship with God just because he couldn't forgive his ex-wife. And it angered her that she kept thinking about it and comparing it to her own situation with her father. True, she couldn't forgive her father, but at least she hadn't walked away from God because of the bad things that had happened in her life. Faith should be stronger than that.

And so should the ability to forgive.

She heard the message loud and clear, knowing that the Lord had forgiven her for plenty of things over the course of her lifetime. But she still couldn't wrap her mind around a father who would betray her mother and then just walk away.

Brooke could remember taking her father's calls in the beginning. She'd been angry and hateful to him, but she'd still hoped he would come home, no matter what he'd done. Eventually, though, she'd stopped taking his calls or opening mail from him. How could her mother have just let him waltz back into her life? It was just . . . wrong.

She sat down on the stool behind the counter and closed her eyes. *Lord, I can't do it. I can't forgive him. I don't know how.* Brooke squeezed her eyes closed. *But show me the way if it's Your will.* She opened her eyes for a moment, then closed them again. *And I pray that Owen won't be such a bitter man and that he'll find his way back to You. Amen.*

She opened her eyes as the bell on the door chimed. Her mother walked in—alone, thank goodness.

"How'd you get here?" Brooke walked toward her and hugged her, noticing that Mom was dressed in another new pants outfit and smelled of her new perfume.

"Your father is in the car." Mom stepped back but kept her hands on Brooke's arms. "We're on our way to get a late breakfast, but I wanted to stop by and check on you. Have you heard there's a storm out in the Gulf? It's about to be a hurricane, and they say we might get some of it."

Brooke had been worrying about the storm too, but now

all her concerns about it flew out the window—along with her good intentions. "Please don't call that man my father. He's not my father."

Mom's face flushed. "He *is* your father, Brooke. And you're being—"

"Really, Mother? Are you going to get mad at me about this? Because we can go through all of this again, and there is no reason for—"

"Stop it! Just stop it!" Mom actually stomped her foot. "Why can't you just accept that I'm happy and find an ounce of forgiveness?"

Brooke's jaw dropped, unsure if she'd ever heard her mother yell like that. She glanced around the store, glad there weren't any customers to hear her mother's childish outburst. Down the aisle, she saw Big Daddy emerge from the back office, concern on his craggy face. "You cannot force me to forgive him or to accept this ridiculous remarriage." This time it was Brooke's voice that rose. "He had an affair, Mother! Then he left us for the other woman. He never tried to come back! He just left and—"

"He did want to come back." Her mother covered her eyes with one hand.

"What?" Brooke looked at her mother, but turned when Big Daddy made it to the front of the store.

"Everything okay?" He stopped a few feet from the register.

"Yes. We're fine."

Mom pasted on a trembling smile. "Hello, Big Daddy. Nice to see you."

Brooke pleaded with her eyes for him to go and he walked away—though she knew he would stay nearby. Then she refocused on her mother. "Answer me, Mom. What were you talking about?"

Her mother sniffled and raised her chin. "Your father did want to come back. He begged to come back. For years."

Brooke walked around the counter and sat down on the stool. "He wanted to come back to us?"

"Yes."

Brooke was quiet for a few moments. "Why didn't you ever tell me that?"

"You were so mad at him, kept saying that you hated him. I didn't think it would be good for him to come back." Her mother pulled her eyes from Brooke's.

Brooke stood again and shook her head. "So you let me believe that he just abandoned me?"

"You abandoned him, Brooke. He tried to stay close to you, and you wouldn't have it."

Brooke covered her face with her hands, then ripped them away. "I wanted him back! Of course I was mad, Mom— mad that he hurt you and did this to our family. But I always wanted him to come home!" She leaned on the counter and stared at her mother. "How could you do this, Mom?" Tears blurred her vision, and she sank back down on the stool. "Did you forgive him back then? Because if you didn't, then tell me the truth. And don't say you kept him away because it was best for me. Let's at least be honest."

Her mother looked away, pushed her glasses up on her nose, and shook her head. "I wish we didn't have to drag all this up. I wish you could just be happy that I'm happy." She turned back to Brooke. "And get to know your father."

"You couldn't forgive him, could you?" Brooke smirked. "You want to preach forgiveness to me, but you couldn't forgive him back then. So you said it was best for me if he wasn't around, and I was left to think he abandoned us." She shook her head. "And all the while, he wanted to come home."

"He made a fool out of me!" Her mother slapped her hands against her slacks. "I couldn't get past that."

"Then why are you forgiving him now?" Brooke lowered her voice as she tried to understand. "And why do you keep nagging me to forgive him?"

Her mother started to cry. "Because I want a life, Brooke. I don't want to finish out my days as a bitter woman. And I've always loved that man, no matter what!" She turned and rushed to the exit, the bell jingling wildly as she slammed the door behind her.

Brooke raced around the counter to go after her, but stopped when she caught a glimpse of her father sitting in an old blue Chevy outside. A large dent marred the right fender of the car. Her father's shoulders slumped in a way she didn't remember.

She walked to pick up her broom and began to sweep again—vigorously. She'd spent her entire life furious at her father for leaving them and never coming back. She'd lived so long with the pain of his abandonment, when all the while her mother wouldn't let him come home?

But can I really blame her?

Was Brooke prepared to make the same mistake her mother had made by not showing forgiveness? That had certainly been the plan, but this new information had confused matters. Her hands tightened on the broom handle as she stirred up a cloud of dust.

❧

Hunter's heart thumped in his chest as he and Owen hammered shingles onto Owen's roof. After everything the guy had done for him, he wasn't about to tell Owen that he was scared of heights.

After a few minutes, Owen said they were done and motioned for Hunter to head back down the ladder. Hunter couldn't get back on the ground fast enough.

"It's not the best job, but if that storm does come our way, hopefully it will keep the rain out." Owen hopped down from the third rung of the ladder. "I'm starving. You ready for lunch?"

Hunter nodded. He was always hungry.

"If you'll put the ladder up and clean up this mess we made, I'll go pick us up something to eat." He pointed to the old shingles they'd tossed off the roof. "How about a barbeque sandwich from Zimmerhanzel's?"

Hunter nodded, then started to pick up the shingles. He had that done and the ladder put away long before Owen got back, so he went and used the bathroom, then looked around. There was still a lot to do in the house, and Hunter was thankful for that. He needed this job. Reaching into his pocket, he felt the twenty-dollar bill—all the money he had left. He was glad he didn't have to spend it on lunch today. Luckily he had given Grandma the money for bills before his parents decided to rob their own kid. He shook his head as he wandered from room to room downstairs.

He tried to picture himself living in a big house like this— maybe with Jenny. He hadn't talked to her online since last week. His mother had hogged the laptop over the weekend, piggybacking off the neighbor's service.

Owen needed furniture to fill up this place, though. All he had was a bed, plus a table and four mismatched chairs that he kept mostly in the living room. Hunter walked through the living room, then sat down in the lawn chair by the small table. The table looked like Owen's dumping ground, kind of like the big bowl on the counter that Hunter and his grandmother put keys and other stuff in.

Hunter picked up Owen's watch, pulled it closer, and saw that it was a Rolex. Probably worth hundreds of dollars. Maybe thousands. He looked over his shoulder toward the window, then turned back around and slipped the watch on his arm, knowing he'd never own anything like that. After a minute, he put it back on the table. There were a few bills in a pile, and underneath that was some change. He swallowed hard, wondering what he was going to do for money for the next week until he got paid again. He'd given his grandma enough to pay the past-due electric bill and buy some food, so the two of them oughta be all right. He didn't care if he ever saw his parents again. *I hope they stay locked up forever.*

Why was life so unfair? Why couldn't he have been born into a different family? He looked around Owen's house again as he counted the cash on the table. A hundred and twenty dollars. He looked over his shoulder toward the window, then back at the money.

A guy like Owen wouldn't miss twenty dollars.

Or even forty.

~ Seventeen ~

Brooke closed the store early on Thursday so every-one could get ready for the coming bad weather. Tropical Storm Bill was headed straight for them and growing in strength. If it kept on its present course, it could bring several inches of much-needed rain, but also high winds and possible tornadoes—especially if it grew into a hurricane as forecasters expected. Smithville residents knew from experience that a big storm didn't always lose its punch after landfall. And this was the first big storm coming their way since the start of hurricane season.

At home, Meghan and Spencer helped Brooke pick up loose objects in the yard that might get tossed around by high winds. It seemed a little extreme to do much else since they were a hundred seventy miles inland. Folks in town had been chattering about it all day, saying Smithville would be on the "dirty side of the storm," the side with the heaviest rainfall. Brooke wasn't sure about that, and she didn't think the weather forecasters were either. Anyone who lived near the coast knew these storms had a mind of their own. She hated storms, so she held tight to the possibility that this one would veer away and miss them.

She stepped onto a kitchen chair and took down her butterfly wind chime. After it was safely stored inside, she carried her potted plants from the porch to the living room and lined them along the box window. Just in case.

"Come on. Let's go turn the TV on and check out the latest." Brooke motioned for Meghan and Spencer to come in the house, and once they were all seated on the couch, Brooke turned on the television and searched for the Weather Channel. Spencer was fixated on the weather coverage, but Meghan just brushed her doll's hair, not paying much attention.

The storm covered almost the entire Gulf of Mexico, and forecasts had the eye of the storm making landfall at Galveston. It would weaken after it hit land, of course, but the sheer size of the thing made Brooke wonder if she'd done enough to prepare.

The phone rang in the kitchen, and Spencer ran to answer it. "It's Mr. Saunders," he said as he passed the phone to her and sighed.

Brooke hadn't talked to Owen since Saturday night, but she'd seen two missed calls from him on her caller ID. She'd toyed with the idea of calling him back, but he hadn't left a message and, truthfully, she wasn't sure she wanted to see him. What had started as a simple friendship now felt way too complicated.

They seemed to have way too much baggage between them to have a healthy relationship. Yet there had been several intimate moments when Brooke had felt things might be moving in that direction—nothing concrete, just the way they looked at each other, how he put his arm around her sometimes. Little things. They'd each been clear about their intentions, but was Owen just protecting his heart the way she was? And what about Owen's feelings about God? The whole thing was beginning to make her a little nervous.

"Are you ready for the storm?" he asked after she said hello.

Brooke settled back onto the couch. "I think so. As ready as we can be. But I saw Mr. Casper across the street putting tape on his windows. I'm not doing all that. I think we're too far inland to get that kind of wind. What do you think?"

"I'm not doing any of that either. I did replace the broken panes I had upstairs and fixed the roof as best I could." He paused. "I called you twice. I was just wondering . . . how you were."

"I'm fine. The kids and I are just watching the storm coverage and planning to eat hot dogs."

Long silence, then Owen asked, "Want some company?"

Brooke tucked a leg underneath her, bit her bottom lip for a moment, then couldn't keep from grinning. Despite the complications, she wanted to see him. "Are you lonely in that big house, Mr. Saunders?"

Meghan nestled up to her mother. "Tell Mr. Saunders to come eat hot dogs with us!"

Brooke put a finger to her lips as she looked at Meghan, then she turned to Spencer. Her son had seemed fine with Owen—until after Brooke's dinner date with him. Since then, Spencer hadn't mentioned going back to his house, and he was scowling now. Brooke suspected that even the possibility of a mysterious bunker wouldn't make him okay with his mother getting too friendly with any man. She covered the mouthpiece on the phone.

"Spence, that okay with you if Mr. Saunders comes over?"

Spencer didn't look at her, just shrugged. "Whatever."

Brooke disliked that word, and Spencer was using it more

and more these days. "We'd love some company," she finally said, keeping her eyes on Spencer.

"What can I bring?"

"Nothing. Unless you don't like hot dogs."

Brooke hung up, and about thirty minutes later there was a knock at the door. She swallowed hard when she opened the front door and saw a beautiful bouquet of yellow roses.

"Here." Owen handed her the flowers. "I felt weird after dinner Saturday, and I think I must have said something or . . ." He shrugged. "I don't know. But . . ." He shrugged again. "These are for you. Not the best since only the grocery store was open."

Brooke stepped back so he could come in. "Thank you. They're beautiful." *So Owen could tell something was wrong. And cared.*

Spencer was quickly by Brooke's side, arms folded across his chest. He nodded toward the roses. "What are those for?"

Meghan sauntered up to them in her bare feet. "Ooh, pretty!"

Brooke motioned for her children to step back. "Let Mr. Saunders in."

Owen followed the kids into the living room while Brooke went to put the flowers in a vase, unsure how she felt about the gesture. Seemed like mixed signals, but Brooke wasn't sure which signal she preferred anyway, which made her as messed up as he was. Either way, she loved yellow roses and briefly scanned her memory, trying to recall if she'd ever told Owen that. She didn't think so.

They all settled on a movie to watch—*Despicable Me*—and while Owen set up the DVD player, Brooke finished chopping onion for the hot dogs. She called Owen and the kids into the kitchen to fix their plates, then they all moved to the living room. Owen sat between Brooke and Meghan on the couch while Spencer curled up in the recliner, not saying much. Brooke and the kids had seen the movie before, an animated comedy that even Brooke thought was funny, but she was used to watching movies that were suitable for a ten-year-old and six-year-old. Owen laughed out loud a couple of times, though, and seemed to be enjoying himself.

When the movie was over, it was Meghan and Spencer's bedtime. "I'll be there to tuck you in shortly." Brooke leaned forward as Meghan kissed her good night. Spencer walked upstairs without his usual argument about bedtime, and Brooke wondered what was going on in his head. She thought maybe Owen was wondering too. His brow furrowed as he watched Spencer go.

Meghan wrapped her arms around Owen's neck and held on for dear life. At first, Owen glanced at Brooke as if he didn't know what to do, but slowly he eased his arms around her. Meghan kissed him on the cheek, and Owen smiled. For a few brief seconds, Brooke felt like Travis was back, like it was old times again.

Owen waited until Meghan was upstairs before he twisted to face Brooke on the couch. "Do you think Spencer is okay? He was awfully quiet."

"Yeah, I noticed that too. I don't know."

"He was dead set on making sure I didn't pursue his mother, but I thought we'd all kind of settled in as friends and that he was okay." He paused, frowning. "Maybe the flowers weren't a good idea."

"No, they're beautiful. I'll talk to him tomorrow." Brooke paused, then got up. "I'd better go tuck them both in."

She walked into Spencer's room first, but he'd already

turned off his light and was nestled down in his covers. That had been the norm for the past month or so, even though she allowed him to keep his light on longer than Meghan did. She missed their old tuck-in routine—a little talk, a prayer, and a kiss on the forehead. "Did you say your prayers?" she asked softly into the darkness, and Spencer responded with a muffled "Yes."

Meghan was pulling on her pajama bottoms when Brooke walked in. Once she was done, Brooke removed the band from Meghan's ponytail, then reached for the brush on the end table. After she'd brushed out the tangles, she and Meghan knelt by the bed and said their prayers. Meghan asked God to watch over the "storm people," which Brooke understood to mean those in the path of the bad weather.

When she got back downstairs, she returned to the couch and flipped to a tropical update. And gulped. She'd been praying the storm would take another path, but the forecast hadn't changed. "That storm is huge. Look." She pointed to the screen. "It's a hurricane now. Hurricane Bill."

"Wild Bill." Owen chuckled, but Brooke envisioned high winds, torrential rains, loud thunder and lightning, and maybe even power outages, and she shivered. Owen didn't seem to notice. He just leaned back and eased his feet up on the coffee table next to Brooke's. When their outer calves brushed against each other, Brooke slowly edged away. They were both barefoot, and she jumped when Owen reached over with his foot and tickled the bottom of hers.

"Don't do that. Very ticklish." She pointed a finger at him, and instead of running his toe along the bottom of her foot, he plopped his foot next to hers.

"Look at those tiny little feet."

Brooke stretched her foot as long as she could. "They're not all that tiny. Yours are just huge." She was secretly flattered, though. Owen kept his leg and foot right next to hers, which sent a tingle up her leg. She wondered if he felt it too.

The televised storm coverage droned on. The hurricane was scheduled to make landfall later that evening. That meant Smithville would begin to feel the effects tomorrow if the storm stayed on course. She'd keep praying the forecast would change, but she felt her anxiety growing as she watched the clouds swirl on the satellite image. It really did look like they were in for it. Maybe she should have had Big Daddy board up the hardware store windows.

She'd called her mother earlier to make sure that the Oaks had taken necessary precautions. Her mother said that Brooke's father had brought in her potted plants and made sure everything on her little patio was secure. Brooke rolled her eyes and told her mother to stay safe. Now she was wondering if she should have begged her to come here.

The truth was, storms terrified her. A neighbor girl had been struck by lightning when Brooke was seven. It had been storming when Travis had his accident too. Brooke could already picture herself huddling upstairs in her bed with the kids, covers over their heads. She'd do her best to comfort them, as she always did, but they wouldn't be fooled.

The whole prospect made her weary, and she yawned as she turned to Owen. "Do you want to watch another movie?"

"I'm thinking I need to go so you can sleep."

Brooke glanced at her watch. It was only nine thirty, and though she was tired, she wasn't ready for him to go. "I can't go to sleep this early. I'd be up at two, which I am half the time anyway. I haven't had a good night's sleep since Travis . . ." She shrugged.

"I don't sleep very well either." Owen put an arm around

her, and at first Brooke tensed. But when he added, "I'll leave if you want, or you can just close your eyes and rest." She couldn't resist how good it felt to be held.

She settled into the nook of his arm and handed him the remote. "Rest sounds good." Closing her eyes, she noticed how different he smelled from Travis. More of a spicy aroma mixed with fabric softener. She'd forgotten how nice it was just to cuddle. In fact, she wished he could be here tomorrow too, especially if the storm predictions proved accurate.

Owen put his hand against the side of her head, then ran his hand gently through her hair. There was every reason to lift her head and pull away from him, but his touch filled her with a warmth she hadn't felt in a long time. But this guy had said he would never trust another woman and he'd lost his faith in God. How could Brooke possibly give him access to her heart? And was she even ready for that anyway?

Owen kept running his hand through her hair as if it were the most natural thing in the world while he flipped channels on the TV. Brooke shifted her weight, wondering if he would stop when she moved, but he just pulled her closer and, surprisingly, kissed her on the forehead. It was the most at peace she'd felt in two years. The next thing she knew, she was opening her eyes, unsure how long she had slept.

She slid her face up his shoulder until she was looking at him. He was asleep too, barely snoring, his head leaning back against the couch. She watched him for a few minutes before she sat up, waking him.

"Wow." Owen pulled his long legs from atop the coffee table and sat up, running a hand through his hair. He checked his watch. "It's two in the morning. I gotta let you get to bed. I'm really sorry."

"Don't be." Brooke stood up when he did. "That's probably

the best sleep I've had in a long time." She followed him to the door.

"Thanks for the hot dogs. And the company." Owen yawned, and so did Brooke.

"You're welcome." She pulled the door open and he turned to leave, but then he spun around and put his arms around her.

He kissed her on the forehead again, then on the cheek, and for a few moments he stared into her eyes. Brooke's heart was pounding.

"I'll talk to you soon." He stepped back, frowning. Then he turned and hurried out the door.

Owen pulled into his driveway but sat in his car for a few minutes as he wondered what was happening between him and Brooke. He'd never felt that comfortable with a woman before, not even his own wife. A certain peace settled over him when he was with her, and he knew why. She didn't expect anything from him. It was okay just to be. With Virginia, there had always been an agenda.

He finally stepped out of the car and trudged up the porch steps to his big, empty house, and again wondered if this whole idea had been a big mistake. What was he going to do with a house this big anyway?

As he put the key in the lock, he thought about Brooke again. He'd wanted so badly to kiss her tonight. Really kiss her, in a way that would resolve this little dance they seemed to be doing together. But at the same time, he'd felt the need to protect himself from her. He was wise enough to know that not all women were like Virginia, but how could you ever know who to trust? He wasn't sure he could take that kind of betrayal again.

He jumped when the cat—Scooter—pounced from the porch swing, hissed, then scrambled down the steps and across the yard. *Crazy animal.* The only person Scooter had taken to was Hunter.

Hunter—that was another thing to figure out. Owen had been a little wounded when he realized the kid had taken forty dollars from him. Owen would have given him the money if he'd just asked. Had he thought Owen wouldn't miss it or didn't know how to count? And what had happened to Hunter's entire paycheck from the previous week?

He'd planned to give Hunter enough time to confess or put the money back, but it had been three days and Hunter hadn't mentioned it. So Owen didn't know what to do. The kid did great work, and just having him around kept the loneliness of his big house at bay. But could Owen afford to have Hunter there every day if he couldn't trust him not to steal?

❧

Early Friday morning Brooke drew an *X* on the calendar in the kitchen, scribbled "15" in the corner, and glanced outside at the rain. Then she took her coffee to the living room to watch the weather coverage. Hurricane Bill was moving into Houston as a category-two hurricane, much of the city was already without power, and extensive flooding was reported. The local forecast was for heavy rain and high winds. At best.

Brooke had already called Juliet and Big Daddy and told them not to go in to work today. She'd asked Juliet if she wanted to come ride out the storm with her, Meghan, and

Spencer. But Juliet had a new love interest she was going to spend the day with. Big Daddy had taken it upon himself to board up the store windows yesterday after she left. Now he was heading out to check on his widowed sister in La Grange. He planned to stay with her until the storm passed.

Brooke slipped off her flip-flops and pulled her legs up under her on the couch. Maybe the worst of the hurricane would miss them. Her mother had already called this morning wanting to know if Brooke and the kids were okay. Brooke had assured her mother they were fine and quickly made up an excuse to get off the phone. Despite everything, she was glad her mother wasn't alone right now.

"Mommy, is the electricity going to go off?" Meghan had just come downstairs. Brooke reached for the remote and turned off the television.

"I don't know, but just think how fun it will be to get out our candles and sit around and play games."

Meghan's eyes started to tear. "I don't want the electricity to go off."

"Quit being such a baby." Spencer threw himself on the couch, grabbed the remote, and turned the TV back on.

Brooke held out her hand. "Give me the remote or watch something else. We'll check on the storm from time to time, but we don't need to keep the Weather Channel on the entire time."

Spencer huffed but started flipping channels. Her son had such an attitude lately, and Brooke wondered how much of it had to do with Owen. She walked to the window and peered out. Even though it was raining, there wasn't even a breeze. The trees were still, as if waiting for something.

As she walked nervously around the house, she pulled out her cell phone, tempted to call Owen. And say what? That she was a huge baby and would he please come over and stay with her and her children while the storm came through?

Why not? They were friends. That should be acceptable. She slid into her bedroom upstairs and called him.

"Ready for the storm?" she asked when he answered.

"Well, I figure this house has been around a hundred years. It must have weathered a few of these. Just hoping the patchwork on the roof holds." He paused, and Brooke thought she heard another voice in the background, but she couldn't tell if his guest was male or female. "What about you? Ready? I saw this morning that it's a category two now. We'll probably have some high winds and thunderstorms out of it."

"At least. But, yeah, I guess we're ready." She sat down on her bed, then lay back, pulling the phone mouthpiece away as she sighed. He had company, so she wasn't going to ask him to come stay with her and the kids. "Hope it doesn't get too bad."

"I think we'll be okay." He paused, and Brooke heard the voice again. She strained to hear if it was a female. "Hey, can I call you back in a little while?" he said. "Would that be okay?"

"Oh, sure." She sat up, wishing she hadn't called. "No big deal. I—I was just—just checking to make sure you were ready." She squeezed her eyes closed, thinking she sounded silly.

"Okay, I'll call you back."

Six hours later Brooke, Meghan, and Spencer were upstairs in her bedroom in the dark, huddled together under the covers as lightning flashed, rain pounded, and wind howled.

And no word from Owen.

Eighteen

Owen had been surprised when Hunter showed up for work at eight o'clock. He'd just assumed the boy would stay at home and ride out the storm with his grandma. Owen had asked him repeatedly if he needed to go be with his grandmother, but Hunter said she'd just be mad if he didn't go to work and that she was fine.

Owen was really glad Hunter was here, though. It took everything they both had to keep the attic from flooding. Less than an hour after the storm hit Smithville, high winds ripped the patches off the roof, and a steady stream of water had been filling the empty planters Hunter had found out in the backyard. The ceramic containers were too heavy to carry up and down the stairs, so every time one filled with water, they poured it out an attic window.

He'd thought about the possibility of a hidden bunker all morning, wondering if the past tenants had hunkered down somewhere during a storm. He doubted they'd been doing this.

"Guess I need to add new roof to the top of my list of things to fix. I should have made that a priority before hurricane season started." Owen lifted one planter while Hunter opened the window. Rain hit them both in the face, but it was the lesser of the two evils. Hunter slammed the window shut as Owen hurried to reposition the container under one hole in the ceiling. "What a mess." He kicked the container. "I don't know why I even bought this house. Stupidest thing I've ever done."

"Why did you buy it?" Hunter lifted the window as Owen picked up the other planter. They both closed their eyes as Owen dumped it and rain pelted them again.

"I guess because I'm a spiteful man." He ran an arm across the sweat on his forehead. It was hot up here—no AC upstairs. Incredibly humid. Two big holes in the roof. It was all just a little too much today.

"By the way . . ." Hunter reached into his pocket and pulled out two soggy twenty-dollar bills. "These are yours. I think I musta picked 'em up by mistake when I was here." He pushed them in Owen's direction, and Owen took them, knowing he should be thankful that Hunter had come clean about it, but irritated with everything in his life at the moment.

"Picked them up by mistake?" He grunted. "I guess that can happen."

"Look, I gave it back, all right?" Hunter was soaking wet like Owen, and as they faced off, Hunter's bottom lip began to tremble.

Owen had hoped that by giving him a job he wouldn't need to steal. "Well, today's payday. You'll have another four hundred dollars to blow."

"I didn't *blow* it!" Hunter gripped his fists at his sides.

Owen nodded for him to open the window so he could dump more water out. When he was done, he took a step toward Hunter, who now had his chest pushed out. "I don't care what you do with it. It's yours to do with as you please."

Hunter shook his head. "You would think, wouldn't ya?"

"What does that mean?"

"Nothing. Never mind."

Owen thought for a few moments. "Did your grandma take *all* the money?" Owen could understand Hunter helping her out with bills and food, but shouldn't the kid be able to keep some of it?

"No." Hunter stepped over to reposition one of the planters. "I gave Grandma some for her pills, food, and stuff. The other half she said was for me, that I'd worked real hard."

"And you did. So I don't care if you did something fun with it. Just don't steal any from me."

"I didn't steal your money! I gave it back!" Hunter's bottom lip was trembling again. "And I didn't do anything with the rest of the money! My dad saw to that!"

Owen put his hands on his hips, looked at the soaked floor, and shook his head. "Your dad stole your money?" He looked up at Hunter, who now had tears in his eyes. Owen couldn't imagine his own father ever doing anything like that. Or blackening his eye.

Hunter blinked back the tears and lifted his chin, breathing hard. "Like father, like son."

Owen realized that it had stopped raining—almost like someone had turned off a faucet. He stared at Hunter long and hard. "You don't have to be like your father, Hunter. That's not something in your genes. You can choose a different life."

Now Hunter seemed to be struggling for air, his mouth opened wide. "I gotta go." He headed for the stairs, but Owen was right behind him.

"Wait. What's wrong?"

Hunter didn't turn around. "I just gotta go." But when he got to the bottom of the attic stairs, he stopped and bent over at the waist. "I can't breathe."

Owen wound around him and squatted down, his own heart racing. "What do you mean you can't breathe? Do you have asthma? What is it? Tell me."

Hunter, still bent over, was fighting for each breath. "Oh man. It's happening, and I think I'm gonna die."

Owen grabbed Hunter's arms and pulled them both to their feet. "Don't move. I'm calling 911."

Hunter grabbed his arm. "No! Don't. Grandma will kill me. That costs money, and . . ." He bent at the waist again. "Just let me go home, and it'll go away."

Owen glanced out the window. It wasn't raining, but the wind was still blowing hard, and he didn't think Wild Bill was done with them yet. "*What* will go away?"

"Oh man." Hunter stood up, gasping for air, and with both hands he grabbed Owen's arms. "I ain't gonna make it, man. I'm gonna pass out."

Owen spoke slowly, unsure what was happening, but he recalled a few times in his life, years ago, when he'd felt something similar. "Hunter, is this a panic attack?"

"That's what Grandma calls 'em, but I don't know. I just know I feel like . . ." He squeezed Owen's arms harder. "Like I'm gonna die."

"Come on. Let's get you to the hospital. Don't worry about the money." Owen put an arm around Hunter, and they walked to the car. Tree branches were down everywhere, and Owen hoped they could get there without incident. He was glad to see his car still intact. Adding a garage was on his growing list of things to do. If this really was a panic attack, Hunter would probably be all right, but Owen wasn't going to take any chances.

They were driving to the Smithville Regional when he remembered that he hadn't called Brooke back. *I hope they're okay.*

When the rain and the lightning let up, Brooke edged out of bed. Meghan had fallen asleep, but Spencer got up and followed her to the window. A lawn chair she'd forgotten to put away had blown out in the middle of the yard amid a lot of small tree branches, but she didn't see any real damage.

"Is it over?" Spencer pressed his nose against the glass pane.

"I don't know."

"When will we have power?"

Brooke walked away from the window. "Don't know that either. But I need to figure out something for dinner."

Spencer followed her downstairs. Brooke fought the irritation she felt, angry at herself for caring as much as she did that Owen hadn't called. She didn't need this kind of aggravation, these hurt feelings.

She opened the door to the pantry, tapping her fingers against the wood as she peered inside. Not many options without a stove or microwave. She glanced at Spencer, who was sitting at the kitchen table eating a banana. "Peanut butter and jelly or ham and cheese sandwiches?"

"Neither," he said through a mouthful.

Brooke wondered how long they'd be without power. She didn't want to lose the food in her refrigerator, and it was getting hot in the house. She also hoped that everything at the hardware store was all right, but she wasn't sure the storm was over, so she didn't want to drag the kids out to go see.

"Well, I can't cook without a stove." She opened the refrigerator and quickly scanned the contents before closing the door. She could remember her father telling her to keep the refrigerator closed when the power went off so everything would stay cold. She wondered how her parents were doing.

Sighing, she sat down at the dining room table. After a few moments, she decided to take advantage of some alone time with Spencer.

"Spencer, is something bothering you?" She propped her elbows up on the table and cupped her chin. "Is it Owen? Or something else?"

Spencer shrugged.

"I thought you liked Owen, and you know I'm not dating him, and—"

"Then why does he come over all the time? And you talk on the phone a lot now. He gave you flowers, Mom. That's more than friends." Spencer reached into the fruit bowl and started turning an orange over and over.

Brooke tried not to smile. Something about her son's statement brought on a tinge of joy, but she tried to stay focused. "I don't think so, Spence." She paused, thinking. "But even if that were true, no one will ever replace your father."

"I know."

Maybe Spencer just needed time to process what was happening. *What* is *happening?* Brooke sat taller and took a deep breath. *Nothing, apparently.* Owen hadn't even called her back. And her cell phone was working, so she assumed his was as well. She decided there wasn't any reason to have this conversation with Spencer, so she stood up and started gathering sandwich fixings.

I wonder who was at Owen's house when I called. She shook her head, wishing she could stop thinking about him.

Then a disturbing image blazed through her mind. Surely Tallie Goodry hadn't gone over there today. She might not be Owen's type, but she was beautiful. And pushy.

⚜

Owen slowed his car down, then stopped in front of Hunter's house.

"Go make sure your grandma is okay before I leave." He put the car in park, glad that the wind and rain had stopped. He still had a big mess upstairs at his house.

Hunter opened the passenger door, but before he stepped out, he turned back to Owen. "You really think these pills will help?"

"The doctor said so." Owen had worried that maybe they wouldn't prescribe anything without one of Hunter's parents or his grandma being present, but they had—maybe because the ER was crowded or they assumed that Owen was his guardian. Or maybe it was because no insurance was involved and Owen was paying cash. "And, Hunter, I've had panic attacks before. I know they can make you feel awful, but I'm glad you got checked to rule out something else. Try the medicine and see if it helps."

"You said it's not like drugs, though, right? Grandma takes some stuff that makes her all loopy. I don't wanna feel like that or get hooked on nothing."

Owen appreciated Hunter's attitude. "No, you take those pills every day, and they won't make you loopy. You heard the doctor. Some people have a chemical imbalance, and the medicine helps."

Hunter sighed. "I sure hope so." He stepped out of the car but didn't shut the door. "I don't know when I'll ever be able to pay you back all that money for the hospital."

Owen smiled. "I'm not worried about it. Now go check on your grandma."

Hunter didn't move. "And about the forty dollars . . . I'm real sorry."

"I know." Owen was ready to go. He wanted to stop by

Brooke's and make sure she and the kids were okay. He felt bad that he hadn't called to check on them, but between the water pouring in his house and worrying about Hunter, he just hadn't gotten around to it. And then, when he did think of it, he had trouble getting through. Maybe a cell-phone tower was damaged.

He nodded at Hunter. "Go check on her."

Hunter finally closed the car door and made his way to the front door. Less than a minute later he stuck his head out the door and waved for Owen to go. As Owen started toward Brooke's house, he got a whiff of himself. He was still wet and sweaty. But before he could decide whether he should go clean up first, he was at her house.

"I can't come in. I'm filthy," he said when she opened the door. He could see the darkness behind her. "No power? That's odd. I have electricity. Phone keeps going in and out, though." He held up the cell phone in his hand.

She was wearing that pink T-shirt Owen liked so much, and when she brushed her hair over her shoulders, Owen had the strangest sensation flood over him.

"We haven't had power since the storm hit. I called the electric co-op. They're working to get it fixed, but we haven't had any power since late this morning." She stepped back. "You can come in."

He glanced down. "I don't know. I had all kinds of problems at my house, and I'm a mess."

She motioned with her hand to come in. "We're eating peanut butter and jelly sandwiches by candlelight in the kitchen. Want one?"

Owen realized that he and Hunter hadn't eaten all day. Once the water had started pouring in, they'd kept busy doing damage control. "That'd be great."

Meghan and Spencer were sitting at the table when Owen walked into the kitchen with Brooke. "Hey, you two."

"You never did call us." Spencer put his sandwich down and eyed Owen.

Brooke stepped toward her son. "Spencer, hush. I'm sure Mr. Saunders was busy. He said he had some problems with his house." She paused, frowning. "What happened?"

Meghan spoke up before Owen could answer. "We were so scared! We were all huddled together in Mommy's bed, and the thunder was so loud I put my hands over my ears and cried."

Owen swallowed hard, then squatted down by Meghan at the table. "I'm really sorry, Meghan." Then he looked up at Brooke. "Sorry."

"I wasn't all that scared." Spencer picked up his sandwich and took a bite. "But Mom and Meghan were crying."

Owen stood up and looked at Brooke. Her face was red as she stared at the floor and shook her head. "Thanks for that, Spence."

Spencer stood up from the table. "Well, it's true. I'm done. Can I go play video games?"

Brooke smiled. "Not without any power."

Spencer let out a heavy sigh. "Come on, Meghan. Finish up, and let's go play a game or something."

Brooke cleared their plates from the table. "I already ate with the kids, but everything is on the table, so sit down and help yourself." She dumped the paper plates and turned to face him. "So what did happen with your house?"

Owen walked toward her, uncomfortably aware that he probably smelled as dirty as he felt. "I'm sorry. Were you really that scared?"

She bit her lip. "I am not a very good role model for my children when it comes to storms."

"Oh, Brooke." Owen rubbed his chin for a moment. He wanted to hug her, but he didn't dare. "I wish I would have been— Oh, excuse me." His cell phone was ringing. He picked it up and pressed Talk, listened a second, then let out an exasperated sigh. "Cut off again."

"That's funny. Mine's been working fine. Anyway, tell me about the house." Sitting down at the table, she moved the peanut butter, jelly, and bread closer to her. "Sit down, tell me, and I'll make you a sandwich."

Owen couldn't remember the last time he'd had a peanut butter and jelly sandwich. Virginia had hated peanut butter— anything with peanuts—so there had never been any in the house. He watched Brooke swiping just the right amount of peanut butter and jelly on two slices of bread.

"Well, I knew I had some bad spots on the roof and that I needed to replace some shingles. When I first looked at the house, the realtor said there was recent hail damage."

"Yeah, I think I remember that storm. Huge hailstones. Hope they gave you some allowance for the price."

He nodded. "But the thing is, I haven't gotten around to replacing it. Everything's been okay with the few showers we've had, but this storm had me worried, so I tried to temporarily patch it with some new shingles."

He thanked her for the sandwich when she pushed it in front of him. "Anyway, the patches didn't hold, and I had water pouring into the attic—lots of water. So now the second-floor ceiling is pretty messed up too." He took a bite of the best peanut butter and jelly sandwich in the world. "This is the most awesome sandwich I've ever had."

Brooke burst out laughing, then covered her mouth. "Sorry. I'm not laughing about the roof. I've just never seen anyone get so excited about a PBJ before."

Owen took another big bite, savoring the flavor, and made a mental note to stock his pantry with plenty of peanut butter. He finished the sandwich and dabbed his mouth with a napkin Brooke had laid out.

"Want another one?" She grinned from where she was sitting next to him.

"Yes, please."

Brooke set to work, and Owen went on with his story. "Anyway, luckily I had hired this kid last week to work with me on the house, and he was there helping me. One of us had to open the window while the other one dumped containers of water. We did that for a long time." He shook his head. "I don't know what I would have done if Hunter hadn't been there."

Brooke froze with a spoon in the jelly jar. "Hunter?"

"Yeah, local kid who needed work." Owen waited for her to finish his sandwich, but she actually pulled the spoon out and put it down.

"Please tell me you don't have Hunter Lewis helping you with your house."

"I know he's known as a troublemaker around here, but I think he's a good kid. He just needs a break, and—"

"A good kid?" She chuckled, but not in the amused sort of way. "I can assure you Hunter Lewis is *not* a good kid."

Owen stared at the unfinished sandwich, then looked back at her, hoping she'd get the hint and go back to the task at hand. "His parents are trouble, and I don't think his grandma has much of a handle on things either. But he's a great worker. Everyone needs a little help now and then." Owen shrugged. *Please make my sandwich.*

Brooke stood up from the table and starting pacing. Owen decided he wasn't going to get that second sandwich. Then she put her hands on her hips and pressed her lips together for a few seconds.

"Well, I'll tell you what. I could have used a *little help* when Hunter Lewis put a gun in my face a couple of years ago." She blinked her eyes a few times, her face red, and Owen lost all interest in food.

Then his cell phone rang again. And hers rang too.

Brooke waved good-bye to Owen as she punched her mother's autodial number. She shook her head as the phone rang, telling herself to stay calm.

"Mom." Brooke paced the kitchen, a hand on her forehead. "Mrs. Doyle at the Oaks called."

Silence for a few moments. "I figured she would."

"She said you are moving out." Brooke circled the kitchen table, popping each chair with her hand as she went around. "Actually, you are being kicked out. A grown woman. And you are being kicked out because you have a man living in your apartment."

"That man is my husband. And he doesn't exactly live here. He's just . . . here. Most of the time, anyway."

Brooke stopped, pulled out a chair, and sat down at the table. "Well, you are only paying for single occupancy. That's why they are tossing you out."

"I know, dear. We tried to upgrade to a double-occupancy apartment, but they don't have any, and the waiting list is a mile long. So I'm moving in with your father at his place right outside of town."

Brooke didn't think she'd ever had high blood pressure—

until now. Her head was splitting, her heart pumping. She was still upset about her mother not letting her father return home all those years ago and never telling her, but at least that made some sense to her. What didn't make sense was Mom letting him back in their lives now. "Mom, just come home. Come back here with me and the kids."

"My home is where your father is."

"You haven't even seen the kids. They miss you. How can you do this to them?"

"I will come and see them soon, I promise. If you would just talk to your father—"

"Quit calling him my father!" Brooke squeezed her eyes shut as she waited for her mother's response.

"If you're going to yell at me, I'm going to hang up."

Brooke beat her to it.

❧

Patsy stared at the phone for a short while, then frowned. "Well, that went well." She pushed her glasses up on her nose and sat down on the couch by her husband. "It's a bad time for this to happen—right after the storm. Brooke has a hard time with storms."

"I remember." Harold held her hand and sighed. "I can't have this, Patsy. I can't live with this tension between you and Brooke. And you hardly see the grandkids. I think this is a mistake."

Patsy swallowed back tears in her throat. "Don't you say that, Harold Miller. I plan to spend every minute I can with you. There will be plenty of time for me to be with Brooke and the children, but this time is ours. Do you hear me?"

"You truly are the only woman I've ever loved. And I

ruined our lives." He paused, blinking a few times. "And yet here you are."

"I wouldn't be anywhere else." She wrapped her arms around his neck and kissed him.

Harold eased her away. "Under different circumstances, I think we would have remained estranged."

"I should have forgiven you twenty years ago. Then we would still be a family." She looked up at him. "I've always loved you. And, despite everything, I've always known that you love me. I have to accept my role in all of this too." She patted him on the leg. "Now, I'm going to finish packing. You rest."

Patsy walked into the bedroom and closed the door behind her. Covering her face with her hands, she let the tears spill. She missed Brooke, Meghan, and Spencer so much she could hardly stand it. But she didn't have much time left with Harold.

Nineteen

rooke was surprised when Owen showed up at the store Saturday afternoon. She had reacted rather harshly about his hiring Hunter, and she knew she should have told him the entire story, but he'd gotten a phone call from his uncle and said he needed to leave before she'd had a chance to explain fully.

"Hey." He strolled up to the counter in his work overalls and white T-shirt. "I need to hire a roofer. That's one job I can't do myself."

Brooke pulled a card from a stack on the counter. "This guy did my house. He's good—and reasonable."

Owen studied the card for a moment, then flipped it between his fingers a few times. "Sorry I had to leave so abruptly yesterday."

"Everything okay?" She sat down on the stool behind the counter and pushed back the rim of her baseball cap.

"Yeah." He stuffed his hands into his pockets. "My uncle is coming to stay with me. He'll be here later this week. He was trying to tell me his travel plans, but my cell service was going in and out."

Brooke sat up a little straighter. "How long is he staying?"

"I'm not sure. He's a bit eccentric." Owen chuckled. "He's my father's brother. He travels the world, and then he'll stop for a while to rest and work on his memoirs. Sometimes he stays with my parents in Florida, and sometimes he stays with friends. But this is a first—staying with me." Owen smirked. "Truthfully, I don't think he cared for Virginia too much— imagine that! Anyway, I've got plenty of room, so when I heard he was coming this way, I invited him." He pulled his hands from his pockets and scratched his forehead. "Maybe he'll help with the house." He paused. "Although I had planned for this project to keep me busy for a long time. If we finish, then what will I do?"

"Listen." She pulled her eyes from his and stacked some papers on the counter as she spoke. "I need to finish telling you about Hunter."

Owen sighed. "I probably heard enough."

"It wasn't a real gun, just a water pistol with a bag over it." Brooke searched his face, and when Owen's eyes met hers, she saw relief in his expression.

"A water gun?" He shook his head. "I guess that's good. Better than the real thing."

"Well, I'm sure you understand that I don't want my children around Hunter."

Owen was quiet for a while. "Everyone deserves another chance. At the heart of Hunter, I see something good. I just want him to have a fair shake."

"I agree that everyone deserves another chance, but that vision of Hunter wearing a ski mask and pointing what I believed to be a real gun in my face—that doesn't just go away. He scares me, Owen."

"I can understand that." He didn't say any more, just looked at her.

Brooke waited, wishing he'd never hired Hunter. She'd done her best the past couple of years to stay away from him. She knew his situation at home, and she and Travis had tried to help him, to include him in family outings. But Hunter had turned on them just the same. "Just don't be surprised if your attempt at giving him a second chance backfires. He's . . ."

She let her voice trail off as she realized Owen was staring at her. His gaze roamed boldly downward, then back up again, until his eyes were locked with hers. He took a step closer. "I've decided I *really* believe in second chances."

Brooke swallowed, suddenly self-conscious, and acutely aware of Owen's seductive tone. *What's happening?*

Owen leaned over, cupped her cheeks, and pressed his lips against hers, gently covering her mouth. It was so random, so unexpected. At first, she tried to pull away, but his lips were persuasive, and his touch sent the pit of her stomach into such a wild swirl that she let out a small moan. When he pulled away, she felt like the breath had been knocked out of her.

"Now"—he smiled—"I have to go call the roofer." He gave her a playful salute. "Have a great day, Brooke Holloway."

"You too," she managed to mumble as he turned to leave. Once he was out of sight, she put a finger to her lips. *Am I falling for my new friend?*

And even more surprising . . . *Is he falling for me?*

❧

Owen had wanted that kiss as much as he'd wanted anything. His favorite place to be these days was around Brooke, but his bold move had gone against everything they'd discussed. He'd only known her a month, and already he felt like his heart was climbing up a ladder and onto a chopping block. She was the kind of woman he could fall in love with. *But could I ever trust another woman?*

He'd done exactly what he said he wouldn't do—led her on. Or had he? Maybe she didn't have any feelings for him at all, so it really couldn't be called leading her on. His thoughts and feelings were jumbled, and he began to question if he really did believe in second chances—for himself.

He spent the rest of the weekend working on the house, and on Monday he scheduled a new roof to be put on the following week. He didn't hear from Brooke, and he didn't call her.

But she was on his mind constantly.

Tuesday morning Owen and Hunter were ripping out kitchen cabinets when he decided to ask the boy about Brooke.

"So, what happened at Miller's Hardware a couple of years ago?" Owen dragged one of the disassembled cabinets across the kitchen floor and piled it with two others.

Hunter was using an electric screwdriver to pull screws from one of the cabinets. He paused for a moment, then went back to work and didn't look up. "She your girlfriend?"

"Just a friend." Owen grabbed a rag from his pocket and wiped his face. "She said you held her up at gunpoint."

Hunter stood up, the screwdriver hanging by his side. "I did not!"

Owen cocked his head to one side. "Really? So she lied?"

Hunter yanked the cabinet he'd been working on free from the wall and pushed it across the floor. "It ain't like you think."

Owen waited, but Hunter didn't offer anything else. "Then how is it?" he finally asked.

Hunter pushed back his red hair and stood up. "It was a water gun with a paper bag over it. I woulda never hurt Mrs. Holloway, no matter what. She and her husband was always nice to me."

Hunter went back to work on the cabinets. Owen just stood there, dumbfounded. "So you chose to rob people who had always been nice to you?"

"I done told you. I'm trash." Hunter pulled out the screw he'd just loosened and tossed it onto the floor.

"I'm just trying to understand." Owen suspected he already knew the motivations behind the crime.

Hunter whirled out another screw. "I needed money, okay? And I seen her load that register with cash before." He pointed the hammer at Owen. "But I woulda never hurt her. Not ever."

Owen grunted. "Hunter, I can imagine who you were probably getting the money for, but can you understand the fear you put her through?"

"I think about it every day."

Owen decided to let the subject drop. Hunter had probably punished himself enough.

"I've got a little bit of furniture being delivered later today. My Uncle Denny is coming to stay with me for a while." Owen opened the door that led to the backyard and dragged some of the cabinet debris out back. When he returned, Hunter was prying the last cabinet from the wall.

"He gonna be helping you now on the house, instead of me?" Hunter wiped his hands on his overalls before giving the cabinet a final tug.

"I'm hoping he'll help. We can use it, don't you think?" Owen paused, but Hunter didn't say anything. "Hunter, you do a good job. I'm not firing you. And your raise will be on your paycheck Friday, just like we talked about."

The kid's face lit up. "Thanks, Owen."

By the end of the day, they'd completely cleared the kitchen of the old cabinets, and Milton's Furniture had delivered some bedroom furniture for upstairs. The large room at the end of the hallway would be Uncle Denny's, so Owen had bought a bed, dresser, two bedside tables, and an armoire. While he was at it, he'd ordered himself a dresser and two tables, a couch for the living room, and a coffee table. It wasn't much, considering the size of the house, but it would make the place a little more livable.

He'd thought about Brooke while he was picking it out, wishing she was there to help him. But every time he considered the possibility of a relationship with her, he thought about Virginia.

❧

Wednesday morning Hunter stood before Judge Landreth. He'd worn his best blue jeans and a new blue short-sleeved shirt, and he'd bought himself some new tennis shoes. Grandma had needed extra money for her medicines and to have someone fix the air conditioner—and he'd found two new bottles of vodka—but it was the first time in Hunter's life he could remember having some money in his pocket. He'd gotten a haircut too.

It was also the first time anyone had ever appeared with him in court.

"With all due respect, Your Honor"—Owen held up a pile of papers as he stood beside Hunter in front of the judge—"there isn't any evidence that Hunter is the one who broke into that store. Just because he was running near the scene doesn't make him guilty. You've already got one witness who said it wasn't Hunter she saw. So how can you press charges against him?"

Hunter had never had anyone go to bat for him. And lots of times, he had to admit, he hadn't deserved help. But Owen had believed him when he said he just ran when he saw the broken glass and heard the sirens. Owen had said, "I don't just believe you. I believe *in* you." Hunter had never wanted to be a better person more in his life than he did now. For Owen Saunders.

"Mr. Lewis has a history in Smithville, Mr. Saunders, and I know you are new to the area, but we have reason to believe that Mr. Lewis is involved in this crime as well."

Judge Landreth was an old man with gray hair and lots of wrinkles. He took off his glasses. "I believe you are the one who captured him and brought him in."

Owen took a step forward. "Well, I turned him over to the police. But I've read the case file, and I am prepared to hire an attorney for Hunter to fight this. There's no evidence to support this case."

Hunter couldn't believe it. Again, he wondered why he couldn't have had a father like Owen.

About ten minutes later, he and Owen left the courtroom, and all charges had been dropped.

"I ain't never seen nothing like that." Hunter couldn't stop the grin from spreading across his face.

"Well, the whole thing was bogus. They were just taking advantage of you because you didn't have legal representation." Owen kept walking past his car, and Hunter followed.

"Where we going?"

"I need to make a stop up here in town, and it's close enough to walk."

Hunter felt on top of the world. Until Owen slowed down at Miller's Hardware.

"I can't go in there." He stopped outside the glass windows and saw Mrs. Holloway sitting at the counter with her son.

Owen kept going, reached for the door, then turned around before he pulled it open. "Yes, you can. Come on."

Hunter started to feel like someone was choking him. That medicine he'd gotten helped him most of the time, but he wasn't sure anything was going to help him with this. He could still remember the scared look on Mrs. Holloway's face. And the way his father had punched him in the gut and told him to do it, to rob the place and bring back some money. He'd woken up lots of nights in a cold sweat thinking about what he'd put Mrs. Holloway through. No way he could face her. He'd avoided her all over town for almost two years.

"I can't." He shook his head. "I'll wait out here."

Owen let go of the door handle and walked back to Hunter. "You're turning your life around, and facing Brooke is part of the process. Have you ever told her you're sorry?"

Hunter could feel his bottom lip trembling the way it did when he was a nervous sissy baby. "No, and I ain't going to now. She'll throw me out if I get two feet inside that door. Or worse yet, Big Daddy will." He swallowed hard. "I ain't going in there."

Owen paced on the sidewalk, rubbing his chin, then stopped in front of Hunter. "You've got to let people see the real person you are. The guy I see has parents who probably aren't the best, but is really trying to be a good member of society. This is a big step, I know, but it's important."

Hunter didn't know what to do. Owen had been so good to him, and he didn't want to let him down, but he was afraid he might pass smooth out if he had to face Mrs. Holloway. He hesitated, then slowly nodded. His heart raced as he walked in behind Owen, and he jumped when the bell on the door rang behind them. He kept his head down. Mrs. Holloway hated him, and he wasn't sure why Owen was making him do this.

"Good morning." Owen walked up to the counter, and Hunter had no choice but to do the same.

"Good morning." Mrs. Holloway sounded just like he remembered. He finally looked up at her just as she was putting an arm around her son and pulling him close. Hunter looked down again.

"Did my cabinets come in?" Owen stuck his hands into the pockets of his black slacks. He'd dressed real nice for court today. He even had on a white shirt and a tie.

"They did. Big Daddy can deliver them later this morning if that's okay." Mrs. Holloway didn't seem to want to look at Hunter any more than he wanted to look at her.

"Hey, Spencer." Owen leaned to his left a little until Mrs. Holloway's son looked up at him. "Whatcha got there?"

Spencer sighed. "It's a plane that used to be my dad's. But it doesn't fly."

"What's wrong with it?" Hunter was surprised at the sound of his own voice, but when Mrs. Holloway pulled her son even closer, Hunter wished he'd stayed quiet. All this wasn't making him feel better like Owen had said. Only worse.

Spencer jerked away from his mother. "Quit, Mom." He offered the plane to Hunter. "I don't know. It's missing some parts."

"It looks old." Hunter studied the wingspan, about two feet, then finally found a date stamped inside. "It says 1963."

"Think it'll fly?" Spencer stood up from the stool he was sitting on, even though his mother frowned.

Hunter shrugged as he handed the plane back to Spencer. "Don't know. Maybe." He was pretty sure that given some time, he could get it to fly. Wasn't nothing Hunter hadn't been able to fix before.

"Hey, Spencer." Owen leaned closer to Spencer. "Why don't you go check with Big Daddy about my cabinets. I need to talk to your mom for a minute." He looked up at Mrs.

Holloway. She nodded right away and almost pushed her son toward the back.

Hunter wasn't sure he'd ever felt more ashamed, and he figured the worst part was coming. He looked at Owen, who just nodded. Hunter forced himself to look at Mrs. Holloway.

"Mrs. Holloway, I'm real sorry for what I did to you. You and Mr. Holloway were always real good to me, and . . ." His lip started to tremble, and it took everything he had not to cry. *Why am I such a sissy baby?* "Anyway, I'm just real sorry." He took a deep breath. "Especially 'cause I scared you. I'm real sorry."

It was hard, but he kept his eyes on hers. Wouldn't it be something if she could forgive him? He'd never gotten away with the money. Big Daddy had seen to that. And the Holloways hadn't pressed charges. *But still.*

She raised her chin a little bit. She didn't smile or anything. "Thank you, Hunter. I appreciate that."

Owen reached in his pocket and pulled out his keys. "Hunter, why don't you go get the car and bring it up to the curb here?"

Hunter's eyes rounded. "Really?"

Owen smiled and nodded. Hunter figured he wanted to be alone with Mrs. Holloway, but he didn't care. He was gonna get to drive Owen's fancy car again. Even if it was just down the street.

⚘

Brooke could hardly take her eyes off Owen, all dressed up in his slacks, crisp white shirt, and tie. It took everything she had not to tell him how amazing he looked.

"How are you?" Owen's forehead wrinkled as he spoke, concern etched in his voice.

"I'm fine. You?"

"I'm okay." He paused. "Listen, I know that was hard for you, but thanks for letting Hunter apologize. I really don't think he's a bad person. Just had a bad upbringing." He grinned. "Can't believe he tried to hold you up with a water gun."

Brooke tipped back the rim of her baseball cap. "Yes, but it was just as scary. And not funny."

"I know. Sorry. I didn't mean to make light of it." Owen sighed. "I'd just like to see Hunter turn his life around."

Brooke was quiet for a few moments. "You're a good guy, Owen Saunders."

He chuckled. "I don't know about that. But I'd like to at least see Hunter have a fair shake. I don't think he would have if I hadn't gone to court with him this morning." He paused. "And all charges were dropped."

Brooke couldn't stop staring at his mouth, and her mind was whirling with random ideas about ways she could spend time with him. But she hadn't even heard from him since he kissed her on Saturday, and she wasn't sure what to make of that.

Owen put his palms on the counter and leaned closer to Brooke. "I want to kiss you so badly I can't stand it. Just like I did last time I was here." He smiled. "What does that mean, Brooke Holloway?"

She bit her bottom lip as the pit of her stomach started to tingle. "What does it mean?" *Kiss me now.*

Owen slowly brought his face to hers, and his gaze was as soft as if he were touching her with his eyes. His spicy, intoxicating cologne hung in the space around him as his lips met hers. Brooke savored every second. He eased away, leaned in to kiss her once more, then stood tall again.

"Would you and the kids like to have dinner with me tomorrow night?"

Brooke stared into Owen's amazing blue eyes and realized that any baggage Owen Saunders might have from his first marriage didn't matter. She had given her heart to only one man.

Until now.

Twenty

Thursday night at Mexico Lindo Brooke felt warmth flow through her as she watched Owen joking around and playing with her children—even though twice she'd had to tell them *all* to settle down. Something was happening between her and Owen despite their vow to remain only friends. Even Spencer was having a good time. But Brooke knew her son, and she could tell that he still had his guard up, often glancing back and forth between Brooke and Owen with questioning eyes.

"There is something I've been meaning to ask you since I first moved here." Owen wiped his mouth with his napkin. "Why is that huge gingerbread man on display by the Chamber of Commerce office?"

"That's Smitty!" Meghan licked vanilla ice cream from her lips.

Brooke picked up Meghan's napkin and wiped ice cream from her daughter's face as she spoke. "Back in 2006, the town decided to do something special for our annual Festival of Lights celebration, so we baked this gigantic gingerbread man. We even got into the 2009 *Guinness Book of World Records* for it. Then the cookie sheet used to bake it was converted into a monument to commemorate the record." She put the napkin down and took a sip of her coffee. "An IKEA store in Norway broke our world record, but we're pretty sure we still hold the American record."

"Good grief." Owen laughed. "Bet that took some serious flour."

"He weighed more than thirteen hundred pounds and measured twenty feet from head to toe. We used seven hundred and fifty pounds of flour, forty-nine gallons of molasses, and seventy-two dozen eggs." She pointed a finger at him. "Separated eggs!"

Owen chuckled again. "That's pretty cool. I would have liked to have seen that."

"There's a video. I'll show it to you sometime." Brooke took a sip of her coffee. "So, your uncle will be here tomorrow, right?"

"Yeah. I had bedroom furniture delivered for the upstairs bedroom that needs the fewest repairs. And I bought a couch. But the place is still a wreck, especially since Hunter and I just ripped out all the cabinets." He paused, taking a sip of coffee. "Thanks for having Big Daddy deliver the new ones."

"You're welcome. We do that for all our customers." Brooke grinned, wishing this night could go on forever. She wondered if she would see a lot less of Owen now that his uncle would be living with him.

Owen threatened to steal a bite of Meghan's ice cream, and they were all laughing and cutting up again when Brooke stopped breathing.

"Oh no." She brought a hand to her chest. Before she could tell Owen what was happening, both Meghan and Spencer jumped up and hurried to the entrance of the restaurant.

Owen twisted in his chair to watch the children. "What is it? Do you know those people?"

"It's my mother." She took a deep breath as she watched

211

Mom hugging Meghan and Spencer. "And my father." She pulled her eyes away. "Oh, Owen. They're coming over here. What am I going to do?"

Owen stood up when Brooke's parents came to the table. He extended his hand to Brooke's mother. "Hello. I'm Owen Saunders."

Mom's eyes lit up as she smiled. "Nice to meet you, Owen. I'm Patsy Miller. And this is Brooke's father, Harold."

Brooke cringed as her father and Owen shook hands.

"You're my grandpa?" Meghan's eyes grew huge.

Brooke almost felt sorry for her father as he nodded, his face beet-red. But she couldn't bring herself to acknowledge him. Her mother's eyes begged her to say something, but she couldn't do it. She just looked down at her coffee.

"Well then, I guess our table's ready," Mom finally said, throwing Brooke a pointed glance. "Owen, it's wonderful to meet you. And I'll see you children soon, I promise. I miss you." Then she and Brooke's dad made their way to a table across the room.

Brooke forced a smile. "Everyone ready to go?" Owen found her hand and squeezed, and the sweet gesture brought tears to her eyes. Things were so messed up. And was there really a happily ever after? She glanced at her parents and their bizarre situation, then she looked up at Owen, this handsome, caring man who'd recently said he was still in love with his wife and would never trust another woman. She gazed at him as he asked for the bill.

Owen quickly threw down cash, then ushered them all to the car. When they got to Brooke's house, he asked, "Do you want me to come in?"

"Yes, yes!" Meghan shouted from the backseat. "Come in, Mr. Saunders."

Brooke waited for Spencer to say something, but he didn't.

Owen leaned over and into the backseat. "I think it's time for you guys to call me Owen." He glanced at Brooke. "If that's okay with your mom."

"How about Mr. Owen?" Brooke suggested. She chewed on her lip, wanting him to come in, but wondering if the kids were going to have a lot of questions about their grandparents. Plus, she had a knot in her throat as if she might cry at any moment. There was something very vulnerable about her father that she hadn't expected. Dark circles lined his eyes, and he was more bent over than she remembered. Despite the anger and hurt, she wondered if maybe she should talk to him.

It was still daylight, and Meghan and Spencer exited the car and ran to the porch. "It's fine with me if you want to come in for a while."

Owen wasted no time turning off the car. "Great. I don't relish the idea of going home to that big empty house."

Once in the house, they went through the same familiar drill as always. Meghan and Spencer argued about going to bed but finally succumbed. Meghan kissed Owen good night again, and this time Owen responded with a warm hug before she ran upstairs. Brooke fielded a few questions about her dad during tuck-in time but was able to get away with a promise to talk more later. Finally she made it downstairs, feeling she had dodged a bullet. For now. But she still had no earthly idea how she would handle the fact that Meghan and Spencer now knew their grandfather was in town.

She sank down on the couch in relief and unbuckled her sandals, tossing them to the side. "Feel free to do the same," she said, nodding to Owen's loafers.

"I love this couch." He kicked off his shoes and frowned. "I don't like the couch I bought. It's too . . . stiff or something."

He leaned back and put an arm around her. "This is possibly the most comfortable couch on the planet."

Brooke laughed. "I bought it on sale at Milton's probably ten years ago. It's just worn in."

"Good to hear you laugh. I could see how upset you were earlier." Owen stroked her shoulder—just as if they were a couple.

"That was the last thing I was expecting, for them to walk in. Though I guess I should have—" Then she couldn't stand it anymore. She twisted to face him. "Owen, what are we doing?"

He smiled. "I knew this was coming."

"This cuddling, the—the kisses." She paused. "I thought we both agreed to be friends, but . . ."

He touched her cheek. "I have no idea what we're doing. But I do know I'm happiest these days when I'm with you. And when I'm not, I—I miss you. So I'm choosing to be with you." He kissed her lightly on the mouth, and Brooke gave in. She ignored the urge to overanalyze and allowed herself this chance to just feel happy in the moment.

He brushed his lips against the top of her nose, cupped her face in his hands, and pressed his mouth to hers again, transporting Brooke to a place she'd forgotten existed. Owen pulled her closer, and Brooke felt like a teenager making out on her parents' couch. But this was her couch, and she had two impressionable children upstairs. She pulled back.

"Sorry." He settled back onto the couch and reached for her hand. "I think I could keep kissing you forever." He kissed her palm. "I hear what you're saying. We should probably talk about whatever is going on." He took a deep breath. "But we've both been duly warned. You're not ready for a relationship. I have trust issues." He flashed a quick grin, then sobered. "But maybe we can just go with it, tread carefully, and see what happens. I love being here."

Brooke nodded. She loved having him here. But she couldn't help but wonder if they each just filled a void for each other, if that's all it was between them. And did Owen just like being in her home because his was big and lonely? But she did take note that while he mentioned the trust issues, he didn't say anything about still being in love with his ex-wife.

"I think that sounds good." Brooke smiled, and Owen put his arm around her again. She laid her head on his shoulder. *Could this be my second shot at happiness?*

⚜

Friday morning Owen and Hunter were installing the new cabinets in the kitchen when there was a knock at the door.

"That would be my uncle." Owen shoved the cabinet a few inches to the left, then wiped his hands on his overalls. He walked down the hallway, through the living room, and to the entryway. He was eager to see Uncle Denny. But when he swung the door wide, Tallie Goodry stood in front of him with a basket in her hands.

"Tallie." Owen raised an eyebrow. "Hi."

"These are for you." She pushed the basket toward him, smiling. Her streaked platinum hair was pulled up into a twist, and her low-cut white blouse and denim capris showed off a tanned, toned body. In her white spike-heel sandals, she was almost as tall as Owen. "I heard that you hired Hunter Lewis to work for you, and I think that's so nice of you. I wanted to bring you boys a little snack."

Owen accepted the gift. "Thanks. Hunter's a good worker." He lifted a red-checkered napkin and inspected the contents.

Tallie took a step closer to him, close enough that he breathed in her musky perfume. It reminded him of Virginia. A lot of things about Tallie reminded him of Virginia, which made him wonder again whatever attracted him to his ex-wife in the first place. Had she changed over the years—or had he?

Tallie pointed to the basket. "Homemade kolaches, muffins, and chocolate-chip cookies."

That was one thing that Virginia didn't do. Bake. Owen eyed the offering. "Thanks again. I know we'll enjoy this." He smiled, hoping he wouldn't have to invite her in. "I'll go share these with Hunter."

"Oh, one more thing." She held up a finger. "A week from tomorrow I'm having a little get-together for some friends at my home. Very casual, just friends from around Smithville. I'd love for you to come. It would be a great chance to meet everyone."

Everyone? Did that mean Brooke too? Probably. She and Tallie were friends, weren't they?

Owen thought for a moment. "I better decline, Tallie. My uncle is due here any minute, and he'll be staying with me for a while."

She waved a hand at him. "Bring your uncle, of course! He can meet everyone too. Cocktails and appetizers at seven, then dinner around eight. Can I count on you both?" She batted long lashes, and Owen hesitated. He wasn't big on parties, especially with Tallie types. But Brooke would be there, so it might be fun.

"Sure. We'll be there. A week from tomorrow." Owen slid one foot backward. "Thank you again, Tallie. And we'll see you next weekend."

She flashed a blinding set of teeth at him and turned to leave, waving back over her shoulder.

Owen plucked a cream-cheese-filled kolache from the

basket and took a big bite. *Excellent.* "Hunter, look what I've got," he said as he made his way back to the kitchen. He set the basket on the only kitchen counter they had installed so far. "Kolaches, muffins, and cookies."

Hunter peeked inside and chose a blueberry muffin. "Cool. Who brought this?"

"Tallie Goodry." Owen reached for a cookie. "She said they're all homemade."

"They're homemade, all right—homemade by Weikel's Bakery in La Grange. I'd know these muffins and kolaches anywhere." Hunter frowned. "Tallie Goodry is a—" He stopped, pressed his lips together, then sighed. "She don't like me at all, and I never did nothing to her."

"Well, she seemed glad you were working here. She didn't say anything bad." Owen scooped out another cookie. "So she didn't make all this? She sort of implied that she did."

"No, this is Weikel's stuff. And they make the best." Hunter picked up a kolache. "You better watch that Tallie. I reckon she's on the prowl for a man, and I feel real sorry for whoever ends up with her."

"Little harsh, don't you think?" Owen grinned, but had to admit that he shared the boy's sentiments somewhat, just from the little he knew about the woman.

Hunter shrugged. "Maybe." He brushed crumbs from his mouth. "I figured Brooke Holloway was your girlfriend anyway."

Owen thought for a moment. "I don't know that she's my girlfriend, but I guess she's become more than just a friend." He shook his head. "Never mind. I guess she's my girlfriend." He sighed. "I don't know. Maybe not."

Hunter laughed. "Wow, man, she's got your head all confused, don't she?"

"I guess so." Owen smiled, thinking that wasn't such a bad thing. A month ago he wouldn't have thought that possible.

Hunter had demolished the kolache and was reaching for a cookie. "I got this girl, Jenny, that I been talking to sometimes on the Internet." He blushed. "We're gonna get together soon, I think. In person, I mean."

"Cool." Owen grabbed two bottles of water from his small refrigerator and handed one to Hunter. "What's she like?"

"She's real pretty. Blond hair. And she knows I have this real good job." Hunter smiled, something he didn't do often.

"A fresh start can be a good thing." Owen heard himself speak the words and realized that there might be some truth in them for himself.

Owen put a half-eaten muffin back in the basket when he heard a loud pounding on the door. "That's bound to be my uncle."

He moved quickly to the front door and opened it. Uncle Denny was exactly as Owen remembered him, only grayer. His grizzled hair hung almost to his shoulders in a wild nest of waves. Bushy gray eyebrows arched high on his forehead, and his mouth naturally crooked up on one side, whether he was smiling or not. He wore a dark-brown shirt, and his khaki pants hung low beneath a protruding belly.

"Owen!" Uncle Denny threw his arms around Owen and squeezed. He smelled like cigars and garlic.

"Good to see you, Uncle Denny." Owen eased out of the hug and reached for the red suitcase on the porch beside his uncle. "Is this all you have?"

"It's all I need." Uncle Denny's left eye twitched as he spoke, a condition he'd had for as long as Owen could remember.

"Well, I'm glad you're here." Owen stepped aside so

his uncle could come in. "Like I told you when you called, I recently bought this place, so it's a mess."

"I'm sure it is quite luxurious compared to my most recent accommodations."

Hunter met them in the entryway. "Uncle Denny, this is Hunter Lewis. He works for me during the week." Owen nodded to Hunter. "And, Hunter, meet Uncle Denny."

Denny and Hunter shook hands, then Owen asked, "So where have you been this time?"

"Motuo County in the Nyingchi area of southeastern Tibet." Uncle Denny rocked back on his heels and closed his eyes, a blissful expression settling on his face. "Unbelievable slice of heaven, I tell you."

Owen turned to Hunter. "Uncle Denny is fulfilling his bucket list, which is to visit the ten most remote places in the world."

Hunter smiled. "Really? That's cool."

Uncle Denny chuckled. "It's cool, all right, but it takes more out of me these days than it used to. Not as young as I once was, you know. So now I've got to rest and work on my memoirs before I head to Peru."

"When are you gonna go there?" Hunter asked.

"Whenever I feel like it!" Uncle Denny laughed and slapped Hunter on the back so hard that it jarred him from his stance. "Where's my room, Owen? I think I may need to sleep for a couple of days."

Owen motioned for his uncle to follow him to the stairs. "What's in here?" he said, hefting the heavy suitcase. "Bricks?"

"Maybe one or two."

Owen was sure the bag must weigh seventy pounds, but he managed to get it up the stairs. Once he had his uncle settled, he walked downstairs smiling. He'd always enjoyed his Uncle

Denny, and it would be nice to have a housemate for a while—especially someone as interesting as Uncle Denny. Owen looked forward to reading those memoirs someday. Uncle Denny wouldn't show them to anyone yet.

When he got back to the kitchen, Hunter was positioning another portion of the kitchen counter. He stopped and wiped sweat from his brow. "That uncle of yours must be loaded to go to all them foreign places."

Owen grinned. "After my aunt died, Uncle Denny sold everything they owned—house, furniture, boat, and everything else they'd acquired over forty years of marriage—and used that to finance his travels. My dad said he'd always hoarded money away too, and they'd never had any children." Owen paused, remembering his uncle as a younger man—a bit thinner and without all the gray hair, but just as jolly and boisterous. "Anyway, he announced to the family about a year after my aunt died that he had this bucket list—you know, a list of things he wanted to do before he kicked the bucket. I think he's already gone to five of the ten places he wanted to visit. The way he does it is to travel for a while, then come back to the US and rest for a while, then take off again. This time he asked to stay with me since he knew I'd just gotten divorced." Owen paused. "He and my ex-wife didn't get along too well."

"The guy's funny." Hunter's toothy full smile made him look even younger than he usually did.

Owen covered his grin with his hand as he rubbed his chin. "Yeah. You could say that."

Hunter picked up a hammer and gently tapped the section of counter into place as if he'd been installing cabinets his entire life. "Bet there won't be no dull moments with him around."

Owen's grin broadened. *I'm sure there won't be.*

Twenty-One

O *nly two days left.*

Brooke stared at the X she'd just marked on the kitchen calendar, then reached up and added the single digit in the corner. She picked up her coffee, but the lump in her throat made it hard to swallow. So she carried the cup upstairs to her bedroom, where she had laid out several outfits on her bed. She was staring at them, contemplating what to wear on Saturday night, when her phone rang.

"How's Meghan?" Owen asked.

"She's fine. I think it's almost run its course, and she's definitely not contagious anymore. You're okay, right?"

Brooke and her kids had been more or less in quarantine since Saturday morning, when Meghan surprised Brooke with a sprinkling of red bumps on her face. Brooke had vaccinated both her children against the itchy disease, but apparently Meghan was among the 2 to 3 percent who got it anyway. Owen had never had the chicken pox or vaccine, so Brooke insisted he go get vaccinated and stay away from the house, just to be sure. Brooke had stayed home from the store with Meghan all week. Spencer had attended the Fourth of July parade on Tuesday with Judy's family, but otherwise he'd been home as well.

"I'm fine. Tell Miss Meghan I miss her almost as much as I miss her mommy." He paused. "Spencer too."

Brooke smiled as the now-familiar warm glow took over. "I'm sure we'll see you soon. How's it going with your uncle?"

Owen laughed. "I can't wait for you to meet him. He slept for two days straight, then started helping me and Hunter around the house. He's strong for an old guy." Owen paused. "And he makes Hunter laugh, which is nice to hear."

Brooke had been trying hard to put her feelings about the boy behind her. The apology had definitely helped. And Owen said he had a great work ethic. "So Hunter is working out okay?"

"Yeah. The kid has all the genes I didn't get—mechanical, woodworking, etc. He can fix just about anything and has a natural knack for working with his hands. It's been a good arrangement for both of us."

"I'm glad." Brooke could almost say that with a full heart.

"You decide whether or not you're going to talk to your dad?"

Brooke had been telling Owen every night when they talked—sometimes for over an hour—that she was thinking about talking to her dad, for her mother's sake, if nothing else. Mom had come by earlier in the week to visit Brooke and the kids, but she'd just seemed so sad. Brooke knew she was the cause of it. But surely Mom understood that her not telling Brooke the entire truth years ago was adding to the distance between them.

"I'm going to do it. Soon."

Silence for a few moments.

"Brooke, I miss you."

"I miss you too."

"Oh!" Owen paused. "I keep forgetting to ask you. Are you going to Tallie's party Saturday night? You can ride with Uncle Denny and me."

Brooke swallowed hard. "Whose party?"

"Tallie Goodry. She was over here last Friday and invited us." He paused. "She made it sound like everyone in town was invited. Don't tell me you're not."

Brooke was surprised he hadn't mentioned this sooner, but she wasn't surprised that Tallie hadn't invited her. "I guess I wasn't on Tallie's list."

"Then I'm not going. You know how I feel about her. But she'd brought that basket of treats over to the house and said that everyone would be at her get-together, that it would be a chance for me to meet the community. So I said I would go, thinking you and I could go together. Now I won't."

"That's ridiculous. You should go. Tallie knows everybody, so it really would be a great opportunity to meet Smithville folks." Brooke deliberately pushed aside the image of Owen at a party with Tallie Goodry. Brooke and Owen had been seen out enough that word on the street was probably spreading, but not enough for Tallie to abandon her efforts to get her hooks in Owen.

"I'll just call her and tell her I'm bringing my girlfriend."

The glow returned, but only briefly. "Tallie and I have the same friends. She didn't invite me because she wants to make a move on you."

"So are you jealous?" Owen snickered.

"Jealousy is a sin." Brooke squeezed her eyes closed, knowing she was a sinner. "I think you should go and meet people, and it will be good for your uncle too."

"You're the only one I want my uncle to meet."

Warm and fuzzy feeling again, but . . . "Besides, I have this thing I have to go to Saturday night." Brooke glanced at the outfits on her bed again, then walked to her closet and pulled out another one.

"What thing?"

She rubbed the side of her face, squinting, not wanting to lie, but not wanting to share either. "Something I committed to a few months ago. A dinner."

"Oh."

Brooke knew he was waiting for more information. But Brooke felt guilty discussing Travis with Owen.

"Who's keeping the kids?" he finally asked.

"They're going with me. It's kind of a family thing, and the doctor said Meghan won't be contagious. You're only contagious for four to five days after the symptoms start."

"I got the shot right when you told me to, and then I'm supposed to get another one in four weeks, but I'm pretty sure I'm not in danger of catching." He paused. "So maybe I could come over tomorrow night? Or after the party on Saturday?"

"I'll see how Meghan is feeling tomorrow, but it will probably be late when we get home Saturday." She closed her eyes, hoping he wouldn't ask more questions.

There was a heavy exaggerated sigh from Owen. "O-kay."

"I'll talk to you later." She smiled as she hung up the phone. But the lump in her throat returned as she eyed the dresses laid out before her.

❧

Patsy paced in the tiny kitchen of Harold's shabby apartment, wishing the constant drip in the kitchen sink would stop. She stepped carefully on the uneven vinyl floor as she wondered what she could do to rid the place of the musty smell. This place made her apartment at the Oaks seem downright luxurious. Worst of all, the air-conditioning was on the fritz. They had it cranked down as low as it would go, but the temperature still hovered at eighty-six degrees. She'd called the apartment manager three times.

Harold was lying on the couch dripping in sweat, and Patsy wasn't sure how much of it was from the heat or how much from the fever he'd been running the past few days.

"I should have taken you to Brooke's, Patsy." Harold was so weak. They'd been to the doctor the day before, and Harold had a bacterial infection, common to advanced liver disease.

She dabbed a cold rag on her husband's forehead. "You're not in any condition to drive. And I wouldn't leave you anyway. But as soon as I have time to look, we will move to a better place."

"I have money saved, and I've already put you on all my accounts." He took a deep, labored breath.

Patsy wondered how much that might be since he'd chosen such a low-budget apartment. It didn't matter. The hardware store was in her and Brooke's names. And she had some money saved, a few investments. They'd get by.

She blotted sweat on his cheeks and smiled. "Remember that first apartment we had when we got married? This reminds me of it."

He smiled back at her. "I think we had better AC at that place."

Patsy shook her head and looked at the clock. "It's been three hours since I left the last message at the manager's office. What's wrong with those people? Don't they know it's supposed to be a hundred degrees tomorrow?"

She was worried about Harold. His fever still hadn't broken after a few doses of the antibiotic. Should she call an ambulance or wait until Monday to see the doctor? They could hardly ask Brooke to take them. Brooke was probably on her way to Houston anyway. Today was the day. Patsy knew Brooke was both anticipating and dreading this evening, which she'd been counting down for months. She hoped it turned out to be a good evening for Brooke and the children. But she couldn't help but be a little worried, knowing her daughter was so far away.

Sighing, she listened to the drip in the kitchen as the temperature continued to rise, hoping to hear from the landlord soon.

∞

Brooke braided Meghan's hair, then twisted it atop her head.

"Daddy always liked my hair like this. He said I looked like a princess."

Brooke smiled, hoping that Meghan would always remember things like that about Travis. "You do look like a beautiful princess." She kissed her on the cheek, glad that only a few small bumps were left, then ran her hand along the white ruffles at the bottom of Meghan's pink dress.

Spencer joined them in the living room wearing black slacks, a white long-sleeved shirt, and no belt, though Brooke had asked him to wear one. Spencer hated belts. *Choose your battles.* She let it go. Today was not the day to get in an argument with her son. "You look very handsome."

Spencer grabbed his trouser legs and fidgeted, avoiding Brooke's eyes. "You look pretty." He spoke softly, but Brooke wasn't sure she'd ever been more touched in her life.

"Thank you," she managed to whisper. She was glad she'd chosen her peach-colored suit. It had been Travis's favorite.

"You ready?" She glanced back and forth between her children, knowing this would be a hard couple of hours for all of them.

Meghan and Spencer nodded, so they set off on their two-hour trip. Brooke had talked briefly to Owen last night, and he'd left her a message earlier today, but she hadn't called him back. This was a day to remember Travis. But the farther out of town she got, the more she thought about Tallie's party and the fact that Owen would be there.

She wasn't surprised when it started to rain on the way to Houston. It had poured the day of Travis's funeral as well. Her mother had said that when it rained during a funeral, it meant the angels were taking the soul to heaven. Brooke smiled, hoping the angels would be with them today too.

It was nearing six o'clock when they arrived at Carrabba's Italian Grill in Houston. She took a deep breath. She hadn't seen Travis's parents since Christmas before last, even though LeeAnn and Chuck had asked Brooke and the kids repeatedly to visit them in Colorado, where they'd lived for the past four years. Going there without Travis had been more than Brooke could bear. But when LeeAnn told Brooke months ago that they'd be stopping in Houston on the way to board a cruise ship, Brooke hadn't been able to think of an excuse for avoiding a reunion.

She latched onto Meghan's hand as they crossed through the parking lot. "Come on, Spence. We're already a little late." Brooke picked up the pace, knowing how LeeAnn felt about tardiness. Her stomach churned, partly from hunger, but mostly in anticipation of the surprise her in-laws said they had for her and the children.

Chuck and LeeAnn had always been full of surprises—some good and some bad. She recalled the time when Travis's parents had bought them two round-trip tickets to Europe. Meghan was barely six months old at the time, and neither Brooke nor Travis was in a position to leave their stores for more than a day or two at a time. But when they politely declined the tickets, LeeAnn threw a fit, repeatedly telling them how ungrateful they were. LeeAnn and Chuck had gotten most of their money back for the tickets, but Brooke and Travis had heard about that one for a long time.

She opened the door to the restaurant. "We're meeting someone," she said to the hostess. "Chuck and LeeAnn Holloway."

Brooke gave each of the kids a once-over and smoothed the wrinkles from her slacks before they followed the young woman to a table at the back of the restaurant. Chuck stood up when they got near and scooped Meghan into his arms. LeeAnn stayed seated.

"Look at my beautiful girl." Chuck kissed Meghan on the cheek, then put her down. He shook Spencer's hand before he hugged Brooke.

"Sorry we're a little late." Brooke walked around the table to LeeAnn. Her mother-in-law dabbed her mouth with her napkin as she stood up.

"We were early." LeeAnn gave Brooke a stiff hug, the familiar smell of her perfume engulfing the space around them. LeeAnn hugged each of the children, then everyone sat down.

Brooke had never understood how Travis shared the same genes with these two people. LeeAnn was as uptight a woman as she'd ever met, even though her intentions were usually good. Chuck was kind but a bit on the formal side. Travis, on the other hand, had been as laid-back and gentle as any man who ever lived, rarely getting upset, and always with his heart on his sleeve.

Chuck and LeeAnn had left Smithville after they both retired from the school district. He'd been an assistant principal and LeeAnn had taught biology. Brooke hated to say it, but she'd been a little relieved when they moved. And even though he wouldn't admit it, she was pretty sure Travis had felt the same way. Travis and Brooke had made a great life for themselves, but his parents couldn't keep from harping on the fact that he'd chosen not to go to college. He'd loved them, but he'd found it hard to live in the light of their disappointment.

"How's your mother, Brooke?" LeeAnn took a sip of white wine, and Brooke wondered if LeeAnn had a radar to know what Brooke would least want to talk about.

"She's doing well. She sends her love." Brooke picked up her menu, glad to see pizza was listed along with all the other Italian offerings. She turned to Spencer, who was seated to her left. "Do y'all want pizza?"

LeeAnn began questioning the kids, asking them what they'd done over the summer and if they were ready for school to start. They all ordered, the food arrived quickly, and Brooke was starting to relax a little until sweet little Meghan began offering up additional information.

"Our friend Mr. Owen likes pizza," she said before she bit into a pepperoni-covered slice. Brooke swallowed hard, hoping Meghan would stop there. She didn't. "When we're at his house, we eat pizza and look for the secret bunker."

Brooke forced a smile and shoved a bite of chicken parmesan into her mouth, avoiding LeeAnn's gaze. *Enough, Meghan.*

"He's not Mom's boyfriend or anything like that." Spence

took a sip of his cola. "So you don't have to worry about someone replacing Dad. Mom said that will never happen."

"I'm sure there will come a time when your mother will start dating again." LeeAnn smiled at Brooke. "When she's ready, though. I'm sure it's too soon still."

It's been two years. Brooke thought about what her mother had said, that she needed to get back out there. Then her head filled with thoughts of Owen—the kisses, all the cuddling. Was LeeAnn right? Was it too soon?

Chuck cleared his throat. "You wouldn't be talking about the Hadley place, would you?" He paused. "Folks always said there was a bunker. Did someone buy it?"

Brooke nodded as she finished chewing. "Yes. A man from Austin. He's living there and restoring it."

"That's a huge place," LeeAnn said. "He must have a big family."

"He doesn't have any kids." Meghan sat taller. "And he doesn't have a wife anymore either."

Brooke could feel LeeAnn's eyes on her, but she kept her head down as she cut another piece of chicken.

"I see." LeeAnn took a gulp of her wine.

Brooke knew her children would both want dessert if offered. She was wishing one of Travis's parents would lend a hint about the surprise. "So what time does your cruise leave tomorrow morning?"

Chuck swirled his ice around what appeared to be a rum and Coke, his usual cocktail. "When we leave here, we'll drive to Galveston, then we start boarding around eleven tomorrow morning." Brooke eyed his glass and hoped one of them would be in a shape to drive to Galveston. It was getting late, and she couldn't help but wonder how much they'd had to drink before she and the kids had gotten there.

LeeAnn gently clinked her fork against her wineglass, grabbing everyone's attention. She smiled warmly at Brooke, and even though Brooke's guard was still up, she smiled back.

"We're so glad you could all meet us here. We miss not being able to see you regularly."

Brooke sat up straighter. *Are they moving back to Smithville? Is that the surprise?* She loved her in-laws, but she was hoping that was not the case.

Spencer seemed to have read her mind. "What's the surprise, Mee-Maw?" He put his elbows on the table, cupping his chin, until Brooke tapped him on the arm as a reminder not to sit like that.

LeeAnn reached beside her and lifted a large item wrapped in brown paper. "Travis was working on something very special before he died, something for all of you. He was planning to give it to you for Christmas." She dabbed at her eyes with her napkin. "When we were here for the funeral, we snuck into your room—sorry about that. But Travis had told us about the gift, and he was so excited about it. We knew it was hidden under your bed, so we took it with us so we could finish it for you all. When Chuck got sick, we had to put that project on hold. But it's just about done now."

Brooke felt a little twinge of guilt thinking about Chuck's heart attack. It had happened shortly after that Christmas when they'd visited. She'd sent flowers and had the children make handmade cards, but she probably should have done more. A lot more. Fortunately, he'd made a full recovery and was doing well now.

LeeAnn carried the item to Brooke and handed it to her. "We did the best we could with it. I know Travis would want you to have it."

The object was heavy, and Brooke couldn't imagine what

Travis would have started that his parents would be able to finish. She started peeling back the brown paper. Meghan and Spencer got out of their chairs and gathered closely around her. Once all the paper was off, she balanced the wooden item in her lap facing her and the children. It looked kind of like a deep picture frame or a very shallow cabinet, about three inches thick and tall enough in her lap that she couldn't see LeeAnn over the top of it. She could tell that it was very old, and as was Travis's way, he'd left it in its original condition and chosen not to sand and repaint it.

There were nine wooden doors, each with a small doorknob and a window. In each window there was a name—Travis, Brooke, Meghan, Spencer, Chuck, LeeAnn, Patsy . . . and Harold. In the middle was a single door that just said "Family." She opened that one first and began flipping through a little booklet of four-by-six photographs inside, groupings of them all together at various events throughout the years.

She let the children ask questions about different pictures as she fought the grief building in her heart. It felt as if no time had passed since Travis had left them.

"Open my door." Spencer reached for the small knob. The booklet there held Spencer's baby pictures, plus shots of his first steps, first haircut, first day of school, baseball games—his entire life. Meghan's door was next, and the compartment behind it held about thirty pictures of her. When Brooke opened her door, she started to cry at the sight of pictures she'd long since forgotten about—group shots of her and both her parents in happier times, photos from when she and Travis were first dating, plus a selection of wedding pictures. More pictures of them together were behind Travis's door, along with Travis's baby and childhood pictures. Chuck and LeeAnn's pages included a few pictures of their own growing-up years along with wedding photos and shots from an anniversary celebration Brooke and the kids had missed.

Brooke's heart raced as she opened her mother's door, filled with the life her mother had led before her father left them. She stared at her parents' wedding picture for a long time, then pulled open the door marked "Harold Holloway." All that was in it was another copy of the wedding picture and a few group shots from Brooke's childhood that included him.

"Brooke, we didn't have any pictures of just your father. Travis did all the pictures of you and the kids, and he'd gathered pictures of you and your mother, but they were loose in a bag under the bed. Honestly, we weren't sure what to do in regard to your father."

Chuck touched Brooke on the arm. "Maybe you'll feel comfortable adding some down the road."

Brooke thought about the bag of pictures that Spencer had found in Travis's store. He must have been planning to add some of those. But the missing pictures didn't really matter. This was the most exquisite, wonderful gift Brooke had ever received. Travis had poured his heart into this, and she missed him now, at this moment, more than she ever had.

"Thank you so much," she managed to say as regret overtook her. She should have kept in better touch, especially when Chuck was sick. She should have made a point of it instead of wallowing in her own pain. These were Travis's parents, and yes, they'd been a little difficult in the past, but they'd loved their son. Their loss was as profound as hers. And for them to have taken such care to finish this unique frame that detailed all their lives . . .

She swiped at her eyes. "I don't know how to explain how special this is."

LeeAnn walked around to Brooke and hugged her. It was

late, so the restaurant wasn't crowded, but a few curious eyes were on them. "We love you all. We've missed you so much. Please come for a visit soon."

Brooke promised they would. She eyed the antique frame with all the doors again, knowing already where she wanted to hang it, but also wondering how she could replace her father's name and spot. He wasn't her family anymore.

Then like lightning, Owen's face flashed into her mind. He wasn't her family either.

What had she done? How could she even think of kissing him? It felt like a betrayal of Travis's memory. Of their love.

Guilt wrapped around her like a thick blanket, so tight that she felt faint. She made a promise to herself.

I have to end things with him. It really is too soon.

Twenty-Two

Owen had told his uncle that a bow tie wasn't necessary for the party, but Uncle Denny was donning the black bow tie with a crisp, white long-sleeved shirt he'd bought in town just for the occasion, along with the black slacks. Black tennis shoes completed his ensemble, and he'd slicked back his long gray hair and pulled it into a ponytail. Owen had chosen a pair of linen slacks, a yellow short-sleeved shirt, and his usual tan loafers.

By the time they arrived at Tallie's, Owen was really missing Brooke. He'd left her two messages that afternoon, and she hadn't called him back or texted or anything. He wasn't sure which emotion was leading the pack—hurt or anger. He would have returned her calls.

Tallie greeted Owen with a hug and kiss on the cheek, which seemed a bit much, but he smiled and introduced his uncle. Owen had already told Uncle Denny about Tallie—and about Brooke.

"Pleasure to meet you." Uncle Denny gave a slight bow, then reached for Tallie's hand and planted a kiss on top of it. Owen stifled a grin. Maybe Uncle Denny was going to make a play for Tallie himself. She was quite tantalizing in a clingy blue blouse, black slacks, and high-heeled sandals like Virginia used to wear, the kind with a lot of skinny little straps.

Tallie looped her arm through Owen's and guided him through the room, making introductions, as Denny followed behind. Everyone seemed to be coupled up except for Tallie, Owen, and Uncle Denny. *Maybe Brooke was right.*

Tallie stayed close to Owen, ushering him to the bar, then frowning when he asked for a glass of water. She was toting a glass of white wine, but Owen had never been a drinker, and he didn't see any reason to start now. Uncle Denny, however, ordered a double scotch on the rocks, belted it down, and ordered another. Owen raised an eyebrow, though he didn't say anything. He'd been around Denny enough to know that the man spoke his mind. He worried a few drinks might intensify that natural instinct.

"So, Denny . . ." Tallie was speaking to Uncle Denny, but she still had her arm looped around Owen's, and he was busy trying to figure out how to escape. "Owen tells me you will be staying with him for a while. Business or pleasure?" She flashed those perfectly straight white teeth and batted her eyelashes as she took a sip from her glass.

Uncle Denny leaned in close. "I foresee a bit of both in my future." Owen smiled at his uncle's unabashed flirting, but he had to admit Denny wasn't a bad-looking man for someone pushing seventy. He hoped he was planning to stay awhile. He enjoyed his uncle's witty sense of humor and his willingness to pitch in with the repairs on the house. With Denny and Hunter helping, Owen was starting to think they'd finish by fall.

Then what will I do?

When Tallie and Denny settled into a conversation, Owen

took the opportunity to ease away from Tallie, excusing himself to make a phone call. He was a little angry at Brooke but also starting to worry.

He closed the patio door behind him and walked away from the few people who were standing around outside. He let the phone ring until it went to voice mail. Glancing around, he was pretty sure he was out of earshot.

"Brooke, where are you? I've left you a couple of messages, and now I'm getting worried. Call me back, okay?"

Owen closed his phone and slowly started back inside, hoping his uncle wouldn't want to stay any longer than was necessary to be polite.

❧

Once Brooke and the children were in the car, she checked her voice mail. Another message from Owen. With a sigh of resolve, she deleted it.

It was all a mistake—the snuggling, the kisses, the time together. She and Owen were a mistake. They weren't a family, and they shouldn't be playing like they were. How far would she have let things get with him, she wondered. She'd only been with one person before. Would she have compromised her values because she was lonely? Temptation had been swimming around her, and she hadn't even seen the dangerous whirlpools. Plus, she'd opened her heart to another man. A man who had told her plainly they had no future.

In her heart, she knew that Travis would want a good man raising his children, someone who loved the kids and Brooke. And Owen qualified in that regard. But she should have never gotten close to a man—or allowed her children to—without a stronger sense that it had somewhere to go. By Owen's own admission, he wasn't over his divorce, and he was still incredibly bitter. *Am I just his rebound person?*

It was almost ten o'clock when Brooke pulled into her driveway with two sleeping children buckled in the backseat. Her breath caught in her throat when she saw Owen's car parked at the curb. He met her when she stepped out of the minivan.

"Thank goodness," he said. "I've been worried about you and the kids."

"We're fine." She opened the back door, roused Meghan and Spencer, and waited while they both climbed out of the backseat. When Meghan stumbled and rubbed her eyes, Owen picked her up and headed toward the house. Like he owned the place.

Brooke got her children tucked in upstairs, but her stomach was churning. She needed to be firm when she talked to Owen.

"Are you upset with me about something?" he asked when she walked into the living room.

Brooke bit her bottom lip. What she really wanted to do was go upstairs, bury her face in her pillow, and cry her eyes out. "I'm not mad. I—I just . . ." She folded her arms across her chest and stared at the hardwood floor. "I just think we need to take a few steps back, that's all."

Owen stared at her, rubbing his chin. Brooke wondered how it had gone at Tallie's party, but she didn't want to lead him on by asking.

Owen walked closer to her. Too close. "Take a few steps back. What does that mean?" Owen's forehead creased as he narrowed his eyes.

Brooke knew she needed to be direct. "Owen, I've enjoyed the time we've spent together, but I just don't see us being in a relationship."

Owen was still rubbing his chin. "Really?"

Brooke nodded. "I told you that, remember? I'm still grieving. And you have issues as well. You told me how you don't trust easily and how you are still in love with your ex-wife." She winced as she heard the words come out of her mouth, but if saying that would put some distance between them, so be it.

Owen stepped closer, and this time Brooke didn't back up. He tucked her hair behind her ears, glanced down at her outfit, and said, "You look beautiful tonight." Then he kissed her on the forehead, and Brooke blinked back tears. "If that's really want you want, Brooke, I'll respect your wishes." He kissed her on the cheek and kissed the tear that trailed down her cheek. "But something else is going on with you."

She gently pushed him away, dabbing at her eyes. "I just can't be with you, Owen. I just can't. And the way we've been lately . . . well, it just isn't right."

Owen hung his head, hands on his hips again. When he looked up at her, his jaw was tense but his eyes were soft. She couldn't tell how mad he was. Or how sad. He pointed a finger at her. "Brooke . . ." He shook his head. "I don't know a lot of things for sure. My life's been kind of a mess lately. But I am sure of one thing, something I don't think I knew until this moment."

She waited, forcing herself not to cry.

He leaned close to her but didn't touch her, even though she wanted nothing more than for him to break all the rules she'd just established and throw his arms around her. He spoke softly as he gazed into her eyes.

"I am *not* in love with my ex-wife. I'm in love with some-one else."

It was a lie—what Owen had said to Brooke. Or half a lie, at least. Because he was sure of *two* things, not one.

First, he wasn't in love with Virginia anymore. That part had been true.

But the second thing he was certain of—even more so than the first—was that he shouldn't have opened his heart and trusted Brooke Holloway with his feelings. If she could so easily walk away from him now, then her feelings hadn't been true for him in the first place.

A few minutes later, he was home and walked to the kitchen, surprised to see his uncle sipping on a cup of coffee. Owen had moved the kitchen table back into the kitchen awhile back and had even purchased matching chairs.

"Well, how did it go with your friend Brooke?" Uncle Denny gestured to his cup. "Want some? It's decaf."

Owen didn't need any coffee, and he was wishing now that he had some of that wine or scotch from the party. He knew that drinking away his sorrows wasn't the answer. He just didn't want to think about any of it anymore.

"Apparently that's all we're going to be." He grabbed a water from the refrigerator. "Friends."

"Hmm." Uncle Denny sipped from his cup as Owen pulled out another chair and sat down. "Women. A confusing lot."

Owen nodded, although he was exasperated with himself for feeling this much for her. He knew better than to trust like this. "I guess neither one of us was ready to move forward." *Although I'm pretty sure I was.*

"Maybe just give her some time. Didn't you say she's a widow?"

"Yeah. Her husband died a couple of years ago." Owen jumped when Scooter ran past them in the kitchen.

"That's the jumpiest critter I've ever seen." Uncle Denny laughed.

Owen shook his head. "I think he's crazy. Only person he lets near him is Hunter."

"Good kid, that Hunter. Seems like a fine boy."

Owen nodded. "He's had a rough time." He filled Denny in on Hunter's past.

"Sounds like a blessing that you came along," Denny said after another sip. "And speaking of blessings, what church are we going to in the morning? I don't much care what denomination, and I don't think the Lord does either." He chuckled.

"I think Brooke and her family attend a nondenominational church in town, but, uh, I haven't been going to church since I moved here."

"Well, I reckon tomorrow is as good a time as any to start, don't you?" Uncle Denny spoke with authority, but Owen wasn't going to be swayed.

"Not for me these days, Uncle Denny." Especially not now. The Lord had allowed him to get over Virginia just in time to set him up for more heartache. Clearly God wasn't on his side.

Uncle Denny raised his chin, eyeing Owen. After a moment or two he said, "All right. Can I borrow your car in the morning?"

"Sure." He gave him directions to Brooke's church. And then, because it seemed that a change of subject was in order, he spent the next half hour telling his uncle about the hidden bunker that might or might not exist.

"Fascinating stuff. Sure you looked everywhere?" Denny got up and put his cup in the sink—which was on the floor, so Owen wasn't sure about the point of that. Hopefully they would finish the cabinets tomorrow and get the new sink installed on Monday.

"Yep. We've checked everywhere in this old place. I don't think it exists." Owen grinned. "Brooke's son, Spencer, was all about finding it. I was hoping we would find it just for his sake. The kid was so excited."

"Oh, I see." Denny smiled, and his eyebrow twitched. "So you fell in love with her kids too?"

Owen frowned. "I never said I'd fallen in love with Brooke. We've only known each other about six weeks." *But I feel like I've known her forever.* "She does have great kids, though."

"I fell in love with your aunt in two weeks and married her the third week." He gave a nod and pointed a finger at Owen. "Fifty-two years we were married."

"That's great." Owen grunted. "Although somewhat rare these days."

They sat there quietly for a minute or two. Then Uncle Denny clapped his hands together and stood. "Well, off to bed for me. Know what time the service is tomorrow morning?"

Owen thought for a few moments. "I think I've heard Brooke say it starts at ten o'clock." He looked at the clock and wondered if she was still awake. Didn't matter, he supposed.

"I'll see you in the morning, then. Good night, Owen."

Owen followed his uncle out of the kitchen, then made his way to his bedroom. If he'd had any intentions of praying tonight, he probably would have said, *Thanks, God . . . for kicking me down again. Why'd You let me fall in love with Brooke?*

The last thing he wanted, as he crawled into bed, was to think about her. But she was the only thing on his mind. And the possibility of not being with her, kissing her, holding her . . . loving her . . . was a sadness he never saw coming.

Twenty-Three

Brooke hurried the children along Sunday morning and, with ten minutes left to spare, got them out the door for church.

She almost stumbled over a bouquet of flowers on the front porch. They looked like they were freshly picked, the stems wrapped in aluminum foil. She recognized the reddish-purple color and the bright yellow tips. They were firewheel daisies. Her mother used to grow them when she was young, and Brooke had seen them growing as wildflowers, but she didn't have any in her yard. Where had they come from?

"Are those from Owen?" Spencer didn't seem angry, but she heard apprehension in his voice.

"I don't know." She picked them up, and two of the blossoms fell out of the makeshift arrangement. "But I don't think so." Picking up the loose flowers, she turned around. "I need to put these in some water. Be right back."

Minutes later she was locking the front door and heading to the car with Spencer and Meghan.

"Someone cut the grass." Spencer pointed as they hurried.

She stopped abruptly. Mowing the yard was Brooke's

exercise, and she usually did it on Wednesdays. "That's odd. They had to have done it while we were gone late yesterday afternoon. I wonder who . . ." She picked up the pace again. "Oh well. Let's go. We're going to be late to church if we don't hurry."

As she crossed the yard, she noticed that someone had also done the weed eating and blowing—even the hard-to-reach places that Brooke often let go.

As they drove to church, she refocused her thoughts and reminded herself that she'd done the right thing by letting Owen go. She'd been doing that since last night, but when they pulled into the church parking lot, she remembered Owen's attitude toward God. Another reason why it was best they went their separate ways. He didn't share her faith.

Once they were seated in church, Brooke looked around for her mother. Mom hadn't been to church the past couple of weeks, and Brooke was sure it was because of her father. He had probably given up his faith a long time ago and now was pulling her mother away as well.

When the service was over, a tall man with a long gray ponytail approached Brooke and the children.

"Brooke Holloway?"

"Yes." Brooke didn't recognize the new attendee, but she suspected he might be Owen's uncle. Not too many men in Smithville—if any—wore a ponytail.

"It is an honor to meet you, Brooke." He extended his hand. "I'm Dennis Saunders. I've heard wonderful things about you." Brooke nodded and shook his hand. Then Dennis squatted down to address the children. "I've heard all about this hidden bunker. Spencer, when are you coming over so we can continue the search?"

"Today!" Spencer looked up at Brooke with pleading eyes. "Can we, Mom?"

Brooke was already shaking her head. "I'm sorry. We can't today."

Spencer actually stomped his foot.

"Another time." Dennis gave them a warm, crooked smile. "I'm sure we'll find it, and how grand that will be." He stood up and caught Brooke's eyes as he added, "That's how it is when you find something special and unexpected." He winked before he walked away, and Brooke didn't think they were talking about the bunker anymore.

She missed Owen already, even though she believed she was right to break off the relationship. But his absence, coupled with the distance between her and her mother, was taking a toll on her heart. So she decided to go see her mother. It was time. Mom had been evasive about where they were living, saying only that it was on the edge of town. But the Oaks would surely have a forwarding address.

After taking the kids for a burger, Brooke called the facility's reception desk and then plugged her mother's new address into her GPS. The weekend manager had finally given it to her after protesting several times that it was against the rules to give out forwarding addresses. She must have found it strange that Brooke's own mother hadn't given her the new address.

Ten minutes later she pulled into a run-down apartment complex. "Wait," she told Spencer and Meghan as she scanned the parking lot, trying to decide if it was safe to bring her children here. She had seen this complex before but only to drive by, and it wasn't in the best part of town. After a few minutes she told them to go ahead and get out of the minivan, but to stay close to her.

They wound their way through the complex until Brooke found apartment 145. Good thing it was on the first floor. One of Mom's knees flared up from time to time.

Brooke knocked on the door, dreading the face-to-face meeting with her father, but needing to know that her mother was all right. She gasped when Mom opened the door. Not only was she not made up the way she had been lately, but she had large bags under her eyes and her hair was a tousled mess. Were they just staying in bed all day? She was torn between disgust and worry.

"Now isn't a good time, Brooke." Her mother pushed at strands of hair that were falling in her face, which Brooke now noticed was dripping with sweat.

"Mom, are you sick?" Brooke tried to look over her mother's shoulder, but the room was dark. It took a moment to realize that she didn't feel any cold air coming out the door. "And why is it so hot in there?"

"Oh, the air-conditioning isn't working very well. The apartment people are supposed to be sending someone."

"We can stand the heat." Brooke pushed against the door until it opened wide, despite her mother's effort to block the entrance. "Meghan, Spencer, come on." She motioned for the kids to follow. Once she was inside, she blinked a few times until the room came into focus. What was that smell? But the odor quickly became the least of her worries when she saw her father lying on the couch, his face pale and glistening with perspiration, his eyes half-closed and unfocused. She ran to his side and put a hand to his forehead.

"Mom, he's burning up with fever." Brooke turned to Spencer. "Go find a cold, wet rag."

His eyes were wide. "What kind of rag?"

"A washcloth or small towel or something. Run cold water on it."

She turned back to her father, whose eyes were barely open. "Daddy, it's Brooke. Can you sit up?"

Her mother was quickly at her side, and together they lifted her father to a sitting position. Spencer handed her a wet kitchen towel, and she dabbed it on her father's forehead.

"Is Grandpa going to die?" Meghan covered her face with her hands. "Like Daddy?"

"No one is going to die, Meghan." She looked at her mother. "Go pack. You can't stay here. It's almost a hundred outside, and it feels almost that hot in here."

"I'm not leaving your father, Brooke. I was going to get us to a hotel if the air-conditioning people didn't come soon." Her mother's voice started to crack. "I just didn't know what to do." She pointed to the worn-out coffee table in front of the couch. "He's on all these medicines, and I'm confused if I gave them to him the right way, and it's hot, and I . . ."

She grabbed Brooke's arm, her face drawn up, her lip trembling. "Is this my fault? Do you think I'm doing things right? I've never seen so much medicine, and . . ." She shook her head, blinking her eyes. "I'm not leaving him."

Brooke tried not to look at her father, but it was almost impossible once he opened his eyes because he couldn't stop staring at her. "Mom, go pack." She paused as she took a deep breath. "For you and Daddy. You're both coming home with us."

"Go help Grandma, Meghan." Brooke pointed to the doorway where her mother had disappeared. Then she pointed to all the bottles of medication on the coffee table—at least twenty bottles. "Spencer, go see if you can find something to put all this in."

As Brooke ran the wet rag along her father's neck, then back up to his forehead, he reached for her hand. "Just take your mother. I've been trying to get her to go to your house for days."

Brooke couldn't look him in the eye. "You're both coming."

He let go of her arm, then reached for a handkerchief in his pocket. For as long as Brooke could remember, her father had always worn short-sleeved white shirts with a handkerchief in the left pocket. He coughed into the dingy rag, a horrible wet cough that sounded like it came from the very bottom of his lungs. His eyes and skin had a yellowish cast, and his abdomen looked distended over his skinny frame.

Brooke was helping him to his feet when her mother returned. "Spencer, you get the suitcase. Meghan, you get the bag of medicine." She looked at her mother's expression, confusion and exhaustion etched across her face. "And, Mom, help me get Daddy to the car."

Her mother started to weep, and her father pulled away from Brooke and threw his arms around her. "Don't cry, Patsy. Please don't cry."

Brooke couldn't see her father's face, but she was pretty sure he was crying too. She gave them a moment before she patted him on the back, wondering why this was happening on the heels of everything else.

✥

Hunter watered the small patch of daisies that grew in the back corner of his yard, as he'd been doing for the past few weeks. It was the only pretty thing at his house, and now he'd found a use for them. Once he was done watering, he went in to check on his grandma. She hadn't cooked anything the past few days, so Hunter had been buying ready-made food in town. But she wouldn't eat. She didn't seem to have any interest in getting off the couch either. And he was thinking she needed a bath about now.

"Grandma, can't you eat that soup I brung you?" Hunter picked up the vodka bottle by the couch, glad to see it was still half-full. He wasn't for sure who was bringing her the liquor, although he suspected it was Pete Jasper. That guy would do anything for a buck. Hunter had seen Pete hand her a bag one day on the front porch, and Grandma had slipped him some money, then told Hunter to mind his business when Hunter asked her about it.

However she got it, the vodka kept showing up, and recently Hunter had been adding water to the bottle every day to weaken it. Today, though, it didn't look like she'd even taken a nip. "Grandma?"

She opened her eyes from where she was lying on the couch. "I ain't hungry, but you be sure to eat now. I got spaghetti warming on the stove for you."

She'd been saying that every day for a week. "Okay, Grandma." He paused. "Maybe you'd feel better if you took a bath."

"Took me one this morning."

Hunter picked up a pile of used tissues, two glasses, and a box of crackers. Maybe she'd eaten something after all. He hauled everything to the kitchen, then started washing the dishes in the sink. Little by little, he was getting the place cleaned up. It wasn't ever going to be fancy like Owen's place, but he'd been surprised what a little elbow grease could do. Their bathroom practically sparkled now except for that stain in the tub he couldn't do anything about.

He stomped on a cockroach that ran across the floor, then bagged up the garbage to take out. Since he'd gotten a job, he'd paid to have a garbage service come pick it up every week like everybody else did.

As he crossed through the living room carrying the trash

bag, he was pretty sure the smell in the air was his grandma more than the trash, but he wasn't sure what to do about it. He couldn't make her bathe. She hadn't been sleeping in her bed, but just stayed on that couch all day and slept.

When he came back in after stuffing the trash bag in the can, he saw that she hadn't moved. "Grandma, when is your next doctor's appointment?"

She shifted her weight but didn't open her eyes. "Hunter, I'm trying to sleep."

He couldn't remember the last time she'd been to the doctor, but he was sure a checkup or something must be coming up. The neighbor lady, Mrs. Kemp, had taken Grandma a couple of times, and she sometimes took the van for Medicaid patients. Hunter was pretty sure Owen would give them a ride if they needed it.

Hunter sat down in the recliner across from the couch, the low buzz of the television in the background, and wondered what he should do. He was in charge. He was worn out from cleaning all day, but as he looked at his grandma, he knew he had to do something.

He stood up, walked over to her, and tapped her gently on the arm. "Get up, Grandma. You gotta get a bath."

She shrugged him off. "I had a bath."

"Grandma, get up. I'm gonna help you in the tub, then we're going to get some soup in you. You hear me? I'll help you."

"Okay, Hunter." She sighed. "Okay."

Hunter put an arm around her, unsure how he was going to do this, but he couldn't stand to see her living in her own filth. He wished he had normal parents, a brother or sister, a friend.

Anyone.

Twenty-Four

Brooke got her parents settled in her mother's old room downstairs, which was unchanged since Mom left for assisted living. She laid out fresh sheets, brought in extra towels, and helped her mother write down a schedule for her father's pills. Then she cooked a chicken-and-rice recipe she knew her mother liked and brought it to them both on trays in the bedroom. She'd called Juliet to let her know she wouldn't be in for at least a couple of days, and she'd spent a lot of time fielding questions from Spencer and Meghan. But she'd avoided being alone with her father since they'd arrived.

It was nearing ten o'clock by the time Brooke got the kids settled down and in bed that night. By this point, she wanted to hole up in her room and have a good cry—about Travis, Owen, her parents, everything. But first she decided to make herself a cup of hot tea. She was sitting down at the kitchen table to drink it when her mother walked in.

"What's wrong with him?" Brooke took a sip of tea as she stared straight ahead.

Mom pulled out a chair. "He has an infection—that's what the fever's about. But beyond that, he has liver cancer."

Brooke swallowed hard. "Is he—"

"Dying?" Her mom took a deep breath. "Yes. He's been through several bouts of chemo, but he's decided against further treatment. He could have months or maybe a year."

They were quiet for a while as Brooke's mother made her own cup of tea. When she sat back down, she said, "The doctor says six months, but he seems to be going down faster than that. I'm sure this infection isn't helping."

Brooke couldn't breathe for a few seconds. She'd just assumed she would have the rest of her life—and her father's—to resent him.

"Is that the reason you accepted him back into your life so easily?"

Mom looked down at her cup, circling the rim with her finger. "Not one thing about any of this has been easy."

Brooke couldn't help but wonder how differently their lives might have been if her mother had let her father come home after his affair. What if it had been Travis who cheated? Would she have let him come home? Could she have forgiven him?

She didn't know.

"I should have told you the truth, I suppose—that he wanted to come home. But back then . . . it was confusing. You hated him." She paused, shrugging. "And I thought I hated him too. But all that seems so long ago now. We just want to spend whatever time he has left together." She blew on her tea, and they were quiet for a while before Mom changed the subject. "How are things going with your friend Owen?"

Brooke swallowed hard, not wanting to talk about it. "We're just friends, so there is nothing to tell." She shrugged.

"That's too bad."

Brooke glared at her mother across the table. "I'm not replacing Travis, Mother."

"No one said anything about replacing. That's your word."

As Brooke shook her head, she said, "You know, Mom, we are two very different women."

"Not so much." Her mother slid the chair back from the table and picked up her cup. "You are going to be hung up on a man who isn't here for the rest of your life. Sound familiar?" Then she walked away and left Brooke with her mouth hanging open.

Owen found excuses to go to Miller's Hardware for the next three days, although Brooke's employee—that huge man she called Big Daddy—wasn't offering up any information about why Brooke wasn't there. "Taking time off," was all he would say. Owen wanted to call her. No matter what had been said the other night, he still missed her and hoped that she and the kids were okay.

He decided to drop by the store again on Thursday, though, and was glad to see Juliet sitting at the counter. *Bingo.* Juliet was a lot more likely to offer up information about Brooke. Or so he hoped.

"Hi, Mr. Saunders. What can I do you for?" She tossed long blond hair over her shoulder, sat taller on the stool, and flashed him a big smile.

"I have a short list." He pointed to a piece of paper in his hand but then lost patience with his cover story. "Where's Brooke?"

Juliet frowned. "Uh, she's taking a few days off."

"Is she sick?"

"No." Juliet looked down and fidgeted.

"Then where is she?"

Juliet looked up. "I don't know what happened with you two, but why don't you just call her?"

Did Juliet know something Owen didn't—maybe that Brooke had changed her mind about things? He certainly had changed his, and he'd decided he wasn't going to let her go without a fight. He turned to go.

"What about your list?" Juliet yelled after him. He waved her off and headed to Brooke's.

Meghan answered the door, pushed it wide, and threw her arms around Owen's legs. Instinctively he picked her up and kissed her on the cheek, surprised how much he'd missed all three of them. "How's your mommy?"

Meghan buried her head in his shoulder. "Sad."

Owen put her down. "Is she here?"

Meghan nodded and stepped back so Owen could go in, but he wasn't sure whether to enter or not. Then Brooke appeared in the doorway.

"Owen. Hi." Her hair was pulled up in a ponytail, but strands were hanging in her face and dark circles shadowed her eyes.

"Are you okay? I haven't seen you at the hardware store, and I—I was just worried about you." *Please just tell me you want to go back to the way we were. That you've missed me the way I've missed you.*

Brooke gave Meghan a gentle push inside. "Go check on Grandpa."

Owen's ears perked up. "Your dad is here?"

Brooke stepped out on the porch and closed the door behind her, obviously not planning to invite him in. "Both my parents are here." She rubbed her forehead as though it ached. "They were living, well, pretty badly in my dad's apartment. And my dad is sick, really sick." She paused. "He has cancer of the liver, and I'm trying to take care of him the best I can because it's the right thing to do."

"Because he's your father," he said softly as he reached out and touched her arm. "Is there anything I can do?"

She blinked rapidly, and Owen could tell she was fighting tears. "No, but thank you. My mother just couldn't handle taking care of him on her own, and I was worried about her health, so I just brought them both here, and . . ."

She sighed, obviously exhausted. He reached out and pulled her into his arms, and she let him. "I've missed you," he said as he kissed the top of her head. "Please let me help you."

She tightened her grip around his waist, and Owen just held her for a while. Finally, she stiffened and backed away. "We're okay. Really."

Owen couldn't stand it any longer. "Brooke, did I misread things between us? I thought everything was going fine. I really don't want to take a step backward, and I don't understand why you do. Please just talk to me."

A tear slid down her cheek as she bit her lip.

"Baby . . ." He stepped closer to her, realizing he'd never called her that before, but it felt so natural. "What is it?" He brushed the tear from her cheek with his thumb.

"I—I just can't talk about this right now. I have a full plate and . . ." She looked up at him and more tears fell. "I loved my husband, Owen. I loved him with all my heart and soul. He was a part of me. I don't know how to love that way again." She paused. "Or if I want to."

Owen grabbed her shoulders. "I understand. I really, really do. But, Brooke, we have something together. I feel it, and I know you do too. And I'm willing to give it as much time as necessary, but please don't push me away. Let me help you with your parents, and when things settle down, we'll see where things are." He pushed back strands of hair from her face. "You're worn out—I can tell. Let me help. What can I do?"

She shrugged. "I really don't know. My dad's fever broke last night, but he doesn't sleep. And he's taking medicine around the clock, so Mom and I are taking turns getting up with him. The kids are driving me bonkers, wanting to go and do things, and—"

"So why don't I take Meghan and Spencer for the day tomorrow? I can pick them up in the morning, and I'll take them to do something fun."

"What about your work on the house?" Brooke dabbed at her eyes.

"Uncle Denny and Hunter have been working really hard. Maybe we'll all take off and go do something."

Brooke's expression had shifted at the mention of Hunter. "I don't—"

"I know what you're thinking, but it'll be okay. Really. Hunter is a great kid who just needed a little help. And I'll be there the whole time anyway. Just leave it to me." Owen cupped her cheek, leaned in, and kissed her on the mouth. She didn't pull away, and Owen found himself thanking God for that. Which was a surprise even to him. Especially to him. It just kind of slipped through his mind when he wasn't looking. But he *was* thankful. Elated, in fact.

"You won't take your eyes off of them, right?"

"I promise. How 'bout I pick them up at eight tomorrow morning?"

She hesitated for a second, then threw her arms around his neck. "Thank you. For everything. I'm just a mess right now." She backed away and met his gaze with a little smile. "I've missed you too."

He couldn't hold back from kissing her again. "I'll see you in the morning."

As he left, he realized that he could analyze the situation until the cows came home, but there was only one conclusion: he was in love with Brooke Holloway. Each time he was with her, he could feel his baggage and burdens getting lighter. And with every day, Virginia's memory got further and further away.

❦

Maybe Brooke should have said no. But she just didn't have the energy right now to fight her growing feelings for Owen. And she had to admit it would be nice to have a day without having the children underfoot. They were restless and a little confused, and a day out would do them good.

She walked back into the living room and found her mother dozing on the couch. The kids were nowhere in sight, probably playing video games upstairs. She glanced down the hall to her parents' bedroom and felt a nudge. Her father was a little better, but he was still very weak. Who knew how much time he had left.

She stood there for several moments, arguing with herself. Then she walked down the hall, knocked lightly on the bedroom door, and pushed it slowly open.

"Daddy?" Brooke had never called him anything else. "Are you awake?" She walked to the side of his bed. He blinked up at her, briefly confused, and she realized she had woken him. But she needed to do this now, while courage prevailed.

"Yes, I'm awake." He pushed himself up in the bed until he was almost sitting up. "I'm much better. Thank you for everything." He reached for his glasses on the bedside table.

"I think your mother was having a hard time." Groaning, he tried to swing his legs over the side of the bed. "She should stay, but I'll go now."

"No one's going anywhere." She put a hand on his shoulder. "Just rest."

Then she pulled a chair close to the bed, sat down, and stared at him for a while, hoping the words would come. *Nothing.*

"What can I do, Brooke? I've hurt you beyond apologies. I'll do anything you want." He leaned forward. "But you have to know that I have always loved you and your mother. I will love you 'til the day I . . ." He stopped, looked away, licked his cracked lips. Then he turned and locked eyes with Brooke. "Your mother will have a hard time when I'm gone. You encourage her to find someone else. She might be pushing seventy, but she has a lot of life left in her. I tried for many years to get her to find someone else, someone better than me."

Brooke had never heard this before, but she sat quietly as her father went on.

"Just tell me what I have to do to share a small part of your life, to get to know my grandchildren. I'll do anything."

Brooke's eyes filled as the answer came to her. "There's nothing for you to do, Daddy. Nothing at all."

The creases in his forehead grew deeper as he looked at her. "There must be something."

Brooke smiled. "No. I'm the one who needs to do something." She reached over and pulled her frail father into her arms until they were both embracing each other. Then she whispered, "I forgive you."

Her father wept in her arms. And Brooke cried too—the kind of freeing sobs that only come when you are cleansed of something that keeps you from moving forward.

❧

Hunter found an old pair of swim trunks he hadn't worn in years, but they still fit. He was excited to have a day off—paid. Owen said they were going to blow off work today and take Mrs. Holloway's kids to a water park. Even Denny was going. He smiled as he tried to picture the older man with his long gray hair and big belly in a bathing suit.

He walked through the living room, glad to see Grandma wasn't on the couch and had slept in her bed again. Seemed once he'd gotten her to take a bath and gotten a little food in her, she'd been doing better. He was almost out the door when he noticed the vodka bottle that had been next to the couch was gone. He'd seen it there the past few days.

Tiptoeing to her room, he slowly pushed the door open. Sure enough, the bottle was next to the nightstand, turned on its side and empty. Good thing he'd watered it down. He walked across the room toward the bed, shaking his head. Couldn't anyone in his family stay sober for more than a week? He picked up the bottle and realized how cold it was in the room. Shivering, he walked over to the window unit and turned the temperature knob.

"Ain't you freezing in here, Grandma?" He folded his arms across his chest and rubbed his arms. When she didn't answer, he walked to her bed and gave her a slight nudge since she was on her side and facing the other way. She was all bundled up in the covers. "I'm leaving."

She didn't move, so he nudged her again. Then again. He walked around to the other side of the bed so he could see her face. It was white as the sheet, and her eyes were wide open.

"Grandma!" Hunter stumbled back, fell over the rocking chair in the corner, and hit his head on the wall. When he stood up, he couldn't breathe—the choking feeling again. But he forced himself to walk closer and touch her face, which was ice cold.

"No!" He kicked the side of the bed, then he kicked it again. "No! No!"

He ran out of the house. This time he was for sure crying like a little sissy baby. He ran as fast as he could to the only other person, besides his grandma, who might care a lick about him. When Owen opened the front door in a blue plaid bathing suit and white T-shirt, Hunter dropped to his knees in front of him.

"Owen, I can't . . . breathe. And . . . and . . ." Tears spilled down his cheek, and within seconds Owen was squatting down in front of him. He could hear Denny in the background asking what was wrong.

"Grandma. She's gone. She's dead." He looked up at Owen. "I thought I'd been taking real good care of her, and now she's dead. She's dead!"

Owen grabbed him by the shoulders and pulled him up. "Are you sure?"

"Oh, I'm sure! Her eyes were all bugged out like them movies on TV." He bent at the waist. "I think I'm going to die too."

Hunter heard Owen telling Denny about the anxiety attacks, but Hunter didn't look up.

"Uncle Denny, stay with Hunter. I'll go over to the house and do whatever needs to be done. Hunter, do I need your keys?"

"Door's open," Hunter managed to gasp.

"Come on, boy. Let's go inside and get you something cold to drink." Denny put his arm around Hunter and led him through the living room and to the kitchen.

Hunter couldn't stop shaking. His grandma. Gone. It didn't seem possible. He put his head on the table and cried.

Brooke had Meghan and Spencer ready to go by eight o'clock Friday morning. When eight thirty rolled around and there was no sign of Owen, she called his cell phone. No answer.

"Where's Owen?" Spencer already had his backpack on with a towel, sunscreen, and a few water toys packed in it.

"I'm sure he's coming, just running late." She was starting to wonder, though.

By nine o'clock she had two unhappy children and was getting a bit irritated herself. She tried Owen's cell phone again, and this time he answered.

"Brooke, I'm so sorry. I totally lost track of the time. Hunter's grandma died, and I'm at his house with the police. They think she overdosed on pills and vodka, but she also had cancer, so I don't really know."

"Oh no." Brooke cringed at the ugly thoughts she'd been having about Owen not showing up. "How's Hunter?"

"I don't know. He was a wreck when I left him at my house with Uncle Denny. He ran to my house as soon as he realized she was dead, so I'm trying to take care of things here. I'm really sorry."

Though Brooke was no fan of Hunter's, her heart hurt for him. His grandma had practically raised him. Everyone in town knew that, and Brooke suspected he was in a bad way. "Don't give it another thought. The kids can go another day. You just take care of Hunter."

"I'll call you when I'm done here."

Brooke hung up the phone and told Meghan and Spencer what had happened. Despite their disappointment, both her children knew about loss, and Brooke was proud when they both focused on Hunter, saying they hoped he'd be okay. She tried to picture Denny tending to Hunter, who was really just a kid.

She went and found her mother sitting on the bed next to her father, showing him the photo album from Brooke's wedding. Brooke swallowed hard, not sure how many more emotional moments she could take.

"Are you two okay if I leave the kids here for a little while? Owen said Hunter's grandmother died, and I want to go see if there's anything I can do."

Mom frowned. "That's terrible. You go. We'll all be fine, dear. And . . ." Her mother seemed to search for words, then decided on, "This is a good thing to do."

Brooke gave a quick wave, pulled her hair into a ponytail as she was walking through the living room, and told Meghan and Spencer she'd be back soon.

As she pulled into Owen's driveway, it occurred to her that Hunter might not be glad to see her. People handled grief in all sorts of ways, and she and Hunter didn't really have a friendly relationship. Brooke had spent the past couple of years making sure of that. But she was here, so she knocked anyway. Denny answered the door.

"I was just stopping by to check on Hunter. Owen told me what happened." Brooke was wishing she hadn't come. She understood loss, but she didn't understand Hunter.

"Nice of you to come," Denny said as he moved back so Brooke could enter. "The boy's in the kitchen. He's a real mess. Sounds like his grandma was all he had."

Brooke noticed all the work that had been done since she'd been there. "The house looks good," she said as Denny led her through the living room.

"Yep. We've been pretty busy." Denny stopped in the kitchen door. "Hunter, somebody to see you."

Hunter's freckled face was red from tears, his bottom lip trembling. His eyes widened when he saw her, and he quickly sat tall and wiped at his nose with his hand. "Mrs. Holloway, what're you doing here?"

Brooke pulled out a chair next to him at the kitchen table. "Brooke. Call me Brooke." She put a hand on his. "I just want to know if there is anything I can do for you."

He pulled his hand away as a tear rolled down his cheek. "Why?" He quickly wiped it away.

"Because I—I know how it feels to lose someone."

"I mean, why would you come see *me*? After what I . . ." He stared down at the floor.

Brooke sent up an emergency prayer. *Help me say the right things.* "The past is the past, Hunter. It's over. And I'm here for you now. At this moment. Is there anything you need?"

He sniffled, shrugged. "I don't know."

"Has anyone called your parents?"

"Oh man!" He threw his head back against his shoulders, then raised it to look at her. "I didn't think 'bout that. I got to, don't I?"

Denny, who had been busy at the kitchen counter, now brought over two cups of coffee and placed the mugs in front of them, then took a seat in a chair across from Brooke and Hunter.

Brooke pushed her cup to the side. "Do you want me to call them and tell them?"

Hunter grabbed his chest. "I don't feel so good. Where's Owen? When's he coming back?"

"I'm sure he'll be here soon." Brooke waited a minute before she asked him again if he would like for her to call his parents.

"Yeah, I guess. It's my mom's mother, so I guess she needs to know." Hunter put his head in his hands.

"If you'll give me the number, I'll call her." She glanced at the daisies in a vase in the middle of Owen's table, the same hybrid variety that someone had laid on her doorstep. "Where did the daisies come from?"

"Hunter brought those." Denny let out a light chuckle. "Said the place needed a woman's touch."

Brooke stared at Hunter for a while. "Did you mow my yard? Put the flowers on my doorstep?"

Hunter kept his head down but nodded. "Just wanted to make up for—" His voice cracked.

Brooke took a chance and put her arms around him. He stiffened at first, but it was only a few seconds before he buried his head in her shoulder and cried. She stroked his stringy hair as she fought her own emotions and wondered how she had any tears left.

Twenty-Five

Owen was pleased with the way the house was coming along, and he was enjoying his uncle's company. Most of all, he was glad that over the past couple of weeks he and Brooke had agreed to roll with whatever was happening between them and quit carrying the past around like a bright torch. The only thing he wasn't pleased about was that Hunter was having a rough time of it.

Owen had stood by the boy through the funeral—which his parents were allowed to attend before being promptly shipped back to the rehab facility. Owen was glad about that. Hunter's father had been a real jerk through the whole process and had even pushed Hunter once. He'd backed off when Owen stepped forward.

Though Brooke hadn't attended the funeral, she was playing a new role in Hunter's life. They had grief in common, and she was able to offer Hunter a comfort that Owen couldn't. But there was only so much anyone could do to make Hunter feel better. He stayed busy working during the days, but Owen worried about him each night when he went back to his house. It wasn't clear if he'd be able to stay there much longer. Owen doubted the landlord would want to keep renting to a seventeen-year-old with a record.

Owen waited until they'd all finished eating lunch one day before broaching a topic he'd been stewing over.

"Hey, Hunter." Owen pulled a handful of chips from the bag. "What's your plan? I mean, for the future?"

Hunter shrugged, his mouth full. Brooke had brought over a huge tub of chicken salad the day before, and they were all enjoying it for lunch again.

"We're going to be through with this house in another month or so."

Hunter stopped chewing for a moment and swallowed hard. He sighed and nodded. "Yeah, I know."

"So I can't keep working with you forever." He glanced at his Uncle Denny and stifled a smile when Hunter's expression fell to the floor. "But I've gotten kinda used to having you around. So I was thinking you could just move in here."

Hunter swallowed as his eyes widened. "Really?"

Owen shrugged. "Why not? Just three bachelors hanging out. It's not like I don't have enough room." He chuckled, then pointed a finger at Hunter. "But you have to have a job."

Hunter grinned. "Denny ain't got no job."

Owen's uncle slammed a palm down on the table. "I work every day at just staying alive."

Owen knew his uncle had plenty of money, and he'd offered a generous amount to Owen for letting him stay there, but Owen had declined. His settlement with Gary had left him with plenty, for the short term at least. He was toying with the idea of working again, though, something that seemed out of reach for him emotionally a few months ago. Maybe when the house was done.

"So, what do you think? Want to be a bachelor with us?"

"Sure," Hunter finally said. His face turned red. "Thanks, Owen."

Owen picked up all three paper plates and tossed them in the trash. "Well, bring your stuff whenever you want and pick a bedroom upstairs." He was glad Hunter had said yes. This way Owen could keep an eye on him, make sure he didn't backslide into his old ways. It was a satisfactory arrangement—for now, anyway. Who knew what would happen in the future.

On more than one occasion, in an incredibly premature daydream, Owen had pictured Brooke and her children in this house. Sometimes he still wondered how long Uncle Denny would stay, where Hunter would end up, and if there really was a possibility that he, Brooke, and the kids could be a family someday. He was wiping down the new ceramic counters when he realized that he and Brooke had never talked about children.

I wonder if she wants more?

⚭

Brooke, Meghan, and Spencer walked into the house loaded down with shopping bags.

"I remember those days." Her mother walked into the living room, sipping on a glass of iced tea. "Always fun to go school-clothes shopping." She put her glass on the coffee table. "Let me see what you got."

They dropped their bags on the couch. Meghan started digging around in the bags and eventually pulled out a pink dress. "This is my favorite!"

Brooke plopped down in the recliner, grabbed a tissue from the box on the table, and dabbed her forehead. "The thermometer in my car said 106 degrees. I thought we were going to melt." She waited until Meghan and Spencer finished showing their grandma their new clothes. "How's Daddy today?"

"Doing very well." Mom smiled. "He loves your chicken salad and ate a healthy portion."

Brooke was glad to see her mother looking less tired. Her father had been sleeping better. Actually, he had been sleeping a lot, which worried Brooke sometimes, but he had a doctor's appointment next week, so maybe they'd learn more about how he was progressing. "I'll go check on him."

Brooke walked into her parents' bedroom and smiled. Her father was sitting up in bed, at least ten pounds lighter than when he'd arrived at the house. But he seemed to have a little more color in his face today, and it was good that he was eating. He was surrounded by photograph albums and little piles of loose pictures.

"I'm trying to memorize everything I missed," he said as he stared at one of the albums. Brooke walked to the edge of the bed, moved a couple of the books, and sat down. She leaned closer to see which one her father was looking at, then she laughed.

"Is that not the goofiest picture in the world?" She laughed again as she pointed to the picture. "I'm fourteen in that picture, and me and my friend Linda were playing hairdresser. Linda thought I needed an Afro. I bet she teased my hair for an hour." Her father chuckled, then turned the page. One of the photos there showed Brooke and her mother at Brooke's high school graduation. "Third in my class," she said softly.

Her father touched the picture with a trembling hand. "You have your mother's smile."

"She always said I had *your* smile." Brooke touched his hand. Then she pulled up a chair, scooted closer, and spent the next hour going through the albums with her father. He cried when he looked at her wedding photos, even though he'd been through that album several times already. Brooke thought about Travis's picture frame and the fact that her father's slot didn't have as many pictures as the rest of them.

"I should have been there to walk you down the aisle."

Brooke fought the urge to say, "Yes, you should have." She'd forgiven him, but even forgiveness came with regret. But now she also wondered how much she and her mother were to blame for their inability to forgive all those years ago.

"I'll be right back." Brooke left her father and returned with Travis's picture frame. "Feel up to a project?"

Her father nodded, and Brooke pulled out the bag of pictures that she'd brought home from the shop recently. For the next couple of hours, they worked together to add more pictures behind the door on the frame and, in the process, filled in a little more of the emptiness Brooke had been feeling in her heart.

Later that evening, after she'd gotten the kids all tucked in, Brooke bathed and climbed in her own bed, waiting for her phone to ring. Owen called her every night at ten.

"All tucked in?" he asked when she answered.

She rolled onto her side and snuggled into her covers. "Yep. I survived school-clothes shopping, and I think I might actually sleep well tonight. What about you? How was your day? How's Hunter?"

"I think he's okay." Owen paused. "I asked him if he wanted to move in with me and Uncle Denny. He seemed pretty excited about that."

"You've been really good to him, Owen. You've completely changed his life."

"Oh, I don't know about that," he answered softly. "But I could see where Hunter was headed. I'm glad he seems to be moving in a new direction."

Brooke rolled onto her back as she twisted a strand of hair. "So how long do you think Denny will stay?"

"I have no idea. He doesn't seem in a hurry to leave, and he's good company. He's helped a lot on the house too." Owen laughed. "When I bought this place, I thought I'd be working on it forever. It's amazing how much the three of us have been able to do."

"It's beautiful, Owen. It really is."

"I miss you."

Brooke smiled. "I just saw you yesterday."

"I know, but I didn't see you today. How's your dad?"

Brooke sighed. "He doesn't eat much, but he's kind of gone from not sleeping much at all to sleeping most of the time. I don't really know what that means." She took a deep breath. "But we're getting to know each other again, and that's good. His face lights up when I walk in the room. It's just all very bittersweet, I guess. I get confused about it all—how much I hated him back then but still always wanted us to be a family and how he'd wanted to come home but I never knew it. But I know in my heart that this is what God wants—for my father and me to reestablish a relationship while we still can. Forgiving him has given me some peace of mind."

Brooke was hoping that Owen was working on his own forgiveness. Until he forgave Virginia, it would be hard for him to move forward. For *them* to move forward. But when she mentioned God, Owen still clammed up, just like he was doing now. She was clear about her role with her father, but she wasn't sure about Owen, whether to push the issue or not. Things had been going so well with them, and Brooke knew that the Lord used to be a big part of Owen's life. He'd told her that. *Please, God*, she prayed for the umpteenth time, *let him find his way back to You.*

"Remember, I'm going to Houston tomorrow," he said. "I'll be there until Saturday."

Brooke knew that Owen had been talking to a public relations firm in Houston about establishing a satellite office out of his house. "Yep, I remember. Are we still on for Saturday night?"

"Absolutely! I can't tell you how much all three of us are looking forward to a home-cooked meal. You'd think that one of us would know how to cook, but we're a pretty pitiful threesome. We've managed to burn some steaks this week, tried our hand at chicken and rice—the recipe you gave me, the rice didn't get done for some reason—and Denny seems to think that eggs are okay for dinner every night we don't have something planned. I'm so sick of eggs." He groaned. "I'm even getting sick of peanut butter."

Brooke laughed. "Well, I'll bring lasagna, salad, and some garlic bread."

"The chicken salad has been great the past couple of days. Have I mentioned that I miss you?"

Twenty-Six

By the time Saturday arrived, Owen was counting the hours until dinnertime. His time in Houston had gone well, and the associates he'd met there were familiar with the work he and Gary had done in Austin. He would probably start back to work out of his home in a couple of weeks, and he was looking forward to it. He couldn't believe the way his life had turned around in just a few months.

He still thought about Virginia from time to time, but he didn't miss her or feel much of anything for her besides a dull resentment. He supposed that after all their years of marriage she would linger in his mind no matter how he felt about her. Every time he thought about Brooke and her father, he knew he needed to forgive Virginia. He just wasn't there yet.

He'd gradually started praying again, but he wasn't comfortable talking about it, even though he could tell Brooke wanted him to. Right now, he was just trying to get straight with the Lord in his own way, on his own time frame. Owen had even been praying for Hunter, who had moved in while Owen was gone, putting most of his grandmother's things in storage. Owen prayed the boy would stay on the right path and not get too derailed by grief.

"There!" Denny emerged from behind the new washing machine. "Hoses are connected. All ready to go."

They'd finished painting the mudroom in the back of the house last week and decided to make it into a laundry room. He and Denny were tired of running back and forth to the local washateria, which meant that dirty clothes tended to pile up. With Hunter under the same roof now, the place was starting to smell.

Denny turned the knob to Start. The washer had a see-through top, and he and Owen watched the water begin to swirl as if they'd created a masterpiece. "Would ya look at that?" Denny snorted. "Glad I remembered how to hook one of these things up. We should have done this a long time ago."

Owen nodded, thinking about how he hadn't heard his uncle mention his memoirs, going on another trip, or how long he would be staying. Not that it mattered.

"Well, it was always on the to-do list, but with the new roof and the electric work, it just kept getting pushed to the back burner."

"Well, I'd have lit that fire long before now." Uncle Denny tucked his long gray hair behind his ears and dabbed his forehead with a rag. Then they both watched the washer move from the first cycle to the second.

"Seems to work fine." Denny pushed the Stop button. "Let's load some clothes for the true test."

Hunter walked in. "We have a washing machine. Thank God!"

Owen knew that was just a figure of speech, not a prayer. But these days, any mention of God tended to trigger regret that he'd walked away from the Lord when things got rough. "Indeed," he said quietly.

Uncle Denny clapped his hands together. "I'm going to wash up before the food gets here." He licked his lips. "Can't wait."

"I'm just glad we ain't having eggs again," Hunter said.

Owen grinned. "Me too."

❧

When Brooke showed up at Owen's, he grabbed her around the waist and almost made her drop the pan of lasagna. "I have a surprise for you," he said as he kissed her on the cheek. Then he finally took the casserole dish and greeted both the kids. Spencer handed Hunter a bag that had the salad, dressings, and bread in it.

"Come on, come on." Owen nodded to his right, and Brooke brought a hand to her mouth when they entered the dining room. A beautiful new dining table with seating for eight spanned the newly painted room. The light amber walls and white trim were a perfect backdrop for the cherrywood table and chairs.

"Owen, it's beautiful!"

"I've had it on order for a while. I was afraid it wouldn't get here before tonight, but it was delivered while I was gone."

"Well, we are certainly going to eat dinner in style." Brooke had always imagined a dining room just like this one—big and roomy and filled with family. An only child, she'd dreamed of having lots of children when she grew up. She'd heard Owen say that when he and Virginia were married, he'd been the one who wanted children. She wondered if that was in his plan anymore—and if that plan included her.

Before they ate, Owen insisted on giving her and the kids yet another tour of the house. It was amazing how much three men could get done in a few days. She laughed when they insisted she watch the new washing machine run as if it were the grandest thing on the planet. "I've seen one of these work before," she said, then giggled.

Once they were all seated for dinner, Brooke looked across the table at Owen and smiled. Hunter and Denny were to her left, Spencer and Meghan to her right. She wished her parents were here, filling the two empty chairs, but her father hadn't felt well enough to get out tonight and her mother had refused to leave him.

Brooke held her hands out to her sides. Meghan latched on immediately, but Hunter just stared at her.

"Let's say grace," Brooke prompted.

"Grab her hand, boy," Denny said as he held his own hands out. Then he grumbled, "We boys should be saying the blessing like this before all our meals. Shame on us, and thanks to Brooke for the reminder."

After the blessing, the room went quiet except for the enthusiastic clinking of silverware against dishes. Travis hadn't been a huge eater, but that was certainly not the case with Owen, Hunter, and Denny.

Brooke didn't mind the silence. In fact, she couldn't stop smiling. The amber walls cast a warm glow through the room. Owen kept catching her eye and smiling back, and all the men interrupted their feasting from time to time to compliment the food. The kids were behaving beautifully. It was shaping up to be the perfect evening. Then Meghan raised her hand and waved it in the air as she stared in Owen's direction.

Brooke thought that seemed odd, but Owen just smiled. "Yes, Meghan. What is it?"

"Are you going to marry my mommy?"

Meghan! Brooke stopped breathing and didn't move,

hoping she would just vanish into thin air. Denny almost choked on his food, covering his mouth with his napkin, and Hunter chuckled. Brooke forced herself to look at Owen, though she knew her face was flaming red. He just smiled and winked. Spencer stopped eating and put his fork down. Like his sister, he was waiting for an answer, but with a scowl on his face.

Brooke wasn't even sure how to reprimand her daughter for this inappropriate question. Her innocent little mind had obviously been working this evening.

Owen cleared his throat. "Well, I don't know, Meghan. Would that be a bad thing?"

Meghan shook her head wildly, pigtails slapping her face. "No! It wouldn't be bad at all!"

Brooke mouthed, "I'm sorry," when Owen locked eyes with her. He just smiled more broadly. Then he saw Spencer's sour expression and his smile faded.

"If your mom and I ever decided to do something like that, I figure it would be a family decision."

Well, no, it wouldn't. But Brooke had to smile, even though she still wished she could snap her fingers and disappear.

"Can I be excused?" Spencer pushed away from the table.

"You didn't eat much," Brooke observed, then decided that maybe it was best for him to leave before he shared his opinions on the subject. "But okay."

Spencer rushed from the room, and a few moments later Brooke heard the television in the living room.

Meghan broke the silence. "I hope we live *here* if you get married! And I hope we find the secret bunker!"

"Okay." Brooke held up one hand. "That's enough. Let's focus on eating."

"I don't think there is a hidden bunker. I've looked everywhere." Hunter helped himself to another serving of lasagna. Brooke didn't think she'd ever seen anyone eat so much. *And he is so thin.* She was just thankful they'd changed topics.

Meghan frowned. "That's why no one has found it. It's hidden real good, but it's here somewhere." She gave a decisive nod, as if that ended the discussion once and for all.

Hunter eased his chair back. "Brooke, the supper was real good." He paused. "I'll go check on Spencer, if that's okay. He said he brought his plane, that you bought him a part online. Maybe I can help him with it."

"That'd be great, Hunter."

Everyone else finished eating, then Denny and Meghan joined the rest of the group in the living room. Owen helped Brooke clear the table. She was loading dishes in the new dishwasher when Owen put his arms around her waist.

"I wish I had a picture of you when Meghan posed her question." He snickered as he moved her hair to one side and kissed the back of her neck. "I've never seen you turn so red."

Brooke kept rinsing the plate in her hand, but the feel of his lips on her neck was a nice distraction. "I'm sorry my children don't have better manners. Apparently when I was teaching them about right and wrong things to say at the table, that subject didn't come up."

Owen waited until she bent over to put the plate in the dishwasher before he put his hands on her hips and turned her to face him. Brooke kept her chin down until he gently cupped it and forced her to look at him.

"If anyone had told me a few months ago that I would be standing here, with you, in this house . . ." He grinned. "And that your daughter would be asking—"

"It's not funny, Owen." She playfully slapped him on the arm. "I have never mentioned anything to the kids about anything like that." She couldn't even bring herself to say the word *marriage*.

Owen brushed her lips with his. "I don't know what the future holds because I don't know how you feel." He kissed her again. "But I know how I feel. I love you, Brooke. I've known that for a while. I just didn't want to scare you off."

"I'm not scared," she whispered. And she wasn't, though she had to admit to a lingering unease. Was it wise to get this involved with a man as conflicted about faith as Owen was?

Too late. She *was* involved. And she couldn't shake the sense that God had brought them together. *If not, please make that clear and help me do what's right. Because I'm afraid I'm in deep.*

She reached up and held his face in her hands. "I love you too."

They held each other for a while before they finished cleaning the kitchen, then walked hand in hand out to the street where everyone else had gathered. Hunter put the plane down on the cement and handed Spencer the remote, giving him a few instructions.

Denny put his hands across his stomach when Brooke and Owen walked up. "Best meal I think I've ever had, Brooke." He grinned at her. "Fun conversation too."

"Thank you, Denny. Glad you liked the meal."

"Now let's see if this plane will fly." Denny used his hand to shield his eyes from the setting sun. They all waited as Hunter showed Spencer how to operate the controls, then stepped back. It was exciting to watch the plane starting to glide forward, but then it made a horrible backfire noise and fell over to one side, balancing on the wing.

"Man!" Spencer walked to the plane and picked it up. "This thing is never going to fly."

Hunter put a hand on Spencer's shoulder. "Dude, we'll get this figured out. You want to leave it with me and I'll work on it?"

Spencer nodded. "But no test flights without me."

"I promise." Hunter stuffed his hands in his pockets, and Brooke didn't even see the same young man who had walked into her store toting a water gun and demanding money. Every once in a while the image still haunted her, but this Hunter was so different—a testament to what a little love and new surroundings could do.

Owen put his arm around her and pulled her close. She felt his pocket buzzing, and he reached inside and pulled out his cell phone.

"Oh no."

Brooke looked up at him. "What's wrong?"

"It's Virginia calling."

Owen let the call go to voice mail, but Brooke felt suddenly uneasy.

❧

Owen listened to Virginia's voice mail three more times after Brooke and her children left. "Hi, Owen. I need to see you. It's really important. I was hoping maybe next weekend. I can come there. Can you please call me back?"

He knew his ex-wife pretty well, and he could tell by the sweet sound of her voice that she wanted something. *To get back together?* Surely not. She and Gary were having a baby. *Money?* She'd seemed happy with their settlement, and Gary made plenty of money.

He tapped the phone to his chin. Uncle Denny had gone to bed, and Hunter was sitting at the other end of the couch from Owen, glued to the television.

"Hey, Hunter, what do you say we go to church in the morning?" Owen shifted his weight on the couch, wishing again that it was comfortable like Brooke's sofa.

"Huh? What for?" Hunter kept his eyes on the television.

Owen sighed. "Do you believe in God?"

"I don't *not* believe in Him." Hunter shrugged, paused the movie, and turned to Owen. "I just never could see that He makes much of a difference. I mean, all this bad stuff happens, and He doesn't stop it."

"But what about the good stuff? Where do you think that comes from?" Owen realized he'd often been guilty of over-looking God's gifts in his life, especially in the last year.

Hunter frowned. "Why are you wanting to go to church all of a sudden?"

"Denny goes. I used to go." Owen paused, knowing he was messing this up. "Let's just go."

Hunter shook his head. "I don't think so. I just don't think I'm the God type." He paused, frowning. "But Jenny is. She talks about Him a lot."

"You ever going to meet that girl or just keep chatting on the Internet?" Owen kicked his feet up on the coffee table, missing Brooke.

Hunter smiled. "One of these days."

"So what does Jenny say about God?"

"That being close to Him makes you different. You believe that?"

Owen smiled. "Yeah, I do. But I guess when my life kind of fell apart, I quit having much of a relationship with Him."

"So why do you need it? You seem to be doing just fine

without God. You got you a nice girlfriend, a cool house, and lots of money. What can God give you that you ain't got?"

Owen stared at Hunter, a sadness wrapping around him. "Salvation," he said. "Through Christ."

Hunter's expression was blank. Clearly, he had no clue what Owen was talking about. So Owen tried again. "When we let God into our hearts, He gives us lots of things—like peace of mind, comfort when we're sad, a reason to keep going when things get rough, and a way to deal with the bad things we've done. We can talk about it someday if you're interested."

Hunter shrugged and resumed the movie. But five minutes later he turned to Owen and said, "Okay."

"What?"

"I'll go to church if you want me to."

That was good enough for Owen . . . for now.

He listened to Virginia's message again, then said good night to Hunter. Once he was in bed, he called Brooke. She didn't ask about Virginia's call, and Owen didn't mention it.

Brooke pushed her father down the aisle in a wheelchair while her mom and the kids followed behind. It was the first time for all of them to attend church together. They'd had a wheelchair delivered last week when her father could barely get up and down to go to the bathroom or to take a bath. He was getting weaker by the day, and Brooke was anxious to see what the doctor would say this week at his appointment.

Once they got settled, her mind drifted back to Owen and the phone call from his ex-wife. She'd felt even more uneasy after their phone call last night, since Owen didn't mention what Virginia wanted. Brooke's mind was awhirl. Had he called her back? Was she having regrets about giving up such a wonderful guy? Were they planning to meet?

Her thoughts were still spiraling when she looked up and saw Owen, Hunter, and Denny coming down the aisle. There was no room near where Brooke and her family were sitting, so the three men took a seat across the aisle. Brooke wanted to run to Owen and hug him, but she just smiled. It felt good to have all her extended family in church this morning.

After the service, they all went to eat together at the Back Door Café, then Brooke helped Mom get Daddy settled back in the bed before she, Meghan, and Spencer went over to Owen's house. Spencer spent the afternoon with Hunter working on the plane. Meghan bounced back and forth between the television and chasing the black cat. And Brooke stayed safely cuddled in Owen's arms on the couch.

"See what I mean about this couch?" Owen shifted his weight, frowning.

"I think it's okay. It just hasn't been broken in like mine." Brooke plucked a handful of popcorn from the bowl on the coffee table and put her feet up beside it. "Where's Denny, by the way? I haven't seen him since we got here."

"I don't know. Probably napping. He does that." Owen reached into his pocket and pulled out his cell phone when it started to ring. He pushed End as he'd done about an hour ago. Both times Brooke had seen Virginia's name flash across the display.

"Do you need to call her back?" Brooke chewed her bottom lip. She hadn't mentioned the phone calls before now.

Owen shook his head. "I'm happy. She'll only mess up my mood." He turned to Brooke and kissed her on the cheek.

Brooke jiggled one foot nervously as she contemplated whether or not to let this go. If Virginia still had the power to mess up Owen's mood, that was worrisome. Finally, she couldn't stop herself. "Maybe it's important."

"That's what she said in her message, but everything is always important if it's about her." He shook his head.

There it was again—the bitterness. She'd thought he was getting over that. And Virginia had left a message apparently. *What did she say?* Both Brooke's feet were in motion now.

Owen leaned over and kissed her. "Nothing Virginia has to say is important enough to warrant my taking time away from us."

Brooke forced a smile, but something in her gut told her that trouble was brewing.

Twenty-Seven

"Y ou should go to work, Brooke." Mom helped her father sip water from a cup while Brooke stood at the end of the bed putting some socks on him. "The doctor said we won't know anything until they get the test results back, and I can call you."

Brooke covered up her father's feet with the blanket again and gave him a little pat on the leg. "I can stay."

They had been at Smithville Regional Hospital since before daybreak. Brooke's father had started running a high fever overnight. Though he was feeling a little better now, the doctors wanted him to stay until they knew what was wrong.

Mom sat down and pulled her father's hand into hers. "Well, we'll be just fine if you need to go." But Brooke didn't want to go. She had to admit that getting to know her father again was stirring up emotions she hadn't expected to feel. At first, she'd written off her growing concern for him as normal nurturing instincts. She would want to help anyone who was ill. But the more time she spent with him, the deeper the fear of losing him burrowed into her heart. She was painfully aware that every moment together was precious.

"Big Daddy and Juliet are fine at the store, and they have Meghan and Spencer, so there's no rush for me to go." Brooke glanced back and forth between her parents, who were lost in each other's eyes, and wondered if maybe they wanted some time alone. *Good grief. They act like teenagers sometimes.* "But I can leave if you want me to."

"No, no . . ." Her father spoke up first, then her mother echoed his words.

A few minutes later her father turned up the television, and both her parents were totally absorbed in *Jeopardy*. Brooke had never been any good at the game show, so she allowed herself some time to think about Owen. *I can't believe he loves me too.*

She had called him a little earlier to let him know where she was. And though he'd rented a sander and planned to do the upstairs floors that morning, he'd promptly offered to come to the hospital. Though she'd assured him there was no need, the fact that he wanted to come meant a lot.

She was really coming to believe that God was giving her a second chance at love, but she couldn't shake the niggling feeling that something wasn't quite right. She'd thought perhaps it was those phone calls from Virginia to Owen that had kept her up last night. But this morning he'd told her that he loved her before they hung up, and he'd wished her father well, so maybe she was worrying for nothing.

"I can see you two are entertained," she said to her parents after about ten minutes. The only talking going on was both her parents voicing answers to the game show. "So I'm going to go after all." She lifted her purse up onto her shoulder. "Mom, I'll come back later this afternoon to pick you up." She kissed her father on the cheek, then her mother.

"Thank you for bringing me and for being here with me today." Daddy's voice cracked as he spoke, and Brooke hoped he wouldn't cry again. He was so emotional these days. She swallowed back her own tears.

"I'll see you this afternoon."

She waved as she walked out the door. She'd spent so long hating him that she'd forgotten how much she loved him.

※

Owen worked all morning on Thursday to set up a home office in one of the upstairs bedrooms, the one with the built-in bookcase. It would feel good to get back to work soon. Denny and Hunter were in Austin picking up two doors, both special orders that Brooke's store didn't carry.

He hadn't seen Brooke the past few days, even though they'd talked every night. She was spending her time going back and forth between the hospital and the hardware store. He decided to take a break and call her now. He headed downstairs and was scanning the kitchen cabinets for lunch options when she answered. She was at the hardware store.

"How's your dad?" Owen pulled a loaf of bread from the shelf and set it on the counter.

"Not so good." She paused. "He can't seem to shake this infection, and he was a little jaundiced when I got there this morning."

Owen wanted to ask her what the prognosis was, how long her father was expected to live, but he didn't want to upset her further. "I guess you don't know how long he'll be in the hospital?"

"No. Just depends. He's getting weaker, though, and losing more weight." She sighed. "You know what worries me the most?" Owen waited for her to go on. "Meghan and Spencer have gotten to know their grandfather, and now they are going to lose someone else. I just hate to see them have to go through that again."

"I know." Owen rummaged around the refrigerator until he found a package of ham. "But I think God sent him back into all your lives for a reason. Several reasons, in fact. So that you could heal and forgive, so the kids would grow up with memories of him, and so both he and your mother can have some closure. If he'd never come back, I think his death would have been much harder on her."

"You may be right," she said. "And it's really nice to hear you talking about God."

Owen smiled. "I'd say He and I are on pretty good terms these days." He thought for a few moments about the ways his life had changed recently. "I miss you."

"I miss you too. I've been meaning to stop by, but between my dad and the shop—"

"I completely understand. Anything I can do?" Owen pushed the Speaker button on his phone, found some mayonnaise, and swiped some onto two pieces of bread.

"No, not really, except to talk to me and cheer me up. Meghan and Spencer have been spending time with Judy's kids, which is good. I want them to enjoy the last of their summer. I just wish I had more time to be with them."

"You're a good mother, Brooke. They'll be okay. And right now your parents need you. But just remember I'm here if *you* need anything."

He told her about his office, which he'd painted a light tan with white trim. He'd opted to keep the bookshelves the way they were. "I just sanded them a little, but left them kinda raw looking. They give the whole room character, even if they don't swing open into a secret room."

Owen took a bite of his sandwich.

"You're eating, aren't you? I can tell you have me on speakerphone."

"Sorry. I was missing you and hungry at the same time." Owen tried to talk as if he didn't have a mouthful.

"Peanut butter and jelly?"

"Ham, actually." He swallowed and took another bite.

"I'll make you guys another batch of chicken salad soon."

"Sweetie, you don't have to do that. You've got a full plate." But chicken salad sure sounded good.

"Well, the kids and I still have to eat, and I can take my parents some at the hospital. I'm sure they are getting sick of hospital food." She paused, and Owen finished off his sandwich. "Maybe we can get together on Saturday."

"Definitely." He smiled. "I love you."

There was a knock at the door, so Owen took Brooke off Speaker and walked to the front entrance.

"I love you too," she responded just as Owen pulled the door open. He was sure his heart stopped.

"Uh, listen, I have to go. But I'll call you later." He hung up without waiting for a response.

Brooke held the phone away from her ear and stared at it for a moment, caught off guard by the abrupt way Owen had ended the conversation so quickly. Then a movement across the street caught her eye. She moved to the front of the store, squinting to see better. Someone was trying to look through the windows of Travis's store—not easy, since the windows were still boarded up. It took just a few seconds for her to recognize that gray ponytail. She watched Denny for another minute, then saw him turn and head her way.

"So tell me about the boarded-up business across the street," he said when he walked in the door. "I hear it belonged to your late husband."

Brooke waited until he got all the way to the counter. "Yes, it did. He sold old books, antique toys, things like that. A mishmash of vintage stuff. Why do you ask?"

Denny scratched the stubble on his chin for a couple of seconds. "Just curious. What are you going to do with the contents?"

Brooke shrugged. "Sell them, I guess. I've been putting it off for two years, but I noticed when I was in there recently that everything is a mess—really dusty."

"Hmm." He took a deep breath. "Can I see inside?"

"Sure." Brooke reached into her purse for the key. "Why?" She grinned. "You want to buy the business?"

"I might." His answer was quick, and Brooke's jaw dropped. "Seriously? What about your travels?"

Denny shrugged. "I have a weakness for old things, particularly books." He took the key when Brooke handed it to him. Blushing a little, he added, "And I have a family now. Not in such a big hurry to run off to Peru."

Brooke nodded. "The lock's a little tricky," she said as he turned to leave. "Lift up on the door a little after you turn the key."

She watched him cross the street and wondered what it would be like to see Travis's business reopened. *Travis would love that.*

Denny returned an hour later.

"Well, what did you think?" Brooke folded her arms across her chest. "You going into the antique books and toy business?" She smiled, doubting it.

"Yes. I believe I am. Let's talk price."

꧁꧂

Owen stared at his ex-wife, then glanced down at the baby carrier she was toting. *You gotta lot of nerve, lady.*

"What are you doing here, Virginia?" Owen fought the bile building in his throat.

She shifted the carrier to her other hand. "Well, I've been calling you and leaving messages. You never would call me back."

"Perhaps that should have told you that I don't want to talk to you . . . or see you." He started to close the door.

"Can we please come in? It's too hot out here for the baby." Virginia nodded toward the child, and Owen reluctantly stepped aside so they could enter. He motioned her toward the living room. Virginia put the baby carrier on the coffee table and slung her purse and a diaper bag on the couch.

Silence for a while. Then Virginia asked, "Are you seeing anyone?"

She wants to get back together. Owen stopped breathing for a few moments. "Uh, yes. I am."

Longer silence this time. "Is it serious?"

"Virginia, why do you care? I mean, really. Did Gary dump you or something?" Owen cringed, wishing he hadn't said that. There was no need for him to engage her in what would surely blow up into a fight.

"No," she said. "We're still together."

"Than what do you want?"

Did she really sniffle? Owen squinted as he tried to determine if what he was seeing was real emotion or the kind that Virginia was able to concoct at will. Either way, his chest was getting tight. Just seeing and talking to Virginia gave him a headache. He couldn't bring himself to congratulate her, but he was trying really hard to keep his cool.

"I see you had the baby." He glanced down at the child nestled beneath a pink cotton blanket.

"I named her Lauren."

Owen didn't say anything, even though he'd always liked that name.

"So does your lady friend have children?"

Owen didn't want to talk about Brooke to Virginia. He was going to wrap this entire visit up momentarily. "Yes. She has a boy and a girl."

"That's wonderful. I know how much you always wanted children."

"And I know how much you didn't." Owen nodded toward Lauren.

More silence, then Virginia responded, "You're right. I never did want children." She reached over and touched the child on her cheek. "Lauren is beautiful, though, isn't she?"

Owen reminded himself that Gary and Virginia's love child wasn't the one to blame. He took a closer look. The baby was sleeping, but she puckered her mouth and moved her tiny fingers atop the pink blanket. "Yes, she is." He pulled his eyes away from the newborn and looked at his ex-wife. She wore white jeans and a blue blouse that showed off a more abundant cleavage than he remembered. Her blond hair was a shade or two darker, and she was packing what Owen assumed was leftover baby weight.

"What brings you here, Virginia?"

Tears filled her eyes and she looked away. She leaned down and kissed her daughter on the cheek, caressing her tiny forehead before she stood and faced Owen. "She's yours. Lauren is your daughter. I've known this was a possibility from the beginning, and now a DNA test has ruled out Gary as the father."

Owen's head swam as his eyes shot to the baby. "What? Are you sure?"

"Yes. And look at her. She looks just like you." A tear rolled down Virginia's cheek, but she quickly swiped it away. "Do you want to hold her?"

Owen nodded, although the realization that he had a daughter was still sinking in.

Virginia unbuckled the protective strap holding Lauren in, then she gently scooped up the baby. "You have to support her head." She placed the baby in his arms.

"She's so tiny. How old is she?" Owen trembled as he gazed down at this little miracle.

"Three weeks today." Virginia dabbed at another tear, and Owen began to speculate. *Does she want to get back together and be a family?* That was impossible, of course. He was in love with Brooke. But there was still a lot to think about. Thoughts of visitations, child support, and other decisions that would have to be made flashed through his head, along with the realization that he'd never seen such a beautiful child. He wished she would wake up.

"What color are her eyes?"

"Blue. But sometimes that changes when they get a little older."

Virginia sat down on the couch, but Owen couldn't move. He felt he could stare at his daughter forever.

"So what does Gary think about this?" Owen finally allowed his eyes to drift back and forth between Lauren and Virginia.

Frowning, she twisted the strap of her purse, which she'd pulled into her lap. "He isn't thrilled."

"Did he know there was a possibility she might be mine?"

Owen recalled only a handful of times that he and Virginia hadn't used birth control.

Virginia sighed. "Yes. But this obviously was not the outcome we were hoping for."

I'm sure it wasn't. And this doesn't change anything between you and me.

Virginia sat taller and folded her hands in her lap. "Tell me about your girlfriend."

"Why?" He finally made his way to the couch and sat down carefully, preparing himself in case Virginia suggested they reunite.

She twisted to face him and shrugged. "Just wondering. You told me she has two children. What does she do for a living?"

"Her family owns the hardware store here in town." Owen smiled when Lauren opened her round blue eyes. "She's awake. Wow." Owen stared down at Lauren, fixated on this tiny person who was a part of him.

"She won't break, Owen." Virginia reached over and moved Lauren's head more into the nook of Owen's arm. "Just support her head."

Owen watched his daughter for a few more moments, then looked up at Virginia. "So what's the plan? I'm assuming you've come here to discuss visitation and child support."

She hung her head for a moment, then looked back at him as tears trailed down her cheeks. "No, that's not exactly what I want to talk about."

Owen couldn't remember seeing Virginia ever cry this hard. "What then?"

"Gary doesn't want to raise another man's child." She pulled a tissue from her purse and dabbed at her eyes, sniffling.

I knew it. "Virginia, I want to be a part of Lauren's life, but I think I should tell you . . . I'm in love with Brooke. There is no chance of us reuniting."

Her eyes widened. "That's not what I want either. I love Gary. I want to be with him." She paused, her eyes glassy as she stared straight off into space. "I want you to raise her."

Owen's mouth fell to the floor. "What?"

Virginia leaned forward. "You know I never wanted children. And Gary is going to leave me if I choose to raise Lauren."

Owen's blood started to boil. "Let me get this straight, Virginia. You would choose Gary over your own child?" He looked down at Lauren, whose eyes were now wide open and focused on him. "And then you would be the one to get her every other weekend and such? Is that what you're proposing?" Owen actually loved the idea, but he couldn't fathom how a mother could choose such a thing.

Virginia shook her head. "No, Owen. I want to sign over all my rights to Lauren." She looked away. "I love Lauren, but I don't want to lose Gary. And I really think you'd be a better parent." She reached into her purse and pulled out a wad of papers. "I've already had the papers drawn up if you're agreeable."

Owen couldn't speak.

"Stop looking at me like I'm a monster." She slammed her palms against her knees.

He paused, shaking his head. "There is no way you've thought this through. Surely you want to be in Lauren's life in some way."

She shook her head. "No."

"Gary won't allow that, or what?"

Virginia scowled. "Do you want to raise her or not?"

"I don't know how I was ever married to you." He gazed

down at the precious bundle in his arms, then looked back up at her. "But, yes, I want to do it."

Virginia sighed. "I'm not as heartless as you think. That's why I was asking about your girlfriend and if it was serious. I'd like to know that Lauren will have a good mother."

"*You're* her mother." Owen shook his head. "Brooke is a great mother, but we haven't talked about marriage. I've only been seeing her for a few months."

Virginia pushed the papers toward him. "I'm sure you'll want to have an attorney look at these, then just sign and mail them to me."

Owen couldn't breathe. "You can't leave her with me now. That's not what you're doing, is it?" His heart started racing. "I don't have any baby stuff. I don't know how to take care of her."

Virginia reached into her purse again as a tear rolled down her cheek. "Here is a complete list of everything you'll need. And there are enough diapers, formula, clothes, and necessities in the diaper bag to get you through a couple of days at least."

"Well, you thought of everything, didn't you?" He paused. "What if I'd said no?"

"I knew you wouldn't. I know you, Owen." She stood and walked over to him, holding out her arms for the baby. Reluctantly, he handed her over. She cradled Lauren on her shoulder and wept.

Owen swallowed the lump in his throat. "Virginia, don't do this. Don't give up your daughter for a man."

She handed Lauren back to Owen, her carefully made-up face streaked with tears. "I have to go." She hurried toward the front door.

"Virginia! Wait!"

She stopped when she got to the door, looked at Lauren, then at Owen. "Take good care of her."

"I don't know how to take care of a baby! I don't know anything about babies!" He was already worried about dropping Lauren as it was.

Virginia stared at him long and hard, her tears subsiding. "Sign the papers, Owen."

Owen stood in the doorway and watched her drive away until she was out of sight. His heart was racing, and the realization that he now had a daughter hadn't even set in when Lauren opened her tiny mouth and began to wail.

He walked carefully back to the couch. *Don't drop her. Just don't drop her.*

He found a bottle in the bag and worked it into her mouth. She latched on hungrily—good! Then he reached for his cell phone and dialed Brooke's number. She answered on the first ring.

"I was just getting ready to call you. An ambulance is here to take my dad to the medical center in Houston. He lost consciousness earlier, and his fever is 104. Juliet has the kids, and me and Mom will follow behind."

"Brooke, I'm so sorry. What can I do?" He looked down at Lauren, knowing his news would have to wait.

"Just pray. I'm not ready for him to go yet, and my mother is a wreck." She paused, and Owen could hear voices in the background. "I have to go, but I'll call you later. Mom and I packed a bag. We might be there a couple of days, maybe get a hotel room nearby. But everything's taken care of. Juliet loves to keep the kids, and Big Daddy will make sure everything is okay at the store."

"I'll definitely pray."

After they hung up, Owen watched Lauren drink the rest of the bottle. "Hungry, weren't you?" He paused, shaking his head. *Unbelievable.* "You are so beautiful."

Then she opened her mouth and threw up everywhere.

As Owen cleaned her up as best he could, Denny called and said they were about thirty minutes from home with both doors in a small U-Haul they'd rented. Hunter was following behind in Owen's car.

"Thank goodness you're almost here. We have company."

Twenty-Eight

unter, Denny, and Owen all sat in a circle around the little baby. Owen had put her on a thick blanket on the living room floor.

"She's just givin' away her kid?" Hunter couldn't believe Owen's ex-wife had gone and done something like this. But then, maybe he would have been better off if his parents had given him away to someone nice like Owen.

Denny's left eye twitched as he leaned forward, a crooked smile on his face. "Well, well, I'm a great-uncle." He smiled more broadly. "Fabulous news!"

"Your ex-wife must be an awful person." Hunter shook his head as he watched Lauren sleeping.

"Well, she's definitely not the maternal type," Owen muttered. He reached over and touched his daughter on the arm. "She was really hungry earlier. She drank the entire bottle but then threw up. Kinda worries me."

"You did burp her, didn't you?" Denny tucked a strand of gray hair behind his ear. "Babies gotta be burped."

"You didn't have any children. How do you know that?"

"Don't you even watch television? Haven't you ever seen someone burp a baby on TV?"

"I think you better call Brooke." Hunter gazed at the cute little baby. "We ain't got no idea what to do with her."

Owen explained that Brooke and her mother were in Houston because Brooke's father had taken a bad turn. Hunter thought about how Brooke had been real good to him when Grandma died. He hoped she'd be okay.

"Anyway, now's obviously not the time to tell her." The baby opened her eyes, and Owen picked her up. Hunter was tempted to reach over and help him. He looked like he was holding something that would break real easily as he finally got the baby settled in his arms. "After all, this is big. She's going to be . . . surprised."

Hunter thought about what this might mean. "You gonna marry Brooke?" He walked to the couch and sat down, then leaned over the coffee table with plane parts scattered about. He was determined to get Spencer's plane to fly.

Owen handed off the baby to Denny. "I hope that's in the future, but we haven't talked about anything like that."

Hunter was relieved to hear that. He imagined that he and Denny would be booted out the door when that happened. Brooke and her kids were great, but surely they wouldn't want others living with them.

But Denny is family. Hunter rethought the situation and figured he would probably be the only one asked to leave. And this was the only real family he'd ever had. It was normal and all. Everyone got along pretty well, there wasn't any yelling or hitting, and everyone helped each other. In the evenings, they even prayed together sometimes. It had felt weird at first, praying with grown men, but now it was starting to feel normal. And maybe the prayer thing worked, because Hunter had noticed things changing inside himself.

"Well, I have some news as well." Denny gently laid the baby back down on the blanket. "I asked Brooke not to mention anything until the deal was closed, but I'm buying her late husband's business."

"What?" Owen's eyes got real big.

Denny sighed. "Yep. Nothing I'm more fond of than vintage books and such—anything old. And that place is filled with fascinating items. I talked at length with Brooke about how she felt about this, and she said it would be a wonderful legacy to her husband and that he would be very happy to have the store reopened."

Owen was still looking confused, with his mouth all twisted in a weird shape. "What about traveling, your bucket list?"

Denny opened out his arms like he wanted to hug someone. "That was before all of you. I have a family now. And we even have a baby. What a bonus!"

Owen reached over and gave Denny a big old bear hug. "I think it's great you're staying."

Denny laughed. "I figure you'll need all the help you can get with little Lauren, but if you and Brooke make this a permanent arrangement, I will be on my way."

Owen shook his head. "I don't think that will ever be necessary."

"Of course it will." Denny gave a little groan as he pushed to his feet. "But that's the way it should be."

Hunter didn't say anything. He was going to have to find another job soon. They were just about done on the house, and now Owen would have the kid he'd always wanted, plus

Meghan and Spencer. He'd probably marry Brooke someday. He pictured them all living here and him gone.

He's right, I reckon. That's the way it should be.

⚬

Friday morning Owen woke up on the living room floor. He'd slept next to Lauren and the diaper bag, with Virginia's brief instructions beside him. He'd been afraid to put her in his bed, worried that he might roll over on her or she would fall off.

First order of business today was to get a crib and the other supplies Virginia had on the list. Denny had been right about the burping, although Owen suspected his uncle didn't know much more about babies than he did. No matter. He'd located a YouTube video that showed him just what to do. There was even one about changing diapers.

It would be easier, of course, if Brooke were here to help him with this, but he hadn't yet told her about Lauren. She'd been so worried about her father each night when Owen talked to her on the phone, and he was nervous about her possible reaction to discovering that he was a father. How would she feel about having this unexpected child in their lives? Owen adored Meghan and Spencer. Surely Brooke would accept Lauren. But her children were older. Would she really want to start over with a new baby?

He smiled, realizing that he was already planning a future for all of them.

"When're we going?" Hunter walked into the living room dressed in denim shorts and what looked like a new blue T-shirt. They'd all decided the night before that they would go to Austin and get all the baby supplies. At first Owen was going to stay home with Lauren while Denny and Hunter made the trip, but he was uncomfortable being alone with her. He thought their best bet would be to all stay together.

"I need to feed her first." Owen slid Lauren toward him and started fumbling with her diaper. "Hunter, I made some bottles, and they're in the refrigerator. Can you go get one?"

Hunter nodded and disappeared. Owen got the sticky tabs loose, pulled the wet diaper away like the video had shown, and slid another underneath her little rear end. Then she smiled, and he thought he might cry. Surely she was the most wonderful gift God could have given him.

"So, how'd that sleeping on the floor work for ya?" Owen hadn't heard Denny come in, but there he was on the floor beside Owen. "She's a beauty, isn't she?"

Owen smiled. "Yeah, she really is."

"How are we going to carry her to town? Do you have a car seat?" Denny shook his head. "I remember back in the day, before seat belts, car seats, and all that other stuff. We turned out okay."

"Virginia said this carrier is a car seat too, and she left directions." Owen handed the piece of paper to Denny.

"She sure went to a lot of trouble to give you notes and instructions for a kid she doesn't care about." Denny shook his head again. "Doesn't make any sense."

Virginia hadn't made sense to Owen in a long time. He knew it hadn't been an easy decision for her. But just the same, it was a choice he couldn't reconcile in his mind.

It took them another hour to feed Lauren, burp her, change her again, and figure out the car seat. "Are you sure she's in there right?" Owen pulled on the straps that held the carrier facing backward. "Denny, you drive. I'll sit back here with her." He heard Hunter grunt, but Owen wanted an experienced driver for this particular trip to Austin.

❦

By Saturday morning, Brooke's father was out of the hospital and doing much better. She was eager to see Owen, but she needed to check on things at the store first. She left the kids with her mother, who insisted she could take care of both Daddy and the kids, and was at the store sorting through receipts when Owen called.

Brooke listened from her stool behind the counter as Owen told her about Virginia's visit—and about the baby daughter he didn't know he had. "I don't get it," she said once she was able to pick her jaw off the floor. "She doesn't want to see her at all?"

His heavy sigh came through loud and clear. "I'll admit this surpasses what I thought Virginia was capable of. But I read over the papers she gave me. And she is signing over all rights to me."

Brooke just sat there. Speechless.

"I know. Unimaginable." Then Owen's voice softened. "But you should see her—Lauren. She's the most beautiful little person I've ever seen."

Brooke smiled, knowing that feeling. But she was still trying to absorb his news. "I can't wait to meet her."

"I can't either, for selfish reasons. I don't know one thing about babies. Not one single thing. Denny, Hunter, and I went to Austin yesterday, and a salesperson helped us buy everything we might possibly need for a baby, but we don't even know what half of it is or what to do with it."

"I do," she said softly.

"Are you . . . okay with this? I mean, as far as you and me and everything. I know it puts a new twist on things—a newborn in the picture."

"Did you think I wouldn't want to be with you anymore

because you have a child?" She smiled. "I have two of those. Remember?"

"I know. And I love Spencer and Meghan. But this came out of nowhere, and it's practically a brand-new baby."

Brooke smiled at his description. "I think you'll be a wonderful father, Owen. I really do."

"Don't know about that, but I've always wanted a child. I just didn't expect it to be like this. But now that your father's better, can you come over soon?"

"Absolutely. I can't wait to meet Lauren." She shifted her weight on the stool and took a deep breath. "Are you 100 percent sure that . . ." She cringed, not sure how to ask.

"Virginia said that they had a DNA test, which ruled Gary out. And she swore to me awhile back that Gary was the only other person she was with throughout our marriage." Brooke heard just a tinge of the old bitterness in that pronouncement. "I guess I could have a DNA test too, but I don't think Virginia would do this unless she was sure." He chuckled. "Plus, I think she kind of looks like me."

They talked for a while longer, and Owen ended the call by saying he loved her and missed her.

"I love you too."

Owen was quiet but didn't hang up, so she asked, "Are you still there?"

"Yeah. I'm just thanking God for you. And the fact that you're such a good mother. What if I hadn't met you? Fallen in love with you?"

Brooke smiled. She'd been thinking the same thing. "God always has a plan." Without either of them saying it, Brooke knew her role in this new scenario, and she was in a hurry to get started. She quickly finished up with the receipts and then hurried to Owen's house, her stomach churning with excitement and nervousness.

When she arrived, Owen was on the porch waiting. He grabbed her and kissed her several times. "I've missed you so much."

"I've missed you too. Now, where is that baby?"

Owen grabbed her hand and pulled her over the threshold. And in the next moment Brooke thought for sure she'd stumbled upon Santa's workshop, with all his elves busily preparing for Christmas. She wasn't sure she'd ever seen so much baby stuff in one place, and both Hunter and Denny were busy in the living room putting it all together.

Brooke paid them no attention. She went straight to the small portable playpen in the living room and scooped up the baby inside it. It seemed like so long since she'd held a little one.

"Owen, she's beautiful." She breathed in the aroma of baby lotion as she cuddled Lauren in her arms.

When Owen didn't answer, she looked over at him, then at Denny and Hunter, who had stopped working. They were all just watching her.

"What is it?" she finally asked.

"You make it look so easy," Owen said.

Hunter ran his sleeve across his forehead. "Yeah, you shoulda seen the three of us trying to give her a bath last night. We was all worried about drownin' her or getting soap in her eyes or something."

Brooke laughed. "I've done this twice before, and most of it is common sense."

"Well, we've all learned the hard way what happens if that little one doesn't have a good burp." Denny went back to screwing the legs on a baby swing.

Brooke carried Lauren over to the couch. She was still processing the fact that this was really Owen's daughter when she heard Owen's phone ring.

She knew right away that it was Virginia. And that there was a problem.

⚜

Thursday morning Patsy kissed Brooke on the cheek before she left to go to the hardware store. Meghan and Spencer were upstairs in their rooms, and Harold was sleeping. Patsy sank down onto the couch, closed her eyes, and basked in the quiet.

Brooke was happier than Patsy had seen her since Travis died, and she seemed excited about what her future might hold, especially with a new baby in the plan. Meghan and Spencer were doing well, although Spencer still seemed on guard where Owen was concerned. Her grandson seemed to want to love Owen, but couldn't shake the fear that he and his mother might be betraying his father. Harold seemed at peace with his situation, although he had one dying wish, and Patsy was afraid he wasn't going to see it fulfilled. He wanted Brooke and Owen to get married so that he could walk Brooke down the aisle—if she would allow him to and he was able.

Patsy knew her daughter didn't move that quickly. She'd only been seeing Owen for a few months. Patsy thought their relationship could eventually lead to marriage, but not anytime soon, even in light of a new baby in the picture. Brooke always made calculated choices.

Still, it had been a special moment for Patsy when she'd spied Brooke and Harold filling the empty door of the photo album that Travis's parents had given Brooke.

Meghan came into the room and cuddled up next to Patsy on the couch. "Mommy said Owen has a new baby."

"That's right." Patsy ran her hand through one of Meghan's pigtails. "Isn't that exciting?"

Meghan nodded. "Spencer says we won't be seeing Owen very much now that he's going to have his own little girl."

"Now, I don't think that's true. But little babies do require a lot of attention. I bet you'll be able to help take care of little Lauren. Won't that be fun?"

Meghan nodded solemnly, and Patsy envisioned them all as one big family. That brought a smile to her face. *Please, Lord, let Harold live long enough to see it.*

As Meghan sat nestled against her, she thought about how she was going to lose Harold all over again, this time permanently. The doctors had said he might make it to Christmas. Patsy prayed every night that this might be true, that he'd live to see Brooke and his grandchildren opening presents on Christmas morning. She remembered with a twinge of pain all the Christmases he had been denied because she wouldn't allow it, just couldn't forgive back then.

Harold started to cough, so Patsy eased Meghan away. "I need to go check on your grandfather."

"He's going to die, isn't he?" Meghan folded her hands in her lap and kept her chin down.

Patsy squatted down in front of her and lifted her chin. "Yes, I think God will call him home soon. But you know what?" She paused. "He will get to meet your daddy in heaven when he gets there. That's a good thing, isn't it?"

Meghan blew on a strand of hair that had escaped a pigtail and hung in her face. "Do you think I can write a letter for Grandpa to give Daddy?"

Patsy fought the tears building in the corners of her eyes as she kissed Meghan on the forehead and stood up. "You know what? I think that would be very nice."

Then Harold started coughing harder, and Patsy hurried to his side.

Twenty-Nine

rooke stood in the middle of Owen's living room on Saturday morning fidgeting, sweating, and pacing. Virginia's phone call had been a demand of sorts: "If you want to keep Lauren, then I want to meet the woman who could be raising her." It was brilliant in a way, even if it was manipulative. Virginia had made sure that Owen had sufficient time to be fully attached to Lauren, then made the demand. How could Brooke say no? Denny and Hunter had bolted out of the house early. Brooke wished she could do the same. She felt like she was being interviewed for a job she hadn't applied for.

"Don't look so nervous," Owen said as he walked into the room and wrapped his arms around her. "She won't bite." He kissed her on the neck. "I don't think."

Brooke pulled away. "I just don't know why she is so insistent about this. We're not even . . ." She looked down, shrugged. "You know."

Owen lifted her chin and smiled. "You know exactly what we are and where we are going."

It wasn't a proposal, but Brooke felt warm all over, even as her stomach continued to churn. She smoothed the wrinkles from the yellow sundress she'd chosen for today, then combed through her hair with her hands.

Owen leaned down and kissed her softly, then whispered, "You look beautiful. And thank you."

"Well, I'm not going to have her denying you your daughter just because I won't meet with her."

"I can't tell you how much I appreciate this." Owen took a deep breath and looked at his watch. "She said ten o'clock, but she's always late." Five minutes—and many paces—later they heard a car pull in. "I bet that's her." Owen walked to the window and pulled back the curtain. "Yep."

Owen walked to the front door and Brooke heard it open, but her feet stayed rooted to the floor in the living room. She straightened her dress again and finally walked to the entryway.

After what seemed like forever, a woman in blue-jean capris, a clingy yellow top, and heeled white sandals stepped over the threshold. She had thick, wavy brown hair and wore black sunglasses. The woman eyed Brooke up and down, and when she seemed to be done, Brooke extended her hand and introduced herself.

Virginia pushed the sunglasses up on her head, and Brooke saw she'd been crying. "Nice to meet you, Brooke."

Owen motioned for them all to go into the living room. Virginia immediately went to the portable playpen in the living room where Lauren was sleeping. Brooke waited for her to pick up the baby, but she just stared down at her for a few moments.

"She's a beautiful baby." Brooke swallowed hard, unsure what to do or say.

Virginia put her purse on the couch. "Owen, I'd like to talk to Brooke alone, if that's all right."

Brooke held her breath, but Owen spoke up right away. "No, it's not all right." His nostrils flared, and Brooke touched his arm.

"Owen, it's really okay with me." They all knew the purpose of the visit.

"Are you sure?" Owen touched her on the arm, and Brooke felt Virginia's eyes blazing into her. Maybe the woman had changed her mind. Maybe she'd realized what a great catch Owen was and wanted him back.

Brooke nodded, not sure about anything, but Owen moved toward his bedroom. Once they heard his door close, Virginia sat down at one end of the couch. Brooke sat down at the other.

"I can't imagine what you must think of me." Virginia pressed her glossy lips tightly together.

"I'm not here to judge."

"Owen tells me that things are serious between the two of you." Virginia eyed Brooke up and down again.

"Yes, I think so."

"Have you talked about getting married?"

"No, not really." Brooke recalled Meghan's outburst and Spencer's reaction. They had a way to go before everyone in her family was fully onboard.

"But it's a possibility?"

I hope so. "Why do you ask, Virginia?"

"I think that's obvious." She rummaged in her Gucci bag and finally pulled out a tissue. "You could be raising Lauren. At the very least, you'll be a big part of her life." A tear rolled down her cheek. "So before I sign her over, I want to make sure you're trustworthy."

Sign her over? She's not a car title. "But you don't have to give up your rights. He hasn't signed the papers yet. He

311

said he wants to wait, to make sure you won't change your mind. There is a way this can work where we can all be part of Lauren's life. A baby can never have too much love."

Virginia smiled. "Owen is a good man."

"Oh yes."

"But it's all been decided." Virginia looked away from Brooke for a few moments, then back at her. "And it's fine." She dabbed at her eye with the tissue. "I just felt like I had to meet you. Believe it or not, I'm trying to do what's best for Lauren. I'm from a broken home, and I don't want her running back and forth between houses like I did. That's not to say I'm doing it all for her, because I'm not. I admit that. But this is still the hardest thing I've ever done." She hesitated, staring at Brooke. "I promise you, I would not be a good mother."

"But you could be. It's a hard job that comes with no instructions, but we all learn. And it's the most rewarding job there is. Virginia, don't do this if you have any doubts whatsoever. Don't let anyone pressure you."

Virginia straightened. "I don't have doubts. Tell Owen to sign the papers. But . . ." Her eyes drifted around the room toward the swing, the carrier, and the playpen. "Can you please send me pictures?" She reached into her purse and pulled out a card. "Here is my e-mail address." Her voice faltered. "Just an occasional picture . . . would be wonderful."

Brooke gazed at the card, still not fully comprehending. "Sure. But—"

"I'm afraid Owen won't do it."

"He would if you asked him to, I'm sure." Brooke took a deep breath and blew it out slowly.

Virginia stood up, so Brooke did too. In that moment, something seemed to shift in her, and all traces of vulnerability disappeared. "I want you to know I won't be interfering in your life. Gary has lots of travel plans lined up for us. A baby didn't really fit into those plans."

"You don't have to choose." Brooke didn't want to step over the invisible lines that had been drawn, but it was true.

Virginia locked eyes with Brooke, a look so intense it would haunt her for months to come. "Yes. I do." She picked up her purse and added, "I'm going." Tears started to stream down her face as she headed toward the entryway, but her expression was stony.

Brooke grabbed her arm, frantic to do something to ease the woman's pain, self-inflicted as it was. "Don't you want to say good-bye to Lauren?"

Virginia threw her arms around Brooke's neck. "I can't. Take care of my baby." Then she ran out the door and slammed it behind her.

Owen came out of the bedroom just in time to see Brooke cover her face and cry. Once it started, she couldn't stop.

"What did that witch say to you? What did she do?" He drew her into an embrace. "I'm so sorry, Brooke. I shouldn't have ever left you alone with her. Baby, what is it?"

Brooke just kept shaking her head and crying. Finally she caught her breath and said, "I just feel so incredibly sorry for her." Then she gently pushed Owen away and looked into his eyes. "She's going to miss everything."

Owen pulled her once more into his arms. "But we are going to have it all."

Brooke knew that both of their lives had changed forever. He held her for another minute before he eased her away and kissed her several times on the lips.

"Everything is going to be okay." After a final kiss on the forehead, he asked, "We are still having dinner here, right?"

Brooke sniffled, glad for a change of subject. "Yes, we're

having dinner. Tell the boys we're having chicken-fried steaks and mashed potatoes. I'll bring the ingredients and cook 'em when we get here." She smiled. "Sure hope Hunter got that plane fixed. Spencer can't wait to try it out." She picked up her purse and slung it over her shoulder. "So I will see you and Miss Lauren tonight."

❧

After Brooke left, Owen picked up Lauren and carried her to the couch. He sat down and stared into his baby girl's blue eyes.

"Hello, daughter."

He felt like he could just watch her forever. Just the sight of her face brought healing to his heart.

❧

"Spence, close my car door, would you, please?" Brooke had her hands full as she walked toward Owen's door. Meghan ran ahead and knocked, and it sounded like Owen, Denny, and Hunter all yelled, "Come in," at the same time. "Meghan, it's okay. Open the door."

Brooke walked in after Meghan, halfway expecting the men to meet her in the entryway so she could unload some of the food she was carrying. But when none of them appeared, she walked into the living room—and smiled. Little Lauren lay on a quilted pad on the floor, and Owen, Hunter, and Denny were sitting in a circle around the baby, eyes glued to her. Meghan and Spencer ran to join them.

"I'll just go get started on dinner," she said. No response. Grinning, she repeated it a little more loudly. Owen stood up and rushed to her.

314

"Sorry." He reached for the bags. "I think I'm getting this down, taking care of her. But you'll have to help me with the bath thing. Hunter has still been doing it with me, but it seems like it should be a one-man job."

"You're going to do just fine. Really." She followed him to the kitchen, then began unloading the groceries.

"Oh. I forgot to tell you." Owen put a hand to his forehead. "She threw up. I tried to call you, but there was no answer."

"When?" She laid the cubed steaks on the counter.

"About an hour ago, I guess. I cleaned her up as best I could without actually putting her in that little bathtub you bought. But what made her do that?"

"Sometimes babies just spit up. Did you remember to burp her?"

"I tried. But I couldn't really tell if she did it."

She turned to face him and smiled. "Welcome to parenthood, Owen. There is a learning curve."

"Do you care if I go back in there?" Owen pointed toward the living room.

"Nope. I have this under control."

Brooke got to work breading the steaks and boiling potatoes. She knew where everything was in Owen's kitchen. She'd been the one to organize it all. No one did much cooking in this room but her, except when Denny made eggs. By now it felt like home.

After they ate, everyone went outside to see if Spencer's plane would fly this time. Brooke wasn't sure who was more nervous, Spencer or Hunter. "You have to do it just like I showed you earlier." Hunter handed Spencer the remote for the airplane.

Brooke carried Lauren, blocking the baby's eyes from the setting sun with a light blanket. She was gently bouncing

Lauren in her arms when she caught Owen staring at them. He winked at her and smiled.

They all watched in suspense as Spencer worked the controls on the remote. Owen and Denny started to clap as the plane inched forward, then gradually accelerated until it lifted off the ground.

"Keep it steady!" Hunter had his hands on either side of his head and didn't look like he was breathing.

Brooke was hoping Spencer didn't fly the plane through someone's window and also was wondering if he knew how to land it, but she loved watching her son's excitement and his confidence at the controls. She looked up as Owen put his arm around her. He kissed her on the cheek, then touched Lauren's cheek with his finger, then nodded toward Meghan. "My three favorite girls," he whispered.

"Careful!" Hunter was jumping up and down now. "Careful!"

"I got it! I got it!" Spencer turned the plane around. Brooke took a few instinctive steps backward, then a few more.

"It's coming right toward us." Brooke turned and hurried back toward the house with Lauren.

"I said I got it!"

Brooke watched from the porch as the plane slid onto the concrete and stopped a few feet in front of where they were all standing. Spencer's face glowed, and Brooke's jaw dropped when her son ran to Hunter and hugged him.

"You did it!" Hunter yelled.

Brooke thought she might be glowing too. It was a perfect night. She'd left her parents cuddled together on the couch watching a movie. Her father had been feeling well enough to get out of bed and move around a little bit, although they'd declined the dinner invitation. Owen beamed like any new father, and Brooke was pretty sure she'd be playing a significant role in this beautiful child's life.

She sniffed at Lauren's few wisps of hair, enjoying that incredible baby smell, as she looked out at her untraditional family. That's exactly what they were—a family. Denny and Hunter leaned over the plane, engaged in intense conversation about something with Spencer. Owen held Meghan's hand. The whole scene was such a gift. *Thank You, God.*

She turned to go in with Lauren. But as soon as she opened the door, she knew something was terribly wrong.

"Owen! Owen!" She clutched the baby tighter and hurried down the porch steps. "Hurry! Inside! Hurry!"

Thirty

Owen knew everyone was safe—he could see them all. But what was happening? Why was Brooke yelling?

His first thought was fire. But when water met him in the entryway, he knew he was dealing with an entirely different problem. He sloshed through water coming into the entryway and followed the noise he heard all the way to the small powder room nearby. Water was shooting straight up from one of the faucets. He squatted down and turned the water under the sink off, but it had apparently been spraying for a while.

"What happened?" Denny walked up beside Owen. After a quick inspection, he said, "Hunter's the one who worked on that faucet."

"Thanks for throwing me under the bus, Denny." Hunter picked up the faucet from the floor where it had landed. "The washer was worn out, so I replaced it and—"

"It doesn't matter, but we need towels—lots and lots of towels." Owen started pulling down towels from the shelf by the door and throwing them onto the wet floor. "We've got to get this water up before we end up having to redo these floors again." He wiped the sweat from his face with his shirtsleeve.

"Hunter, go into the linen closet in the big bathroom down the hall. There's a big bag of towels in there. I bought new ones to put in all the bathrooms when we were completely done, but I think we're going to need them now. Hopefully we can keep the water contained to the entryway and hall."

Brooke was busy keeping the kids back and holding Lauren. "Can we do anything to help?"

"See if you can find any towels in the kitchen." Owen started mopping up the water with the towels he had, then dumping them into the trash can when they were saturated. Denny disappeared for a few minutes, then returned with a blue plastic storage tub. "For the towels. It's bigger." Owen heard Brooke and the kids in the kitchen opening drawers. But there was no sign of Hunter.

"Denny, can you go see what's taking Hunter so long? If he can't find the bag, it's at the very back of the bathroom closet, thrown in the corner. I only have three or four towels that I use on the shelf. We'll need more than that."

"Will do."

Brooke returned with her arms full—two kitchen towels, two rolls of paper towels, and a bag of shop rags. "This is all I can find. I put Lauren in the playpen in the living room. What else can I do?"

Owen sighed, straining to see down the hall toward the entryway, where water still puddled atop his newly sanded and stained floors. He closed his eyes and took a deep breath, then looked at Brooke. "Apparently the boys can't find those towels. Can you please go see what the holdup is? They are in plain sight in the back left corner, inside a gray shopping bag."

"Sure."

❧

Brooke held Meghan's hand with Spencer close behind as they sloshed through the water in the entryway, making their way toward the full bath next to Owen's bedroom. Meghan and Spencer lingered behind as Brooke entered the large bathroom. She loved the claw-foot tub and portable shower unit Owen had installed, and the new tile and countertops managed to look both vintage and up-to-date.

"Owen needs the towels. Did you find them? A big bag at the—"

She stopped, confused. Hunter stood in the middle of the floor holding a few towels in his hand. Denny tossed the big shopping bag of towels from inside the closet where he was standing. It was a sizable closet for a house this old, big enough to walk in about four steps. Denny and Hunter were both staring at the floor.

"Better go get Owen," Denny said, hands on his hips.

"And hurry!" Hunter added. "Tell him we found the bunker."

Brooke's heart began to race as Spencer pushed past her. "Where?" he asked. "Where?"

Denny pointed to the floor, and Brooke edged closer. "I don't see anything." Spencer was stepping on everyone's toes as he inched closer as well. Brooke gently grabbed him by the sleeve and pulled him back. "Just wait, Spence."

Denny squatted down about the time Owen came rushing into the bathroom.

"Hello? Anyone got the towels?" He threw his hands up in frustration as he spotted the bag in the middle of the floor. "And what is everyone doing in the closet?"

Meghan pulled on his pant leg. "Mr. Denny found the bunker."

"What?" Owen poked his head in where they were all

standing. "Are you kidding? Because I've still got water in the entryway."

Denny motioned with his hand for everyone to stand back. "See how the wood grain here is just a little different from the rest of the flooring?" He rubbed his hand along the seams. "Here's two little holes, and I'm thinking there was a handle here at one time. It's really hard to see, though. You'd have to know what to look for."

"Well, I certainly didn't." Owen peered down at the floor, squinting. "Are you sure?"

Denny groaned as he stood up. "We'll have to get a screwdriver or something and pry it open to know for sure. But I've got a pretty strong feeling about this."

"Oh man, oh man, oh man." Spencer's eyes were round as saucers.

"Okay, let's clean the water up as best we can, then we'll check it out." Brooke left the bathroom with the bag of towels. As she hoped, they all followed.

Brooke had never seen a group sop up water as quickly as they all did, dumping all the wet towels into the plastic storage tub to worry about later. Then everyone followed Owen back to the closet and stood outside the small space while Owen gathered up several pairs of shoes, a set of golf clubs, and two duffel bags. He handed the items to Hunter, who put them in the bedroom.

Denny then squeezed in beside Owen and handed him a screwdriver while everyone else stood in the bathroom, heads poking inside the closet. "I think if you pry it up right where those two holes are, it will open."

Everyone went silent as Owen lifted a section of the floor. Grabbing it with two hands, he nodded to Denny to step out of the closet, then he laid the door back. The opening in the floor was about two feet by two feet. Brooke had Spencer by the shirtsleeve but barely managed to hold him back.

"Need a flashlight." Owen pointed at Hunter. "There's one in the kitchen, second drawer from the stove."

Hunter sprinted out of the room.

Owen smiled at Spencer. "Looks like you're going to get your secret bunker after all."

"This is so cool." Spencer tried to edge closer, but Brooke kept a firm hold on his sleeve. "I said wait. We don't know what's down there." Brooke's heart was racing, and she found herself moving closer as well.

Only Meghan stayed patiently in the background. She was afraid of the dark, and Brooke knew she wouldn't be in any big hurry to venture down into that hole.

Footsteps pounded in the hallway, then Hunter appeared with the flashlight. Owen switched it on and shined the light down the opening.

Hunter gasped. "Staircase! Who's going first?"

Brooke could feel Spencer actually trembling.

Owen pushed his arm farther down the hole and shined the light in a circular motion. "I'll go down first. We don't know what's down there or if it's safe." He turned around and held each step with one hand on his way down, since there was no handrail, shining the flashlight below him with the other.

"Be careful, Owen." Brooke let go of Spencer so he could move closer now, and she brought a hand to her chest, her heart still pounding.

"Don't anyone come down here until I say it's okay." Owen paused, his head even with the floor now as he spoke to Brooke. "Listen for Lauren, okay?"

"I will. Just be careful."

Brooke decided to quickly check on Lauren, who still slept

soundly. When she returned, Denny, Hunter, and Spencer were all on their hands and knees, staring down into the darkness.

"Well?" Denny called out to Owen.

Brooke moved in closer and knelt down with the others. They were so close together, their heads were lightly touching.

"We're going to need more light, but you guys are not going to believe this."

"What? What?" Spencer's voice practically squeaked with excitement. "Owen, can I come down?" He looked up at Brooke. "Please, Mom. You've got to let me go down there!"

"No. You wait until Owen says it's safe." Brooke heard the baby cry. She leaned down toward the flickering light from below. "Owen, I've got to go check on Lauren. Do not let Spencer or Meghan down there until you know it's safe."

"Okay."

Brooke hurried to Lauren and picked her up. She stopped crying right away, and Brooke quickly determined she just needed a diaper change. It wasn't time for her to eat yet, so Brooke changed her and then rocked her a little in the new rocking chair the men had picked out. Sighing, Brooke held the infant against her chest, enjoying the feel of this tiny person against her, but also wondering what was happening in Owen's bathroom. She knew Owen would keep her children safe, just as she was making sure Lauren was taken care of.

When the baby finally drifted to sleep, Brooke laid her back in the portable playpen and rushed to join the others. Her heart skipped a beat when she found no one in the bathroom—not even Meghan. She peeked into the closet, where a glowing light shone from the hole in the floor.

"Are you all okay?"

"Yes!" Spencer yelled from below.

"Hurry!" Meghan squealed. "Come see."

Brooke carefully made her way down the steps and turned to find herself in a long narrow room, maybe twenty feet by ten feet. The flashlight beam bounced off concrete walls. Metal shelves lined the walls, stocked with dusty canned goods, an old radio, boxes that had been chewed at the corners, lanterns, and what looked to be an old generator. Two dusty shotguns leaned in the corner.

"Stay away from those guns." Brooke latched onto both Meghan's and Spencer's arms.

Spencer tried to wiggle free. "What's that?" He pointed to a chest on the shelf, and Owen shined the light on it as they all moved forward.

"Maybe it's full of gold, like from pirates or something!" Spencer leaned closer.

Owen brushed away dirt from atop the chest, which indeed did look like a miniature pirate's chest—about two feet long and a foot deep. "It's locked." He stuck the flashlight between his arm and waist, keeping the light on the box, and picked it up. "Doesn't weigh much."

Brooke jumped and Meghan screamed when Owen's flashlight went dim for a few seconds. He banged it on his hand, but the effort only brought a trickle of light. "This flashlight is about done." He motioned toward the ladder. "Let's all get out of here before we don't have any light."

They clustered around the staircase, but Denny lagged behind, holding a lit cigarette lighter above one of the boxes on the shelf. "Books. Lots and lots of books. Fantastic."

Owen hurried Denny along. Once everyone but Owen had made it back up the stairs into the bathroom, he handed up the trunk and climbed out as well.

They all hurried to the living room. Owen set the trunk down on the coffee table, then hurried over to the playpen.

"She's still breathing," he whispered to Brooke when he returned. She just smiled, remembering those moments of watching her children sleep when they were babies.

Hunter was fiddling with the lock. "I think we're gonna have to break this thing."

"Brilliant minds think alike." They looked up to see Denny in the doorway, a hammer in his hand.

It took a few swings, but the lock eventually broke. They all gathered close as Owen removed the fragments of lock and reached to open the trunk.

Travis breezed into Brooke's mind momentarily. He'd always been fascinated by the idea of a bunker in the Hadley mansion, and he would have loved to be here. But he wasn't here, and Brooke realized she could accept that. God was in charge, and there could be no regrets right now. Just hope for the future.

Owen carefully lifted the lid of the trunk, and they all crowded closer to see inside.

"Doesn't look like pirates' gold to me." Spencer shrugged as Owen lifted a handful of folded papers.

Owen picked up one of the unsealed envelopes. "Letters." He flipped through a few. "Letters between Adeline and John Hadley."

"That's it?" Spencer let out an exasperated gasp. "Just a bunch of letters? That's not a treasure."

Denny was still flipping through them. "The oldest is postmarked 1938. Some are from San Antonio. Lots of 'em from John in Smithville to Adeline in San Antonio, but some from her to him. And a few of them are addressed to John in the service. This one is still sealed."

"Adeline was from San Antonio. She must have written those letters to John while they were courting." Brooke was lost in the past, picturing that long-ago love story playing out through the mail. Then she thought about Adeline's letter to the attorney. *"All my worldly treasures are of the heart and buried beneath this house that love built." But I wonder why she didn't take them when she left.*

Meghan walked to the playpen, clearly bored with the treasure. "Can I hold Lauren, Mommy? She's awake."

Brooke scooped up Lauren, who was yawning. "Sit down on the couch, and I'll give her to you." She eased the baby into Meghan's arms. "Can you sit here and hold her while I go get her bottle ready?"

When Brooke returned, Owen, Hunter, and Denny had each pulled out one of the letters and were reading them back and forth to one another. "What are you guys doing?" They all looked up with wide-eyed innocence. "Those letters aren't ours to read. They belong to Mr. Hadley, and we need to take them to him."

She walked to the couch and handed the bottle to Meghan. "Only this much, then we need to burp her, plus she probably needs her diaper changed."

She turned back to the men. Hunter and Owen were stuffing their letters back in the envelopes, but Denny was still reading. He wore a pair of black glasses she hadn't seen before.

Brooke scowled at him and cleared her throat, but Denny held up one finger and didn't look up.

"She's right, Uncle Denny." Owen stood up from where he was sitting on the floor and looked down at the chest on the coffee table. "These aren't ours to read."

Denny pulled off the glasses slowly, then looked up at Owen from his spot on the floor. "Well, well. Our heroine in this story, Mrs. Adeline Hadley, was pregnant when she fled town. Listen to this. It's postmarked November 1942." Denny put his glasses back on and read the letter out loud. Brooke was too curious to tell him not to.

"'My dearest John, With each passing day, my heart grows heavier, and I pray that God will send you home to me. I wonder if you will ever know that we are with child, since all of my letters with mention of it have been returned. I pray this one will reach you. As my womb grows, so does my despair. I was so happy the day I got the news. I thought our dreams for a family would finally come true. But you are somewhere in the Pacific, far from my arms, and I can't help but worry if I'll ever see you again.

"'Forgive me my fears, my love. But I have tried so hard to be cheerful, to put on a good face, when all the while my heart is breaking. I wander around this big house you built for us, longing for you to return to me and this precious little one who is growing inside me. My days are long, my nights even longer. Sometimes I wake in the middle of the night, reach for you, then remember that you aren't there.'"

Brooke swallowed hard as she thought about how many times she'd done that exact same thing. The room was silent as Denny went on.

"'My hired man helps me with the garden and repairs on the house, trying his best to keep it tended until your return. I reckon that without him this place would be as run-down as many others whose owners are off to war. I don't know what I'd do without Jesse Lewis. He feels bad that the army wouldn't take him, but he is doing true service here on the home front. I know you will want to shake his hand when you return—and that must be soon, my love. I want to be strong, but some days it's very hard.

"'So come home to me, John. Be brave—I know you can't be anything else—but remember you are needed here as well and be careful. Our child needs a father. And I need my husband. Your loving wife, Adeline.'"

Brooke took Lauren from Meghan's arms and put her on her shoulder to burp as she fought the tears building in her eyes. *She never knew he returned for her after all.*

Owen paced the living room, shaking his head. "There was no mention of the pregnancy in Adeline's letter to the attorney. John Hadley never knew he had a child."

Denny stuffed the letter back in the envelope. "That's how it appears. But Brooke's right. These all belong to John Hadley, as bittersweet as it is. Didn't you tell me when I first moved in that he was still alive? That's pretty amazing in itself."

"I don't know Mr. Hadley personally, but he lives in the same retirement place where my Mom was." Brooke gently patted Lauren on the back. "Mom said he pretty much kept to himself—he's in his nineties, after all—but they knew each other to say hello. She said there was such a big production when he returned after the war; he was treated like quite the war hero. But as things settled down, he kind of withdrew into himself. Just ran his business, never talked much about himself or the war. Or Adeline."

"Is he strong enough to hear about all of this, do you think?"

"I don't know, but I can find out. I think we need to give him the letters, though. There might still be time for him to connect with some of his family. Oh, and, Owen, I think Lauren needs a diaper change. Where do you keep the fresh ones?"

He hurried out of the room while Hunter and Denny began packing the letters back into the trunk. Meghan was now lying on the couch, seemingly bored with the happenings around her. Even Spencer was yawning. Brooke knew this wasn't the type of treasure he'd been hoping for.

But family really was a true treasure, wasn't it? Love was a treasure. Brooke scanned the room and realized she was seeing riches in abundance. Even Scooter, the black cat, seemed aware of it. He'd taken to staying in the house and was curled up in the far corner.

Hunter crossed his ankles and leaned back in his chair, shaking his head. "Man, that's one pitiful story." He yawned as he stretched his legs out farther. "Funny, I think my great-grandma and grandpa was named Adeline and Jesse."

Brooke glanced at Owen and Denny, who seemed to be holding their breath the way she was. "Hunter, do you know where your great-grandparents lived?"

Shifting his weight in the chair, Hunter yawned again. "Yeah. I remember Dad talking about his grandpa, but he died real young, before I was born. He said I came from a long line of boys, no girls." He shrugged. "Anyway, they lived in Wichita Falls, Texas, way up there close to Oklahoma. Dad even grew up there, but then he moved to Austin and met my mom, and she was from La Grange. Don't know why they ended up in Smithville, though, except that Grandma lived—"

"Son?" Denny had walked over to Hunter and was looking down at him. "Are you not putting this together?"

Hunter sat up straight, a confused expression on his face. "What?"

Denny leaned closer. "For a sharp kid, you're not acting too bright. If Adeline Hadley was pregnant with John Hadley's baby and ended up in Wichita Falls, and if her hired man—Jesse Lewis—disappeared too, don't you think it's possible that Adeline and Jesse Lewis are the same ones talked about in these letters?"

Hunter crinkled his brow. "You mean—"

"Yup. You could be John Hadley's great-grandson."

Thirty-One

The following Monday Brooke took Hunter to the Oaks to speak with John Hadley. Brooke had explained the situation on the phone to the old man. Mr. Hadley had actually started crying while they were talking, so Brooke was prepared for an emotional meeting between Hunter and his potential great-grandfather. Hunter was skeptical that he could actually be related to a war hero, someone with honor and a respected background.

John Hadley met them at the door of his apartment. He was a tall man, only slightly bent over his walker, with wispy gray hair under a Houston Astros baseball cap. His blue jeans rose high above his hips, held up by a brown belt, and his dark green shirt brought out kind green eyes beneath bushy gray brows. His face was a road map of a long life, but when he smiled, there was a tenderness that made Brooke want to rush into his arms. Instead, she extended her hand.

"Mr. Hadley, I'm Brooke Holloway." She turned to Hunter and smiled. "And this is Hunter."

"Did you say Hunter?" He reached up to adjust something, and Brooke realized he wore a hearing aid.

"Yes, Hunter. The one I told you about?"

Hunter reached out to grasp Mr. Hadley's hand. "Hello, sir." His lip was trembling, and Brooke knew he was struggling not to cry.

Mr. Hadley had tears in his eyes as well. He gazed at Hunter for a long time, then slowly maneuvered his walker around so they could enter his small apartment, furnished much like the one Brooke's mother had lived in. A plate of cookies sat on the coffee table, along with three glasses of water.

"I didn't make the cookies," he said, grinning. "Nellie Rutter in number 219 brings me treats." He winked at Hunter. "I think she fancies me." He chuckled. "Imagine that. At my age." He motioned for Brooke and Hunter to sit down, then carefully lowered himself into a chair. Once they were seated, Brooke handed him the chest with the letters, and his eyes behind their thick glasses filled instantly. "Thank you. You don't know what this means to me."

She'd already explained—and apologized—about the letters they had read, including the one that held news of the pregnancy. She had also mentioned the possible connection between him and Hunter.

"What about my son or daughter? My grandchildren?" he asked now, smiling at Hunter. "Are there more like this handsome fellow?"

Brooke glanced at the boy and waited, but Hunter nodded for her to do the talking. "I'm so sorry to tell you that your son died young, Mr. Hadley. His name was Richard Lewis, and he got cancer at an early age."

"Oh." A little of the old man's eagerness deflated. "That's too bad. I would've liked to know my boy."

"Your grandson is alive, but I'm afraid he's in a correctional institution, so I don't know—"

"But I ain't bad. I promise." Hunter leaned forward. "I have me a good job."

John Hadley stared long and hard at Hunter, then chuckled. "You know, I think you got my eyes, son." He laughed. "Not everyone is blessed with these green eyes we both got." He pointed to Hunter's head. "And my mother's hair was exactly that same color."

Hunter seemed to be holding his breath, and Brooke worried he might have another panic attack. She was having a hard time holding herself together too. But there was only one way to be sure if all of their speculations were on target.

"Mr. Hadley, would you be willing to do a DNA test to prove that Hunter is indeed your great-grandson?" Brooke paused, unsure how he'd feel about that. Was he even aware of what DNA tests were?

The older man shrugged. "I guess so, but it's not really necessary. I know this young man is my great-grandson—I see it in his face. But why not make it official." He reached for a cookie.

Hunter wasn't smiling, and his lips were pressed firmly together. "What about my father? Do you want to meet him too?"

Mr. Hadley stared at Hunter for a long time, almost to the point of it being awkward. Finally he said, "I believe I would like to get to know you first. How does that sound?"

Hunter lit up like a jack-o'-lantern, his crooked teeth stretched into the biggest smile Brooke had ever seen on him. "That sounds really good, sir."

"Mr. Hadley, we can do the test tomorrow if you'd like. The results usually take three to ten working days, but I know someone at the hospital, and I think we can get the results sooner." She glanced at Hunter, who was still grinning. "However the results come out, the owner of your former home—Owen Saunders—would like you to join us for dinner Saturday night. I'd be happy to pick you up. We thought you might like to see the way he has restored your old homestead."

Brooke couldn't read the man's expression at first, but then he seemed to force a smile. "Maybe I can get back to you about that. Not sure I'm ready for that."

"I understand." Brooke was disappointed, but she supposed they should have expected that. Visiting the home he'd built for the only woman he ever loved might be too much.

They chatted for a while longer, then Brooke said they should probably go. Mr. Hadley asked if Hunter could stay, and Brooke just smiled and said, "Of course. Just call me when you're ready to go, and I'll pick you up."

Hunter held up his new cell phone. "Sure."

"Then I'll see you later." Mr. Hadley stood up when she did and held out his hand. "Thank you for this." He nodded to the chest of letters, then to Hunter.

"You are very welcome."

❖

Saturday arrived, and they were expecting a crowd.

Mr. Hadley had decided he did want to join them, so Brooke drove to pick him up around four o'clock. Her mom and dad were already at Owen's house cooking. Brooke's father still had to use his wheelchair, but he sat at the kitchen table peeling vegetables while his wife chopped and stirred. Brooke and her mom had been cooking most of the afternoon, and the aroma of turkey, dressing, pumpkin—a complete Thanksgiving meal—wafted through the house. They'd decided there was so much to be thankful for, and they didn't want to wait for November to celebrate.

"You've done a fine job with the house, Owen." Mr. Hadley maneuvered his walker slowly into the dining room and sank down into a chair at one end of the table. "It makes me happy to see it filled with love and family." There was a sadness in his voice, but Brooke suspected it wouldn't last long. She had news that would brighten his day, and she planned to share it during dinner.

Owen had bought one of those little baby slings and had Lauren with him most of the day—when she wasn't being passed off to others anxious to hold her. His awkwardness in handling her had vanished. Brooke felt like grinning whenever she saw him with the baby. He was a born father.

Brooke still couldn't grasp Virginia's decision to abandon her child, but she was glad of it for Owen's sake. He'd already signed the papers and mailed them. But he'd also made it clear to Brooke that if Virginia ever changed her mind, he wanted to make a place in Lauren's life for her biological mother. Brooke was glad of that too. He hadn't actually said anything about forgiving his ex-wife, but Brooke could see him gradually letting go of the bitterness. That was an important step—a necessary step—toward the future she now envisioned with him and Lauren and her kids. But she was willing to wait for that, to walk by his side as he worked it out for himself. She knew that forgiveness took time . . . and a lot of grace.

When everything was on the table, the group took their seats. Owen positioned himself at the other end of the table across from Mr. Hadley, with Brooke by his side, then Brooke's parents were seated next to her. Denny, Spencer, and Hunter were on the other side, and Meghan was squeezed into an extra chair next to Spencer. The portable playpen—with Lauren sleeping inside—sat within arm's reach of Owen.

Owen asked everyone to join hands for the blessing, and

Brooke was prepared for him to nod in her direction as he'd done in the past. But he didn't. He simply bowed his head, and everyone else followed suit.

"Dear Lord, we give thanks for everyone gathered here today. In ways we couldn't have foreseen, You have brought us all together and blessed us beyond what we could have imagined or hoped for. We ask You to bless this wonderful meal laid out before us and to guide us as we all strive to walk the path You've chosen for us. In Jesus's name, we pray."

Brooke swallowed hard as Owen squeezed her hand. She waited until he had carved the turkey and everyone had filled their plates, then she couldn't stand it any longer. She glanced around the room and thought about what they'd all gone through this past summer, how God had worked miracles in their lives. But there was still one thing she needed to do. She tapped her fork to her glass, pushed back her chair, and stood up.

"Attention, please." She cleared her throat as everyone put down their forks and stopped talking. She held Mr. Hadley's eyes as she spoke—loudly to make sure he could hear. "I heard from the hospital yesterday, and it's official. Hunter Lewis is indeed your great-grandson."

Mr. Hadley's lip trembled, the same way Hunter's did sometimes when he got very emotional, and his voice cracked when he spoke. "I didn't think I would ever see a day like this." He turned toward Hunter. "I'm as proud and happy as a man can be to be included in this family." Then he did start to cry. Brooke started to walk toward him, but Hunter was already there. Mr. Hadley slowly stood up, and Hunter gently put his arms around him. No one spoke. Even Meghan and Spencer seemed to understand the importance of what was happening.

After a few moments, Hunter returned to his seat, and everyone resumed eating. Brooke couldn't stop looking around at their untraditional family and reveling in the joy that filled the room. She couldn't think of anything else that could make it more perfect. Then there was a knock at the door.

"We expecting someone?" Denny stood up and walked to the entryway as they all waited quietly. He returned, ushering in a tall girl with blond hair.

Hunter bolted to his feet.

"I'm so sorry to interrupt." The girl's eyes widened when she saw how many people were in the room, but then she focused on Hunter. Her voice was soft. "Hey, Hunter. Did you get my e-mail?"

Hunter's shocked expression relaxed into a smile. "Hi, Jenny." Something unspoken passed between them as he walked toward her. Then he turned and faced everyone in the dining room. "This is Jenny, and . . . uh . . ." He introduced each one of them by name. "They are *all* my—my family."

Brooke wanted to laugh aloud. *Just when you think life can't get any better, God comes up with another surprise.*

She smiled as she stood up. "Hunter, go get another chair, and let's make room for our guest."

As she walked to the kitchen to get another place setting, she thought about how far they'd all come this past summer. She couldn't wait to see what God had in store.

Epilogue

Brooke was flipping pancakes when Owen walked into the kitchen on Saturday morning.

"Mmm. Smells good." He wrapped his arms around her waist, kissing her neck. "You *could* just turn the burner off and come back to bed since no one is up yet."

She smiled, pulling away from him. "Stop that, now. Our herd will be ready for pancakes when they get up. Is Lauren awake yet?"

"No. Even she is still sleeping, giving you permission to come back to bed." Owen tried to snuggle up to her again, but she slipped away from him, pointing the spatula at him. "Behave."

It had been three months since their wedding in February. Because Lauren was still so little, they hadn't gone away after they took their vows. But in a sense, every day had been a honeymoon since they'd committed to love each other for the rest of their lives. And while much had changed, Saturday pancakes had remained.

"I smell bacon and pancakes." Denny shuffled into the kitchen and went straight to the coffeepot.

"You and Hunter will get the first pancakes," Brooke said as she flipped another one. Hunter had been working at the hardware store since before the Christmas rush, and last month Brooke had left the store in his and Big Daddy's capable hands. Juliet was back in college, and Brooke was enjoying being a full-time mommy. So it was a Saturday pancake rule that Hunter and Denny got the first batch off the griddle since they had to leave on Saturday mornings. Denny had reopened Travis's store, and Brooke was sure Travis was smiling from heaven to know it was back in business.

Owen had signed with the public relations firm in Houston and had been working from home for six months. Life was good, even though she missed her father every day. He'd passed away a month after their wedding, but she would be forever grateful to God that he had been well enough on that day to walk her down the aisle—and that he was able to watch his grandchildren open their Christmas presents before that.

"I hear Lauren." Owen rushed from the room toward their bedroom just as Spencer rounded the corner rubbing his eyes. Meghan was behind him, and Hunter scooted past both of them.

"I get the first batch." He reached for a piece of bacon.

Hunter and Denny had both offered to move out after Brooke and Owen married, but Owen kept finding more projects for the men to work on in the evenings and on the weekends. The new garage was currently under construction. And she was pretty sure Owen would never run out of home improvement chores or reasons for them to stay. She didn't mind. She enjoyed having them around as much as he did. Who said a big family had to be just parents and children?

Hunter crunched his bacon. "Miss Patsy here yet?"

"Her friend Audra is bringing her." Brooke's mother, who

had moved back to the Oaks when they sold Brooke's house, rarely missed pancake Saturday these days, and sometimes she brought her friends, including Mr. Hadley. They'd all celebrated his ninety-fourth birthday with him last month, and at this rate they thought he might live forever. He surely would in their hearts. He'd become very dear to all of them, but especially to Hunter.

Every now and then, even Jenny would make the drive from Houston to have pancakes with the family, then busy herself in town until Hunter got off work.

Brooke carried a plate of pancakes into the dining room, stepping deftly over the orange cat and the black cat stretched out together in the doorway. Introducing Kiki and Scooter had been challenging at first, but even the feline members of their new combined family had made peace.

Their new life was sometimes noisy and often chaotic, with people running in all directions. Even their big old house seemed crowded these days.

But Brooke didn't mind. Because it was family.

And it was perfect.

Reading Group Guide

1. Brooke and Owen's friendship matures into something much more despite both of their reservations in the beginning. Who do you think had the most "baggage" going into the relationship, and how did each of them work through it?

2. Brooke clung to God after Travis died—even though she admits to questioning His will. Owen did exactly the opposite and was angry at God. How do you react during an emotional upheaval in your life? Do you lean on God? Or turn away from Him?

3. Many of the characters grow and change throughout the story. Who do you think changed the most?

4. What did you think about Hunter? Was he a product of his environment? How much was he responsible for the choices he made? How much blame do you place on his parents?

5. Brooke and Patsy's close relationship becomes strained when Brooke's father comes into the picture. What do you think would have happened if Patsy and Harold

had reunited—and if Harold hadn't been dying? Do you think Brooke would have still opened her heart to him anyway and forgiven him?

6. Uncle Denny had a bucket list. But fulfilling those dreams became less important to him once he became part of a family. Do you think he'll ever resume his travels? Or, do you think that he and Patsy might make a good match someday?

7. Spencer goes to some pretty wild extremes to keep Owen from wanting to date Brooke. The boy is conflicted on several levels—loyalty to his father, but also a growing fondness for Owen. What are some instances when Spencer struggles with his feelings, and when do you begin to see resolve for him?

8. Forgiveness of self and others are strong themes throughout the story. Who do you think struggles with this the most? Who do you think had the most to forgive?

9. Each character had a unique set of circumstances. Was there one character in the story that you identified with more than the others?

10. Virginia does some awful things, but we don't really know much about her except through Owen's eyes. Based on her brief interactions with Owen and Brooke, what do you surmise has brought her to where she is in her life? Is she truly just an evil woman? Is she lost? Will she regret her choices some day? Did you feel any sympathy for her?

Acknowledgments

When I started writing *The House That Love Built*, I knew that it would be a love story, and I knew that there would be a family living in the house. But I had no idea how many characters would show up along the way to be a part of the fun! Hunter was quite a surprise when he popped into my mind, demanding a large part in the story.

I still wasn't sure who I would dedicate the book to until I wrote the very last page. Then it became clear to me. Diana and Terry Newcomer have their own love story and six children. To me they represent *The House That Love Built* in their own lives. They are loving, kind, and nurturing, and if I didn't already have such a great family, I'd beg them to adopt me. Many times, Diana and I went on our daily walks and discussed the plot for this book. It's an honor to dedicate this story to you, my dear friend.

God makes all things possible, but second to Him would have to be my husband, Patrick. Thank you, dear, for all that you do. To my entire family, while we aren't all under the same roof, I'm so grateful for all of you. And many of my friends (you know who you are) are included in my fabulous 'family'.

Thanks to my agent—Natasha Kern—for her keen insight and career guidance. Special thanks to my editors on this project, Natalie Hanemann and Anne Buchanan, and to my entire publishing team at Thomas Nelson.

Abbie and Joe Navarro, thanks for answering all of my Smithville-related questions. And to my assistant Janet, you continue to rock!

Praying God continues to bless me with stories to tell. ☺

About the Author

Photo by Saxton Creations

Beth Wiseman is hailed as a top voice in Amish fiction. She is a Carol-award winner and author of numerous bestsellers including the Daughters of the Promise and the Land of Canaan series. She and her family live in Texas.

Beth can be found at her website (BethWiseman.com), on Facebook (Fans-of-Beth-Wiseman), or on Twitter (@bethwiseman).